Losin Control

Ladii Nesha

Contents

Books by Nesha

Series

Bambi-1-3
Catching Flights/Feelings

Spin Off

Holiday's With The Carter's
Here We Go Again
Emotionally Scarred

Standalone

Envy Me
Fraud
Stay Schemin'
You'll Always Be My Baby
We Could've Been
Lucid Dreams
Finally Famous
Santa's Little Pleaser's

This book is dedicated to my favorite girl.

You were more than my grandma. You were my superwoman, you were my safe space, and my bestfriend. I'm so thankful to have been blessed with you.
#Fuckcancer.

Prologue

"What do you have a taste for?" Benny asked his girlfriend Marley, who was sitting in the passenger seat drawing in her notebook. Her right foot was tucked underneath her butt while her left foot danced to the music pouring from the speakers. Marley wasn't a big fan of rap, but whenever she was riding shotgun with Benny, she was his little trap queen.

Glancing up, Marley put the end of the pencil in her mouth and cocked her head to the side. The question was simple, but the answer still required a little thought. Benny was doing pickups, which meant she wouldn't have access to a bathroom, so eating anything heavy was out of the question. Then again, she hadn't eaten since that morning, so she didn't want to get a salad and be hungry in the next ten minutes.

"Come on, love, it's not that hard," Benny stressed, taking the pencil from her. "And what I tell you about chewing on these?"

"How many more stops do we have?" she asked, pushing her hair out of her face.

"Six. I need to go to the East side and then downriver."

"So that's like 3 or 4 hours?"

"Marley." Benny peered over at her.

"Fine, I want some vegan stir-fry."

"You killing me with this vegan shit," he huffed. "How my seed supposed to grow if all you eat is fake meat and plants?"

"Why does my diet concern you? I still cook whatever you ask me to, even if I detest the smell. Your child is getting more than enough nutrition. Probably more than you."

"I'm just saying." Benny held his hand up in defense. She was right. As much as she gagged while doing it, Marley cooked whatever meal he requested. From fried chicken to oven baked ribs, she did it all. "I hope you don't think you're about to be feeding my baby that shit."

"I am." Marley smacked her lips. "My baby will eat fruits and veggies daily. None of this factory bullshit you eat."

"I hear you talking." Benny reached over and touched her stomach. "I trust your judgment. They say mama knows best."

"As long as you know." She blew him a kiss.

Marley took one more look at him before focusing back on her notebook. Her pencil slowly moved across the piece of paper as she filled in the eyes, then moved down to the nose. With Benny rapping to 42 Dug, she stole peeks of his handsome face, making sure she didn't miss a detail. From his thin eyebrows to his brown eyes and big lips, she captured it all.

"I'm going to start charging yo ass.""Now why you wanna do something like that?" Marley snickered. "You should be happy I want to draw yo funny looking ass. I make you look good."

"Yea, aight. If I'm funny looking, my seed growing in your

womb is funny looking too," Benny teased, leaning over to stroke her round belly.

"I doubt it. She's going to have all my genes."

"She?"

"Yea, God wouldn't make me suffer with another you."

"You got jokes," Benny laughed, tapping the earpiece in his ear to answer his vibrating phone. "Yo."

Marley zoned out while he talked on the phone. She could tell it was business from the way he spoke in code. With one hand on the steering wheel, Benny's other hand continued to caress her stomach.

"Fuck outta here!" Benny bellowed. "I'm not worried about no nigga that bleed like me. I been getting money and I'm going to keep getting it. The fuck they thought!"

Shifting in her seat, Marley watched the vein in the side of his neck throb as he popped his shit. Benny was hard because he had to be. Soft niggas didn't make it out of the jungle, and Benny didn't just make it out, he ran it. Anything that moved through the East Side of Detroit touched his hands. Everything needed his stamp of approval and moving without his permission came at a cost.

"Look, I'm not about to keep talking. Send Tech and Shooter over there and let them handle it," Benny calmly stated as if he didn't just order a hit on someone's life. Ending the call, Benny removed the earpiece and gazed over at Marley. Without him saying anything, she knew what that look meant. The streets were calling.

"I'm about to drop you off. Shit is probably going to get ugly and-"

"And that doesn't change the fact that I'm hungry. Take me to get something to eat and then drop me off at home," Marley snapped.

"Why you mad?"

"Just take me to get something to eat, Benny."

"Oh, now I'm Benny?" He stopped at the light and turned to face her. "Don't be mad, baby. Let me take care of the streets and then I'm going to come home and take care of you. It's not like I'm out here with other bitches."

"I only know what you tell me," Marley sarcastically grunted.

"Chill. I've been on my best behavior since that last situation. Plus, you're always with me."

"So you need a babysitter to make sure you keep your dick in your pants?"

Benny stroked his beard. Marley's insecurities were a result of his wrongdoings. The minute he started getting money, hoes who previously wouldn't give him the time of day started flirting with him. It started with a couple of 'hey big head' texts and that later turned to him fucking those same girls in the back of his truck. Benny felt like the man. For a while, he was flying under the radar until someone left panties tucked in his seat. Marley not only bust all the windows out of his car, but she bust out his mama's house windows too.

"Don't put words in my mouth. I'm not thinking about these bitches. I hustle, Mars baby. I run the streets and I bring the money home to you."

"Money isn't everything, Benny." Marley waved him off. "I'd rather have you."

"And you got me," he promised.

She wanted to be mad, but she only had herself to blame. Benny was deep in the streets for years and expecting him to change was foolish. He was the man all his family members could count on, the boyfriend who paid for the whole tab at the restaurant or club, and the lover who whisked her away to Miami or Las Vegas for a quick trip to get her mind right. He was everything and it was hard being mad at him because his actions were genuine.

"Gimme kiss."

Beeeeep!

The cars behind them impatiently blew their horns, signaling that the light had changed colors, but Benny didn't budge. His gaze stayed fixed upon Marley, whose face still held a frown.

"Benny," Marley groaned.

"Nah. These muthafuckas can wait. I can't move out in these streets if I know you're mad at me. I need you on my side, Mars," he pouted, giving her his saddest eyes.

Marley glared in his direction. Benny was very handsome and his sad face didn't help the storm he created between her thighs. At a little over 6ft, Benny rocked a low cut and clean face except for a small red heart that was tattooed under his right eye. His golden-brown skin was a little rough from years of trapping, but thanks to Marley and her home remedies, it was improving by the day. Although he had money, Benny wore the typical Nikes, basic white tees, and jeans. It was rare to catch him in something other than a crisp tee and fresh white Nikes. His jewelry was a different story. Benny was a boss ass nigga, so it only made sense for the diamonds on his neck and wrist to shine in the dark. His wrist alone could feed a third-world country, yet he sported it around town without a care in the world. Benny's reputation proceeded him, so niggas knew what it was.

"Gimme a kiss before you make all these people late." Benny puckered his lips.

"You not cute." She rolled her eyes but leaned over the armrest to kiss him.

"You know I love you, right?" he questioned, inches away from her lips.

Marley smiled. She believed he loved her with all his heart and he had been doing it since he was in the fifth grade. What started out as him giving her cookies and Bazooka gum later turned into name brand clothing, jewelry, and weekend trips. Benny was her first love, but his first love was the streets.

"I know you love me, and I love you, but I also love you free and alive."

"And I'm going to stay that way. The fuck these niggas gone do to me? I run-"

Before he could finish the sentence, screeching tires and loud footsteps pounding the pavement caught his attention. Benny didn't have any time to react before Marley's car door was snatched open and she was yanked out of the car by her hair.

"The fuck?" Benny snapped out of it, trying to reach for his gun, but was punched in the face and pulled out of the car by his shirt.

"Aye, let my girl go," he ordered with blood dripping from his mouth. His heart broke watching two masked men roughly grope her while snatching the diamonds from around her neck.

"Ahh," Marley cried as the custom-made diamond earrings were yanked from her earlobes, ripping them in the process.

It was broad daylight and instead of someone helping them, cars sped around, not wanting to get hit by a stray bullet. Pedestrians took cover, hiding behind other cars and buildings, knowing how quickly the streets of Detroit could turn into the wild wild west.

"Shut the fuck up, Mr. Untouchable," one of the masked

men roared before pulling the trigger, sending a bullet into Marley's stomach. He dropped her to the ground and pulled the trigger once more, silencing her loud cries.

"B-ba-baby!" Benny tried to break free. He felt like he was in a twilight zone as he watched the love of his life, the mother of his unborn child, his best friend, bleed out on the pavement while holding her stomach.

"Next time be careful where you lay yo head at nigga." The shooter smirked before pulling the trigger, turning Benny's world black.

Chapter 1

"Everybody 'round me family, nigga, we don't do recruitin'. Everybody 'round me shooters, ain't no tellin' who was shootin' nigga," Czar rapped with a fifth of Hennessy tucked at his side.

Peezy had the club rocking, but nobody was partying harder than Czar's section. Nobody repped Detroit harder than them and they wore the wounds from the streets as a badge of honor. Envious stares were shot in their direction, but that's all they were— stares. Nobody was stupid enough to put their life on the line, and even if they were, Czar wasn't worried. He might've been a well-known rapper, but he was a hood nigga first and didn't mind knocking a nigga's head off his shoulders if the opportunity presented itself.

"If we locked in, ain't no switchin' up," he rapped, locking index fingers with his brother Nova, who did the same thing with their younger brother Romeo. The trio held their locked fingers in the air while lights flashed around them. As impaired as he was, the moment made Czar's heart full. There was nothing better than making it to the top with his people standing beside him. Never behind, always at his side where they belonged.

"I love you niggas." Czar held his bottle up, prompting his brothers to do the same.

"Today and tomorrow," they said in unison, clicking their bottles together.

The DJ switched up the vibe and dropped a mixture of house music and current hits causing the club to go wild. Women shook their asses on tables and couches like they didn't have any home training while hood niggas posted up around the section enjoying the show. Weed smoke filled the air like oxygen, fifths of top-shelf liquor were passed around like bottles of water, and a few pills and lines could be found if you were into that kinda shit.

Fuck you good off a Perc bitch (mm-hm). Get activated or get hurt bitch (on God)

Czar placed the bottle to his mouth and guzzled it down like it was Gatorade as Sada Baby blared over the speakers. Beads of sweat rolled down his face, prompting him to swipe them away with the towel that rested around his neck.

Faded didn't even begin to express how fucked up he was. His body swayed from side to side as the woman in front of him shook her ass faster than the beat. Czar wanted to tell her to chill because her movements mirrored a person having a seizure and it was getting a little scary. Her long weave was hanging down her back when she entered his section, but now that she was hot and sweaty, it was pulled back into a ponytail. Since it was dark she thought no one could see the mini fro that peeked out the back, but Czar saw it. He didn't mind though because her hair was the last thing on his mind. All he wanted to do was fuck and he prayed her pussy was as soft as her ass. He couldn't stand a pretty bitch with trash pussy and wished shit like that came with a warning label. The trickery was getting a little out of hand.

"You straight, bro?" Nova asked, posted up next to his older brother. He too was tipsy, but his protective nature wouldn't allow him to let loose. His job was to be on guard when his brother wasn't, and from Czar's hooded eyes, it was easy to tell he was on cloud nine, and he had every right to be.

"Life is good," he smirked, quoting his favorite rapper.

Czar spoke the truth. After finishing up a 30-city sold out tour, he was ready to bask in his success. The tour stretched across the entire East Coast, and he left every city yearning for more. Czar was more than a rapper. His music told the story of his life, and he left it all on the track every time.

"You see this nigga?" Nova tossed his head in the direction of their younger brother.

Leaning against the wall, Romeo fisted his companion's long braids while she sexily bounced her ass on him. It didn't matter that he was in a very public relationship with a crazy ass girl who was known to cut up. He reasoned the way ole girl was throwing her soft ass against him was worth the trouble it was going to cause.

"Sammy gone fuck that nigga up," Czar mumbled, looking down at his dip for the night. "Excuse me, sweetheart." He stepped back, putting space between him and Lil Ms. Saltshaker.

"Everything ok?" she asked, hoping that he didn't change his mind. Leaving with Czar was a must. She didn't care if she had to share him; as long as she got her claws in Detroit's bad boy, she was good.

"What's your name again?"

"Honey."

"Aight, Honey, you starting to make me sweat, and I think you need to drink some water before you overheat. Go sit by the fan or something because if yo pussy musty, it's a wrap," Czar dismissed her. Any other woman would've been offended, but not Honey. Czar could've told her to play in traffic for the dick and she would've did it.

"I'll be at the bar. Don't forget me when you're ready to leave." Honey stood up straight, retrieving her purse from the floor beside them.

"I got you, lil baby," he promised, watching her switch away from him. She had nothing else to prove. His only hope was that she could twerk on his dick the same way she popping on it through his jeans.

"Damn, she thick as fuck." Nova admired her frame. "Gotta ass like a donkey and twisting that muthafucka like a corgi."

"She looks like the rest of them," Czar uttered. "Every Instagram influencer and Fashion Nova model look the same. Slim waist, big booty, and long weave. Basic as fuck."

Czar spoke from experience. He had knocked down some of the baddest bitches the industry had to offer, and still, none of them stood out to him. They all aspired to look and act the same. They all wanted clothing boutiques that sold the same shit, long weaves they put on payment plans, and bodies that doctors made from scratch. Czar would never knock the next person's hustle, but he often wondered where the originality was. Then again, it could be because he found his women swinging on poles and in the back of clubs snorting coke.

"You still gone fuck though."

"Duh nigga." He grinned, glancing back at Honey. "I'm a sucker for big booties and pretty faces and lil baby dragging a wagon with the thighs to match."

"Aye, but did you peep ole girl?" Nova discreetly tossed his head to the left.

Instead of asking who, Czar's eyes scanned the club before landing on the section to the left of them. He wasn't surprised to see her there because she was always on the scene if it was popping. When their eyes locked, she winked and discreetly started tapping on her phone.

"Nah, I didn't know she was here," Czar replied, glancing down at the Apple watch on his wrist.

Head Hunter: Meet me in the bathroom.

Czar took another sip of his drink and stared at her. The skintight mesh body suit she wore left little to be desired and he wouldn't mind peeling it off of her, but he wasn't on that type of time tonight. Tati was playing with fire, and she knew it. She was standing in another man's section, drinking his liquor and grinding on his dick, but her attention was across the room.

From the moment Czar and his clique filed into the club, her eyes were on him. His mannerisms screamed drug dealer and the way people flocked to let you know he was that nigga. As if he was her prey, Tati watched him walk through the club, commanding everyone's attention without even trying. People stopped talking when he walked by, trying to show him love, hoping the gesture would be reciprocated, but Czar wasn't a friendly nigga. He didn't acknowledge everybody and when he did, it was a quick nod.

The cub owner cleared the biggest section for Czar and his crew, moving another party without even asking. Czar didn't have to request bottle service because the second he sat down, the bottle girls walked out holding sparklers, a sign with his name on it, and all of his favorite liquor. The DJ started playing all his music and his section went crazy. In a matter of seconds, ass and titties were everywhere. On any other night Tati would've joined him, but her new lil boo Yaro didn't like their situationship, so to keep the peace between the rappers, Tati avoided being seen with Czar in public.

"Fuck you looking over there for?" Yaro roughly grabbed her chin, making her face him. Tati could almost taste the liquor that seeped from between his lips as he glared at her.

His red eyes were big and glossy from all the extracurricular activities he did before the club and Tati could tell he was on tip.

"Boy, stop!" She snatched away from him. "You drunk."

"Nah, I just know how you like to play with my head. Fuck is you staring at that nigga for when I'm right here?" he slurred, throwing his arm around her neck. "You my bitch or nah?"

"I am."

"Then act like it and give me a kiss."

Rolling her eyes, Tati did as she was told and kissed him. She tried to give him a cute peck, but Yaro wasn't having it. Grabbing a handful of her ass, he placed a sloppy kiss on her lips while locking eyes with Czar. For good measure, Yaro slapped Tati's ass and roughly kissed her neck before he released her.

Unmoved, Czar smirked and turned his bottle up. If he were the kiss-and-tell type of nigga, he'd tell Yaro that he probably had the same amount of his DNA in his mouth as Tati. The same lips he attacked were the same lips that stayed wrapped around his dick.

"It wasn't that serious." Tati frowned, knowing he was trying to put on a show for Czar.

"It's always that serious," Yaro disagreed, pulling her to his side.

He didn't know what kind of games Tati was playing, but she had him fucked up if she thought she was about to leave him to go be with the next nigga. Yaro spent so much money on Tati in the first few weeks of them dating that he could have filed her on his taxes. He assumed Czar was cashing Tati out, so he needed to upstage him. Unbeknownst to Yaro, Czar didn't spend a dime on Tati. He'd never trick on pussy that was available to any and everyone.

"Ok, Yaro." Tati rolled her eyes, over the beef Yaro made up his head.

It was no secret that Yaro felt some kind of way about Czar and he never missed an opportunity to let it be known. He lived for interviewers to ask him about the beef. Not only did it stir up old shit, but Yaro's music streams skyrocketed when the world thought they were beefing. Everyone wanted to pick a side, and although most of the listeners sided with Czar, Yaro still had a few loyal ones who stuck with him through it all. He wasn't as established as Czar, but he was signed to a label that capitalized off his pretty boy looks versus his music. If anything, Yaro was a show pony.

On the other side of the club, Czar laughed to himself and took another swig of his drink. He thought Yaro was funny and he loved fucking with him. Czar didn't remember when the beef started, but apparently, it was his fault. When an interviewer asked him how he felt about the new Detroit rapper Yaro, Czar chuckled and said Yaro was from Westland and that didn't count as being from Detroit. Czar even called him a suburban rapper like he was some white boy. It was bad enough nobody took him seriously, and since the interview, people were calling him 'B-rad,' the white dude from *Malibu's Most Wanted.* Yaro felt played but it was the truth. Westland wasn't Detroit. The black people who were raised in Westland weren't even allowed to say nigga and black people from Detroit didn't go to Westland because it was too far and cops stayed on bullshit.

Yaro called himself hooking up with Tati because he thought it would bother Czar, but he was wrong as two left shoes. Tati was an industry hoe, and for the right price she would fuck Flavor Flav. Wifing her was supposed to be temporary, but Yaro fell in love with her wet mouth and warm walls.

"Why you fucking with that man?" Nova chortled,

knowing how petty his brother was. Yaro was now standing on the couch rapping to Yo Gotti's *Fuck You* like a lil bitch. His middle finger was pointed to Czar's section, but per usual, Czar was unbothered. He was actually tickled.

"Watch this." Czar removed his phone from his pocket. He sent a quick text and then looked up. Nova was confused until he looked over and saw Tati leaving out of the section with urgency.

"The fuck you about to do?" Nova questioned.

"None of your business, nigga." Czar patted his shoulder and sat the bottle on the table. "I'll be back." He started walking off. Nova shook his head but silently told two of their cousins, Shortie and Biggie, who doubled as security guards, to follow him.

Tati stood against the bathroom wall waiting for Czar. She knew what type of time he was on and she was ready. It had been a while since she had some *good* dick and her body craved it. Her mind immediately shifted to Yaro and she almost felt sorry for him. He was a good boy trying to be bad and it was tainting his image.

Yaro was fine. Not just any fine either, he was pretty boy fine. People often compared him to Justin Combs, and he hated it, claiming the nigga didn't have shit on him. Yaro possessed fair skin that was covered in ink of all shades. Half of them didn't make sense, but they complimented his toned body nicely. Standing at 6ft, he sported a low cut with tiny black curls that spiraled around his head and often looked wet. His style was immaculate, but Tati hated that he tried to act harder than he really was and to top it all off, he couldn't fuck. His below average size dick didn't do anything for her, which created yet another insecurity. While he was a good guy, his handicap kept Tati running back to Czar.

"Hey," her sultry voice greeted when he bopped into the bathroom.

Czar was the complete opposite of Yaro, and she loved it. His skin was the color of cocoa beans and his pretty teeth were as white as fresh snow. People swore he had veneers, but it was the furthest thing from the truth. Czar didn't bother clearing it up because the world was so fake that claiming something was real sent the world into an uproar. His long thick locs hung over his shoulders with auburn tips and were accompanied by a tapered line-up. His eyebrows were wild and full, but his long lashes were fuller. Tati loved laying on his chiseled chest and staring in his face. His voice was deep and it sounded even better when he was talking shit while hitting her from the back. He had a few tattoos, but they blended in with his skin unless he was standing under a light. Czar was the type of man you fell in love with over and over, even when he warned you that all he wanted was pussy. Falling for him was like breaking your own heart, and she did it every time.

"What up doe," Czar replied, locking the door behind him. He wasn't worried about nobody running up on him because he saw his cousins following behind him and they were ready for whatever. "You trying to piss your nigga off?"

"I missed you." Tati pushed off the wall, wrapping her arms around his neck. "He don't fuck me like you do."

"Aye, back up, you smell like that nigga." He turned his nose up in disgust while removing her arms.

"Oh god. He was all over me," she complained, walking over to the sink. Czar watched her through the mirror as she wet a paper towel, lightly wiped her neck and then patted her face, careful not to mess up her makeup. Reaching into her purse, Tati sprayed her wrist with YSL perfume and her face with Rosewater. Going a step further, she brushed her teeth and gargled for good measure.

"Better?" She spun around, poking her lips out.

"Yea, come here and let me mess it up," Czar demanded and Tati's pussy purred.

There was no other man on God's green earth that could handle her the way Czar did. He wasn't even her man and she jumped at his command like he paid her bills. Czar made her freshen up in a public bathroom and she was still ready to drop to her knees and swallow his dick. The charisma Czar possessed couldn't be taught. It radiated from his body like a powerful pheromone and captured anything with a split.

Tati pushed her shoulders back and walked over to the chair in the corner. Taking a seat, she lifted her finger, motioning for Czar to come to her.

"Nah, you come here." He cockily posted up against the door and Tati wasted no time doing as she was told.

"You swear you run shit," she complained but still squatted down in front of him.

The fact that he had her in the bathroom kneeling in a five-thousand-dollar bodysuit her nigga bought said he ran shit, but Czar kept the comment to himself. Tati reached out to unbuckle his pants and released his thick crooked dick. His curve alone made her throat ache, but there wasn't any bitch in her blood. Taking the thick, yam-like vessel into her hand, Tati kissed the tip before placing kisses all over the shaft. Staring into his eyes, she slowly submerged his dick between her cheeks and proceeded to swallow him. Tati stroked his dick in her mouth while lovingly looking into his eyes.

"Don't make love to my shit." Czar grabbed a handful of her hair and thrusted his dick further down her throat causing her to choke. "Eat this dick," he groaned, grinding in her face.

Like the pro she was, Tati switched gears. With one hand on the base of his dick, she massaged his balls while choking on his shaft. Saliva ran down the sides of her mouth as tears formed in her eyes. She couldn't breathe, but the pleasure etched across his face told her she was doing a good job, breathless and all.

"Uh huh," Czar grunted, fucking her face, not caring that he was messing up her makeup. Grabbing his ass, Tati pulled him closer as she gobbled his dick up like a $5 foot long. Massaging his balls with her free hand, Tati's mouth worked overtime to keep up with his thrusts.

"Aye," Czar snatched his dick out of her mouth and disrespectfully tapped it on her lips. "Stop playing and get a nut out the muthafucka."

"I got it." Tati accepted the challenge and took him back into her mouth. All that cute shit went out the window as she sucked the nut out of his dick like a shock vac.

"Hell yeah." He closed his eyes and held on tight as she delivered head that would make Karrine Steffans proud.

Shamelessly, Tati swallowed his salty nut like it was the best thing she ever tasted.

"Am I seeing you later?" she asked, wiping her mouth.

"Nah," Czar shook his head. "Do me a favor though."

"What?" Tati asked, cocking her head to the side, watching him wipe the remaining nut off the tip of his dick. Reaching out, Czar used his thumb to smear it on her lips. "What do you want me to do?"

"Go kiss that nigga. He wanna be on my dick so bad, go show the nigga how it tastes," he laughed.

"You can't be serious."

"I'm dead ass serious. Go kiss that nigga and enjoy the rest of your night."

"Wait, I can't get no dick?" She pouted.

"Nah, I gotta save a couple nuts for shorty at the bar," Czar said, walking over to the sink to wash his hands. "Thank you for the head though. You a real one," he swore before drying his hands and bopping out the bathroom as smoothly as he entered.

"You straight?" Biggie asked, guiding him back to the section.

Czar opened his mouth to respond, but an angry Yaro stomping in their direction caught his attention. His yellow complexion was bright red. It could've been his drunken state, but Czar swore smoke was coming from his ears. The thought made him laugh out loud.

"Fuck is you laughing for?" Biggie quizzed, looking upside his head.

"Cause this nigga look like a cartoon character," Czar cracked. "Ole Shaggy Doo looking ass nigga," he continued, making Bigge laugh loudly.

"You think shit sweet?" Yaro barked with spit flying from his mouth.

Bystanders had their cameras out recording the moment. Some were going live on Instagram and fans were in the comments instigating, placing bets on who'd win the fight.

"Hell yea, now what?" Czar's jaw twitched, knowing that Yaro wasn't about the life he rapped about. He grew up in a two-parent household and was an honor roll student. His parents wanted him to go to college to be a lawyer like his father, but Yaro went in a completely different direction. When he graduated high school, he started hanging out with his long-lost cousins and shit went downhill from there. They were into a bunch of shit Yaro had never heard of and it intrigued him. Since he was green to the streets, he was the first person to raise his hand to do some dumb shit. While

Yaro was so busy trying to get in the hood, most residents of Detroit were trying to get out, like Czar.

The shit he rapped about was real. He had the scars from gang fights, the marks on his wrists from police cuffs being too tight, and a shit load of emotional trauma that he wouldn't wish on his worst enemy.

"Where my bitch?" Yaro snarled, this time taking a step forward.

"You sound weak as fuck asking another nigga where yo bitch at. Move the fuck around before I shake shit up in this fine establishment," Nova warned, appearing out of thin air. Czar was capable of handling Yaro with his eyes closed, but he had shooters. There was never a time when he needed to lift a finger.

"I'm supposed to be scared?" Yaro's eyebrows dipped, meeting in the middle of his forehead.

"No. You're supposed to be smart because you fucking with the wrong niggas. I'll stomp a hole in your chest and start a GoFundMe to pay for your lung transplant."

"Yall niggas swear yall the only ones with shooters."

"The difference is my niggas really get shit done, so what's up?" Czar stretched his arms out. "You sure you wanna start some shit you can't finish?"

Yaro's heart skipped a beat, and for a split second, the fear that flooded his veins was displayed across his face. He wouldn't back down from a fight, but under normal circumstances he didn't start them. The liquid courage and jealousy gave him a boost of confidence, but not enough to make a fool of himself in front of the entire club.

"Baby?" Tati moved through the crowd with her friend on her heels. "What's going on?" She feigned dumbfounded, peering between him and Czar.

"Where the fuck was you at?" Yaro grabbed her by the arm.

"The bathroom, my stomach was hurting," Tati hissed, completely mortified. Normally, she liked all the cameras on her, but not in this manner.

"See," Czar hunched his shoulders. "Yo girl had to shit," he added, making the crowd laugh. Tati shot him a death stare before turning her attention to Yaro.

"Come on, it's getting late." She pulled at his arm. "Let's go back to the room," Tati pleaded, kissing the corner of his mouth. Yaro kept his eyes on Czar but allowed Tati to place kisses on his mouth while begging him to leave with her.

"Weak ass nigga ain't gone do shit," Yaro popped his shit, turning away from Czar a few moments too soon.

Without warning, Czar cocked back and punched him in the jaw, sending the crowd into a frenzy. Wanting to give him a fair fight, Czar waited until Yaro caught his balance before he started going in. Yaro's boys tried to get at Czar, but Shortie, Biggie, Nova, and Romeo started snatching niggas and tossing them like wet clothes. The chaotic scene caused people to start running as club security tried to fight their way through the crowd.

Czar ignored the pandemonium around them as he laid haymakers to Yaro's face and body. Tati begged him to stop, but the Hennessy in his system was screaming, 'Whoop that trick,' so that's what he did until blood leaked from Yaro's mouth and nose. Nova grabbed his brother, stopping him from catching a murder charge. Yaro or his slick ass mouth wasn't worth a prison sentence.

"Now who the weak ass nigga?" Czar spat, kicking Yaro as he passed him. "And since you wanted my attention so bad, every time I see you I'm going to embarrass yo bitch ass."

"On God," Romeo co-signed, following his brother out of

the club.

"Fuck that nigga and his bitch," he stated as valet opened the truck door for him. "Matter fact," Czar pulled out his phone and made a call. "Aye, drop that nigga off at urgent care and bring yo ass on. You wanted the dick, now you about to swallow this muthafucka until your jaws are numb."

Chapter 2

"Welcome back, Detroit! This is ya girl Nesha Re and I have all the hottest gossip around the city," the radio host clearly spoke into the microphone.

"Can we start with ya boy? He out here snatching wigs, whooping ass, and taking names." Her co-host Felix chortled. "I don't know why they trying that man and he repeatedly proved that he doesn't have any sense."

"Not too much on my boy. Ole girl should have made sure her lace was tight before she got her happy ass on stage and started bending over. The way I see it, she needs to be thanking him and suing her hairdresser," Nesha Re snorted. "As far as the brawl, Yaro started it. He should keep his hands to himself, especially since he can't fight."

Terri ended the recording and pinched the brim of his nose. By now he was sure a few more gray hairs were starting to sprout from his roots. The amount of stress Czar caused him was unreal, and if he didn't rake in millions, Terri would have dropped him days after he was signed. The twenty-nine-year-old rapper was a master at his craft but a pain in the ass to manage. He didn't follow the rules and his behavior at times could be considered reckless.

"Czar, I need you to break this down for me because I'm not understanding." Terri rubbed his temples. At this point, he was ready to switch careers. Instead of managing grown ass men, he felt like he was a chaperon for annoying fifth grade boys who couldn't conduct themselves in public. "A brawl on your first night home?"

"Ain't nobody thinking about that nigga." Czar waved him off. "He got exactly what he wanted. A black eye and ten minutes of fame."

"Is he a problem? This isn't the first altercation between yall."

"Not at all, he's a bitch."

"And the lady with the lace front? What was that about?" Terri quizzed.

"Look, the bitch jumped on stage and," Czar started explaining but was cut off by his brother.

"And he snatched her wig off and started swinging it around like a helicopter," Romeo laughed.

"Nigga, I about dieeeeed," Nova snickered. "Sis braids was fighting for they life to connect."

"That's not funny." Terri glared at Nova. "Do you know how that made him look? The PR team is having a field day trying to clean this up."

"I mean the name of the song is *Lace Front Bully*," Czar scoffed.

"*Bitch stop talking, bend over, let me see it*," Nova rapped, reciting his brother's lyrics. "*I'm trying to fuck you in my Timbs and a skully. Dick all in her back, now the chick swear she love me. I hope her wig tight because I'm snatchin' laces, call me bully*,"

"Whew," Romeo clapped. "T-dog, the crowd went wild with that one. Well, everybody but the chick with the toddler braids. I know she didn't get on stage thinking that she was about to salsa. She knew what it was, and it was not my brother's fault her shit was loose as hell."

"Czar, do you have anybody on your team that doesn't act like a damn child?" Terri quizzed. Czar glanced at his brothers, their security, and then back at Terri.

"Aight yall, be serious." He cleared his throat. "What's the move?"

"She's suing you for two million dollars." He dropped a folder on the table.

"Ain't no fucking way!" Czar jumped out of his seat, knocking the chair over.

The money wasn't a problem because he spent that on family vacations and Christmas gifts. He made two million in his sleep and spent it even faster, but the thought of giving it to a money-hungry gold digger made his ass itch. Had she asked for a few thousand, Czar would have happily given it to her and the phone number to a hair stylist that could help her out, but since she wanted to play in his face, she wasn't getting shit.

"I'm not giving that hoe shit," Czar snorted. "She hopped her funny looking ass on stage in a five-dollar Temu outfit and beauty supply store sandals and she thinks she's about to get 2 million dollars from me?" he snapped.

"The point is the girl is embarrassed and you need to make it right," Terri stressed. "Cut her a check, offer an apology on social media, and stop snatching lace fronts on stage!"

Czar was by far one of the most talented rappers Terri had the pleasure of working with outside of Southwest Rah, but he was a knucklehead. He rarely accepted Terri's guidance and it drove him up the wall. At times he wanted to drop Czar as a client, but his talent was unmatched.

"Aight, fuck it. Send her bucket head ass $500 and a picture of my dick and tell her to choke on it." He grabbed his keys, phone, and bottle of water off the table.

"I'll send her two thousand and you'll issue an apology on your Instagram page."

"You know what, Terri; if you wasn't my boy, I'd knock all this shit over. Send the check, but she's not getting a second of clout off my name. So that apology shit is out the window."

"We'll see if that works."

"Cool, I'm out."

"And don't forget we set up a table for you at Belle Isle tomorrow," Terri reminded him. "I'm going to be in Atlanta, so I won't be here to hold your hand through it."

"Fuck outta here, Terri. I know how to handle my shit when you're not around." Czar waved him off.

"Sure you do."

"Look, just give Romeo the information and we'll go from there."

"You should really think about hiring another assistant," Terri insisted.

"The fuck I need an assistant for when I have my brother?" Czar inquired as if Terri's statement was the most illogical request in the world.

Terri didn't bother arguing with him because it was a road they had been down before. When it came to his business and letting people into his circle, Czar was very selective. Romeo handled his day-to-day tasks, Nova hired and overlooked the security details, his mother handled all of his finances, and his father managed all of his businesses outside of rapping. Czar created a family empire and made sure everyone had the tools to succeed.

"Second thought, send me a few. Bad bitches only though.

I might need assistance unbuckling my pants," he smugly grinned.

"Just go." Terri pointed to the door.

"Let me stop fucking with you before you have a stroke in this bitch. I got it, damn. The fair bullshit tomorrow at noon," Czar recited the information.

"It's a *mental* health fair and it's good for the community. Maybe you should seek some kind of counseling."

"And maybe you should get some pussy, it's good for the mental."

"Don't worry about me. I get plenty of pussy."

"Nigga you don't even say pussy right. Sound like Braxton and shit," Nova cracked. *"I get plenty of pussy,"* he mocked, earning a middle finger.

"Like I was saying," Terri redirected as he straightened the sleeve of his Tom Ford suit jacket. He didn't need to get into a dick measuring contest because, contrary to popular belief, Terri had his fair share of women. "There are over one hundred vendors, including food trucks, games for the kids, and more. Health care workers will be there checking for pre-diabetes, high blood pressure, and STD screenings."

"Oh shit, Romeo. You might need to check that out." Nova bumped his shoulder.

"I'll check when you do. We ran through the same women, so whatever I have, you have too," Romeo rebutted, wiping the smirk from his brother's face. Czar let out a low laugh because it was true. His younger brothers didn't mind swapping women and had run more trains than Amtrak station. Being that they were related to one of the most remarkably successful rappers of all time, women threw themselves at their feet, hoping it would get them to the real prize. *Czar.*

"Like I was saying," Terri interrupted them before it could go any further. "There is a little bit of everything, and Czar will be talking about releasing stress through music. He's going to help write a few bars and teach kids about YouTube and streaming."

"That's not the only way I release stress," Czar grinned, stroking his beard. "You feel me, sweetheart?" He winked at Terri's assistant Ebony, who was sitting in the corner looking like she was holding her breath.

Ebony clamped her mouth closed and shifted in her seat. She should've been used to his flirtatious ways, but she wasn't. One smile from Czar had her flicking the bean on her lunch break.

"Leave her alone and get out of my office," Terri warned.

"Eb, if you ever wanna switch up, let me know. Apparently, I'm on the market for a new assistant."

"Have a great day, Mr. Czar," Ebony dismissed his advances. As bad as she wanted to bust it open for him in the utility closet, she couldn't. Terri told her if she messed around with any of his clients, she would be unemployed.

"Mr. Czar," Czar taunted. "I'm not on the market for good girls anyway. I'd ruin your life."

"What you say, bro?" Romeo instigated.

"Tell the chicken touch her toes, don't want no nice chick, point me to the freak hoes," he rapped, bopping out of the door.

Terri shook his head, praying that everything went as planned. Although Romeo and Nova were rowdy, they knew when to step back and allow Czar to do his thing. It was Czar he worried about. The man went from 0 to 100 in seconds, and anybody standing in his crossfire was hit. The last thing he needed was for Czar to do something stupid and end up in the media once again.

∞∞∞

Czar cruised down I94 with the music blasting. With ease, he weaved in and out of lanes while the earthy Detroit wind whipped across his face. In other cities, he hired a driver or security did the driving, but in his city, he dominated the streets. No one knew the tattered streets like he did. Czar was familiar with all the shortcuts, backroads, and side streets. On a good day it took twenty to thirty to travel from east to west, but he could do it in ten...fifteen max.

Today was different though. Czar dismissed his security team and driver. While he was in Michigan city limits, they weren't needed. He was home. Czar embraced the muggy summer breeze, crowded freeway, and impatient drivers. Everyone had somewhere to be, and due to the continuous construction, they were all stuck in traffic, going nowhere fast.

After being gone for two months, Czar appreciated the moment to sit still and take it all in. With five songs on the Top 100 chart, a new album in the works, and ending a sold-out tour, Czar had a lot to be proud of. After his last album dropped, he secured brand endorsements with Pepsi, Beats by Dre, and a few local companies. His YouTube channel and Twitch account were whole different conversations. All he had to do was go live once a week, talk shit, or freestyle, and his fans went wild. Those checks alone were enough to retire.

Dragging his hand across his face, Czar reached for his Red Bull and took a sip. The sugary drink gave him just enough energy to get through the drive. Anything other than that was in God's hands. All the sleepless nights and clubbing were starting to catch up to him. Tour life was lit, but Czar wanted nothing more than to eat a home-cooked meal and fall face first into the bed. Not just any bed, his custom-made Hastens mattress was calling his name.

"You still tired?" Romeo questioned, catching him yawning out of the corner of his eyes.

"Fuck yeah," Czar replied, slouching a little further down in his seat. Tired didn't even begin to convey the exhaustion that coursed through his veins.

"I'mma slap this broad," Romeo mumbled, peering down at his phone. Reading the text message on the screen, his face contorted into a frown before he sucked his teeth and looked back up at his brother.

"What's wrong with you?"

"Sammy hoe ass," he scoffed. "She in Miami with her sister and best friend on some fuck that nigga shit."

"That's what she said?" Nova chuckled from the back seat. Instead of repeating it, Romeo handed him the phone so he could view her Instagram story. "Oh shit, Sammy showing out." He raised his eyebrow in adoration. Sammy was short and thick as fuck. On any given day she resembled Jayda Wayda and she had the stank walk to match.

Romeo sat in the passenger seat vexed. He didn't see shit funny and couldn't wait for Sammy to bring her short ass home. She was barely 5ft and wanted to be on LIVE shaking her ass for the world to see. Romeo had something for her hot ass though, and he was reporting the video for child nudity. Her and her hood rat ass posse had him fucked up.

"Damn, have I ever met ole girl in the white?" Nova asked, handing the phone back to him.

"Yea nigga, you fucked her and ducked her."

"Oh shit. See, these wigs make 'em look like a new person." He shook his head, sitting back in the seat. "And why you keep yawning? You making me tired."

"Tati had some of her friends pull up last night," Czar admitted, rubbing his eyes.

"You disrespectful as fuck. You beat that nigga up, shipped his ass to urgent care, and-

"Had his bitch sucking my toes."

"You let Tati suck your toes?" Romeo asked, intrigued. He'd done a lot of freaky shit, but toe sucking was a new one.

"I didn't let her do anything. She was riding my dick backwards and started sucking them muthafuckas." Czar shrugged. "I almost punched her in the back of the head, but that shit started feeling good. Had a nigga feeling feminine as fuck."

"You sick," Nova laughed but made a mental note to have the next chick he fucked suck his toes. "Why you ain't call us?" he interrogated, prompting Czar to turn the radio down.

"Because I'm not with that tunnel buddy bullshit. I'm not sticking my dick in no pussy that's lubricated from another nigga's nut. That's like slipping and sliding in each other's juices."

"Why you make it sound like that?" Romeo furrowed his eyebrows, grossed out by the thought of using his brother's nut as lube.

"I mean that's what it is," Czar chortled. "Yall niggas nasty anyway, so I know yall don't care."

Instead of refuting his claim, Romeo cut the radio up and sat back. Czar had a point. There wasn't much that they didn't do together. Born 11 months apart, Nova and Romeo shared everything. The way they ran through women could be considered reckless, but it was nothing new. The ghetto twins took young, dumb, and full of cum to another level. The moment they discovered the power of the tools between their legs, it was a wrap. They could blame their sexual escapades on their brother's success, but it started way before Czar signed his first deal. Nova and Romeo were in ninth grade with senior chicks on their jock. Girls couldn't get enough of the suave teens with good hair, deep voices, and big hands.

Now at twenty-one and twenty-two, they were at what they considered their sexual peek. When Romeo called himself settling down with Sammy, Nova was devastated. They should've been passing out dick like government cheese, but Sammy put a stop to it all. She came right in sucking the soul from Romeo's dick and fucking up all his common sense in the process. He went from loving her to fighting her to fucking her brains out within a matter of hours. Their young, toxic love was draining, but Romeo didn't play about his girl.

"I say dump her," Nova shrugged. "You can move back in with me, and we can resume twerk fest Thursdays. Shit ain't been the same without you."

"Nah, I'm straight." Romeo shook his head, still examining Sammy's pictures. "I'mma fuck around a catch a case. Bitch out here shaking an ass I paid for. I wish they could repo that muthafucka and have her around this bitch looking like her flat back mama."

"Damn, what her mama do?" Nova laughed out loud.

"Her bald-headed ass raised a hoe."

Forty-five minutes later, Czar pulled up on the east side of Detroit. His parents lived in a mini mansion in Indian Village. The six-bedroom, four-bathroom, three-car garage home was his first *major* purchase. Without blinking, he dropped 2.5 million on the house and then furnished it with whatever his mother wanted. His parents tried to fight him on it, but quite frankly, they didn't have a choice. For all they had done for him, buying them a house was the least he could do. Czar had taken them through the wringer and the house was his apology gift.

Whipping into the driveway, Czar parked behind his father's truck and hopped out of the car with his brothers not far behind. He prayed like hell his mama cooked because a meal and a good night's sleep would give him enough energy to get through the health fair that Terri signed him up for against his will.

"Mama," Nova hollered out, crossing the threshold.

"I'm in the kitchen, Casanova, and stop yelling in my house like that."

"He don't have no home training, Mama," Romeo said, turning the corner to find his mother standing over the stove frying chicken.

Whirling around, Ada watched the trio fall into the kitchen one after the other. Had someone told her she'd have three grown ass sons by the time she was forty-five, Ada would have told them to kiss her round ass. Yet, there she was, staring at three different versions of herself. The protector, the player, and the lover.

"My favorite lady." Romeo leaned down and kissed her on the cheek while simultaneously stealing a piece of chicken off the plate beside her.

"I know that's a lie because my boys are very well-mannered," Ada swore. "Even when they yelling through my house acting like heathens." Her eyes darted over to Nova.

"Get off my mama nigga." Czar pushed his brother to the side and pulled his favorite lady into his arms.

"You're home," she beamed.

Ada wrapped her arms around her big baby and patted

him on the back. She loved all three of her boys, but Czar was her heart. Being that she had him at seventeen, they grew up together. He witnessed all of her bad decision-making and weathered the storm with her. Czar had seen more than he should have, yet he still came out on top. He was her biggest accomplishment and she thanked God every day that their checkered past didn't affect him too much. Sure, he was a little rough around the edges, but things could have been worse. *He* could have been worse.

"How you doing, Ma?" he asked, kissing her on the forehead.

"I cannot complain." She smiled, still holding onto him. "Between the bi-weekly trips to the spa and the chef Slim hired for the weekend, I've been in heaven. I don't have to lift a finger."

"You deserve the world." Czar kissed the top of her head.

"How about you? You taking care of yourself?" Ada touched his face, noticing the bags forming under his eyes.

"Of course." He gave her a sly grin.

"I'm serious, Julius. Are you taking your medicine? Eating right? Getting enough sleep?"

"Yea," Czar nodded, saying whatever she needed to hear.

Ada glared at him with a knowing look. She knew her son like the back of her hand and taking medicine wasn't his forte. It never was, but it was something he needed. Czar hated the man-made drug, but it stabilized his mood, eased his mind, and helped him sleep. He could get away without taking them for about a week before his world started to grow a little darker.

"Aight, I'm lying, but I been good," he promised, releasing her. "Plus, you got these guard dogs watching my every move. I can't even piss in peace."

"Shut up," Nova laughed, giving him the finger. Czar told no lies. The day he hired his brothers to be a permanent part of his team is the day he gave up all his privacy. Nova and Romeo paid close attention to his health. They were good at reading him. It was easy for them to tell when he was irritable, hungry, sleepy, and everything else. When he became irate, they knew it was time for him to take his medicine and disconnect from the world.

"Damn nigga, share my mama," Romeo fussed, pulling Ada into his arms.

"She was mine before she was yours. You only exist because Pops wouldn't let her abort you."

"Czar!" Ada popped him in the back. "Don't tell my baby that. He's wanted, he's loved."

"See, she feels guilty. That's why she's always speaking positive affirmations in your ear."

"You gay for knowing what affirmations are," Nova tittered.

"What? I need positive reassurance too."

"What did you do to my girl?" Ada popped Romeo in the back of the head.

"What she say I do?" He cocked his head to the side, not wanting to divulge any information that wasn't already out there.

"Doesn't matter because I know you did it."

"So you just take her word for it?"

"No, but I also went through fifteen hours of labor with you and raised you. I know what you're capable of. I'm not one of those mothers with wool over their eyes when it comes to their sons. Sammy ain't lying." Ada twisted her lips. "Plus, she sent me pictures."

"He did that ish, Ma," Nova advocated, biting into another

piece of chicken.

"Shut up. You was right there with me," Romeo dry snitched. "*Tag me in Ro*."

"The difference is he's single," Ada reminded him.

"Period, Ma. I don't love 'em. I just get the sex and then duck 'em," Nova rapped.

"That's still not ok, and yall need to stop sharing women. That's nasty. What self-respectable woman sleeps with brothers?"

"Ma let's be real. You named me Casanova. I was born to spread my love. Instead of shooting girls with bows, I shoot 'em with my-

"Don't you dare," Ada raised her hand.

"Just saying, Ma."

"You stupid," Czar chortled.

"I'm dead ass. Mama knew what she was doing. Ro is a sucker for love, I'm a player by nature, and you're-" Nova glanced over at his brother. "Well I don't know what you are."

"Good. Keep you niggas guessing."

While it was intended to be a joke, Czar was sort of a mystery to his brothers. Since there was an eight-year age gap between them, they didn't necessarily grow up together. By the time Nova and Romeo came again, Czar felt like he had lived three lifetimes.

"What's all this ruckus I hear?" Slim inquired, strolling into the kitchen. "Boy, unhand my wife." He frowned at his baby boy.

Ada snickered while releasing her son to give her husband a little attention. Living in a house with four possessive male egos once drove her up the wall, but now she was used to it. Between broken bones and prank calls from girls they played, Ada mastered it all. On any given day, she was a nurse, banker, therapist, cook, and whatever else they needed. She could talk one son off the edge while cooking dinner, helping another with their homework, and sew a costume for her baby without blinking. Ada talked her shit, but she wouldn't trade her family for anything in the world.

"Y'all some haters," Romeo snorted, making his way over to the stove.

"Chill, yall know he a crybaby," Nova taunted.

"Leave my baby alone. You ready to eat, Love?" Ada asked, standing under her husband's gaze.

Slim was almost a foot taller than his wife. At 6ft 7, his tall stature towered over her and made him stand out in a room full of people. A salt and pepper blend covered the top of his head and ran down the sides of his face and chin. Slim was in his early sixties but could easily pass for a man in his early forties. His style was a blend of Steve Harvey and Fabulous. It was nothing for him to throw on a three-piece suit and later swap out his Tom Ford dress shoes for some Timbs and Armani jeans. Between the home-cooked meals, daily workouts, and golf outings, Slim stayed in shape. Ada had him taking yoga classes, water aerobics, pottery classes, and whatever else she wanted to try. When they weren't traveling, they were living their best life, and for Slim, making his wife happy was his purpose.

"Yes, make my plate, please." He kissed her lips. "C, let me talk to you for a minute."

"Ah shit, what I do?" Czar questioned but followed him to the basement.

The basement was Slim's mancave and one of his greatest accomplishments. It took him years to get the right furniture, sports memorabilia, and custom-made pool table he had imported from Spain. His cigar and liquor collection was top notch, and the only time he invited his boys into his space was when he had to get a few things off his mind.

"Terri called you?" Czar guessed.

"He didn't have to. You snatching that girl's wig off is the topic of everybody's gossip blog." Slim moved behind the bar and started making them a drink. "What was that about?"

"I was fucked up, but it wasn't that serious."

"It's your image." Slim pushed the shot glass in his direction. "In a world full of sensitive ass muthafuckas and cancel culture at an all-time high, you can't do shit like that."

"What you know about cancel culture?" Czar grinned, cocking his head to the side.

"I know that everybody and their mama is sensitive nowadays. The world loves you, but saying or doing the wrong thing will cause them to turn on you. She can say she has alopecia and boom, there's a whole community of people trying to boycott you."

"With all due respect, fuck these people, Pops. Am I supposed to walk on eggshells because of this soft ass generation? I love the ones who are for me, and the rest can go to hell. I'm going to be me and whoever don't like it can get the fuck on."

"And the beef shit you got going on with the lil suburban kid?"

"I'm not worried about him."

"Yea, well don't ever underestimate a nigga that you embarrassed."

"Like I said, I'm not worried about that nigga. With that being said, I know this ain't the reason you called me down here. You could've said this upstairs. What's going on? Ma alright?"

"You think you know me?" Slim smirked.

"I know you enough," Czar countered, knowing when Slim was beating around the bush. He was normally a straight-to-the-point type of person, and Slim's hesitation made the hairs on the back of his neck stand up.

"So listen," he cleared his throat. "A couple of weeks ago, your mother's lawyer called and informed us that Cain was granted parole."

"W-what?" Czar stuttered, feeling like he couldn't breathe all of a sudden. The liquor he'd just consumed slowly made its way back to the top, causing his mouth to water. His forehead broke out in a light sweat and the walls felt like they were closing in on him. Reaching for the collar of his shirt, Czar yanked at it, feeling as if the fabric was tightening around his throat.

"Breathe, C," Slim coached, rubbing his back, but Czar backed away.

He wasn't some weak ass nigga who needed comforting. He didn't need Slim to rub his back and tell him everything was going to be ok. Czar needed answers. Reaching into his pocket, Czar removed the pill bottle and twisted the cap. Shaking two tiny pills in his hand, he popped them in his mouth and took a couple of deep breaths.

"Fuck you telling me for?" Czar questioned once his breathing returned to normal.

"I heard that he's been asking about you, and I want you to be prepared."

"I don't have shit for that nigga but hands. If he tryna square up then send the nigga the addy."

"I know you're upset-

"Upset?" Czar snorted, thumbing his nose. "I don't think upset begins to explain what I feel. If the nigga knows like I know, he'll stay the fuck away from me and mines, and that's on God."

"Everything ok down here?" Ada asked, standing on the bottom of the steps.

Czar glanced back at his mother and his heart broke. No longer was she the confident woman she was moments ago. She now appeared timid standing there pulling at the bottom of her shirt with slumped shoulders. Cain did that to her. *To them*. The mention of his name sent them back to a tiny apartment with black eyes and bruised ribs.

"Why you ain't tell me?" Czar gazed at her.

"Because I wanted to be the one to tell you," Slim spoke up.

"You aight?" Czar ignored Slim and focused on his mother. He was worried about her mental state, although he felt sick to his stomach. Ada wiped her face and walked across the basement to him.

"I'm good, baby," she swore, rubbing his arm. "We are good."

"I have someone keeping tabs on him, and if he tries to reach out to either of you, he's going back to prison," Slim assured them both.

"Prison?" Czar wiped his face. "That nigga come looking for me, he leaving in a body bag."

"Czar," Ada warned. "Violence is not the way to solve this."

Violence. It was the world he was born into. Instead of being delivered at a hospital surrounded by nurses, doctors, and loved ones, Czar was beaten from his mother's womb by the hands of his father. Her pimp. There were no machines to make sure he was breathing properly or time to bond with his mother. Cain didn't care if his son lived or not because he didn't want the baby anyway. Czar was literally ripped from his mother's arms while she cried at the top of her lungs. Between bleeding out and screaming for her son, Ada passed out. It took three days for her to regain consciousness and another week before she was forced to get back to work.

Czar's childhood was anything but ordinary. His mother was the bottom bitch to a pimp who was in love with her, and it killed him. It didn't matter what Ada did, Cain beat her ass. He couldn't take the thought of another man touching her, yet he sold her pussy to the highest bidder because it provided them with a lifestyle he could never pay for on his own. Sure, he sold drugs here and there, but it was nothing like the money Ada brought him. There was something about her long legs, high cheekbones, and pretty smile that drove men crazy, Cain included.

"Do you hear me, Czar? Violence isn't going to solve anything."

"You sure about that?" He rubbed his jawline. "That was always his go-to."

"That's enough, C," Slim warned.

"I love you, Mama, but I'm not a lil nigga no more, and I promise you that if I see him, I'm going to shoot him." Czar walked around her. "I'm not hungry anymore. I'll catch up to yall later."

"Czar," Slim called out, but it was too late.

Chapter 3

Marley kneeled before her daughter's grave and let out a painful sigh. For the last three years, the weight of the world rested on her shoulders. Leaving her barely standing, hell, barely breathing. The dates on the marble headstone didn't make sense to her. How could you die before you even lived? Her baby girl didn't get a chance to inhale her first breath before her life was taken.

The epitaph scribbled across the stone made her stomach churn '*Billie, The angel who was born sleep.*" Marley didn't even know who came up with that shit, but she hated it as much as she hated praying to a God she didn't believe in. Marley reasoned that God would have saved her baby. He would have saved Benny, but that wasn't the case. Every day she was forced to deal with constant grief because God failed them. He failed her.

"Mommy's sweet girl," Marley cooed, rubbing the top of the marble headstone. "I brought you a gift," she smiled, reaching to her left to retrieve the gift bag.

Marley was aware that her baby girl was gone, but she couldn't let her birthday pass without getting her a toy she'd never play with and a cake she'd never eat. According to her grief counselor, it was supposed to help, but Marley didn't know if it was helping her or driving her crazy. She wanted her baby to open the gift and to smash the cake in her face. Knowing that she'd never do that left her worse than when she arrived.

"I should slap you!" Marley's older sister Harper huffed, walking up behind her and holding a bag of her own. "I asked yo narrow ass if you were coming up here and you lied."

"I didn't lie." Marley quickly swiped the tears from her eyes. "I said I didn't know what I was going to do."

"Girl bye. It's your baby's third birthday. You knew what you were going to do. You just wanted to do it alone."

"Would you have respected that?"

"No," Harper quickly replied.

Instead of responding, Marley inwardly laughed. Her sister was right. She knew exactly what her plans were for the day, but she wanted to do it alone. Celebrating Billie's birthday was always a bitter moment. There was nothing sweet about it, but she did it, hoping it would bring her some kind of comfort, but it never did. If anything, it pissed her off. At times she didn't know who to blame for her anger, but on Billie's birthday, she blamed God.

"Got me hiking up this hill by myself," Harper huffed, carefully sitting the bag of wine on the ground. "You know my back too big for shit like this."

"Harper, please," Marley snickered. "Your big back is beautiful."

"Shut up and give me a hug."

Doing as she told, Marley turned around and fell into her sister's arms. A loud sob escaped her parted lips as tears fell from her eyes. She never understood how she missed something she never had, someone she never got the chance to hold or kiss, yet she felt empty. Marley missed Billie's kicks and the way she balled up under her rib cage when Marley drank something cold. She missed the sound of her heartbeat and the calmness it offered her.

"Let it all out, baby." Harper rubbed her sister's back.

"I really miss herrrrrrrr," she sobbed.

"I know you do. It'll get better."

"It's not," Marley shook her head. "It's not getting better. Some days I'm ok, and other days I can't breathe."

"That's grief, baby. It comes in waves that are worse than the North Sea. Just know they won't last forever." Harper rubbed her sister's back until her breathing returned to normal.

"Why do you sound like an old ass lady," Marley sniffed, pulling away.

"Girl, hanging with them PTA hoes. I swear, when Jaxon said he wanted me to be a stay-at-home mom, I didn't know it meant being involved in all JJ's school shit. If I get another email about gluten-free snacks, I'm going to lose my mind. Like bitch we know Timmy's weak stomach ass can't have gluten, peanut butter, and soy products."

"That's what happens when you move to the suburbs and send your kid to private school. They want you to be *involved.*"

"Girl, kill me now. Ain't no way I can keep going to those boring ass meetings sober. Next time I'm going to bake they ass some weed brownies. Have they uptight asses sitting there high as hell," Harper ranted.

"I believe you too," Marley side-eyed her.

"You should because when you have to bail me out of jail, you know why."

"Where is my nephew at anyway?"

"On a playdate. Jaxon moved my ass to the boondocks and that's what they do out there. Go on playdates, drink wine, bitch about the neighbor's grass while fucking the pool boy. Some straight white people shit."

"You like it."

"I do." Harper smiled, removing a bottle of wine from the bag she sat on the ground. "I be feeling like I'm on the set of *Desperate Housewives*. What's in the bag?"

"A small cake and a gift for Billie."

"I'm right on time. Crack that cake open. I didn't walk that big ass hill for nothing. Here."

"You need to stop." Marley accepted the glass of wine.

"Cheers to my lil Billie goat."

"Bitch, don't call my baby a Billie goat."

"It's all out of love. Happy third birthday, TT's baby." Harper held her glass in the air, and Marley did the same as tears flowed freely down her cheeks.

"Happy Birthday Billie. Kiss your daddy for me."

"Thank you for coming."

"Crack that cake open and let's get sugar wasted before serving our community."

"Ugh. I don't even wanna go to that shit." Marley sighed.

"Well, too bad." Harper smacked her lips. "Drink up. I need a buzz because I know these people are about to irritate my soul."

"In that case," Marley downed the wine in her glass and stretched her hand out for a refill. "Beam me up, Scotty."

"Perioddddd. We about to get wasted and go sell these hoes some detox tea."

∞∞∞

A few hours later, Marley was still in her feelings. With her eyes closed, she practiced her breathing while trying to stay grounded. After visiting Billie, she always thought about Benny. Behind her eyelids was the only place she saw him, and if she closed her eyes tight enough, she could feel his touch or smell his favorite cologne in the wind. Half of the time, Marley didn't know if she was coming or going. After three years, she should have been over it. Benny should've been a memory from her past, she should have been able to move on, but no. Most of the time, she was angry and wanted revenge; other times, she wanted to crawl under the earth and join him.

Everyone kept telling her to give it time, but Marley lived in a world where time didn't exist. Time hadn't healed the hole in her heart, and it hadn't made her forget. If anything, it made her bitter and sometimes unbearable to be around. At this point in her life, Marley was simply existing, a shell of the person she used to be.

"Are you even listening to me?" Harper snapped her fingers in her sister's face. Marley opened her eyes and peered over to her left.

"Not really, what did you say?" She shielded her eyes from the beaming sun. Marley didn't know whose idea it was to host a fair on one of the hottest days of the summer, but she hated them. It was sticky, crowded and all she wanted to do was catch a buzz and hide in the shade.

"I asked if you needed anything else out of the car."

"Oh," Marley glanced around the tent, doing a quick inventory survey, "No. I think I have everything. If I run out of anything, I'll run back to the van."

"Ok, I'm about to run to the bathroom. Please try to smile when people walk up to the table," Harper pleaded with her hands in the prayer position. Marley gave her sister a blank stare until she was no longer in her line of vision.

Smile. A five-letter word, a simple gesture of kindness that could turn a person's day around, yet Marley rarely did it. The muscles in her face were so used to frowning that smiling felt foreign. Her resting bitch face and furrowed brows were the norm.

"What's in your organic peppermint tea? Does it help you lose weight?" A voice chirped, snapping Marley from her trance.

"Crushed peppermint leaves with hints of mint," she answered without looking at the lady.

"And it help with all this?" the woman asked skeptically, reading the back of the box. "Headaches, bloating, and can give you energy?"

"Yes," Marley answered, trying to muster up the energy to engage with the potential customer.

"Tuh," she scoffed. "And it's thirty dollars? This is a *free* health fair, you think people about to pay $30 for some whack ass tea? Yall black business owners be killing me. Wanna charge your own people an arm and a leg for simple shit."

"If it's not in your price range, then I apologize," Marley calmly told her.

"Oh, hell no!" the woman screeched, causing a few people to peer in their direction. "Are you calling me broke?" She clapped loudly, drawing attention to them.

"If I was going to call you anything, I'd call you a ticking time bomb. Your stomach is hanging over your belt, which I'm pretty sure is causing back problems. You're leaning to the side, and the yellow in your eyes indicates that you are either suffering from liver failure or you drink too much. Either way, your days are numbered, and peppermint tea won't help you with anything but your breath. What you need is a doctor and life coach. I think they have that over in tent three, and guess what?" Marley plastered a fake smile on her face. "It's free."

"Oh fuck no! This lil bitch got me fucked up." The woman dropped her bags, ready to charge at Marley, but was stopped when Harper jumped in front of her.

"Excuse me, what seems to be the problem?" She glanced at the raging bull and then back at her sister, who was sitting there unbothered.

"Her! Just because she's skin and bones doesn't mean she can talk about me. I have a thyroid condition."

"Yet you have grease stains on your shirt and your fingertips are stained with red dye. I'm guessing you just left the snack table and those hot Cheetos got the best of you. Pick a side, sis, you sick or hungry?" Marley taunted her.

"Marley!" Harper hissed. "Take a walk."

"Gladly," she mumbled, snatching her knitted bag from underneath the table.

"I think I deserve something free for being verbally attacked by your employee," the woman crossed her thick arms.

"Sure, I have a free sample over here," Harper replied with a tight smile.

Participating in the health fair was Harper's idea. She wanted to give back to the community while gaining a few customers in the process. Harper could have handled it alone, but she wanted to get Marley out of the house. At first it sounded like a good idea, but now that they were out, Harper was second-guessing her decision. Marley kept staring off into space and ignoring customers. She refused to engage and had even acted deaf.

"Take five minutes and come back!" Harper called after her, and in return, Marley stuck her middle finger in the air. She had a good mind to leave Harper's ass right there.

Walking toward her van, Marley took in the scene around her. Anything free brought out the city. It didn't matter that it was a mental health fair; Detroiters used it as an excuse to get together. Nice weather equaled BBQ in Detroit, and that's exactly what was taking place. A mixture of charcoal and kerosene polluted the air, and joyful giggles from children could be heard between cat calls and loud cursing. Marley noticed groups of men gathered near their tricked-out cars that were equipped with big, eye catching rims and loud bass systems. They rocked name brand clothing and custom jewelry with diamond studded charms. Their demeanor screamed drug dealers and the girls were eating it up. Smoke lingered in the air while they loudly talked shit, each trying to out talk the next. Women of all ages flocked around them, wearing too small outfits as if it wasn't a family event. As if they didn't have enough problems in their lives, but the thought of having a dope boy had them acting out of character. Movies and Urban Fiction books had melted their brains, leaving them thinking that every hood nigga tricked and had a big dick.

Marley shook her head. She wished she could warn them about the pain and sacrifices that come with men like that. Sure, the parties, unlimited shopping sprees, random women, and hood respect were good, but the shootouts, jail bids, and death weren't worth the risk, or at least it wasn't in her eyes. She knew about that life all too well and had plenty of war wounds from the battle.

"Benny, who is this bitch?" Marley quizzed, shaking him from his sleep.

"What bitch?" He groaned through his sleepy eyes. It

had been a long night and Benny didn't get home until three in the morning. He hopped in the shower and slid in the bed behind Marely. She was a harder sleeper and didn't flinch when he wrapped his hand around her waist and rubbed her stomach until he fell asleep.

"This bitch!" She held the phone in his face. Benny focused in on the screen with one eye and chortled. Bitches were bold as fuck. He had just fucked the girl on the screen and she was already sending Marley messages about how they were sharing the dick.

"I don't know who that bitch is," he lied, turning over.

"You a fucking lie." Marley threw the phone at him before hopping on his back. Pregnant and all, she held his head under the pillow while his arms flung.

"Get the fuck up," he mumbled as she attempted to smother him.

Benny didn't suffer for long because Marley's bedroom door flew open, and her mama barged in. Pam shook her head as her baby girl went ape shit on her boyfriend like he wasn't twice her size.

"That's enough, Marley!" Pam tried to pull Marley off him, but she snatched away from her.

"Don't touch me!" She climbed out of the bed. "I want him gone and you better not let his ugly ass back in this house or I swear I'm going to move out!"

"Baby," Benny pleaded. "That bitch lying."

"Shut up, dummy!" Marley threw a pillow at him. "I'm going over to my sister's house and when I get back you better be gone," she hissed.

Pam waited until the bathroom door closed and glanced over at Benny.

"Give her some time to cool off. I'll leave the back door open

for you, just give me a few dollars to get my nails done."

"Good looking," Benny nodded, reaching into his pants. He peeled off a couple hundred dollars for her and watched as she stuffed them in her bra.

"Gone on and let her cool off. I'll call you when she gets home."

"Aye, you know where table 12 at?" The deep voice forced Marley back to reality.

Instead of answering, she stared at the tall man for a few seconds and then slowly allowed her eyes to roam over to his entourage. They all towered over her, waiting for her to point them in the right direction, but she was at a loss for words. The entire clique was clad in diamonds and gold. Gucci this, Cartier that. The combination of cologne scents entered her nose, prompting her to close her eyes.

"Hellooooo!!" Czar waved his hand in her face, forcing her back to reality. "Do you understand English?" He snapped his fingers, causing her eyes to flutter open. "Hola."

Unbothered by the frenzy his appearance caused, Czar stared at Marley, waiting for something to slip from her pretty little lips, but she stood there taking deep breaths. He had to be at least six feet something because the way he towered over her 5'7 frame was ridiculous. His smooth skin was the perfect shade of Hershey Chocolate. His locs were long and thick with auburn tips. His eyebrows were black and bushy and his lashes were long and wild. Facial hair wasn't her thing, but his mustache/beard combo was perfectly lined. Marley's eyes fell to his mouth. She caught a glimpse of his grill when his tongue rolled across his bottom lip. They looked soft, almost delicate. He was perfect, well almost, until he opened his mouth.

"Nigga you know Spanish?" Nova snickered. "Say something else.

"I know a lil bit of everything," Czar smirked. "Hola, amigo."

"Oh shit, somebody call Bad Bunny. They need to put my brother on a track," Romeo cosigned, tickled that Czar really thought he could speak Spanish.

Marley stared at them but still said nothing.

"What kinda event this nigga signed me up for? She don't even talk and she nodding off. Somebody get Terri on the phone," Czar said aloud, not caring who called. "Should you have a seeing eye dog or cane?"

"That would mean I'm blind, and I believe what you're trying to insinuate is that I'm deaf or mute." Marley scowled. "Your fans know you slow?"

"Aye, don't talk to my brother like that," Nova warned her.

"Boy, fuck you and your brother. Y'all are in my way, but because he's famous, I have to bow at his feet?"

"So you know who I am?" Czar ignored her obvious dig at his intelligence.

Again, Marley stared blankly at him. Czar was a legend around the city, you'd have to live in a hole not to know who he was. There was a street, library, and basketball court named after him. The mayor had handed him the keys to the city and declared a day in his honor. The media painted him as the biggest asshole that ever walked God's green earth, but in Detroit, he could do no wrong.

"Duh." Marley eyed him from head to toe. "I don't need to stroke your ego, you know who you are." She stepped to the side.

"So you don't want no autograph, picture, social media post?" Czar cockily grinned. "Top me off in the back?" The men with him laughed and gave each other pound as if Czar's words weren't offensive. As if he didn't just ask a complete stranger if she wanted to suck his dick.

"You serious?" She laughed out loud, causing them all to look at her like she was crazy. "If you're looking for groupies, there are a ton of women to your left and a few men, if I might add."

"Where the manager? They gone fire yo ass. My brother doing yall a favor," Romeo snapped.

"Your brother ain't doing shit for me because this is not my event. Now, perhaps if you took off your sunglasses and looked around, you'd see that every table is numbered. There is also an information desk to your left and people dressed in uniforms with badges to your right."

"You couldn't just say that before yo lil head ass started talking shit?" Czar snapped.

"And you couldn't look around before you started asking questions, or are you just used to everyone giving you the answer?"

"Bitch, you don't know me," he snapped.

"And you don't know me. Calling the wrong person a bitch can end your life," Marley winked, stepping around them. Czar tucked his bottom lip into his mouth as he watched her walk away. Marley's small frame didn't have much of an ass, but he couldn't help but notice the gap between her thighs. The way she walked said she had some fire pussy, and if he didn't have somewhere to be, he'd chase behind her and make her back up all the smart shit that spewed from her pretty little lips.

"Come on nigga." Romeo pushed Czar so he could get back on track. "Terri said we're table 12 and someone is already over there setting up."

"Aight." Czar gave Marley one last look before he bopped away with his team.

Once Marley made it to her van, she slipped into the back and climbed into her bed. People exhausted her and large crowds gave her anxiety, which was why she didn't want to do the event, but for Harper, she'd do anything.

Reaching above her headboard, she grabbed the stone ashtray that housed her lighter and joint. Removing the pre-roll filled with Detroit's finest, she placed the tip in her mouth and lit the other end.

Sharply inhaling, Marley waited for the potent contents to invade her system and cloud her mind. She welcomed the foggy feeling Mary Jane provided. It tucked her in at night and gave her an appetite when food made her gag. It comforted her during long nights and mellowed her out when she thought she was losing her mind. Doctors tried to pump her with man-made drugs, but none of them compared to Mary Jane. It was the sole cure for all her pain.

"Marley!" Harper hollered, standing over her.

"What? And how long you been standing there?" Marley peeled her eyes open, wondering how long she had been lying there. When she was with Mary Jane, time didn't exist.

"Long enough to know that you're high as hell. Come on. The raspberry tea sold out and I need your help."

"Sold out?" Marley asked, ashing her joint.

"The rapper Czar and his friends bought it all. I'm not complaining because they are tipping, but they keep buying out everything faster than I can stock it."

"Ugh. I ran into his arrogant ass."

"Well good. You can make conversation and ask him to share our tea."

"Eh, no. I don't even wanna share the same air as his rude ass."

"Whatever, come on. His people are watching the table."

"Do I gotta go?"

"Bitch, yes, you have to go. I need help and it's your freaking tea!"

"I just make it, you sell it."

"You damn right I sell it because it's too good not to." Harper pursed her lips.

Sippin' Tea was Harper's baby. While Marley was the mastermind behind the blends, it was Harper who designed the logo, worked on the marketing, and convinced her sister to sell it. If it were up to Marley, she'd only make it for people who asked, and free at that. Harper wasn't having it. She put an end to all the freebies, registered their name, and Sippin' Tea was born. Harper's hope was that they'd one day open up a shop. She had visions of them owning a cute boutique eatery that specialized in clean eating.

"Ugh, ok." Marley pushed herself from the bed and stopped at the sink to wash her hands. She quickly brushed her teeth and applied coconut oil to her lips. Once she was satisfied with her appearance, she exited her van and locked it up.

Taking her time, Marley enjoyed the feel of the sun on her skin as she headed back to the tent. Summer was her favorite season. Not only did it stay daylight longer, but she was able to travel across the state as much as she wanted to without a care in the world. It was nothing for her to park alongside the lake and meditate while listening to the beautiful sounds of nature.

"Oh hell nah," Marley sighed heavily as she slowly approached her table. At this point, she was ready to go because there was no way she was going to survive another three hours next to Czar and his posse. Thanks to him, their area now looked like a VIP lounge. The music was loud, but the crowd surrounding him was much worse. Marley hated large gatherings, and Czar being next to them was fucking up her vibe. Women were dancing, men were gawking, and kids were surrounding Czar, all vying for his attention.

"Aye look, it's the deaf girl," Nova said aloud, making Czar lift his head.

"Ah, fuck nah! this who you had to go get?" He frowned, looking at Harper.

"Yep, this my sister and I would introduce yall, but she said yall already met."

"So you was talking about me?" Czar simpered.

"You wish," Marley blurted.

"You fried as hell. Your tent is 11, you couldn't just walk me over here?"

"You couldn't use your common sense? I know you see everything is numbered."

"And she got a smart-ass mouth." Romeo licked his lips. "Just my type. You got a man?"

"Yep, come a lil closer and I'll let you meet him," she patted her pocket.

"Oh, and you violent." Nova eyed her. She was a little on the slimmer side and Nova liked his women thicker than southern grits, but she could still get the work.

"Marley," Harper hissed and bumped her shoulder. "Be nice. They are paying customers."

"Wait, Lil Booty made this tea?" Czar asked, holding up the bottle in his hand.

"If you are referring to my sister, then yes. This is actually her company," Harper proudly boasted, knowing Czar loved pouring into black businesses. All she needed was for him to share their business on his page or even tag her. Harper wasn't looking for handouts, but a little exposure ain't never hurt nobody.

"Well, in that case, I want my money back. She mean as fuck, and because of her, I almost got lost."

"We don't do refunds." Marley shrugged her shoulders, moving around the table to take her seat.

Intrigued, Czar watched her sit back in the chair and kick her legs up near the end of the table. He didn't know why, but her '*I don't give a fuck mentality*' turned him on. It was rare to be in a woman's presence and she wasn't throwing herself at him. It was refreshing and he welcomed the challenge.

"So you still don't want an autograph?" Czar questioned, licking his lips.

"Just on your credit card receipt and make sure you leave a tip." She winked, pulling the shades over her eyes. "And stop yelling over here. It's giving ghetto."

"So you not star-struck or nothing?"

"Sir, please, climb off of the high horse and join us in the real world. What does your being famous do for me?"

Czar let out a low chortle before turning his attention back to the crowd that was patiently waiting for him. While he did his thing, Marley watched him out of the corner of her eye. She couldn't front. The man was fine, and his deep voice sounded so much better in person. Like a natural-born leader, Marley watched Czar work the crowd. His music played in the background while he moved around his table, taking pictures, signing autographs, and flirting with women he deemed fuckable.

"You want a picture?" Harper teased, standing next to Marley, who still had her sights set on Czar, who was now listening to people rap to him.

"No. Do you?" Marley shot back, turning her head.

"I already have one and he signed a hat for Jax," she said a matter of factly. "He's going to be so happy."

"My nephew don't want that shit."

"Your nephew loves Czar. Maybe you can flirt with him and get us some tickets to a show."

"Maybe you can rub your coochie on a porcupine," Marley shot back.

"You know being mean is just a defense mechanism. I still love you though." Harper kissed her on the forehead.

"Mm," Marley sucked her teeth. "Got me out here in this hot ass sun. You should be happy I didn't leave yet."

"Yea, yea, yea, now about those tickets. Look out for your girl one time. Your nephew will love you for years to come."

"We gotta introduce him to some better music. Now if you asked me to fuck on Southwest Rah, I'd do it. Shit, I'm not even gay and I'd let him and his wife slut me out."

"Period," Harper agreed. "But we're talking about Czar."

"I'll pass. He's not my type."

"Oh, girl please. I know for a fact you have a few of his songs on your playlist. Don't even try to act like you aren't fangirling right now."

"I'm not," Marley denied, glancing back at their neighbors. "Just because I listen to his music doesn't mean I like him as a person."

This time Czar was staring at her. When their eyes met, she quickly turned her head, making him chuckle. Marley was acting as if he were a lame ass nigga that hung on the corner asking people for change versus a multi-millionaire who could change her world with the snap of his fingers.

"I'mma be a rapper just like you," the little voice said, staring at a Czar with stars in his eyes. Pulling his attention away from Marley, he turned to face the young boy standing in front of him.

"Oh yea?" Czar grinned. "What's your name?"

"Ryan and I practice too. Wanna hear it?"

"Spit something for me, lil homie."

"Ok." Ryan bobbed his head, trying to catch a beat. Noticing the struggle, Czar whipped out his phone and played a beat his producer sent over to him.

"Uh, I like this." Ryan's fingers tapped against his leg. *"Yea, they call me the playground king. Mean left hook guaranteed to leave a sting. Uh. Lil voice but I hit hard, might have ya girl giving me kisses on the schoolyard. Dang Ry, why you do 'em like that? No time for explanations, you don't know me like that."*

"Ooooooh," the crowd howled as his friends patted his head and back.

"Nice, how old are you?" Czar asked.

"I'm ten, but I'll be eleven next year." Ryan grinned confidently.

"Ok, I'm going to give you my card. The next time I'm in the studio, I want you to drop by."

"For real?" His eyes lit up.

"On God."

"Thanks, man." Ryan straightened his posture to give his favorite rapper dap before running to catch up with his friends.

"Who next?" Czar asked his team.

They had only been there for a little over an hour and the line in front of his table was steadily growing. There were a few more kids, a couple of men, but women outnumbered them all. Some wanted a picture, a few wanted to audition to sing on a track with him or be in his next video, and then there were the ones that wanted to fuck. Their motives were very clear. The mental health fair was a kid friendly event, yet they were wearing one-piece rompers that made some of them look like wrestlers, short shorts that allowed their asses to peek from the bottom, and licking their lips at him as if he were a cold drink on a hot day.

"Aye, clear the line. This ain't no muthafuckin' BET uncut video audition." Czar stood up from his seat.

"Why not though? I can do a lot better than them lil hoes." A loudmouth woman in the middle of the line swore, placing her hand on her hip. "You got something against big girls?"

"Nah," Czar denied. "I have something against hoes who wear they kid's clothes. Go take that shit off before you get a yeast infection."

"Oop," People cackled, glancing back at her.

"Boy, fuck you and yo music ain't all that." The woman stuck her middle finger up at him.

"Yet you have a bag full of rap snacks with my picture on them. Put my shit back."

"Let me find out yall favorite rapper is an Indian Giver."

"Get yo high cholesterol ass outta my line and go get your blood pressure took." Czar waved her off. "Matter of fact, yall can thank Ms. Cankles for me taking a break."

"Mannn," the crowd murmured and sucked their teeth as they watched him walk away from his table.

Czar started walking back to his car with Biggie not too far behind. He had a few choice words for Terri. While he didn't mind giving back, sitting in the hot ass sun, talking to a bunch of muthafuckas wasn't his idea of a chill Saturday afternoon. Just as he was about to click on Terri's contact, his eyes fell on Marley. She was leaning back in her chair, drawing in a small notebook. Her bushy curls were pushed to the side, reminding him of the singer H.E.R while her slim frame and style resembled Lisa Bonnet. Marley wasn't his type at all. There was nothing like a big stupid booty and double D breasts, but Marley had him wanting to see if she could talk shit while riding his dick.

"Aye, Lil Booty," Czar called out.

Marley ignored him.

Harper snickered. She knew her sister was hell on wheels and if Czar kept playing he was going to get burned.

"Why you so mean?" he asked, lifting his hand to block the sunlight.

"Why do you care?" she countered.

"Because you almost ruined my day."

"Yet you're still talking to me."

"Cause," Czar walked toward her. "I wanna know who turned you bitter."

"Life," her top lip curled.

"Then you ain't fucking with the right type of nigga."

"I'm not fucking with *no* nigga," she informed him.

"Oh shit, that makes sense." He slapped his forehead as if a lightbulb went off.

"What does?" Marley squinted her eyes in confusion.

"You a lesbo."

"Excuse me?"

"You ain't trying to fuck with a nigga because you like bitches. Well, guess what?" Czar cheesed, stretching his arms out like he solved world hunger. "I do too."

"Wow!" Marley laughed, slowly rising from her chair.

"Marley," Harper groaned, knowing things were about to

take a turn for the worse.

"Why you misogynistic, arrogant asshole. I gotta be a lesbian because I don't want to give your ill-mannered ass the time of day."

"Basically," Czar stood his ground. "Or are you playing hard to get? I mean, I don't mind chasing you for the pussy, but I need to know if I am going to get some at the end of the chase."

"What you can get is a one-way ticket to kiss my ass town."

"What ass?" he jested. "Ain't shit back there, Lil Booty."

"Boy, fuck you." Marley stormed away.

"Just let me know when!" he called after her. "I can put some meat on that lil muthafucka." In return, Marley stuck her middle finger up at him.

"Aye," Czar turned to Harper. "Gimme her number."

Chapter 4

Marley sat in the last pew of her mother's church, trying to find solace in the words that harshly spewed from the pastor's mouth. Church wasn't her thing, but Harper begged her to attend. For Harper, it was go to church with her mother or going to another birthday party, and that shit was out of the question. Marley sat there looking for her purpose on Earth but was having a hard time concentrating when the Pastor was on the pulpit spitting on everybody in the first row. Sweat rolled down the sides of his face as his hand slapped the podium for emphasis. Every time he dropped low, Marley prayed he didn't hit his head on the edge of the stage because she surely wouldn't be able to contain her laughter. Whenever he lifted his arms to praise the Lord, she caught a glimpse of the yellow stains under his pits, and she could only imagine the funk that was produced from them.

"If there is anybody in the house tonight that needs prayer, please make your way to the altar," Pastor Jones whispered into the microphone. "If you're in need of the Lord's shoulder today, step forward." He stretched his arm, encouraging members of the congregation to come to him.

Marley sat there waiting to see if the spirit would move

her to the front, but it never did. She didn't catch a chill, nor did she have the urge to jump up and yell hallelujah like everyone else around her. In fact, it pissed her off that she felt nothing. For three years, she had been waiting to feel something. Some type of message from the Man Above that He had a plan for her. A plan that didn't include more suffering and pain. She needed a sign and wasn't getting it from church or its hyperactive pastor.

"Allow my team...ha- God's team to bestow a blessing upon you," he continued. "A closed mouth doesn't get fed. That's what the kids say, right?" He pulled the microphone away from his mouth and chuckled at his own joke. "How about a closed mouth don't get a blessing? Let me get a Amen this morning."

"Period," Harper clapped her hands. "I mean Amen," she corrected herself, causing Marley to snicker.

"Keep playing and yo mama gone toss some holy water on you."

"Girl, please," Harper snorted. "She acts all holier than thou when just a few short years ago she was thotting her way across the west side of Detroit on a quest to find love."

For as long as she'd been alive, Pam had never stepped foot inside of a church, but going after hustlers and ballers wasn't working, so she figured she would try the Lord's servants. In her mind they had to be good if they praised The Most High. So, every Sunday Pam dressed up in her tightest clothing, put on her fake voice, and marched into the Lord's house on a mission.

Marley personally didn't know how her mother did it. Pam had been in so much bullshit that walking into a church should have sent her ass up in flames, yet wearing a big hat and tight dress, she walked through the big brown doors with the wrong mindset.

"That's yo mama," Marley hunched her shoulders. She didn't have time to think about Pam's reasons for getting closer to the Lord when she was struggling with her own.

"You know it's true. She needs a lil dick to help her snap out of this holy trance. Don't get me wrong though, I kinda like this side of her. It's a far cry from her dealing with them young boys who eat all her food and trap out of her house. I just wish she'd stop acting like she doesn't have a past."

"Jesus washed her sins away."

"He needs to anoint her some dick," Harper whispered, watching her mother jump up and down. The thin white camisole barely contained her breasts, and she didn't seem to mind...neither did the pastor who stole peeks in between prayers. "Some holy dick. Maybe then she'd stay out of our business."

"You going to hell."

"Right along with the rest of these sinners," she mumbled.

Marley laughed under her breath, but her sister had a point. They were all hypocrites. Damn near everybody in the first few pews had been involved in some kind of scandal that shamed the church. From stealing money to sleeping with a person they didn't exchange vows with, they were all dirty, yet they were the most judgmental people she had ever seen. On Monday through Saturday, they got drunk, smoked like a chimney, and cursed like sailors. Come Sunday morning, they rolled out of the bed with stale breath, got dressed, and marched down to the Lord's house to tell someone else's business. It didn't matter whose business it was as long as it wasn't their own.

"Don't be shy," Pastor Jones murmured into the mic. "I'm here to help you get through those long nights. To bring you comfort in your time of despair."

"I bet," Harper whispered.

"I'm not sitting next to you no more," Marley swore as the pastor asked everyone to stand for a final prayer.

The second he dismissed the congregation, Marley and Harper were the first ones out of the church. They weren't up for awkward hugs, fake smiles, and forced conversation. Together, they dodged the pungent perfumes and perverted men who wanted hugs and kisses on the cheeks.

"What are you about to get into?" Harper asked while they walked back to the car.

"Drive toward Traverse City for a couple of days."

"For what?"

"Sit by the water," Marley sighed, pulling her glasses down over her eyes. "Meditate."

It was a nice summer day and she wanted to take advantage of the good weather they were having. Michigan weather was so wishy-washy that it could snow, rain and still be 90 degrees.

"Girl, you are depressing me." Harper tooted her lips up. "Let's go out or something. Get some drinks and people watch."

"I'll pass."

"Ugh, why though? We haven't hung out in foreverrrrr."

"We see each other almost every day."

"Marley, bye. The only time I see you is when I'm picking up orders or we're packing. You never wanna come over and chill, and let's not forget you're always standing me up. How long are you going to isolate yourself from the world?"

"Harper," Marley groaned, not in the mood for another lecture.

"I'm just saying that it's ok to live your life and still miss them."

Missing them was an understatement. Marley didn't know if she was mad because they were taken away or mad because they didn't take her with them on that horrendous day. Waking up to find out that the love of her life was gone and his body had been shipped down south was a slap in the face. Learning her unborn child died inside of her was the icing on the cake. Marley went crazy. No amount of pleading from her sister and mother could stop her from snatching the tubes from her body or the mask off her face. Marley stopped eating, she refused treatment and cursed out every doctor who tried to help her. She wanted to die and hated them for saving her when she had nothing to live for.

Marley wanted her to hang out, but the mere thought of getting dressed, doing her hair, and pretending to have a good time was too overwhelming, and Marley preferred to just be alone. With no one around she was able to sulk in her sadness without pretending to be ok.

"Look at yo mama," Harper snickered. "These church women gone jump her ass."

Marley snapped out of her thoughts and glanced in her mother's direction. Pam was standing next to the Pastor as if she was the First Lady. As if his real wife wasn't a few feet away watching them like a hawk. Pam loudly laughed at whatever he was saying and followed up with a *'Won't He do it."* Pastor leaned in and said something in her ear and Pam nodded before walking away. Marley laughed to herself. It was a different setting, but Pam's intentions were always the same. As sad as it was, she was one of those women who needed a man to validate them, and it didn't matter if said man belonged to another woman.

"Well, that was a lovely service." Pam clapped her hands together as she approached her daughters.

Marley and Harper shared a knowing look. The soft voice

was as fake as her press on nails and to keep from laughing in her face, they simply tucked their lips. Pam was a beautiful woman. Her skin was the color of roasted almonds, and her thick golden-brown hair complimented her oval face. She was on the heavier side of the scale, but that never stopped her from getting a man. Pam's problem was keeping one. She wanted love so bad that she turned a blind eye to the lies and cheating. Her need to be wanted caused her to ignore the red flags and accept the verbal abuse, refusing to believe that there was anyone better out there for her.

"Mm, lovely is a lil far-fetched, Ma," Harper disagreed.

"Maybe if you weren't talking you would have caught the message." Pam arched her eyebrow. "You know it's a sin to play in the Lord's house."

"Oh, Mama please. Don't make me call off the long list of sins you've committed. Plus, it's kinda hard to focus with your titties bouncing around. You didn't wear a bra?"

"For your information, this shirt has a built-in bra." She smacked her lips. "My blazer was a little too hot."

"Mama, please. You know your boobs are too big to fit in those flimsy shirts." Harper twisted her mouth.

"Watch your tongue," Pam scolded, turning to her youngest daughter, who hadn't said a peep. "Well, hello Marley. I didn't even notice you slide in. What's the point of coming if you're going to miss half of the service."

"Hey Ma," Marley dryly responded.

"Did you learn anything?"

"Not really."

"Why not?"

"Yall do too much. Let your Pastor know he doesn't need to do all that hollering to get his point across. I mean we can't even hear the message over all that screaming."

"Swear," Harper commented. "It's like a mega church on crack. All the noise without the money. If he passes that bent up collection plate one more time at the end of the service, I'm going to scream."

"And he needs to change his shirts. I'm tired of seeing those same yellow armpit stains," Marley added.

"The Lord says come as you are." Pam pursed her lips. "I mean aren't you high right now?"

"I was born high," Marley shot back, causing her mother to frown. "And I think we can make an exception for him."

"Swear, and you couldn't find a better church to start attending? They don't even give out thin slices of cake and fruit cups but want somebody to keep digging in their pockets," Harper added.

"Well, instead of judging, yall need to be listening and asking the Lord to heal your soul."

"I don't have a soul."

"Marley!" Pam hissed. "Don't talk like that. I think you just need the right influence. The Pastor and his wife invited us-

"Ma, please, that lady didn't invite us anywhere."

"Harper, hush. They invited us over for dinner next Sunday and their son is single-

"He not single, Ma, he gay," Harper told her.

"That man is not gay," Pam exclaimed.

"Mama, please. His pants are tighter than the straps on your heels, and he gets more dick than a dog in heat."

"You are in front of the Lord's house!"

"And you were just bouncing your titties in his house, so what's the difference?"

"I honestly don't care. Either way, I'm not going," Marley

interrupted them, causing Pam to suck her teeth.

"Why not? Don't you think it's time you got back out there?"

"Where exactly?"

"Back to the dating scene. I wish I had your body and your looks. You can keep the attitude though because you inherited that from your father. You are young and beautiful, you should have all the boys chasing you. Benny, God rest his soul, is gone and you are still here. His death should have been a sign that you weren't living right."

"Ma, you don't wanna go down that road with me."

"Unlike you, I'm an open book. There is nothing you can tell me about myself that I don't already know. I've done things in the past that I'm not proud of, but I know how to move on. It's your life though; if you want to be sad and miserable, go right ahead." Pam shrugged, getting into the front seat. "Hurry up, Harper. I need to cook before the evening service starts. I promised the Pastor I'd bring him a plate."

"I'm not bringing you back over here."

"Marley can bring me then."

"No I'm not. I'll be laying under the stars somewhere."

"Whatever, keep acting like a crazy person and I'll have you recommitted." Pam shut the car door in their face. She shook her head, not knowing where she had gone wrong with her youngest child.

From the day she started walking and talking, Marley gave Pam a run for her money. Harper was the chill one. She had a smart mouth, but she followed the rules, whereas Marley did whatever she wanted when she wanted. Marley was headstrong and challenged Pam from the day she was born. Marley wouldn't take formula, forcing her mother to breastfeed. She refused to take naps in school and confronted her teachers when she felt like they were wrong. Marley's rebellious nature kept her on punishment and sitting in the principal's office.

Being that Pam was always on the prowl to find a new man, she wasn't the best role model. At every turn she contradicted herself, making it impossible for Marley to take her seriously. She'd tell Marley not to go outside, but the moment one of her male friends came over, she was pushing her girls out of the door. She hardly cooked, but if one of her male companions requested a Thanksgiving meal on a Wednesday, Betty Crocker rolled up her sleeves and got to work. As if that wasn't bad enough, Pam morphed into whatever the man in her life needed her to be. She had been a getaway driver in a robbery, a stick-up girl, and a few more things to please men who had no intentions of making her theirs.

"Ignore her," Harper sighed, walking around to the driver's door.

"I always do." Marley chucked the deuces before heading over to her van.

"At least call me when you make it."

"Will do."

Shirtless, Czar stood on his balcony with a blunt hanging from his lips. It was a little after eight in the evening and the sun was starting to set. The orange and red arrays of light radiated over the inner city, providing a fullness in his chest. Residing in one of the tallest buildings downtown gave him a view of everything from Little Caesar's Arena to Belle Isle. The panoramic view with floor to ceiling windows was well worth the money he paid for it.

For a lil nigga from the grimy streets of Detroit, he was doing quite well for himself. His bank account had more zeros than he knew what to do with, he had access to some of the most beautiful women on the planet, and every night he knew where his next meal was coming from. Yet, with all of that, something was missing. He wasn't sure how a rich young nigga was supposed to feel, but he didn't feel it. In fact, he didn't feel anything.

Sitting the blunt down, Czar reached into his pocket and removed the unlabeled pill bottle. Popping the top, he shook the bottle until two pills fell in the palm of his hand. Defying the instructions, Czar picked up his glass of Hennessy neat. Tossing the pills in his mouth, he took a sip of the liquor and let out a low howl. When the burn had subsided, he picked up the blunt to finish his smoke session.

"You want something to eat?" Tati asked, poking her head out of the door.

Czar blew the smoke out of his mouth and turned to face her. For a minute, he forgot she was even there. Then again, maybe he wanted to because she didn't do what she was there to do. Tati had one job and she failed miserably, yet that didn't stop him from admiring her curvy frame.

Boldly, Czar's eyes roamed her body, starting at her perky breasts and then down to her slim waist and thick thighs. Tati was bad and she knew it, which is why she had cupped her breasts and licked her lips when she caught his lingering gaze. Her long, dirty blonde weave was parted down the middle and even though he had been sexing her like crazy for two hours, it was still intact. Her roasted coffee color skin was smooth and her normally thin lips were a little fuller thanks to the lips fillers she received like clockwork.

"You want some more?" she purred, effortlessly making her thighs clap. Usually, the move made his dick hard, but this time it did nothing. In fact, it pissed him off. Tati was becoming a pillow princess and it annoyed him. He almost wanted to call Yaro and tell him to come get his bitch because she kept lying there like a corpse and it irritated his soul. Tati used to be a slut for him, but now she liked to lay on her stomach with her ass tooted in the air. Her arch was sexy as fuck, but her lazy ass couldn't hold it for long without complaining about her back. Tati was about as stiff as a piece of plywood and he was ready to drop her ass out of rotation. The fact that they had been fucking for hours and Czar hadn't nutted once said a lot. Tati had pulled out all her best tricks, but nothing worked. After a while, Czar simply pulled out and told her he was done for the night.

"Nah. What you ordering?" he questioned, unimpressed by her sexual gestures.

When Czar first started fucking with Tati, she was new in the industry and low key. She started out with Fashion Nova endorsements, but with a little fame and a couple hundred thousand followers came a big head. Certain rappers started to mention her name in their songs, she was requested to be in videos as the main girl, and before Tati knew it, she was the *It Girl*. She started dating NFL players, rappers, and movie stars. None of that mattered to Czar because whenever he wanted some pussy, she flew across the world to bust it open for him. What other niggas were paying for, he got it for free. Their situation wasn't exclusive, so he didn't bat an eye when she was photographed with some random nigga after doing a bunch of nasty shit with him. It was niggas like Yaro who couldn't accept that they fell for public ass.

"I was going to cook-

"Fuck nah. Don't cook shit in my kitchen. Order something from Urban Soul Food. Tell them it's for me."

"Why you acting like I can't cook?" Tati questioned, placing her hand on her hip.

“Because you can’t.” He frowned. “Instead of watching twerking videos, you should have been in the kitchen watching yo mama cook.”

“Why do I need to cook when there are millions of restaurants and thousands of niggas that will buy me something to eat?”

“And you wonder why yo PH balance be off. All that fucking for food gone fuck up your insides.”

“Oh, C, please. My shit was off one time because of a douche and you swear my pussy stank all the time.”

“The point is that the muthafucka was sour and brittle. Had my whole room smelling like salt and vinegar chips,” he snorted.

Czar chuckled to himself before taking another puff of his blunt. He could laugh about it now, but when he thought Tati burned him, he almost beat her ass. Czar knew he wasn’t the only one Tati was fucking, and he didn’t care because they used condoms, but when she spread her legs and it smelt like he opened a bag of Lays chips, he pushed her off the bed. As if that wasn’t bad enough, Czar made her take a shower and then dragged her to the clinic. Tati was beyond humiliated as he sat there explaining the smell to the nurse. After that ordeal, he didn’t fuck her for three months, and he made her submit to an STD screening when she wanted to climb back in his bed.

“Fuck you, Czar.” Tati gave him the finger. “Well, do you wanna go out? I know a few low key spots, something romantic.”

“Gone on, Tati. Do I look like a romantic nigga to you?” he gritted, blowing smoke in her direction.

“I mean you could be. I could teach you,” she proposed, walking toward him and straddling his lap. “I can make you the perfect man.” She kissed his chest.

"You can't make me shit, Tati. I'm straight, maybe it's you who's not perfect."

Tati sat up, not sure why the comment felt like a dagger in her chest.

"Whatever. I'm about to order the food." She slid off his lap and went back into the house, closing the door behind her.

Glancing down at his phone, Czar watched his mother's name dance across his screen. It had been a few days since he stormed out of the house and he hadn't answered any of her calls. Czar wasn't mad at her, but he didn't feel like coddling her feelings when his was all over the place. The thought of Cain walking around in the free world didn't sit right in his chest. The abuse he bestowed on them should have been enough to lock him under the jail, yet he was slapped with twenty years and eligible for parole after fifteen.

"I'll call you later, Ma," he mumbled, watching the call go to voicemail.

Czar didn't know why, but he found himself on Sippin' Tea's Instagram page. Scrolling through the pictures, he watched videos of Marley making the tea bags he fell in love with after one sip. The way the herbs and spices worked together sat his taste buds on fire. Clicking on her newest post, Czar sat back in his seat and cut the volume up. To say he was impressed was an understatement. Her whole setup was a vibe. Low music played in the background while she sat at a small counter. He watched as she showed the organic products and then the video sped up as she continued to make the bags, one by one. After sharing her video and encouraging his fans to tap in, he decided to put her number to use.

"Hello?" Marley's hushed voice answered on the first ring.

"Damn, you whispering and shit. Yo nigga must be in the

bed with you."

"Who is this?"

"Santa Claus."

"I don't believe in Santa." Marley ended the call. It took her a minute to catch on to his voice, and the smart comment only confirmed what she knew. It was Czar's ill-mannered ass.

On the other end of the phone, Czar chortled at her feistiness and called her right back. This time the phone rang three times before she picked up his call.

"My sister gave you my number?" she questioned, answering the phone.

"Nah, don't try to clear your voice. Put Barry White back on the phone."

"Boy, fuck you. How did you get my number?" Marley stifled her laughter. Because she was smoking, her voice was a little heavier than normal, making her sound like an adolescent boy, but she didn't care. He called her phone, it wasn't the other way around.

"I have connections. Yo sister ain't give me shit," Czar lied.

"I'm pretty sure it was her because she doesn't know how to mind her own business." Marley twisted her lips, not buying his lie. "Is it normal for famous people to stalk us regular folks?"

"Fuck you mean? I'm regular too. I just got a lil money."

"Sure you are."

"Why you acting all mean and shit like a call from a rap mogul not one of your wildest dreams." Czar grinned, slouching down in his chair.

"You're so full of yourself." Marley snorted at his cockiness. "Does that work? Like, do women usually fall for that?"

"All the time. I don't know why you're acting all hard, knowing damn well I got your panties all wet and shit."

"What do you want, Julius?"

"Fuck outta here! How you know my real name?" He furrowed his eyebrows.

"Google, it's public knowledge, my boy. Now answer my question. Why are you calling me?"

"I wanted to see if you were having a bad day."

"Why?"

"Cause your mean ass been on my mind," he answered honestly. Czar didn't know what it was, but since the mental health fair, Marley ran across his mind more times than he cared to admit. Although her mouth was a little too smart for his liking, her eyes were sad as hell. Something about her sadness felt familiar and made him gravitate toward her.

"You coming inside to eat, or are we eating out here?" Tati asked, standing in the doorway holding up the bags of food.

"I'll be in there in a minute," he answered without looking back.

"Is that Nova?" she asked, making her presence known.

"Go back in there, Tati, before I hurt your feelings," Czar snapped.

"Don't be mean to your little girlfriend because you're on the phone with me."

"She's not my girlfriend."

"Right. I almost forgot you're Detroit's bad boy. You got all the hoes."

"That's what I'm talking about. Act like you know. You trying to join the team?"

"As if." Marley rolled her eyes.

"*As if*," Czar mocked. "So what's up, you wanna be my friend or nah?"

"Nah, I'm good on friends at the moment."

"Damn, cold world."

"Oh please. Like me turning down your friendship hurts your feelings."

"It does. I'm pouring out my heart and you're giving me your ass to kiss," Czar scoffed.

"I didn't give you any part of me to kiss. I just know how you can be."

"You don't know shit about me, shorty."

"You're right. I don't know you, but whenever you're in the media, it's because you did something stupid or like the day at the park. You called me a bitch."

Czar mulled over her words before responding. She had a point, but it wasn't always as it seemed. Most of the time, he was simply responding to someone else's actions. It was a well-known fact that Czar hated to be touched, yet groupies and reporters tested their luck and cried wolf when he snapped on them. Czar didn't mind the cameras in his face, but they always took it too far. It was like jumping into a lion's den at the zoo and expecting it not to bite you. His personal space was his and crossing the line triggered him.

"My fault for calling you out of your name," he apologized, something he didn't do.

"Apology accepted."

"Aight cool, so we can fuck now?"

"No," Marley giggled.

"But look, I'm really cool as fuck. People just take shit way too serious and they don't respect personal boundaries."

"That's your story?"

"It's the truth," Czar stated. "Your turn."

"My turn for what?" Marley furrowed her eyebrows.

"I told you something personal about me and now I want to know something about you."

"That wasn't personal. It's a well-known fact that you are a heathen."

"Aight. I can't swim, I don't sleep with the lights off, and I hate the smell of old grease," he ranted.

"That was random as hell," Marley replied. "And why can't your grown ass swim?"

"Never learned, you gone teach me?"

"No, and who says I want to get to know you?"

"The fact that you're still on the phone says it. Your turn."

"Fine, I'm not a people person."

"Obliviously," Czar snorted.

"You want me to finish, or are you going to keep making snide remarks?"

"My fault, go ahead."

"I'm vegan, and one day I want to travel around the world in my van."

"Vegan, so you like grass and tofu?"

"I don't eat grass and I hate tofu. I'm going to need you to expand your palate."

"Nah, I'm straight. Give me all the unhealthy shit with a side of extra pork."

"Just nasty," Marley snickered.

"And where are you trying to travel to? Can I come?"

"Nope."

"You mean as hell, man."

"Am I mean, or are you just not used to someone being closed off toward you?" Marley countered.

"Both, but I'll let you make it." Czar changed the subject. "Where you at?"

"By the water looking at the sky."

"You downtown?"

"No. Traverse City."

"Yo nigga live out there?" Czar questioned. For some reason, the thought of her laid up with some nigga bothered him.

"Didn't I tell you I don't have a nigga?"

"Then what the fuck you doing out there by yourself?"

"Looking at the stars, smoking, and sipping my tea," Marley said, blowing the smoke into the night sky.

"Now what if a bear comes and gobbles yo ass up," he cracked.

"Then it's my time."

"Death don't scare you?"

"Nope, attachments scare me."

"Why?"

"Because nothing is really yours. Everything has an expiration date."

"Aw shit," Czar loudly exhaled. "You one of those."

"One of what?"

"One of them muthafuckas that wanna get all deep and shit when they high."

Marley choked on the smoke in her mouth. Harper had told her that more than once and to hear someone else say it tickled her. When she regained her composure, Marley opened her mouth to tell him to kiss her ass, but his company spoke first.

"Your food is going to get cold," Tati reappeared.

"Go eat." Marley abruptly ended the call.

Czar looked down at the phone and then over at Tati, who was standing there biting into her chicken. The smug grin on her face let him know she knew exactly what she was doing. Normally, it wouldn't bother him because he was single and neither party's feelings mattered, but Marley hanging up in his face rubbed him the wrong way.

"Aye, put your shit on and leave." Czar put his blunt out.

"Why? Because you out here skinning and grinning with another bitch like I'm not standing right here, and since when do you talk on the phone? I can't even get you to text me back, but you have time to talk on the phone."

"Then that should tell yo slow ass something."

"I know you not mad for real. Aren't you the same person that had me suck your dick while I was with another nigga?"

"That's on yo dumb ass."

"Whatever, Czar. Are you coming to eat?"

"Didn't I just tell you to leave?"

"But why?" Tati snaked her neck.

"Because I fucking said so!" he bellowed, making her jump.

Standing up, Czar snatched the plate of food from her hands and tossed it off the balcony before she could utter a word. In shock, Tati stood there with her mouth wide open.

"I know you didn't just throw my fucking food like that," she uttered.

"It shouldn't be a problem. Go get one of them other

thousands of niggas to feed your hungry ass," he sarcastically grunted, pushing past her.

"Wow. I can't believe you right now. All because I wanted you to eat with me?" Tati frowned, following him inside.

"Nah, because you don't know your place. Hurry the fuck up before I toss yo clothes next," Czar warned. "Matter of fact, hold on." He walked over to the table to check his food. "You better had ordered me a extra cornbread or I'm sending your botched lip ass back."

"I don't know why I continue to lower my standards by allowing you to treat me like this."

"I only treat you how you allow me to," Czar shrugged, biting into the buttery cornbread. "Damn, you should have grabbed you one of these."

"I had one before you threw it out," Tati sneered.

"Oh, well if you hurry up you might have a chance to get it. God made dirt and dirt don't hurt."

"Asshole!" she screamed and stomped away.

"Yea, yea, and pick up your big ass feet before you burn a hole in my rug."

Chapter 5

"TT Marley, you wanna hear a joke?" Harper's six-year-old son Jax asked, dancing around the kitchen counter and climbing on the bar stool next to her.

"Yep," she answered, giving him her undivided attention.

"What do you call a angry carrot?" He covered his mouth, hiding his toothless grin.

"Hmmm, I don't know." Marley rubbed her chin.

"Steamed Veggie," Jax revealed before doubling over in laughter at his own joke while his aunt stood there waiting for the joke to hit her the same way.

"Laugh bitch," Harper hissed in between her fake laugh. She had heard the joke fifty times and each time she laughed to keep from crying. If she heard one more dad joke, she was going to pull her hair out.

"That was a good one," Marley clapped her hands.

"My dad brought me a jokester kit and I have a book, whoopie cushion, fake flower, and everything. When I grow up, I'm going to be a clown," Jax expressed. This time, Marley laughed so hard tears fell from her eyes.

"I'm going to go get the book to tell more jokes." He hopped off the bar stool and ran to the back of the house toward his room.

"That's not funny." Harper popped her on the arm. "Out of all the shit in the world, my baby wanna be a damn clown."

"My poor baby." Marley shook her head. "Ain't no way I could sit up and listen to them corny ass jokes all day."

"Forget all that. Spill the beans! How the hell did we go from two thousand followers to over two *hundred* thousand in a three-day time span? He called you, huh?"

"Yea, because you gave him my number."

"Omg, what did he say? What did yall talk about?" Harper gushed, picking up her glass.

It was Wednesday afternoon, and the sisters were sipping wine and packing orders they received over the weekend. Normally, they'd have between twenty and thirty orders to fulfill, but when Harper checked their website Tuesday evening, there were over three thousand orders. She didn't know whether to cry or praise God. For the first time since they started their business, they sold out of everything on their site.

"Why would you give him my number?" Marley squinted. "Isn't that like some kind of invasion of privacy?"

"He asked." Harper bucked her eyes. "Plus, you need a little fun in your life, and as your big sister, it's my job to steer you in the right direction... or right dick in your case."

"Now what if I gave him your number?"

"Then the nigga would come up missing, and your sister would be walking around looking like a raccoon." Harper's husband Jaxon swaggered into the kitchen. He walked right over to his wife, took the glass from her hand, and placed a kiss on her lips. "I'd black both of her eyes and body that nigga."

"You'd kill for me?" Harper cheesed, staring up at him as if he told her he loved her for the first time.

"What Scissors say?" he asked, looking at his wife. *"Mobbin', schemin', lootin', hide your bodies,"* Jaxon sang off-key while rocking her from side to side. *"Long as you got me, you don't need nobody."*

"You mean SZA?" Marley furrowed her eyebrows.

"That's what I said." He rounded the counter and pulled her into his arms. "What's up, sis."

"Hey, brother," she hugged him back. "You over here listening to SZA?"

"Hell yeah," Jaxon chuckled, releasing her. "Your sister be having me over here on some simp shit. Listening to SZA, sipping wine, and reading them nasty ass books."

"It's ok as long as you're my simp." Harper blew him a kiss.

"Fuck outta here." He waved her off.

Marley picked up her glass as they continued to flirt like they were the only two in the room. She didn't mind their display of affection for one another. It was cute and she loved the way Jaxon loved on her sister and nephew. He was street through and through, but for Harper, he was the softest man in the world. Marley tried not to watch them, but it was hard not to. Their love was pure, and it reminded her of the love she once had.

"What do you think?" Benny asked, standing against the wall while Marley looked around the spacious living room.

"Wait, so this is ours?" She squinted, wanting to be sure before she started screaming.

"Yep. I had my aunt put it in her name, and as soon as we get your credit together, I'm going to switch shit over."

Thanks to her mother, Marley had so much credit debt that it would take her years to climb out of the hole. From utility bills to Rent-A-Center arrangements, she had it all. When Marley confronted Pam about it, she was dismissed as if what she did wasn't illegal and identity theft.

"Oh my godddddd!" Marley held the bottom of her stomach and wobbled over to him. "I love it. I love you!" She smothered him with kisses. "When can I decorate?"

"Whenever you are ready. I have a plug from Value City. All you have to do is go look at the shit you want, write down the item number, and I'll handle the rest."

"I gotta call Harper! This is so amazing." She kissed his lips. "My mama about to be so mad."

"That's her problem. I want to raise our baby in our own house."

"I love you."

"I love you like a fat kid love cake. You know my style, I'll do anything to make you smile," Benny rapped.

"You so corny," Marley laughed out loud.

"You love this corny ass nigga though," he smirked.

"Fuck yea, who else gone thug me like you do?" She winked.

"MARLEY!" Harper yelled her name for the third time. "I'm going to need you to get some hearing aids."

"My bad, what did you say?" Marley cleared her throat.

"We wanna know what Czar said when he called."

"We?" She looked back and forth between them.

"Yea, we." Jaxon poured himself a glass of wine. "Me and my wife share everything. So tell us together, or she'll tell me tonight."

"Bitch, you be telling my business?"

"Not all the time," Harper denied. "But come on, spill the beans."

"Yall belong together because yall both nosey as hell." Marley playfully rolled her eyes. "He called me Sunday night and we chatted for a minute."

"Abouttttt?"

"Well, first he called me Barry White because I was smoking and my voice was deep. He asked if I wanted to be on his team and then I hung up on him because some bitch was in the background."

"But you answered?" Harper questioned with a smirk on her lips.

"Well, duh."

"And you talked to him?"

"Obviously."

"Then that's a start. My job is done. I'll let the universe do its thing." Harper clapped her hands.

"And let me know if the nigga get outta line," Jaxon voiced. "Famous or not, I got a couple hot ones in the chamber."

"That's right! Cause my man keeps the blickey and don't mind pulling it out when shit get sticky." Harper wagged her tongue.

"You ghetto," Marley giggled.

"My hubby like it."

"All jokes aside, do I really want to be connected to a man of his caliber?"

"A man of his caliber? What does that mean?" Harper questioned. "You don't think you're good enough?"

"I'm not saying that, but Czar is a freaking megastar, and I'm…" Marley dragged, not bothering to finish her sentence.

"You're what?"

"I'm sad, depressed, broken, and all the other synonyms. My heart still belongs to a man who's no longer breathing. I don't have time to entertain a relationship when I'm broken from the last one. I'm barely standing." Marley picked up her glass. "I don't have the mindset to even think about being with a man like him."

"Then just have fun with him." Harper rounded the corner. "Let him help you get back on the horse... or dick."

"Say something else about that nigga dick and I'm going to beat yo ass," Jaxon promised, making the sisters laugh.

"Baby, you know the only dick I care about is yours." Harper reached across the counter to grab his hand. Jaxon dismissed her gesture, making them laugh harder.

"That's what the fuck I know, but since we hooking sis up, my boy Lucky been asking about you," Jaxon noted.

"You didn't tell me." Harper arched her eyebrow.

"See, and you over here sharing my business and he keeping his tea to himself." Marley twisted her lips. "Seems a little unbalanced to me."

"Stop being messy." Jaxon tossed a tea bag at her. "And just for that, I'm going to slide your number to Lucky."

"Don't play with me. You are one of my favorite people, but if you give Lucky's round ass my number, we're going to have a problem."

"Oh my god, he is round as hell," Harper laughed loudly. "He reminds me of CeeLo Green."

"You play all day," Marley laughed.

"Somebody at the doorrrr," Jax sang from the front of the house.

"I got it." Jaxon sat his glass down and jogged toward the

front door. There were only a select few who knew where he rested his head, and only two who would pop up without announcing themselves. Peeking through the peephole, Jaxon let out a low groan before he pulled the door open.

"Oh, you're here." Pam turned her nose up as soon as she laid eyes on her daughter's husband.

Dressed in a skintight floral dress and red kitten heels, she bypassed him as if he were the doorman. As if she wasn't stepping foot in the house where he paid bills. Turning to face him, Pam straightened her posture and pushed her hair behind her ear.

"I live here, don't I?" Jaxon squinted.

"Well, I'm just saying," Pam twisted her lips. "I know how you like being out in the streets doing God knows what," she rolled her eyes.

"Could've sworn doing God knows what use to pay your bills," he retorted.

"Hm, speaking of money, it's been a while since-

"Who was at the d-" Harper asked but stopped seeing her mother standing there. "Ma, what are you doing here?"

"I need an invitation to come see my child?" Pam gawked, putting a little space between herself and Jaxon, who was now sporting a frown.

"I mean yea, it's the polite thing to do."

"Oh, girl please. Is your sister here? I saw that god-awful van out front."

"She's in the kitchen," Harper told her. Pam didn't bother to respond. She switched around them and headed toward the back of the house as if she owned it.

"Yea, I'm about to head out. Call me when your company leaves and give sis a hug for me." Jaxon pulled his wife into his arms.

"You sure you don't want to stay?"

"Fuck nah. Yo mama be on one. I'll fuck around and cuss her ass out and the whole congregation will be at our doorstep."

Harper giggled. Jaxon played all day, but he didn't fuck around with his mother-in-law. Back when she was on the other side of the bible, Pam was cool. There were plenty of times he smoked and shared a drink with her. He had even extended relationship advice, letting her know she was too friendly and needed to stand up and stop allowing men to use her. Harper didn't know when, but something changed. Jaxon stopped coming over, and Pam started expressing her dislike for him.

"Take your son," Harper told him.

"I'm already on it. We're going to stop at my parents' crib."

"K. Love you."

"I love you more." Jaxon kissed her lips.

Back in the kitchen, Marley shuffled through orders to avoid talking to her mother. From the moment Pam stepped into the kitchen, she was on her why shit. *Why are you still sleeping in the van? Why do those tea bags look like that? Why they smell like that? Why don't you do something with all this hair? Why are you wasting your life?*

The questions were back-to-back, and before Marley could answer one, another one rolled off her tongue. At some point, Marley started to ignore her, hoping she'd catch on.

"How much do you charge for these anyway?" Pam asked, picking up a bag of tea like it was a snotty tissue.

"Please don't touch." Marley snatched it from her. "It's not sanitary."

"Hm. You got your nerve talking about sanitary when you sleep, cook and shit in a van like a freaking hobo."

"Oh, not sister Pam using words like that and judging. What would your musty lil Pastor say about that?"

"You always did have a smart mouth." Pam twisted her lips.

"You call it smart, I call it speaking my mind," Marley shot back.

"You should come back and live with me." She switched gears. "I could use the money and you need the space."

"Ma, I'll Double Dutch on hot coal before I come live with you."

"What's so bad about living with me?"

Marley blankly stared at her mother. She often wondered if on her trip to glory did she fall and bump her head. It was as if she blocked out everything that transpired between them over the years and made up her own story. Pam talked a good game, but her offer wasn't sincere, and even if it were, Marley wouldn't dare accept it. God almighty himself couldn't convince her to go home.

"Everything," Marley replied without hesitation. She smoked before they started packing orders, but now she wished she would have hit her joint once more.

"Ma, you need to start calling before you just pop up," Harper insisted, strolling back into the kitchen. Taking another glass out of the cabinet, she poured her mother a glass of wine and slid it to her.

"Why? Because Jaxon said so?" Pam jeered, rolling her eyes. "Did he ever call before he popped up at my house? I'm pretty sure he had a key."

"First of all, I was living there, and he was paying the bills, so yes, he had the right to pop up whenever he wanted. And second, I said it. I don't need him to speak for me."

"Tuh. Yall move out to the suburbs and start acting real

funny," she said with pursed lips.

"If me establishing boundaries is considered acting funny, then that's your opinion."

"Whatever, Harper. This will be my last time coming over to your lil house. I actually needed to borrow your Chanel purse, but since you actin funny, keep your little purse to yourself."

Marley bit her inner cheek in order to keep her negative comments to herself. She'd never understand how their mother could minimize Harper's accomplishments but ask to borrow her nice things in the same breath. Pam hadn't once commended them on starting a business, but her hand was out more than the homeless people on the I-75 service drive. She bragged about them to her church *'friends'* but was quick to criticize them in private.

"You drinking and being moody on this good Wednesday, huh, sister Pam," Marley hinted.

"Grow up, Marley. A lil wine ain't never hurt nobody." She took a sip. "What kind is this anyway?"

"It's Issa Rae's new brand."

"I don't like it."

"Anyway, Ma, what's going on? I know you didn't drive all the way to Rochester Hills to harass my sister and insult my wine." Harper rolled her eyes. Her mother had only been there for twenty minutes tops and she was ready for her to leave. "What purse do you want to borrow?"

"You don't have to say it like I'm one of your little friends," Pam spat but went on to tell Harper she wanted the pink Chanel bag with the matching scarf.

Again, Marley chose to keep quiet because at times Pam was one of their little friends, but that era didn't last long. As soon as they started sprouting out and developing their own voice, things changed. She criticized her daughters at every turn and mocked their bad decisions instead of comforting them. In fact, she was in competition with her girls. The more Harper and Marley matured, the more Pam grew jealous of them. Since they were active in sports, their bodies were toned while she walked around with a body built from processed food and years of bad habits. Instead of being their mother, she acted like their friend and only wanted to put her foot down when it benefited her. Other than that, she didn't care if their boyfriends stayed the night. As long as they were paying a bill, both Benny and Jaxon were free to walk in and out of the house as they pleased. Pam turned a blind eye to the catty fights between the couples and even encouraged her daughters to go a little easier on the men who provided them with comfortable lifestyles. That advice normally went in one ear and out the other because if Pam didn't teach them anything, they learned not to be like her.

"Well, actually, I met someone." Pam smiled broadly.

"Here we go again." Marley downed the remaining wine in her glass and reached for the bottle. "What are you about to morph into now?"

"Look, everybody isn't ok with being alone like you. I need a man in my life," she reasoned, setting her glass down. "Now like I was saying, he's into the whole church thing and I really like him."

"How long have yall been dating?" Harper asked, using the word dating loosely. She knew firsthand that her mother didn't know how to date. Pam went from liking a man to loving him all in the same week.

"Well, it's still early, but it's promising. He's getting a divorce and-

"And let me guess, he wants to keep your relationship a secret," Marley pondered, placing her finger on her chin.

"Well, for now, yes, and I understand it." Pam uncomfortably shifted in her seat, hating how Marley always called her out on her bullshit.

"Aren't you tired of making the same mistakes?"

"Excuse me?" She arched her eyebrow.

"I'm just saying. Every man that breathes on you isn't the love of your life. You need to practice loving yourself before you allow a man to enter your space. Learn your self-worth first."

"Self-worth," Pam snorted. "Let's not act like Benny was perfect. He walked all over you. I can remember a couple of times he sent you home with a wet ass and broken heart."

"I was sixteen. What's your excuse for all the shoe prints on your back?"

"You have a lot to say for a lil girl that's pining over a dead man."

"Ma don't," Harper warned. She was used to her mother and sister bickering, but like always, Pam took it too far when Marley started calling her out on her bullshit.

"Don't what? Tell her how it is?" Pam snorted. "You have so much to say about my love life, but what about yours? The man you loved was murdered, and his family took everything from you and left you living in a van. If that's not pitiful, I don't know what is."

"Well, at least I know where I get my bad decision-making from."

"Marley, you can go to hell."

"Right after you, Sister Pam," Marley stated and polished off the rest of her wine. "At least make sure this one takes you out to eat or to a movie before he gets the Pam experience." She sat the glass down.

"Go ahead and run away like you always do," Pam

continued.

"Ma, I'd advise you to chill. You keep hollering this open book mess, but I know a few untold stories." Marley wickedly smiled before backing away from the table. "I'll be back when she leaves."

∞∞∞

Czar sat in the director's chair watching his dancers struggle to stay on beat. He was beyond irritated and it was taking all his might not to fire them all. Czar could blame his attitude on the fact that he hadn't gotten any sleep or the anxiety attack he had that morning, but it was them. This was the last shot for the video and the dancers kept fucking up like they hadn't been doing the same dance for three weeks.

Shaking the pills in his hand, Czar went back and forth on whether he should take them. Being that he was directing, it wasn't ideal. His judgment would be clouded and his creative streak would be nonexistent. Opting for a drink instead, Czar lifted the cup to his lips and took a sip of the liquor, hoping it would calm his nerves, but it did just the opposite. His fingers impatiently drummed against his thigh as he watched the dancer continue to fuck up a simple two-step.

"Cut," he hollered in the bullhorn, causing half of the set to suck their teeth. They had been there since five in the morning, and it was going on eight in the evening. "Aye, what the fuck is going on?" he yelled. "Why the fuck yall moving so slow?"

"We tired," the lead fucker-upper mumbled.

"Aight, cool. Take the rest of the night off."

"Seriously?" She started walking to the end of the stage.

"Yea," Czar nodded. "And while you're at it, clean out your locker, and don't bring your saggy booty ass back."

"You're firing me?"

"You're firing your damn self. Your ass so big you can't even keep up with the beat. Go back to your doctor and tell them to take some of that fat out of your ass. You can't control the big muthafucka."

"Fuck you, Czar!" she shouted, charging toward him. Nova and Romeo jumped into action, restraining her from going any further.

"You did last night and I felt like I was fucking a bounce house. I'm all for a little cushion, but you took that shit to the next level and your pussy smelt like burnt plastic."

"Oh, you got me fucked up." She threw her shoe at him. "I'm going to sue you nigga!"

"Get in line, bubble booty." Czar waved her off as his brothers dragged her out of the warehouse. "Now for the rest of yall. If you can't keep up, just say that, and I'll have you replaced. Ain't no half-stepping around these parts. Take twenty minutes and come back with your mind right, or yall can follow Ms. New Booty."

Besides a couple of groans and low mummers, no one said anything. Czar was known to fire his entire staff and start over from scratch. His need for things to be flawless wouldn't allow him to accept anything less than perfection. He worked too hard to make it to the top and his fans deserved nothing but the best. Sitting the bullhorn down, he took a seat and ran his hands down his face.

"You pissing off everybody today," Nova stated, dropping in the chair next to Czar.

"Black Twitter not about to drag me because she's in the background looking like she having a stroke."

"And what the fuck you do to Tati?"

"Why? What she post?" Czar frowned, knowing that was Tati's thing. Whatever went on in her life, the internet was the first to know about it. It didn't matter if she broke her nail while pulling the price tags off a Chanel bag, she'd tweet and ask her followers to pray for a speedy recovery.

"Some shit about not fucking with rude ass niggas no more."

"I'm going to make her thin lip ass stand on that. I'm the one who should be mad."

"What she do?" Nova quizzed.

"I was on the phone with Lil Booty-

"From the park?" Nova grinned, recalling the cutie that cursed his brother out in front of everybody.

"Yea." Czar stroked his chin.

"How you swing that? I just knew her lil mean ass wasn't going to answer the phone."

"Fuck outta here. You know who I am?" He cocked his head to the side. "Anyway, we was kicking it. Wasn't even no deep shit, just vibing."

"Aight, you was caking and what else?" Nova urged him to get to the good part.

"I don't cake, but yea, so Tati kept coming to the door talking about some food. Lil Booty hung up on me, and I tossed Tati's food off the balcony."

"You what?"

"Played frisbee with her food. She talks too much. All she had to do was eat her food and shut the fuck up."

"Wait, so were you mad that Lil Booty heard her voice or because Tati was being messy?"

"Both," Czar answered. "I was enjoying my conversation."

"You know Tati can be possessive. I'm pretty sure she thought she had a chance to be your girl."

"Again, none of that is on me because I never alluded to no shit like that. She's an industry hoe and I'll never settle down with a bitch like her," Czar replied, watching Romeo bop over to them. The guilty look plastered across his face said he had been up to no good.

"The fuck you just do?"

"Aye, I need you to put ole girl back in the video," he told Czar.

"You fucked her?"

"Nah. I calmed her down and she sucked my dick like a pacifier. I need you to put her in the video."

"Nigga, no!" Czar bucked. "You better get a restraining order on her ass because I'm not putting her in the video, and when she realizes she gave up that head for free, she's going to go postal on you."

"Speaking of postal," Romeo nodded his head in the direction of their mother hastily headed in their direction. The scowl etched across her face let them all know she was out for blood.

If there was one thing Ada didn't play about, it was disrespect. She had been abused and misused by several men in her life, and she didn't play that shit when it came to the boys she pushed from her womb. Czar ignoring her calls was a sign of disrespect, and since he still wasn't answering her calls, she decided to bring her concerns straight to his doorstep.

"Hey, mama," Romeo was the first one to greet her and then Nova.

"Hey, my loves." Ada hugged them, placing a kiss on their cheeks. Czar stood there with his hands in his pocket, waiting for the storm. "Is the cell service out over here?" she asked, stepping back and glaring at her oldest son.

"Ma-" he started but was cut off when she raised her hand.

"I asked if the cell service was off."

"Nah, Ma," Czar answered, shifting on his feet. He glanced up and could see the staff from the set peering in their direction. "Aye, go do something," he yelled, making a few of them jump from the thunder in his voice.

"Don't yell at them. I'm pretty sure they answer the phone for their mamas."

"Ma, I'm sorry."

"Nova and Romeo, give us a minute," Ada calmly said, taking a seat in the chair with Czar's name etched across the back.

Doing as they were told, the duo paddled away from the tension while making faces at Czar. He wanted to curse them out, but testing Ada wasn't a good idea. She was no taller than 5ft 7 but would have no problem bringing him to his knees.

"So, you too busy for ya mama?" she asked, turning to face Czar.

"Never."

"Then why haven't I heard from you since you stormed out of my house?"

"Been working, Ma." Czar shifted on his feet.

"And picking up the phone to say that is such a hassle, huh?"

"I didn't say that."

"Then what are you saying, Julius?" Ada quizzed, using his real name to let him know she wasn't about to talk in circles.

"I'm not gone lie. Hearing ole boy is out of prison is messing with my head. I grew up around the nigga and I know he's not about to let you be happy. I know that if he finds you, he'll try to break you down and make you come back to him."

"You gotta give me more credit than that," she sighed. "There's nothing he can say or do to me now. Back then I was young, and I'm not that little girl anymore. If Cain tries anything, you or Slim won't have to worry because I'll take his life myself." Ada patted her purse where her pretty little nine was sitting. "And that's on God," she mocked him.

Czar cracked a smile, but her words did nothing to soothe the uneasy feeling in his stomach. He had seen Cain in action and knew he was a piece of work. His mouth game was so cold that he could talk a nun into busting the pussy open for him. A week later, he'd have her on the stroll fucking niggas in her habit. His deep voice, fine features, and lengthy dick made women willingly walk the plank and deep dive into a life full of toxicity.

"I hear you, Ma," Czar nodded. He heard everything she was saying, but it wouldn't stop him from taking matters into his own hands. Cain was unpredictable and he had years to think about his next move. That's what bothered Czar the most.

"Good, now stop acting funny and give me a hug." Ada stood up. Czar did the same and pulled her into him. Hugging her tight, Czar silently said a quick prayer. He needed God to give her strength because going back wasn't an option.

"I really don't feel good," Ada groaned, holding the bottom of her stomach.

"Baby, come on now." Cain lovingly kissed her forehead. "I'll make it up to you when the night is over."

"I really can't today."

"So fuck me and what I need?" He barked, making three-year-old Czar pop his head up. He was only a few feet away, flipping through his comic book, but stopped moving when he heard the thunder in his father's voice.

"I'm not saying that bae, but I'm cramping," Ada whined.

"Then take something and let's get this money. You have a full schedule today." Cain clapped his hands.

Ada rolled her eyes but pulled herself up from the couch. She knew no matter what she said, she was working. It simply depended on whether she was going to do it willingly or with a black eye. Ada tried to walk by him, but Cain grabbed her wrist and planted a kiss on her cheek.

"Let's get this money, baby, because that's what we do," he charmed her.

Ada hated how confused she felt by his touch. One minute, he was stroking her cheek like he did when they first met, but in the next breath, that same hand could strike her to the ground. The wrong words could leave her with a busted lip, but agreeing to do what he wanted had a different reward.

"Ok," Ada sighed, giving in to his touch.

"Good girl, and make sure you don't kiss none of them niggas. Those lips are reserved for me."

"Never," she promised, wiping the tears that slipped from her eye.

Czar sat on the floor flipping through his Captain Underpants comic book. He didn't have to look up to know his mother was crying. He was used to it because that's all she ever did. Even when he thought they were having fun, Ada could be found quickly swiping tears from her eyes.

"Go get cleaned up and come see me before you go," Cain ordered, getting back to the money. He didn't have time to coddle

her when money was on the line.

"Ok," Ada cleared her throat. "Let me get Czar settled before I go."

"That nigga straight," Cain grunted. "Do what the fuck I said." His loud voice bounced off the walls making Ada jump.

"I'll bring you something, sweet baby boy." She stroked his cheek. Cain couldn't fight the frown that covered his face. Ada looked at Czar in a way that she never looked at him and it rubbed Cain the wrong way. Deep down, he knew that she'd never love him as much as she loved their son. As crazy as it was, the thought of Ada loving someone other than him got under his skin.

"I should have made you abort his scrawny ass. How the fuck he about to be five and little as shit?" Cain taunted as if Czar wasn't produced from his sack. "And stop reading this gay shit. A white man in his draws shouldn't be something you want to read about." Cain snatched the comic book from his hands, ripping the pages.

"I can take him to Trina's house," Ada insisted, catching a backhand that ended with her flying into the wall. Czar jumped up and ran over to her as she held her face.

"The fuck you gone do?" Cain laughed, finding humor in the fear in Czar's eyes. "Go get ready, Ada, and don't make me say that shit again."

"You know I love you, right?" Ada touched Czar's cheek, bringing him back to reality.

"Yea, I know." He nodded. There was never a doubt that she did. Ada simply did what she had to do. She learned at an early age that if you didn't make lemonade with the lemons life threw your way, someone else would.

"Good, show me what you're working on."

"Maybe you can help. Get up there and show them how

yall used to do it back in the day," Czar joked.

"Don't threaten me with a good time. I'll get up there and turn this whole set out," Ada smirked. "I might not be a spring chicken anymore, but I still make the roosters holla."

"Yo, I don't know if that was supposed to be a sex joke or not, but you gotta go."

"Oh, now I gotta go because your mama still got it."

"Ma, you ain't got nothing but a sore back and swollen ankles."

"See, I almost went off on you." Ada punched him in the arm. "I'm going home since you wanna call me old," she pouted.

"I'm playing." Czar took her hand and walked her to the edge of the set. "Break over!" he shouted. "Show my mama what yall working on, and if yall embarrass me, everybody fired."

Chapter 6

Czar rolled over for what felt like the millionth time. Lack of sleep was another downside of not taking the medicine that was prescribed to him. He wasn't sleepy per se, but he knew he needed to rest because he had a shitload of things to do when the sun came up. Czar thought about calling a female to help put him to sleep, but then again, he didn't feel like dealing with the aftermath of delivering A1 dick. The women he fucked didn't know how to take the dick and keep it pushing. They wanted to lay up and daydream about a future with him. That's all it was, a daydream because though he wasn't against the idea of love, it wasn't at his forefront.

As soon as he thought about rolling a blunt, his phone started to vibrate. Picking it up, Czar saw the notifications from Twitter, Instagram, and text messages from his people. Before he could even open it, a FaceTime from his brothers came in.

"The fuck yall calling me on three-way for?" he asked, answering the phone.

"What you doing?" Romeo quizzed.

"Nigga, it's one in the morning. Don't call my phone on some what you doing bullshit like you a bitch."

"Fuck outta here."

"You been on Twitter?" Nova asked, cutting them both off.

"Nah, why?"

"Ya boy Yaro on there popping big shit."

"What's new? His eye must've healed."

"I'm about to share my screen," Nova insisted, not giving his brother a chance to protest.

Czar switched on the light to watch the video.

"What up doe Detroit, this ya boy Yaro. Tonight at a pop-up location, I'll be shooting an impromptu video for my new single 'My Hood.'" Yaro spoke into the camera. It was dark, but Czar could still see the shiner around his left eye. *"Tell a friend to tell a friend that at 2:30 am, we about to turn Rouge Park out."*

"Fuck outta here," Czar scoffed. "Who told that nigga he can shoot his whack ass video in my city?"

"Same shit I said, so I rounded up the boys and we're downstairs. Don't take all day." Nova ended the call.

Czar scratched the top of his head and stood up from the bed. He didn't plan on attending a video shoot, but since the hood needed saving, he was the person for the job.

"Super C to the rescue," he joked to himself.

Yaro stood in the middle of the crowd, rapping the lyrics to his latest hit. The song was released on YouTube right after his fight at the club and fans were eager to see what he had to say. Videos of him being knocked out floated around the internet and Yaro swore Czar snuck him. The diss track was aimed at Czar. To add icing to the cake, his team decided to shoot the video in Detroit, Czar's stomping ground.

"*Who want beef with the illest? Wasn't raised in the city, but my whole team killas,*" Yaro rapped, pointing his index finger and thumb at the camera.

With a stack of money pressed to his face, Yaro shot his imaginary gun in the air. The thick girls of all shades bent over next to him, shaking everything their plastic surgeon gave them. A few of Yaro's homeboys stood beside him, throwing up a gang they didn't belong to. A gang that many had died for, yet they carelessly threw up the sign like they were a part of that life.

"*And run up lil nigga, try me. Keep a bad bitch, call her Tati,*" Yaro rapped, blowing a kiss in Tati's direction, who was sitting on top of a Charger, wearing a thong bathing suit and fur coat.

"What the hell?" Yaro's videographer mumbled, slowly lowering his camera. "Yall hear that shit?"

The sound of burning rubber and bikes revving could be heard, but because it was dark, they couldn't see anything.

"Go see," Yaro snapped at his security team, who was standing there just as puzzled. "Ain't that what I'm paying you niggas for?!"

"Nigga, no. It's dark as fuck and we told you not to shoot here." The head security guard frowned. "You not my mama, so I'm not jumping in front of a bullet for you either."

"Yall some bitches," Yaro's cousin Free chuckled. "Don't worry, fam. I got the strap." He lifted his shirt, revealing the butt of the gun he had tucked in his pants.

"Oh shit, look!" One of the dancers pointed toward the noise.

Three masked men on Yamaha R3s sped around the perimeter of Yaro's video set, creating a thick cloud of smoke. Like something out of the Purge movie, loud sirens and flashing lights took over the scene, causing a slight panic. Yaro knew that his video shoot was going to stir up a little commotion, but he wasn't willing to die for it.

When the smoke cleared, Ram trucks the size of monster trucks led the way. Again, men in ski masks drove while women hung out of the passenger windows in black bodysuits waving black bandanas in the air. Yaro's cameraman caught on quickly and started filming the scene. Whether Yaro wanted it or not, he was recording everything.

"These niggas foolin'," Free voiced, as the trucks and motorcycles formed an aisle way. A slingshot slowly drove down the middle as Chief Keef's *Love Sosa* instrumental loudly played. Two women in ski masks dangled from the sides of the slingshot while the shirtless driver bobbed their head to the beat.

"These niggas love Czar," he rapped, coming to a stop right in front of Yaro.

Like the cocky ass nigga he was, Czar hopped out of the slingshot, removed his ski mask, and tossed it at Yaro's feet. He wasn't hiding and wanted the world to know who the King of Detroit was. Like clockwork, all of Czar's crew jumped out of their trucks and stormed Yaro's video shoot. They stood behind his dancers, sat on the car next to Tati and posted up as if they were invited. Yaro was bewildered and couldn't believe that Czar was hoeing his life.

"Bro, the fuck is you doing? This is a closed set," he gritted, finding his voice.

"Who told you that you could shoot your bum ass video here?" Nova questioned.

"Nobody, we don't need permission." Free stepped

forward, lifting his shirt. "I suggest you niggas hop back on them lil toys and get the fuck on."

Nova looked down at the gun and grinned. He snapped his fingers and goons circled around them, holding choppers that could end their lives in seconds. Free slowly lowered his shirt, and Yaro wanted to shit on himself. All that hot shit Free was talking went right out the window.

"Man, what do you want?" Yaro asked Czar with his head held high even though his heart was beating at dangerous levels.

"I should be asking you that. You brought yo pale ass to my fucking city and tried to record a video to that whack ass diss track."

"I live here too, you don't own this park."

"I live here too," Czar mocked. "You think I give a fuck because you bought a block on the east side and fixed that shit up. You a fucking puppet with money. These niggas don't really fuck with you."

"Fuck you, Czar."

"This nigga turning red and everything," Romeo joked.

"Whatever, can I get back to my video?"

"Nah," Czar answered. "I told you every chance I get I'm clowning your ass."

On cue, the *Love Sosa* instrumental started playing, lights started flashing, and Czar started rapping. The freestyle went crazy and even Yaro's people had to stop themselves from rocking. Yaro's dancers were now dancing with Czar's crew and the cameraman was moving as if Czar wrote his checks.

"These niggas hate Czar, but he's a lady pleaser, took his main bitch and I turnt her to a skeezer," Czar rapped, winking at Tati who was shaking her head. *"Claiming he want work, but he ain't got no heaters, looking like a character, call that boy a*

creature."

"Ahhh," Romeo laughed into the camera.

Outnumbered, Yaro nodded his head and tucked his tail. He wasn't a freestyle rapper and it normally took a whole team to write his lyrics. Even if he wanted to clap back, there was nothing he could say that would make sense, so Yaro did the next best thing. Grabbing Tati's hand, he walked around Czar and headed back to his car with Free on his heels. The cameraman recorded him walking away and he almost felt bad for him. He would have respected him more if Yaro put up a fight, but he got punked out of his set and team. There was no coming back from that kind of humiliation. As he pulled off, Yaro could hear the crowd chanting Czar's name like it was a prayer.

"Czarrrrrrrr, Czarrrrrrrr, Czarrrrrrr!"

A few days later, Czar's video and song charted at number one on almost every platform. Once again, Yaro was the laughingstock of the music industry.

∞∞∞

Marley lay in her bed listening to the sound of Jhene Aiko humming in the background about being alive and well. Her windows were down, and the fresh rain scent flowed through the van, putting her mind at ease. With her eyes closed, Marley placed the joint in her mouth and pulled. This was how she reset, and after seeing her mother, it was much needed. As much as Pam talked about her van, for Marley, it was home.

1990 Chevrolet G20 served as her home on wheels. After watching tons of TikToks, Marley had the van gutted from the front to the rear. With the help of her sister and Jaxon, she installed padding and insulation to control the temperature. She had a twin bed, running water, a hotplate, a refrigerator, and plenty of storage. On top of all the essentials, Marley made it home by hanging her drawings on the wall, adding a few plants to the roof, and a small bookshelf over her bed. The van was the only thing she had left of Benny. It was something he planned to work on once he slowed down in the streets. Instead of selling it, Marley fixed it up and lived in it.

The vibrating of her phone pulled her from the Zen place. Picking it up off the bed, she answered without looking at the number. It was a little after midnight, and unless something was wrong, she knew that it wasn't her sister.

"Aye, why you hang up on me?" His deep voice vibrated against her eardrum, causing her to close her eyes and exhale. It had been years since she melted at the sound of a male voice. "I thought we were getting along."

"How long ago was that?" Marley tittered.

"And you think the shit is funny. People who hang up on me don't get a callback. Now say sorry because you hurt my feelings."

"I'm not apologizing. You need to be apologizing to me because your little friend was rude as hell."

"Oh, so you one of those," he scoffed.

"What's that?"

"A person who can't take accountability for your actions."

"Your food was getting cold." She blew the smoke out of her mouth. "I didn't want your little friend to starve waiting on you. Sis was dependent on your company."

"Deep ass voice," Czar teased, listening to her try to clear her scratchy throat.

"Shut up. Don't call my phone talking shit."

"You smoking?"

"Yep." Marley inhaled. "I have a prescription."

"You smoke a lot?"

"Every day," she answered proudly.

"You be that stressed?"

"Nope, Mary Jane relaxes me, and according to my doctor, a joint a day keeps the anxiety away."

"Man, yo doctor ain't told you no shit like that." Czar laughed into the phone.

"I mean she didn't say those exact words. I summed it up for her. Mary Jane is like a support animal to me."

"So, weed is your support animal?"

"No, Mary Jane. Weed sounds so ghetto."

"You funny as fuck," Czar chortled, allowing them to fall into a comfortable silence. He didn't know what to say because he didn't know why he had called her.

"Why are you calling me this late?" Marley quizzed.

"Fuck if I know," he sighed, sitting back on the couch. "It's crazy 'cause I don't even like talking on the phone."

"Should I feel honored?" She arched her eyebrow.

"Do you?"

"Nope. I couldn't care less," Marley lied. She felt something but didn't know if honored was the correct term.

"You mean as hell," Czar simpered, running his tongue across his teeth. "So, you trying to be my friend or not?"

"Let me find out your rich ass ain't got no friends." Marley twisted her lips as if he could see her.

"I don't and I'm not that rich," he dismissed the comment, but they both knew it was the furthest thing from the truth.

"I checked your net worth," she divulged.

"How much am I worth?"

"Couple grand," Marley fibbed. She was way off and she knew it. According to Google, Czar was worth millions and counting.

"Sounds about right," Czar agreed. "Let me hold a couple of dollars, especially since I had my followers go cop your tea."

"I didn't tell you to do that."

"But I did and I know they came through and showed out."

"They did," Marley admitted. "I made so many tea bags this week that my hands hurt."

"You be doing all that by yourself?"

"No, my sister helps. I make the tea bags and she handles everything else."

"That's what's up. Teamwork makes the dream work." Czar picked up his glass and took a sip of the warm brown liquor. "How you get into that shit?"

"Making tea?"

"Yea."

"Julius," Marley sighed. She was having a hard time believing that he was on her line asking about her life as if they talked every day.

"And I'm about to sue Google. Why you keep calling me that shit? If you not gone call me Czar, call me daddy."

"Definitely not calling you that," Marley laughed out loud. "For real though, why are you on my phone? I know you have plenty of Instagram bitches to entertain you, and their story is far more interesting than mine."

"Their stories are all the same. It's all surface."

"Mm."

"For real and talking to you is refreshing. I mean you sad as shit, but you so unfazed by who I am, and I'm not going to lie, that shit attractive. It's been a minute since I've talked to a female that wasn't trying to fuck me. Plus, you from Detroit and Detroit girls do it better. Them out of town hoes be fake as fuck. I mean you ain't got no ass but you be dragging that lil muthafucka."

"You're an asshole," Marley laughed. "Me not wanting to jump your bones turns you on?"

"Yep. Makes me wanna jump your bones," he mocked her.

"Well, you can forget it because you won't be jumping anything this way."

"Why?"

"I'm celibate." Marley blew the smoke in the air.

The statement was semi-true. She hadn't been with anyone since Benny, and she wasn't looking. The toys under her bed got the job done just fine. Marley was almost sure no man could make her climb the walls like her late lover, and she didn't want to test the theory.

"Fuck outta here." Czar snorted, reaching for his ashtray. "Shit, you about to make me smoke."

"I'm serious. I haven't had sex in a little over three years."

"Now why would you tell me some shit like that?" He closed his eyes. "I bet that bad boy tight as fuck too. Let me get a lil bit before we start being friends."

"No, and who says I want to be your friend?"

"You might not want to be my friend, but shorty you need one. Those big ass eyes are full of sadness."

Marley didn't respond. She took another pull from her joint and gazed up at the sky through the sunroof. By now she was aware that sadness radiated from her pores. As far as she was concerned, she had nothing to smile about.

Happiness was temporary and she learned that the hard way. So instead of setting herself up for failure, Marley chose to simply exist.

"Hello?" Czar removed the phone from his ear to make sure she didn't hang up on him again.

"I'm still here."

"Aight, so back to what I was getting at, you a virgin?"

"I never said that."

"So, what the last nigga had a lil dick or something? If that's the case, you ain't got nothing to worry about, my shit b-

"He died," Marley blurted.

"In the pussy?" He coughed. "On some *Color Purple* shit?"

"Oh my god, I don't know why I'm entertaining you right now."

"Cause I'm a real ass nigga and you like that," Czar stated.

"I guess."

"So you wanna tell me why you're always sad?"

"No, I'm about to go to bed."

"Then get yo Luther Vandross sounding ass off my phone."

"Bye Julius."

"Don't call me that sh-" Czar fussed, but Marley ended the call.

Tossing the phone to the other side of the bed, Marley picked up Benny's sweater and buried her face in his shirt. She missed their nightly conversations and talking to Czar reminded her of that. The faint scent from the sweater brought tears to her eyes because she knew once it was gone, she'd never smell him again. That was the downside of grieving. One minute she was on the phone laughing, and the next she was crying and trying to catch her next breath.

∞∞∞

On the other side of town, Czar couldn't help the unsettled feeling in the pit of his stomach. The sadness in Marley's tone made him feel anxious, kicking his Superman complex into gear. He wasn't used to the women he talked to sounding so helpless. Czar was used to man-eaters. Without putting much thought into it, Czar grabbed his phone to FaceTime her.

"Anybody ever call you annoying?" Marley answered the phone, wiping the tears from her eyes.

"Nope." Czar squinted, zooming in on her face. "The fuck you sitting in the dark crying for?"

"None of your business. Why are you FaceTiming me after you just called me Luther?"

"Cause I'm trying to chill. Pull up on me, or I can send you a car."

"A car for what?"

"To come to my crib, or I can come to yours. Either way I wanna chill, so how you wanna play it?"

"Julius, are you high right now?" Marley bucked her eyes. "I literally just met you, and I also told you I didn't want to have sex with you."

"Girl, calm down. You can keep that lil pussy. I just wanna chill, that's it. I have like five guest rooms and you can stay in one of them."

Pulling her lip into her mouth, Marley thought about what Harper would do. That wasn't even a logical question because Harper would have already been halfway out the door.

"Fine, I'll come, but I'm not staying the night and you better not try no funny shit. I have pepper spray."

"Aight. I'll text you the address, but don't post my shit online."

"Boy, just send me the address," Marley mumbled before ending the call.

Doing as he was told, Czar sent her the address and scratched the top of his head. This was new territory for him. Usually, Tati would come through with one of her homegirls, they'd fuck and suck each other all night, and he'd send them home. He didn't really have to talk to them besides telling them which body part to suck on one another.

Ding

The elevator to Czar's penthouse went off, signaling that someone was on their way up. Pushing off the couch, he went over to the camera and sucked his teeth when he saw Nova, Romeo, and a bunch of black trash bags at their feet. Taking a closer look, he could see that Romeo had tears running down his face.

"Oh hell nah," Czar mumbled, instantly getting a headache.

Ding

The doors opened and the brothers walked off arguing while dragging the bags behind them. Pinching the brim of his nose, Czar watched them go back and forth like he wasn't standing there.

"I don't see why you crying and shit. You been cheating for as long as yall been together and now that she on some get back you wanna kill yo self," Nova fussed.

"Fuck you nigga." Romeo pushed him, dropping the bags

on the floor. "We don't even know if she really cheated."

"The nigga texted her phone and said thank you for breakfast and *head*."

"She said he meant bed."

"You had a gun to the girl's head. I bet she did," Nova chortled.

The call from Romeo's neighbors made Nova's heart skip a beat. They only had his number because they watched the house when Romeo was on tour with Czar. Skeptically, Nova picked up the phone to hear his brother in the background beating down the bathroom door, threatening to kill Sammy if she didn't bring her hoe ass out.

"What the fuck are yall doing here?" Czar asked, interrupting their argument. "And why yall bringing all this shit up here?"

"Sammy cheated on this nigga, he fucked up their condo, and she put him out," Nova gave him the cliff notes while flopping on the couch.

"How she put you out of your own shit?" Czar frowned, whipping his head around to face Romeo, who was standing by the wall looking like a lost puppy.

"When we moved in, I put her name on the lease," he mumbled. "While we was on tour her sneaky ass removed my name and changed the locks."

"Dummy," Nova snorted. "Now look at you, standing on your brother's doorstep with all of your shit in garbage bags."

"Why didn't you drop his crybaby ass off at a hotel? The fuck you bring him here for?" Czar's bushy eyebrows met in the middle of his forehead, displaying the annoyance he felt.

"Because he didn't wanna go to a hotel and he can't stay at my crib."

"Why the fuck not?"

"Cause I fuck hoes, I don't cry about them. Now if he wanted to have a good time, I'm the man for the job, but I'm not about to get drunk while listening to him replay *When a woman's fed up*. I got a headache just from listening to him sing off-key and leaving voicemails on her phone."

"Fuck you, Nova, for real. I know I be out in the streets fucking up, but she my girl," Romeo said, choking on his tears. "C, can I call her off your phone?"

"Aww, hell nah. Drag yo shit to the back and go lay yo crybaby ass down somewhere." Czar walked over to the bar to pour himself a shot. "Marley about to pull up on me."

"The deaf girl?" Romeo cocked his head to the side.

"She not deaf nigga," Czar corrected him.

"Oh shit, why you ain't say that." Nova rubbed his hands together. "She bringing a friend?"

"Nah, just her."

"Oh. That's boring. Call her back and tell her to bring her friends. Who I'm supposed to cake with?"

"Nigga yall ain't even supposed to be here. You dropped this nigga off so you can go on about your business."

"Nope, I think I'll chill. You acting all funny style because you about to have company. You must like her." Nova eyed him.

"She cool," Czar admitted.

"And that's about it because she ain't got no ass, and according to her medical history, she tried to commit suicide."

"You did a background check on her?"

"Yep," Nova replied. "My job is to see a threat before it harms you. I filter everybody you come in contact with. You wanna know what else I found?"

"Nah, it ain't that serious," Czar told him. "If it's not something that'll put me in a fucked-up situation, keep it. She'll tell me."

"You like her?"

"Nah. She just remind me of Mama."

"The fuck kinda freaky shit you on?" Nova side-eyed him.

"Not sexually, dumb ass. Her eyes. They all sad and shit like Mama's," Czar revealed.

"Fuck is you talking about? Mama ain't sad," he refuted with a scowl, and Czar had to remember his brothers didn't know that side of her. They've never witnessed her in tears from being slapped down or sad because there was no way out.

"So, what am I supposed to do since you about to have company?" Romeo interjected.

"Fuck if I know, but get lost."

"You think you can call Ray J and ask him to serenade Sammy like he be doing Princess?"

"Nigga, no," he groaned.

"Shit, I might as well chill here since yall both here." Nova picked up the half blunt in the ashtray and lit it.

Before Czar could tell him to get the fuck out, the elevator dinged, alerting him that someone was on the way up. Walking over to the camera, Czar intently watched Marley as she fiddled with her phone. He could tell she was nervous and probably overthinking. To mess with her, he tapped on the intercom.

"Not yo mean ass standing in there all scary and shit," his voice boomed, making her jump. Marley grabbed her chest with one hand and stuck up the middle finger with the other.

Ding

"You're such an asshole," Marley sneered as the doors opened. She started to step off the elevator but paused, seeing three pairs of eyes staring at her. "Oh, hell nah." She reached in her purse and removed the pepper spray.

"Girl, put that shit up," Nova laughed but backed up in case she was trigger happy.

"I knew this was a mistake." Marley backed into the elevator and rapidly tapped the door close button.

"Aye, stop before you break my shit. You can't make enough tea bags to get it fixed," Czar scolded, sticking his foot in the door. "Come on, these my brothers."

"I don't give a fuck if they were The Jackson Five. This ain't that type of party." Marley shook her head. She didn't care how fine or rich he was; there was no way she was about to let them drug her and slut her out.

"Sweetheart, chill. You don't have enough booty for us to pass around." Nova blew smoke in her direction. "And this crybaby nigga ain't thinking about you unless you can give him advice on how to get his girl back."

"Oh shit, you might be on to something." Romeo pulled at his barely there beard. "How many times do a nigga get to fuck up before yall women say it's over for real?"

"Nigga get the fuck on." Czar waved them off. "You coming in or not?" He turned his attention back to Marley, who was still staring at them. Her eyes traveled between the brothers, trying to find one red flag, but she didn't see any. From where she was standing, they didn't look devious, so she stepped forward, allowing the doors to close behind her.

"Yes, but I swear if yall try to drug me and-

"Girl, shut up and get yo scary ass in here. You can't be a shit talker and scared. Pick a side."

"I'm both," Marley giggled, stepping into the penthouse.

"Wow," she peered around in amazement. From where she was standing, she could see the entire Detroit skyline. "This is breathtaking,"

"It's straight." Czar stuck his hands in the pockets of his jogging pants and followed Marley's movements with his eyes.

"Nigga, is you nervous?" Nova put him on blast. Quickly removing his hands, Czar gave his brother the middle finger.

"Fuck outta here," he mumbled, watching Marley walk over to the window.

Taking the time to check her out, he eyed the big curls that were scattered across the top of her head. She had on a pair of black tights and a long gray distressed shirt. On her feet were a pair of black Croc sandals. As she walked around the living room, Marley left behind a faint lavender and mint scent that made his dick jump. Czar laughed to himself. She didn't even try to impress him by wearing tight clothing she couldn't breathe in or shoes she couldn't walk in. Marley walked into his house like she was one of the homeboys, yet she still had his attention.

"Damn, can I get a hug, or you just gone keep walking around my shit like you looking for roaches?" Czar jested, tilting his head to the side.

"I'd hope you didn't have roaches in this fancy ass apartment, but then again, apartment buildings are prone to have ants, bed bugs, and roaches." Marley tooted her nose up. "Should I even be in here?"

"You wild as fuck," Nova chuckled. "Saying this man got bedbugs is next level."

"Fuck outta here." Czar waved them off. "I was about to offer yo little head something to drink, but you can drink your saliva since you wanna keep talking shit."

"Let me find out you on the sensitive side," Marley

taunted.

"And you just gone keep talking shit." He furrowed his eyebrows.

"Ok, ok, I'm sorry," she giggled. "I'mma chill."

"Fuck that, my feelings already hurt. Now gimme a hug so I can forgive you."

"Fine, but don't try to touch my booty." She pointed her index finger at him.

"Girl, you don't have a booty." Czar roped her in his arms. "You smell good," he murmured in her hair. Marley couldn't even say anything smart because she nearly melted in his embrace. A cologne and weed mixture clung to his T-shirt, liquor and peppermint lingered on his breath, and lust filled his eyes as he loomed over her. Being in his arms felt good, too good.

"I know." Marley pulled away.

"You want something to drink?"

"Yea, gimme a shot glass and the strongest liquor you have in there," Romeo requested, reminding Czar that he was still in the room. "Thanks."

"Do I look like a bartender? I'm not talking to you." Czar reluctantly released Marley.

"Water is fine." She twirled around and made her way to the couch. Taking off her shoes, Marley tucked her feet under her butt and sunk into the big pillows that decorated the couch.

"How much you weigh?" Nova wondered out loud, sitting across from her.

"Why?"

"Cause I think I want my next girl to be your height and size. You're like snack size. Can I try to pick you up?"

"Sir, if you touch me, I'm going to chop your ass in the throat."

"Nova," Czar warned. "Stop that weird shit."

"You said she look like Mama, but I'm weird."

"You think I look like yo mama?" Marley arched her eyebrow while taking the bottle of water from him.

"I didn't say you look like her. You remind me of her."

"And you still wanna freak on me?" She cocked her head to the side.

"Same shit I said," Nova dragged. "You know what, Lil Booty, you might be alright with me. I thought this nigga was on some weird shit too."

"Aye, let me ask you a question." Romeo took a seat next to Marley. "If a chick sent you a picture of your dude licking sugar off her nipples, would you leave him?"

"What?" Marley laughed. "Is he serious?" She glanced at his brothers, who were both shaking their heads.

"Yall gotta go." Czar walked back to the bar to pour himself another shot.

"Humor me," Romeo pleaded. "What would you do?"

"If a nigga sent you a picture of your girl sucking sugar off his tip, are you leaving her?" Marley quizzed.

"I'd kill her hoe ass." Romeo's heart dropped at the thought. "Damn, I think I lost her for good," he whined, knowing he couldn't handle the bullshit he dished out. "My god, can you please call Ray J, Tank, JPay the nigga R Kelly or something."

"Romeo," Czar snapped.

"And you wanted me to take this crying ass nigga back to the King's palace. I'll be damned if he gets tear stains on my suede couch," Nova commented.

"Wait, your name is Romeo?" Marley asked. "Like Juliet and Romeo?"

"Yea," he sniffed. "And I'mma die without my Juliet."

"And you're Czar, like Julius Caesar?" She turned to Czar.

"The one and only." He winked.

"What's your name again?" She doubled back, pointing to Nova.

"Casanova. Guardian of the hoes for short." He grinned.

"That's unique," Marley gushed. "Your mama likes ancient literature?"

"Yea. She wanted to be an English professor."

"That's so dope. Do yall rap too?" She glanced over at Nova and Romeo.

"Nah," Romeo shook his head. "This nigga started rapping in speech therapy."

"Speech therapy?" Marley raised her eyebrows.

"Yea, this nigga stopped talking when he was ten." He chuckled. "Oh shit, my fault."

"Nigga go call Sammy or something. You doing too much," Czar warned.

"Don't worry," Marley gazed up at him, "I won't tell."

"So you wanna be my lil diary?" he flirted.

"No, but I also won't run to the press and tell them your business."

"That's good to know. Aight, yall can bounce." Czar clapped his hands, wanting to chill with Marley by himself.

"Nigga, you can't hog her. She don't even like you like that." Nova frowned. "Do you mind if we chill with you, or are you trying to chill with this big nigga by yourself?"

Marley's eyes roamed over in Czar's direction, and he was

staring at her, waiting for her to answer. Tucking her bottom lip into her mouth, Marley's eyes fell from his face and slowly made their way down his chiseled chest, which was rippled with tattoos and old scars. Her eyes paused at his waist and examined the jogging pants that loosely clung to his hips. The lump on his left thigh made her jaw twitch.

"No," Marley swallowed. "Yall can stay."

"Scary ass," Czar taunted, walking back to the bar. "And get yo feet off my shit."

"Nope, you pulled me out of the comforts of my bed, so I'm going to make myself comfortable," she sassed. "Matter fact, can I smoke in here?" Marley reached for her purse.

"Hell yea!" Nova rubbed his hands together. "Light that shit up and it better not be no weak shit."

"Can I ask you some more hypothetical questions?" Romeo quizzed.

"Sure, but I can tell you right now that I'm not going to say what you wanna hear. You sound like you be on bullshit."

"Why you say that?" He cocked his head to the side.

"You just told me you sucked sugar off somebody's titties. Since you're still breathing, I'm guessing she just went off and put you out." Marley lit her joint and passed it to Nova.

"She did, how can I get her back?"

"Stop being a dog!" She bucked her eyes. "You got off easy. I would have stabbed you."

"Damn, yo little ass crazy." Nova took a couple of pulls and attempted to pass the joint to Czar.

"I don't want that little ass shit." He waved them off. "My fingers too big for that shit."

"Come here." Marley sat up straight and leaned forward. Czar pulled up his joggers and quizzically gazed at her. Her wild hair was pushed to the side and her pouty lips were glossy. Czar was a sucker for pretty lips and he would bet the lips between her thighs were identical.

“Come here, Julius.”

“Didn’t I tell you don’t call me that shit?” Czar gritted but still walked over to her, closing the space between them. Even with marijuana smoke lingering in the air, he still caught a whiff of her enticing scent.

“What are you wearing?” He sniffed her hair.

“Shampoo,” Marley gulped, praying she didn’t choke on the ball of nerves that brewed in the pit of her stomach. Taking the joint from Nova, Marley took a big pull and held it in her mouth. Inches away from Czar’s lips, she slowly blew the smoke into his mouth, careful not to touch his lips.

“Problem solved,” Marley raised her hand and lightly pushed him out of her face.

“Damn, can you do that to me?” Romeo asked, staring at them.

“Nope,” Marley snickered, passing the joint back to him. “And that’s why I said you be on bullshit. You over here crying about your girl and asking me to give you a shotgun. You either heartbroken or a horn dog, pick a side.”

“Both.”

“And both gone have yo ass sitting in the ICU with internal bleeding.”

“Yea, you are alright with me, Lil Booty.” Nova nodded his head while Czar tried to snap out of the trance Marley put him in. She was going to be a problem.

Chapter 7

Czar stood on stage in front of the lively crowd with sweat dripping from his face onto his tatted chest. The adrenaline pumping through his veins had him jumping around on stage like he took a molly, but that wasn't the case. Czar was high on life. Nothing compared to thousands of people chanting his name, rapping the lyrics he wrote, and begging him for an encore.

"Detroit! Stand the fuck up!" Czar thundered in the microphone causing the crowd to yell out in response. The mixture of voices brought a smile to his face. He had songs that made women drop their panties, and he had songs that made hood niggas grab their Glocks. It was balance. His music catered to every mood and his fans loved him for that.

Detroit was one of those cities that showed up and showed out for him, so when Terri asked him to do the last-minute show, he did it. The sold-out concert was so packed that the Fire Marshal had to close the doors, preventing anyone else from entering. The entire stadium was smoked out, and it didn't help that Czar's people were on the stage throwing pre-rolled blunts out into the crowd.

"In the fast lane it's hard to slow down, I'm in love with

the limelight. Making music, gettin' high, fucking a different bad bitch every night," Czar rapped, two-stepping across the stage.

"And we don't do the lovey dovey shit, save it for yo nigga," Nova rapped with a dancer bent over in front of him.

"And if a nigga talking shit, we nice with the trigga!" The crowd finished the sentence while aiming their imaginary guns in the air. Czar grinned, hoping that somebody from his team caught the moment.

After rapping a few more songs, Czar thanked the crowd and walked off the stage. As soon as he hit the stairs he was handed a glass of Hennessy neat and a towel to wipe the sweat from his forehead. Downing the liquor, he handed the glass to a random person walking by and gave the towel to one of the dancers.

"Detroit muthafuckin' finest!" Southwest Rah, another rapper signed to Eastwood, greeted him once he made it backstage. "What up doe nigga!"

"Walking in the footsteps set forth by the greatest," Czar praised, giving Rah his flowers. "I see you got the whole family with you and shit," he nodded toward Rah's wife and two small children.

"Hell yea, ain't many places I go without them." Rah looked back at his wife Taylor and winked. Blushing, Taylor pushed her hair behind her ear and focused on the conversation she was having with another woman.

"I dig it." Czar nodded. "And congrats on your Grammy. You're making the city proud."

"Nah, *we're* making the city proud. Two lil niggas out of the hood making millions and walking in doors that were once sealed is a big deal."

"We big shit, baby!"

"Been that," Rah cockily smirked. "Let me get out here

and give these people a show. I'm going to have Terri set up something to get us in the booth together."

"Hell yea! Drop me the details and it's a done deal."

"You got it." Rah gave Czar a brotherly hug before nodding his head at security, who tapped his wife. Ending her conversation, Taylor hoisted their baby on her hip and fell into stride with her husband, who was holding hands with their toddler.

"Yo, that nigga wife thick as fuck. She could walk around in one of them Walmart gowns and I'd still hit that shit," Nova whistled.

"Swear," Romeo cosigned, stroking his chin. Czar chuckled at his brothers. He felt the same way when he first laid eyes on Taylor. She was so fucking thick that he had to look at his phone to keep from staring at her.

Further backstage, Tati and her friends were seated on the couch talking amongst themselves as if they were too good to talk to anyone else. Czar wasn't surprised to see her because he had been ignoring her posts and text messages. He almost wanted to call Yaro and tell him to come pick up his bitch.

"Aye, that shit was lit!" Nova stretched his hand out to dap his brother.

"It was. Detroit showed out," Czar agreed. "Have Romeo take half of the money from this show and donate it to a women's shelter."

"Anonymous?"

"Duh. I don't need a bunch of fake muthafuckas all in my face thanking me for shit. I don't do it for the recognition."

"Why you always donating to women's shelters?"

"Cause I want to."

"Nice show." Tati slid between them, placing her hand on

Czar's chest. "And you was up there looking so damn fine."

"Fuck you doing here?" He frowned, knocking her hand to the side. "Wasn't you just on Twitter talking about not fucking with rude niggas? I didn't get any nicer since I tossed your food in the air and made yo nigga go on a social media rampage, so why are you here?"

"I missed you, and I even brought you a treat," She turned around and glanced at the three women sitting on the couch with their eyes glued to Czar.

Tati knew what it took to get back in his good graces, and if she had to munch on a lil pussy to get her boo back, then so be it. Czar would fuck the three girls and put them out, but she'd hopefully have him all night.

"I'm straight, I'm not in the mood," Czar replied, unimpressed.

"And don't you see us talking?" Nova raised his eyebrow. "How did you and the rat gang even get back here?"

"Your brother isn't the only famous one around here," she replied with an attitude. "I do have status and it gets me places," Tati boasted.

"It gets you skeeted on, that doesn't make you famous."

"And being a flunky for your brother doesn't make you famous," she rebutted.

"Watch your mouth," Czar warned her.

"Lil baby, I have a bachelor's degree in business management. I have three businesses that are self-managed, which means I make money while I sleep. I own my house and three cars. What the fuck do yo uneven lip ass have besides a stomach full of nut?"

"Wow, you just gone let him talk to me like that?" Tati grabbed her chest, highly offended.

"He a grown man, and maybe you should stop speaking

on shit you don't know nothing about. I don't surround myself with flunkies and broke niggas." Czar bypassed her. "All my niggas got they own shit, but they travel with me because we got it like that. Go sit down before you get your feelings hurt."

"I'm just going to leave," Tati suggested as if he would stop her.

"Be safe." Czar chucked her the deuces, leaving her standing in the middle of the floor. "Leave your friends though. Shorty with the red hair got some pretty ass lips, and the other ones thick as fuck. Thank you for the gift." He winked. "Aye, I'm about to grab my shit, get us a section at Glitz."

Czar didn't bother waiting for a response because he knew his brothers had it under control. As he walked away he could hear Tati and her friends arguing. She wanted to leave, but they wanted to stay, knowing that the after-party was about to be ten times better than the concert. Czar hoped they stayed so he could fuck them and send them back to Tati with stories of their own.

Not paying attention to his surroundings, Czar bypassed the men standing outside his dressing room while reading the text messages from Tati. Just that quickly, she was apologizing for how she spoke to his brother and begging him not to fuck her friends. Laughing to himself, Czar sent her a devil emoji. If they left with him, it was over!

"These hoes crazy," he mumbled to himself, opening the dressing room door.

"Same shit I used to say," The deep voice made the hairs on the back of Czar's neck stand up. Reaching for the gun on his hip, Czar cut on the lights, locking eyes with the man who helped create him.

Calling Cain a father was giving him too much credit.

He was nothing more than a man who impregnated an underage girl. At almost sixty years old, Cain didn't look a day over thirty. Instead of prison breaking him and turning him into a feeble old man, it did just the opposite. Like Czar, he sported long, thick locs that hung down his back. His facial hair was full but neatly trimmed. A few tattoos covered his neck and hands, and he now rocked a pair of Gucci eyeglasses, giving him a more innocent look, but Czar knew the real him. Wasn't shit innocent about the man standing in front of him even if he looked like a reformed prison pastor.

"I see you still jumpy as fuck," Cain chuckled.

"How the fuck you get in my shit?" Czar removed the gun and pointed it at the older version of himself. The lump in his throat grew, but Czar wouldn't let Cain see him sweat.

"Your balls finally dropped."

Czar lightly tugged at his mother's curls while she read him a bedtime story. Actually, it was the third story, but Czar was having a hard time falling asleep. Ada thought it was because he was scared of the dark, but in reality, Czar knew that when he fell asleep, his mother was going to leave. He also knew that when she left, she never came back the same way. Even at his young age, he knew something was wrong.

"Ok, C, it's time for bed." Ada closed the book.

"Nooo, just one more," he pleaded.

"Nope, but if you go to bed, we'll find something fun to do tomorrow."

"A!" Cain's voice roared through the apartment, causing them both to freeze. "Where you at, girl? I have someone I want you to meet."

"Just putting Czar to bed," she answered, fighting the urge to smack her lips.

"Always worried about that lil nigga," Cain snorted, talking

to the other person in the living room. "Get the fuck out here before shit get ugly."

"Ok," Ada sighed, pushing up from the bed. "Get some rest, baby. We'll have some fun in the morning."

"Why can't we just move," Czar pouted. "I hate it here. I hate him!" His little voice barked.

"Hey now, we don't do that. You don't yell at me."

"But he does! He's always mean and we stay. We just stay," Czar's voice grew louder, shocking his mother.

Ada knew he was watching, listening, taking it all in, but this was the first time he reacted in such an aggressive way. The pain and disappointment in his eyes broke her heart.

"The fuck taking you so long?" Cain roughly pushed the door open. "You trying to embarrass me in front of my fucking family?" Spit flew from the corners of his mouth.

"Uh, no." Ada pushed her hair behind her ear. "Czar was having a bad dream and I wanted-

"You think I give a fuck about a bad dream?" His wild eyes bounced around the room. "I'll make it so this nigga won't be having no dreams." Cain snatched the pillow off the bed. "I'll smother him and make you bury his body."

"Cain don't talk like that in front of him." Ada wiped the tears from her face. "Come on, show me to your friend."

"Oh, you don't wanna bury this lil nigga," Cain laughed. Without warning he launched forward, pressing the pillow to Czar's face.

"No!" Ada screamed, using all of her strength to pound on his back, but Cain was coked out of his mind and unfazed by the hits to his back.

"Aye, bro-" The man from the living room entered the room. "What the fuck are you doing?" He pulled Cain off of the bed. Czar couldn't even cry; he was in shock, and the air was having a

hard time finding its way back to his lungs.

"Breathe, baby." Ada ran to his side, patting his back. When Czar took a deep breath, she wrapped her arms around him, placing kisses on the top of his head.

"Just teaching this bitch a lesson." He wiped the beads of sweat from his forehead.

"You high and out of your mind. The fuck you trying to do, kill your son?" The man questioned, staring at his little brother with disappointment in his eyes. Ada turned around to catch a glimpse of the man shoving Cain through the door. Her eyes widened. Cain whooped her ass on the regular, and to see him being manhandled made her look at him differently. At the moment, he didn't seem so scary. In fact, the way he cowered under the man's gaze was amusing.

"Aye, big bro, don't come in my shit thinking you running it. This is how I run my household." Cain beat his chest. "He too fucking soft!"

"Look, let's just go get a drink."

"Nah, I promised you a good time and this bitch gone make it happen." He pointed to Ada. "Go get ready."

Ada wanted to turn around and comfort Czar a little more, but it was in their best interest for her to do as she was told.

"Bro, don't make me paint this room with your brains." Czar pulled the hammer back, dropping a bullet into the chamber. "What the fuck do you want?"

"I'm proud of you." Cain clasped his hands together and then folded them across his chest. "I mean a seed from my sack is a fucking rap star." He grinned. "I swore I told niggas in the pen that you were mine, but they didn't believe me. The whole time I kept thinking *nigga we made it.*"

"I'm not your shit," Czar spewed.

"You sure? I've followed you over the years and you're just

like me. You stand on business and make these muthafuckas respect you. I taught you that! You keep these hoes in line and you about your money. Like father, like son if you ask me."

"You didn't teach me shit!" Czar gritted, itching to release the bullet in the chamber. Cain could see the hate in his eyes and he didn't blame him. If it were the other way around, Cain would hate him too.

"Aight, calm down, son, it's not that serious. I just came for what's mine."

"Don't call me that shit, and what the fuck is you talking about. I ain't got shit that belongs to you."

"You sure about that?" Cain raised his eyebrow. "I told you from day one that she was mine."

"Are you talking about my *mama*?"

"What do you think? I just spent over a decade of my life in prison because you called the police and testified against me like a lil bitch. Now how would your fans feel if they knew their beloved favorite rapper was a snitch?"

"Fuck outta here, I was a kid," Czar snorted.

"Yea, well I think a lil restitution should set us straight." Cain rubbed his hands together. "I mean you got it." His eyes bounced around from the jewels on Czar's neck down to the watch that adorned his wrist.

"Wait," Czar chuckled, thumbing the tip of his nose. "Are you trying to extort me?"

"If that's how you wanna put it, then yea." Cain wiped the corners of his mouth. "I'mma need a nice portion of your earnings to rebuild my life. A life you and yo mama-

"Don't mention my mama again." Czar took a step forward, gripping his gun.

"Whoa, whoa. You sure you wanna do something like that? I'd hate for you to get arrested for shooting a fan." Cain raised his hands in the air. "Look, I'm not here for trouble. I just want what's mine. The way I see it, you took my bottom bitch, and I need to be paid for mine."

"I'm not sure if you snorted Boric Acid or drunk too much of that fermented fake liquor bullshit, but you got me fucked up. Get yo Rev Run wanna be ass out of my shit."

"Look, I see you need some time to think about it, and I'll give you that, but don't take too long. I have a few pictures the media will pay a pretty penny for, if you know what I mean." A sinister smile etched across Cain's face, sending a shiver down Czar's spine.

"You think I give a fuck about some old ass pictures?"

"You might not, but your mama will." Cain nodded his head toward the table where a brown envelope set. "How much is her privacy worth to you? Give me a call with a price and I'll talk it over with my people."

"On some real shit, I'm not some little ass boy, and you not about to son me. I'm not giving you shit, and that's on God."

Cain opened his mouth to reiterate his threat, but the door to the dressing room flew open. In seconds, the room was flooded with Czar's brothers, security, and two random men who posted up behind Cain.

"Who the fuck is these niggas?" Nova questioned, posting up next to his brother, ready for whatever.

"We strictly pussy this way. Yall taking this fan shit to the next level." Romeo frowned.

"I'm nobody," Cain promised. "Czar, I'll see you around and give your mama my love." He winked before bopping out of the room with the two silent men walking behind him.

"Who the fuck was that?" Nova inquired.

"Fuck all that," Czar roared. "Why the fuck am I paying

thousands of dollars for security and it's niggas just posted inside my dress room?"

Silence

"Oh, nobody wanna talk?" he sneered, full of anger. "All of you muthafuckas fired! If my blood not running through your veins, get the fuck out!" Czar roared. "Useless ass niggas."

One by one, the security guards filed out of the dressing room. There was no point in arguing because they knew they fucked up. Instead of securing their posts, they were flirting with the dancers and trying to catch a glimpse of Southwest Rah's performance. Being in the wrong place at the wrong time cost them their jobs.

"Aye, make sure yall grab my key and badges from them," Czar told his brothers, who were still standing there trying to figure out what was going on. They didn't know about Cain or their mother's past, and it wasn't Czar's story to tell, so he ignored their curious stares.

Once the cost was clear, Czar slowly removed the pictures from the brown envelope. The first picture was an image of Ada lying in bed laughing. The second picture was of Ada, Cain, and another man on the same bed talking, and the third picture made Czar clamp his eyes shut. Vomit rose to the top of his throat and violently expelled from his mouth like he was possessed. There were more, but he couldn't bring himself to look at them. He couldn't see her like that again.

"Fuckkkk!" Czar balled the pictures into his hand and swung his fist into the mirror. "Fuck! Fuck! Fuck!" He punched the broken mirror over and over until glass was sticking out of his hand.

"Fuck!" he whispered, dropping down into the chair. Killing Cain was the only solution because Czar wasn't giving him a dime, nor would he allow his mother's past to be used against her.

"We got the-" Nova stopped at the door and covered his mouth.

"Call Terri." Czar bypassed him, leaving a trail of blood behind him.

∞∞∞

Marley pushed her cart around Walmart, picking up a few things she'd need for the week. Since she was Vegan and ate mostly fresh vegetables, Marley shopped more frequently than she liked to. Not to mention it was a little expensive.

"I'm about to trip you," Harper hissed, dropping a box of half-eaten cookies in the cart. "I want details!"

"What else do you want me to say? I chilled with him and his brothers. We talked, got high as hell, and Czar ordered a bunch of food."

"And you stayed the night?"

"I did. We actually all fell asleep in the living room and I left before they woke up."

"I'm going to need commission or something." Harper cheesed. "I definitely hooked yall up and I want all the credit."

"Harper, please."

"I'm just saying. I hooked you up with a millionaire."

"Hm. Hooked me up is a little far-fetched. I didn't do anything with him."

"Let me say this." Harper stopped walking.

"Oh lord. Here you go preaching,"

"No, for real, listen. Let him blow your back out, cash out on you, and all that good shit. I know you miss dick. There's only so much a toy can do for you. Wait, you still like dick, right?"

"Yes, fool," Marley sighed.

She couldn't front like her pussy didn't throb the entire time he sat next to her, but she didn't know if she was in the right headspace to have meaningless sex.

"Don't think too much about it." Harper threw her arm around her shoulder. "But I do think a good dick down will make you smile a little more."

"Shut up." Marley bumped her hip. "I think I'm too scared to put myself out there like that again."

"And I expect nothing less. I know that you're scared, but you still have to do it, scared and all."

"Marley?" The voice came from behind them, making the sisters turn around.

"Char?" Marley squinted her eyes at Benny's aunt. Harper sucked her teeth.

"Girl, come here. I haven't seen you in years. How are you?" Char reached out to hug Marley, but she stepped back like she had shit on her hands.

Although years had passed, Marley didn't forget about everything she went through once she was released from the hospital.

"You want me to go up with you?" Harper asked, looking over at Marley, who was sitting in the passenger seat with tears streaming down her face. It was two months after the shooting and she'd finally gathered the strength to return to the place she once called home.

"No, but don't leave yet. I called the leasing office and they said the rent was paid up through the end of the year," Marley sniffed. "I guess he did that to keep from asking his aunt to do it every month."

"Have you talked to her?"

"No, but I hope they didn't touch my shit. It's bad enough they buried him while I was in a coma."

"It'll be ok." Harper rubbed her back.

Marley wanted to believe her words, she wanted to have faith, but she knew it would never be ok. Nothing would ever be the same again.

Using her key to unlock the door, Marley entered her condo but frowned when she was greeted by a host of Benny's cousins and their kids. From the amount of trash and dirty dishes piled up around the living room she could tell they had been there a while. Bags of clothes lined the wall, her furniture looked dingy, and it reeked of dirty diapers.

"Marley," Char greeted her with alarm in her tone as she pushed off the couch. "What are you doing here?" She smoothed out her shirt as if it would magically make the grease stains disappear.

"What am I doing here?" She scoffed. "I could say the same thing. What is all this?"

"Uh, well you know the place is in my name, and with Benny being gone, we didn't have anywhere to go."

"Well, I'm back so yall can pack up and leave."

"Marley, Benny was helping us all and with him being gone, I think it's only right we get the condo. I mean it is in my name. I thought you-

"And you think I care about all of that?" Marley snapped, becoming more irritated by the second.

"Look, girl, we not going nowhere. You wasn't shit but his girlfriend. We're family," Char's daughter Serra spoke up.

Marley zoomed in on her clothes and laughed to herself. She hated broke bitches and Serra was just that. She had some nerve talking shit while wearing another woman's clothing. Marley started to let it go, but when she looked around the room, they all had something of hers on, and their kids were playing with her baby's toys. Toys that she and Benny bought for their baby, toys her baby never had a chance to play with. As petty as it was, Marley was triggered, and she couldn't help the rage that took over her body.

"Get the fuck out of my house now!" Marley screamed.

"Yea, you can do all that and we're still not going anywhere."

Marley couldn't pinpoint when the camel's back broke, but she snapped. Picking up the end table, she swung it into the TV, shattering the screen.

"Oh, this bitch crazy," Serra gasped, picking up her baby and moving to the back of the condo because Marley had completely lost her mind.

"Look, Marley, I didn't get a chance to tell you back then, but your mama said I could move in the condo." Char cleared her throat, bringing Marley back to their current situation. "I came to see you at the hospital, and they had you on a psych hold. She said you weren't getting out anytime soon, so we could just stay there. She even said we could keep everything, which is why I was surprised you came back for the van."

"She what?" Harper spoke up because her sister couldn't.

"Yea, she made me a copy of the key, which is why I was shocked you popped up all rowdy. I thought you knew."

"I gotta go." Marley pushed past her. Harper left the cart right there in the middle of the aisle and ran behind her sister. She didn't have to ask where they were going because Harper already knew the answer.

Marley wasn't surprised by Pam's actions because her treacherous ways had no end. Instead of her telling Marley the truth, she allowed her to think that Benny's family fucked her over and left her out in the cold. Marley had to rebuild her life from scratch, and she could almost bet that

Pam got a kick out of watching her suffer.

∞∞∞

Twenty minutes later, Harper pulled up at her mother's house and parked behind a truck that looked awfully familiar. She was sure the owner had no business being at her mother's house and wondered if he was the mystery man Pam was so gone over. Marley barely waited for Harper to park before she jumped out of the car and stomped up the long driveway. Without thinking, she snatched the front door open and barged inside the house.

"What the hell?" Marley gasped, taken aback by the scene in front of her. His back was to her, but it wasn't hard to see what was happening. His yellow ass thrusted back and forth, trying to keep up with her jaw movements.

The same Pastor that preached about being faithful and honest had his pants around his ankles while Sister Pam went to town on his little yellow dick. He was so busy calling on the Lord that he didn't notice Marley standing there watching them.

"Oh, yall going straight to hell." Harper covered her eyes but kept enough space so she could see the drama unfold.

"I-uh-oh lord." Pam stood up, wiping the corners of her mouth. "What are yall doing here?"

"I can explain." The pastor quickly buckled his pants.

"Oh no, allow me." Marley folded her arms. "You told her you were leaving your wife, and she foolishly believed you. She invited you here for her signature dish, fed you, and then proceeded to empty your nuts."

"Watch your mouth!" Pam screeched. "You will respect the Pastor in my house."

"Girl bye. Are you respecting him? Wait, is this the man you're so in love with?"

"I should go." Pastor wiped his forehead.

"Ya think?" Harper bucked her eyes. "You creepin' on Saturday and preachin' on Sunday. You should be ashamed of yourself. Does your wife know you are anointing members with more than prayers and holy oil?"

"Can we keep this between us?" he pleaded.

"Sir, just leave." Marley shooed him away, not wanting to hear his reasoning.

Pam waited until he was outside the door before she turned to face her daughters. Now that she was standing in front of them, she felt naked. The strings on her yellow sundress were hanging off her shoulders, her hair was all over her head, and the red lipstick she wore was smeared across her cheeks.

"What are yall doing here?" Pam questioned, running her hands through her hair.

"So you don't wanna talk about why you were just sucking the Pastor's-" Harper started but was cut off by her sister.

"Is this the man you were just bragging about?" Marley cocked her head to the side. "Is this why all of sudden you're being extra at church because you're trying to win brownie points with a married man?"

"Watch yourself, Marley. My business doesn't have anything to do with you."

"Oh, but you can be in mine?"

"Girl, what are you talking about? Your boring ass don't have no business. All you do is cry behind a dead man." Pam flicked her wrist in the air. "Shit," she mumbled, reaching for the pack of cigarettes.

"I thought you stopped smoking," Harper side-eyed her.

"Ha," Marley loudly laughed. "She never stopped; she simply hid the habit while she transformed into a new person. I mean do you even know the real you?"

"Marley save the dramatics. Why are yall in my house?"

"I ran into Char and she said you gave them the key to my condo."

"I did," Pam admitted, blowing smoke in her direction. "You tried to kill yourself and you think it was smart for you to go back there?"

"It wasn't your fucking decision!" Marley shouted, feeling her emotions get the best of her. "You had no right to give them my key. That was my place, those were my things, and you gave them away and watched me struggle."

"Get over it, girl, damn. Please find something better to do than to cry over spilled milk."

"Wow."

"What was your plan, Marley? To go back there and do what? Cry yourself to death? Try to kill yourself *again*?"

"Really, Ma?" Harper frowned.

"Yes, really. She was going crazy, and as her mother, I made a decision. You were trying to coddle her feelings, but I stepped up. I did what needed to be done."

"What needed to be done?" Marley laughed to keep from crying. "Fine time for you to wanna be a mother after you retired from being the set-up Queen of Detroit. Does Pastor know his lil side piece wasn't always so holy?"

"That was the past. You should thank me if anything. I helped you grieve."

"I had nothing. I slept on your couch for months while you walked around talking about me to your church friends."

“I took you in!” Pam snapped. “I could have left you in that fucking Looney bin and let them dope you up.”

“You spent all the money in my account, leaving me with nothing, and then you put me out. You call that being there for me? You used me!”

“I told you Benny wasn’t shit, but you didn’t want to listen. You let that bum knock you up and move you out of here like you were better than me.”

“I’ve always been better than you.”

“Says the homeless ass lil girl that’s sleeping in a van.” Pam taunted.

“You have a lot to say with married dick on your breath,” Marley countered.

Whap!

Pam's heavy right hand went across Marley’s face, splitting her lip in the process.

“Respect me! This is my fucking house and you will respect me.”

“Ok, I think yall both should calm down.” Harper stepped in the middle of them, praying her sister didn’t knock their mother across the living room. “Marley, let’s just go.”

“Respect?” Marley licked the blood from her lip, pulling away from Harper. “You don’t even know the meaning of respect.”

“Get out of my house! Get your ungrateful ass out of my house. The Bible says a child that doesn’t respect their parents lives a short life.”

“Please don’t quote that bullshit to me while the scent of your Pastor's ball sack is on your top lip. But while you’re speaking the good word, it also says you shouldn’t covet your neighbor’s house and look at you over here sucking your neighbor’s dick. Seems like we’re both headed for an early grave." Marley glared at her mother one more time before stomping out of the house.

Chapter 8

"Give me the beat back," Czar requested, lifting the cup to his lips. Taking a sip of the dark liquor, he sat the cup down and bobbed his head to the Makaveli instrumental.

Normally, when his head was clouded, Czar spent hours in the studio listening to all of his favorite artists. He studied their words, memorized the beats, and then created a remix of his own. Pac's albums were by far his favorite. The way he combined poetry, politics, and music was unmatched, and Czar would forever be a fan. The new style of music couldn't touch none of the artists from that decade.

"Wasn't born a killer, but don't push me. Done seen it all, been through the storm and ain't shit about me pussy," he rapped. *"Been running so fast, my past bout to catch me. It be the pussiest niggas tryna test me."*

The producer and his brothers watched on as Czar released his thoughts on a track that would never be released. The mixtape served as his diary and held some of his deepest feelings. It was Czar's way of expressing himself without explaining the meaning behind the words to anyone. For the men in the studio, it was an unspoken agreement. What was said during those sessions stayed in the booth.

For as long as he could remember, Czar loved music. His tastes varied from blues to country, back to dancehall and R&B. On Sunday mornings, it was nothing for Ada to open all the windows in their tiny apartment and blast the music while spraying everything down with bleach. Czar would sit at the table eating cereal and flipping through his comic book, secretly watching her. She was free, she was happy, and for him, that was enough. When their eyes met, Ada would chase him around the house, hugging him and singing in his ear. Back then he acted like he hated it, but deep down he loved it. It made them seem normal even when their world was anything but such.

Czar opened his eyes when the door to the studio chimed. It was a private session so he started to go off until he saw Terri, along with the label's PR, enter the room. Picking up his cup, Czar took another sip while watching Terri hand his phone to the producer, who hooked it up to the Bluetooth system in the studio. In seconds, a radio interview began playing in the headphones.

"He's a monster," the radio host yelled into the microphone. "These promoters invite him out and what does he do? Trash the dressing room. Did you see the picture?"

"I did," the cohost answered. "I wouldn't say he's a monster, but these young artists are cut different. They don't respect anything."

"Well, I think they should press charges. Paying to clean up the mess isn't enough. Czar needs to clean up his act because this bad boy act is played out."

"We aren't even going to address the situation with him and Yaro. The man gets off on bullying people. In my opinion he's a troublemaker, bad for business if you will."

The photos of the wrecked dressing room hit the media a few hours after the incident. People speculated that Czar was on drugs and had an episode, while others swore it had something to do with Tati. Right after the dressing room ordeal, she was photographed hopping on a private jet with Yaro.

"Cut this shit off," Czar barked, snatching the headphones off. He had heard the interview multiple times over the course of the last five days, and he didn't need to hear it again. The owner of the stadium was suing him for property damage even after he cut them a check. Apparently, it wasn't enough, and Czar told him to drop dead because he wasn't coughing up shit else.

"We need to talk about this," Terri stated, taking a seat on the couch next to Nova. "I know something triggered you to act out like that, and if something or someone did something, then this can work in our favor."

"The fuck they tripping for? He cut them a check," Romeo questioned.

"Money doesn't fix everything. The company wants to make an example out of him. Czar isn't the first artist to tear up a dressing room."

"And he not gone be the last," Nova retorted. "But look, it was my fault. I should have made sure them niggas was on the job and I didn't. I was having a good time and I slipped," he admitted.

"I'm just trying to understand what happened. Rah said he saw you and you were cool," Terri sighed.

"Bro, you straight," Czar assured Nova for what felt like the millionth time.

Nova took what happened personally. As the head of security, he took his job seriously, and the fact that three unknown niggas were able to slide by him wasn't sitting right with him. He combed through all of the footage and still didn't understand how they were able to get backstage without a pass. It didn't help that Czar wouldn't give him information about the men.

"Cancel the studio time for the week and the interview with Nesha Re. I need to clear my head." He bypassed Terri.

"Czar, we need to come up with a story," his publicist pleaded. "Was it the Yaro and Tati situation?"

"I honestly don't give a fuck what you say." Czar pulled the door open. "Make some shit up... they do."

"You want them to bring the car around?" Nova called after him.

"Nah, just give me your keys. I'll be back later."

"Love you nigga, be safe. "

"Today and tomorrow," Czar tossed over his shoulder.

∞∞∞

Marley was parked near the end of Belle Isle with her doors shut. Surprisingly, the park was quiet, and she welcomed the silence. Sitting in the middle of the bed, Marley practiced her breathing while trying to fight away the negative thoughts that seemed to slip through the cracks.

Her phone had been ringing off the hook. She knew it was Harper, but she didn't have the strength to act like she was ok. Pam's words affected her more than she thought they would. Marley's mind couldn't help but drift back to those days when she could barely get off the couch. She hardly ate and her mind and body were always tired. Pam's only concern was whether she had money on the rent.

"I'm fine, Harp," Marley pressed the speaker button on her vibrating phone.

"Call me another nigga's name again and see what happens."

"Czar?"

"Nah, the ghost of Christmas past."

"I'm not in the mood," she sighed.

"Good, me either, so let's cut to the chase. Pull up on me," Czar demanded.

"No. I'm not good company right now."

"Me either, but I want to see you," he admitted. Marley couldn't put her finger on it, but something was different about his voice. It was almost desperate.

"How about you come see me?"

"What's your address?"

"I'll just share my location."

"Aight," Czar ended the phone.

Marley didn't know why she did it, but it was too late to renege, so she rolled out of the bed and started straightening up her space. She had no idea how his tall ass was going to fit, but it would have to work because she wasn't ashamed of her home. It was her safe space.

"Aw hell." Marley slapped her forehead and reached for the phone. She tried to call Czar back, but he didn't answer, so she called Harper.

"Are you hurt?" she questioned, making Marley cringe.

"No."

"Then where the fuck yo trout mouth ass been? I've been calling you for days and you keep sending me to voicemail!"

"I'm sorry. I was in my feelings and-

"I get it. What Mama said was wrong, but you can't disappear like that."

"I won't do it again."

"And you need to make more of an effort to be my sister. I

miss the old you."

"I'll do better, Harp."

"And you're going to make it up to me. I want to double date like we used to. You and Lucky-

"Nope." Marley shook her head. "I'll have tea with yo mama before I go on a date with that man."

"Then bye!" Harper hung up in her face. Marley rolled her eyes and loudly exhaled before calling her back.

"I'll do it," she hissed as soon as the phone picked up. "But not with Lucky, find somebody else."

"Cool. I'll make reservations at that new restaurant downtown."

"You know I hate you, right?"

"You love me, now what's popping?"

"Well, I was calling to tell you I invited Czar over."

Silence

"Hello?" Marley pulled the phone away from her ear to make sure the call didn't drop. Being that she was close to Canada, her phone tended to roam at odd times.

"I'm still here, just trying to make sure I heard you right."

"Stop being dramatic."

"I'm just saying. I don't know if I should be pissed that you've been talking to him and not me or praising the Lord that you about to get some dick."

"Who about to get some dick?" Jaxon asked in the background.

"Marley. She invited Czar over."

"She got a room?"

"No, fool, her van."

"Can that tall ass nigga fit in there?"

"Tell Jaxon to mind his business," Marley smacked her lips. "Yall think I should call him back and tell him not to come? I mean he's a freaking millionaire and I just invited him to my vanhouse."

"First of all, calm down," Harper told her. "Think of this as a trial run. If he comes over and doesn't act all funny, then cool, but if he walks in there turning up his nose, tell him to get the fuck on."

Marley heard what she was saying, but it didn't ease the nervousness that brewed in the pit of her stomach. Before her thoughts could run wild, the roar of an engine outside the window caught her attention. Peeking through the blinds, she nearly passed out when she saw Czar step out of the truck.

"Oh shit, he's here," Marley panicked. "Oh my God, this was so stupid. I'm so stupid."

"Lil Booty, you in there?" Czar knocked on the door while trying to peek through the curtain.

"Ah shit, call me later," Harper giggled, hanging up the phone.

Marley took a deep breath and slipped on her Crocs. She pushed her hair behind her ear and adjusted her sports bra. She wanted to kick herself for not changing, but then again, she wasn't expecting company, so her unkempt hair, biker shorts, and sports bra would have to suffice. Taking a deep breath, Marley opened the door to see Czar standing there checking out her van.

As hard as she tried not to stare, Marley found herself damn near drooling. His hair was freshly twisted and pulled up on the top of his head and his lineup was cut to perfection. Cartier sunglasses covered his eyes and he rocked a fresh white t-shirt with a pair of Nike tech joggers. A couple of gold rope chains hung around his neck and his signature gold watch rested against his wrist.

"You bullshittin,' right?" He glanced at the van then back at her.

"No. You said you wanted to come over, well this is it. This is my home." She pushed the side door open for him. "You coming in or nah?"

"If you didn't want to share your address, you could have came to my crib. To act homeless is taking shit to a new level. I ain't never had a chick act homeless."

"Julius, first of all, this is my home. I live here 365 days out of the year. Now, you can either come in or leave, but don't talk about my house."

"This is a fucking van with a twin-size mattress in the trunk." Czar peered over her shoulder. "Wait, am I being punked?"

"Bye asshole." She rolled her eyes.

"Aight." He caught the door, stopping it from closing in his face. Their fingers touched, prompting Marley to gaze up at him. She sharply inhaled, catching a hint of the liquor on his breath.

"Are you drunk?"

"Not as drunk as I would like to be. You gone let me in?"

"Fine, and you better not say nothing smart or I'm putting you out."

"Girl, shut up. Now are you going to give me a tour or what?"

"Strike one!" Marley pushed him.

"Aight, damn girl, stop being so damn serious and let me in this shoebox." Czar moved around her, ducking lower than he needed to. "And yo strong ass better stop pushing me."

"You're such an asshole." Marley shut the door and locked it.

Awkwardly, Marley watched Czar examine the pictures on her wall, the books on her shelf, and everything else in between. When he stopped at a picture of Benny kissing her pregnant stomach, he paused.

"You have a kid?" he inquired, looking closely at the picture. Marley was younger and the smile on her face was so contagious that it caused the corner of his lips to lift. Her eyes were full of life and he wondered if the dude in the picture was responsible for her heartache.

"Umm, no." Marley rubbed the back of her neck. "I lost her when I was eight months," she murmured.

"Oh shit, I'm sorry to hear that." Czar backed up and sat on her bed. "I'm not gone lie, I have hella questions."

"I know," Marley sighed. "Go ahead."

"You homeless?"

"No, this is my home, and before you start, I have more than enough money to get a place if I want one."

"Who is the nigga in the picture?"

"My boy-" she paused. "My ex-boyfriend."

"He's the one that died?" he asked, recalling the conversation they had on the phone.

"Yes."

"How?"

"We were gunned down at a stoplight. Benny and our daughter were m-murdered," Marley forced out as if the words were blocking her airway. Knowing what happened was one thing, saying it out loud was another. "I was shot twice, once in the stomach, and by the time I made it to the hospital, she was gone. They were gone."

"Damn, sweetheart, I'm sorry that happened to you." Czar touched her hand. "He was in the streets or some shit?"

"Yep, heavy in the streets and my dumb ass was right there for the ride."

"We live and we learn, right?"

"Right, but living and learning almost cost me my life."

"You mad at him?"

"No. Mad at myself. I should've known better." She dropped her head and rubbed the back of her neck.

"Come here." Czar reached out for her.

"It's fine." Marley cleared her throat. "Do you want some tea?"

"You can make tea in here?"

"Yes, fool."

"Like how? You start up the engine and sit the kettle on the hood?"

"Oh my god," Marley laughed out loud. "Do you ever think about the crazy shit you say?"

"Not really," Czar shrugged, kicking off his shoes. "I ain't go lie, this bad boy nice," he complimented, touching her dreamcatcher. "Look all homey and shit."

"What kind of tea do you want?" she asked, pulling out her hotplate and glass kettle.

"Surprise me." He laid back on her pillows, catching a whiff of the lavender and lemongrass scent she wore. "You don't be scared in here?"

"Nope, I have pepper spray."

"You killing me with this pepper spray shit. We gotta get you a gun."

"I don't like guns."

"Then a taser."

"My pepper spray is just fine as long as your crazy ass fans don't find us, then I'm good."

"I drove my brother's car, so we straight."

"How are you this rap star but move around so freely? You're not scared of Jack boys and aggressive fans?"

"I'm not scared of anything that bleeds like me. All that bodyguard shit is a show. Those be the same niggas that turn on you. I have security guards when I travel, at home I'm straight."

"Oh ok, Mr. Badass."

"That shit turns you on, huh?"

"No, fool!" Marley rolled her eyes. "Where are you coming from?"

"The studio."

"I bet that's so dope."

"What?"

"Recording in a studio. Is it like the movies?"

"What do you mean?"

"Smoked out, naked women doing lines of coke, unlimited liquor, twerk contests. You know, the works."

"The fuck?" Czar laughed out loud. "You need to stop watching Tubi movies."

"Not just Tubi. I know you saw *Notorious*. Biggie was in there going wild! Shit, even Southwest Rah posts videos of his studio sessions and they can get wild."

"That's not my style." Czar stroked his chin. "I'm not a fan of people being in my space. Being in the studio is my peace. You never disturb your peace with negative energy."

"Okkkk," Marley snapped her fingers. "Let me find out

you on your Zen shit."

"It made your pussy wet, huh?"

"And there you go fucking it up."

Czar sat back in bed, watching Marley pull out the same counter from her Instagram videos. In her zone, he watched as she easily moved around the van as if it were a full kitchen. She hit a switch on the ceiling and plugged the hot plate up. Leaning down, Marley grabbed two bottles of water and poured them into the kettle before closing the lid. Reaching under the cabinet, she removed two tea glasses and a tray of pre-rolled joints.

"Here you go with these little ass joints," Czar chortled.

"Shut up and light one."

"I'm not about to burn my fingers with these little shits. Remind me to bring some wraps next time."

"You're such a princess," Marley teased. "I have a clip." She handed him the tray. "Sometimes my nails are too long and this is a lifesaver."

Czar took the tray from her and picked up the long gold bedazzled clip.

"What kinda shit is this?" He held the tool in the air.

"It's an extended weed clip." Marley sat on the bed next to him and placed the joint between the clamps. Sparking the tip, she took a pull and handed it to him.

"Real niggas don't use clips, but then again, real niggas don't have they feet kicked up in the back of Barbie's camper, so I'm going to try it."

"Shut up," Marley giggled. "Anyway, what's up? What are you doing here? I thought millionaires spent their days on yachts with half-naked women. You know, Diddy style."

"Nah, not me shorty. I don't really fuck with too many

people in the industry. I drop albums, do concerts, and from time to time, I get a little easy pussy."

"And that's what you thought you was getting from me?" Marley arched her eyebrow.

"Nah, ain't shit easy about you. I still don't know how old you are."

"I'm twenty-four."

"Finally, one step closer to the golden gates." Czar rubbed his hands together.

"Unless you're talking about meeting your maker, you aren't touching these golden gates," Marley insisted. "So because you don't mess with people, is that the reason you don't do features?"

"I do features, just not for everyone. My prices aren't cheap and my shit exclusive."

"So you're all that?" She arched her eyebrow.

"And a bag of chips," he winked cockily.

"Anyway, why are you here? What's on your mind?"

"I needed my best friend." He reached up and tugged at one of her curls. "This your real hair?"

"Damn, that escalated quickly. I'm at best friend status now? And yes, this is my real hair."

"I mean you could be more, but you don't want to give up that lil booty." Czar's hand dropped to her waistband, tugging at her shorts. "And you ain't got no clothes on. You trying to flaunt this lil muthafucka, huh?"

"Stop." She popped his good hand.

"Aight." He sat back as the kettle started to whistle. "Be stingy then."

Marley hit the joint once more to calm her nerves and then passed it to him. It only took her a few minutes to make their tea and rejoin him on the bed. Kicking off her slides, Marley climbed beside him, praying he couldn't hear her thumping heart.

"So Julius, why are you here?" she asked again. "And what happened to your hand?"

"I got into a fight with a mirror," he joked.

"Ouch. Does it still hurt?"

"Not as much as them corny muthafuckas suing me."

"Oh, well I mean I know that's not the first time you've been sued."

"The fuck that's supposed to mean?" Czar furrowed his eyebrows.

"Don't act like you don't know you have a reputation." Marley twisted her lips. Bringing the tea to his mouth, Czar took a sip and exhaled. He didn't know if it was the tea, the joint, or her company, but he felt relaxed, probably the most relaxed he'd ever felt.

"What flavor is this?"

"Lavender honey chamomile with hints of vanilla."

"I like it."

"I didn't take you for a tea drinker." Marley leaned back on her pillows.

"I'm not, but since my best friend is into this type of shit, I'm trying to catch the vibe." He took another sip. "I'm not that bad."

"Huh?"

"I'm not a bad person. The media just catches me at the worst times, and people believe anything nowadays."

"Now that I'm getting to know you, you aren't that bad. Talk shit, but you're not that bad."

"So that means you trying to fuck?"

"See, there you go messing up the vibe." Marley sucked her teeth.

"Nah, I'm playing Lil Booty. Put some music on and lay back. You a whole vibe, got a nigga thinking about some acoustic type shit."

"You ain't said nothing but a word." She grabbed her phone.

Tapping on the screen, Marley clicked on her Pandora app and selected Hip Hop and R&B. In seconds, *Snooze*, the acoustic version, started playing. Marley lightly hummed along with the melody while rocking from side to side.

"Ok, I fucks with this," Czar nodded, placing the clip to his lips. "This some fancy ass shit. I'll never smoke bud the same again."

"See, I knew you liked it." Marley bumped his shoulder.

"Don't get all big headed and shit."

"I been big headed," she smirked.

"You do got a big ass head," Czar joked, placing the clip in the ashtray and his tea on the shelf above her bed. "Come here," he spread his legs so she could sit between them.

"I'm fine right here," Marley claimed. It wasn't what he was trying to hear, so Czar picked her up, placing her between his legs with her back to his chest. "Czar," she squealed.

"Stop acting like you weigh more than a buck fifty." He positioned her between his legs.

When Czar's fingertips touched her scalp, Marley's eyes closed and her lips slightly parted. He applied the right amount of pressure and moved at a nice pace. It was as if his fingers synced with the music and danced through her curls with ease. The act itself wasn't sexual, but it caused her legs to twitch and her pussy to pulsate.

"Not rich ass Czar sitting in my bed, massaging my scalp," Marley mumbled.

"I can massage something else if you let me." He made his dick jump against her back.

"Don't ruin the mood."

"Aye-" Czar's hand traveled to her neck and traced the scar that stretched from ear to ear. "What happened here?"

"I was in a dark place," Marley admitted, surprised that it took him so long to say something about it.

The ugly scar stood out on her body like a sore thumb. Marley used to try to cover it with turtlenecks and chokers, but after a while, she stopped. The scar was part of her healing and she wasn't ashamed of what she did... or at least tried to do.

"And now?" Czar caressed her neck.

"Now I just take it one day at a time," Marley murmured, lying in his arms.

For a minute, they fell into a comfortable silence. Czar wanted to tell her that he was all too familiar with those thoughts. That they consumed him, and the thought of taking his life crossed his mind more than once. He understood how sometimes life became so loud that the need to shut it out intensified with each passing day, but Czar could never do that. He could never leave his family with the burden of knowing he had given up.

"Aye, don't do that shit again." He broke the silence.

"I don't plan to."

"Good." Czar moved his hands from her hair to relight the joint. "You cool with your people?"

"My sister is my best friend, and my mom is just that... my

mom."

"Bad blood?"

"Bad everything."

"What about your Pops?" Czar quizzed, passing her the joint. Marley took a deep pull and released a thick cloud before answering his question.

"He's dead. He took his life when I was fourteen. According to my mama, he suffered from depression after his wife left him."

"Aw, damn LB. I'm sorry to hear that."

"LB?" She lifted her head to look at him.

"Yea. You don't like when I call you Lil Booty so I'm trying to switch it up."

"I guess I should be thanking you."

"Kissing me or something, damn."

"I'm not kissing you, Julius."

"You like saying my name, huh?"

"Maybe." Marley handed him the joint back. "Are you cool with your parents?"

"Yea. I love my family."

"That's cool." She snuggled closer to him. "Can I ask you a question?"

"Shoot," he exhaled.

"Why were you in speech therapy?"

"I had this project in fifth grade and it required me to write about my family tree," Czar began explaining, pulling from the joint. "All the kids in my class was happy as fuck, but for me, the shit was depressing. I didn't even bother to tell my mama about the project. On the day I was supposed to present it, kids in my class laughed because my tree was empty. Just me and my mama."

"Why didn't you add anyone else."

"Because up until I was seven, she was the only family I had. When Ro and Nova were born, I wasn't fond of them. I ended up throwing a chair at my teacher for making me do that dumb shit and then I stopped talking to muthafuckas. For like a year, the only person who heard me talk was my mama, and even then, it was only a few words."

"Speech therapy helped?"

"Not really. I had no problem with talking; I just didn't want to. They called it post-traumatic stress." He shrugged. "Enough of that shit though, you got me feelin' like a bitch, pouring my heart out and shit."

"Talking helps."

"Aight, so talk. Why haven't you been with anyone since your ex died?"

"Because," Marley exhaled. "He was my first everything, and I'm still getting used to the fact that he's never coming back."

"Then why are you sharing your space with me?" he countered, and it was a good question.

"For one, I didn't willingly share my space with you. If I'm not mistaken, you bullied your way into my life."

"True," he chuckled. "But you still could've sent a nigga packing."

"I might think it's cool to have a famous friend."

"Oh yea?"

"Yea, just don't fall in love with me. I'm not that kinda girl."

"Damn, a nigga get the dandruff out of yo hair and you think he about to propose?"

"I'm just letting you know."

"Shut up and catch this smoke." Czar bowed his head and slowly blew a stream of smoke into her mouth. "Soft ass lips," he mumbled, stealing a kiss, and to his surprise, she didn't fight it, so he did it again and again until their tongues started to wrestle.

Chapter 9

Marley chewed on her bottom lip while skimming through Czar's posts on Instagram. Almost a week had passed since they chilled and she found herself thinking about him more than she should. But because she was stubborn as a bull, calling him was out of the question, so she stalked his page, hoping it would soothe her craving to be near him.

The night Czar stayed in her van, they talked all night about nothing. They were both high as hell and their conversations ranged from why do cats have nine lives and not humans to Marley trying to convince Czar that drinking cow milk was just as bad as eating chicken's unborn babies. Czar, of course, couldn't keep his hands to himself, and Marley didn't seem to mind. She allowed his fingers to graze her panty line and brush across her breasts.

"TT Marley, wanna see a trick mommy taught me?" JJ asked, plopping down on the couch next to her.

"Of course." Marley turned to him, sitting her phone on her lap.

"I can make a heart on your screen." Without warning, he

quickly tapped on a shirtless picture of Czar from two years ago. "Tadaaaaa!" He smiled when the red heart appeared on her screen.

"JJ, nooooo," Marley whined, snatching her phone only to change the picture and like a video of Czar at the gym. "Oh my goooood," she shrieked.

"What's going on?" Harper waltzed into the living room, taking a seat beside JJ.

"You showed him how to heart people's pictures?"

"Yea, he saw me doing it and wanted to know how it worked. Why?"

"He just liked Czar's picture!"

"Ok, and?" Harper frowned, confused as to why her sister was so hyped.

"From two years ago!" Marley exclaimed.

"Ohhhh, you got caught lurkin'," she laughed out loud.

"That's not funny! He probably thinks I'm a creep."

"You lurkin' through that man page and not liking shit is the exact definition of a creep. Luckily for you, he probably won't notice it. I mean famous people probably get about thousands of notifications a day."

"Ok, you're right," Marley exhaled. "Yea, you're right," she assured herself.

"Wanna see another trick?" JJ quizzed.

"No, don't you dare touch my phone again."

"Lurker, lurker, TT Marley is a lurker," he sang, bouncing out of the living room.

Before Marley could tell him that Santa wasn't real, her phone rang and Czar's name flashed across the screen. Immediately, Marley's heart went into overdrive. She clutched the phone to her chest and took deep breaths.

“Girl, answer the phone.” Harper rolled her eyes, over the dramatics.

Giving her sister the middle finger, Marley pulled the phone away from her chest and answered the call.

“If you want the dick just say that. You don’t have to flick your bean to my old pictures,” Czar lowly spoke into the phone.

“You wish.”

“Nah, wishes are for people who don’t have faith. I wholeheartedly believe that God is going to bless me with you.”

“You can’t be serious,” Marley snickered.

“I am, but we’ll leave the plans of our future up to the Big Man. Where are you and the paddy wagon parked at today?”

“Julius, please don’t make me hang up on you.”

“I’m fucking with you. I like your lil get up. Throw some hydraulics on that bitch and we really got some action. A waterbed on wheels,’ he joked.

“I hate you.” Marley held her stomach.

“So, what’s up? Besides stalking my page, what you on?”

“I’m getting ready to go to hot yoga.”

“The fuck is that?”

“Just what it sounds like. Yoga in a heated room.”

“And it’s good for what? Because I know that shit ain’t fun.”

“Mental health, sleeping, skin… plus, I like it.”

“Aight, can I come?”

“No, the class is sold out and-

“Don’t worry about that. Just say yes.”

"Yes, you can come," Marley answered, pulling the corner of her lip into her mouth.

"Send me the addy," he ended the call.

∞∞∞

Czar put his phone on the nightstand and looked over his shoulder. Honey was laid out on her stomach with her ass tooted in the air. As much as he wanted to hit it again, his desire to see Marley outweighed his horniness.

"Aye," he called out, standing to his feet.

"Hmm?" Honey moaned, lifting her head up.

"I'm about to dip."

"Ok, you wanna meet up later?" she asked, rolling over and shamelessly displaying her bare breasts. Her perky melon sized breasts were a sight for sore eyes and as hard as his dick was he had other business to attend to.

"Nah, I'm straight," Czar declined, moving around the hotel and collecting his personal items.

"Well, let me know if you change your mind. I'll be in town for a few more days," Honey purred, watching Czar pile his locs on the top of his head.

"Aight." He dropped a few bills on the nightstand before picking up their used condoms.

Honey rolled her eyes. This was the third time they hooked up and it never failed. Czar only used condoms he bought, and he always picked them up before he left. Even when they were both drunk as fuck he rolled out of the bed and flushed them down the toilet or dropped them inside a water bottle. She tried to hop on his dick between condom changes and he knocked her into the nightstand.

"Aye," Czar called out when he reached the door. "What's a good brand for yoga gear?"

"Lululemon. You do yoga?"

"I do today." He winked before closing the door.

Biggie was sitting in front of the door with his hands in his hoodie. Loud snores caused his big stomach to vibrate while his lip trembled like it was playing the flute. Czar reached out to pop him in the head, but Shortie rounded the corner with his nine in hand.

"Leave my brother alone, bitch boy."

"Stop playing so much." Biggie removed his hands, removing the nine he had tucked.

"Just making sure yall niggas not sleep on the job." Czar bypassed him on the way to the elevators.

"Never that, plus Captain Nova called up here all night. That nigga should have just came up here and waited outside."

"Aye, why ole girl was in there screaming like you was shoving pop bottles up her ass?" Shortie asked.

"Fuck if I know," Czar grunted. "I had to tell her ass to knock it off. I know I'm serving work, but damn. She almost burst my eardrum."

"Swear, and I had to stop hotel security from entering a few times," Biggie snorted.

"I'm surprised you stayed all night." Shortie side-eyed him.

"I tried to leave while she was sleeping, but she kept waking up with some new shit. I don't know what's up with these hoes and sucking toes. Shorty was sucking my big toe like a bomb pop and then tried to kiss me. I almost kneed her ass in the pussy," Czar yawned. "I need to go to the crib to shower and then I'm headed to some yoga shit with LB."

"Yoga?" Biggie and Shortie paused as the elevator doors opened for them to exit.

"Yea niggas, yoga. Just because yall haven't been exposed to some new shit don't mean I haven't."

"On God, you ain't never did yoga in yo life."

"So what? Today is a new day." Czar grinned. "And I need to go to Lululemon."

"See, now we're on the same page. I'm hungry as hell." Biggie rubbed his stomach. "What's the name again? I wanna look at the menu."

"Nigga, it's not a fucking restaurant with yo hungry ass. It's a clothing store. I need to pick some shit up for LB."

"Man, can we stop and get something to eat? I'm hungry as hell."

"Biggie, what's new?" Czar chuckled, sliding in the back seat. "Drop me off and yall can go eat."

Retrieving his phone from his pocket, Czar opened up the text from Marley, read it, and forwarded the information to Romeo. Seconds later, his phone vibrated, and of course, it was Romeo.

"You want me to do what?" he laughed.

"What the fuck the text say?"

"I'm saying, since when do you do yoga?"

"Why yall keep asking me that like I can't try new shit."

"Cause you don't try new shit. I mean you been fucking the same bitch forever. Shit, I'm surprised you banging this new chick."

"Look, do I need to call the studio myself and then look for a new assistant, or do you got the shit?" Czar barked.

"Aight damn, you kinda testy today. Lil miss twinkle pussy must've been whack."

"Nah, she was straight. It's the questions yall niggas keep asking. Call the studio and make sure they're onboard."

"Aight, I'm on it, but you need to ch-" Czar ended the call and closed his eyes as Biggie zoomed through the city with his stomach growling louder than the radio.

∞∞∞

Peas in a Pod Yoga studio was located in Royal Oak, a twenty-minute drive outside of Detroit. Instead of driving her van, Marley opted to take an Uber. The parking was horrible, and the last thing she wanted was to get a ticket or, worse, towed. Royal Oak parking attendants stayed on bullshit, and Marley wanted to enjoy her much-needed session without worrying if her baby was being tampered with.

"Alright, here we are." The Uber driver pulled up in front of the studio in record time. Marley sat up and stared out of the window. She was surprised to see that there wasn't a line wrapped around the corner. In fact, there were only two cars in the parking lot. One belonged to the owner and the second one was a black truck. Marley didn't have to wonder who it belonged to because Czar hopped out of the back seat holding up shopping bags with a big grin plastered on his face.

"Best Frienddddd," he sang, bopping over to her.

"Julius, what is this?" Marley exited the car, meeting him halfway.

"Yoga shit. I got us some matching fits from Lululemon."

"I know you lying," she giggled. "Who told you about Lululemon?"

"That's not important. Now come on so we can get dressed and do best friend shit."

"You do know it's about to be a room full of women lusting over you."

"Wrong." Czar held the front door open for her. "Just one."

"Huh?" Marley furrowed her eyebrows in confusion, but Czar hit her on the booty with the bag in his hand, encouraging her to walk up. "Boy, stop," she hissed, crossing the threshold to the studio.

"Welcome to Peas in a Pod," the instructor greeted. "My name is Remi and I'll be guiding you through this exhilarating experience."

"Nice to meet you, Re." Czar tossed her a head nod.

"Let me just fan girl really quick and then I'll be professional," she swore.

"Do ya thang."

"Oh my god, Detroit's finest is in my yoga studio and I'm geeked as fuck. Thank you so much for coming through, and no disrespect, but you fine as hell in person, and I love your music," Remi blurted out in one breath, making Marley laugh out loud.

"Thank you, sweetheart. I want you to put my card on file. Whenever she comes in here, it's on me." Czar winked.

"Julius." Marley shook her head. "I don't need you paying for my yoga sessions, and I'm confused. I thought I signed up for a class today." Marley frowned, peering around the empty studio.

"Uh, well Mr. Czar paid to have the studio shut down. You two will be my only students. The session is two hours, and at Czar's request, it'll be a mix between hot yoga and acro yoga," Remi explained in her best customer service voice.

"Acro? Julius, what do you know about acro yoga?"

"It's a bonding experience," he smirked. "Right?" He looked over at Remi for confirmation.

"Right, so go ahead and get changed. We'll be in studio one today. The locker rooms are around the corner. Remember no oils, perfume, or deodorant."

"Oh hell nah. What if she gets musty?" Czar turned up his nose.

"Trust me, her being musty will be the least of your problems. I'll see you inside." Remi winked before disappearing into her office.

"The fuck that's supposed to mean, like she trying to say yo pussy gone stank?"

"No, fool! But Julius, what is all of this?" Marley questioned, shifting on her feet. "I mean you trying a little too hard now."

"This is me trying to get to know you on a personal level. Now come on, I got us some matching yoga shit and you better post it on yo story."

"I didn't need you to buy me anything. I have clothing."

"And I have money, so take yo ass in there and try this shit on. Lululemon expensive as fuck and you got the nerve to be standing here acting like you don't want it."

"I-" Marley never got the chance to finish her sentence because Czar was in her face with his large hand loosely wrapped around her neck.

"Aye-" He stared into her eyes, allowing his thumb to brush against her bottom lip. "Go put that shit on so we can go get hot and sweaty. Stop giving me a hard time."

"Ok." Marley swallowed the lump in her throat.

Doing as she was told, Marley went into the women's locker room and changed her clothes. Not only did Czar have the right size, but he picked out a cute pair of hunter green leggings with the matching sports bra. The soft fabric felt good against her skin and hugged her body like it was made for her. Using the brush in her bag, Marley quickly parted her hair down the middle and tried her best to gather each side without all her hair products. The two braids weren't perfect, but they kept the hair out of her face. After applying a thin layer of coconut oil to her lips, Marley exited the locker room to see Czar standing there matching her fly. His dreads were in a bun, and instead of a sports bra, he was shirtless, exposing his tattooed cover chest.

"You wanna be like me so bad," she teased.

"Nah," he gazed at her. "I wanna be in you." Czar kissed her cheek. "Come on, let's do this yoga shit."

Remi had the room set up for two people. A menthol fragrance flowed through the room. It wasn't overpowering but it felt good when you took a deep breath. Two yoga mats sat on the floor in front of one another, along with a couple of tools, just in case they needed help getting into position.

"Yall cute," Remi cooed when they stepped into the room. Marley bit the inside of her cheek so the smile that pulled at her lips wouldn't be revealed.

"Thanks, take our picture," Czar requested, handing her one of his phones.

"Julius, no!" Marley declined, but again, her wants were ignored as Czar pulled her into him. Without much of a choice, Marley smiled and posed alongside him.

"Damn, it's hot as hell in here." Czar fanned himself when they parted.

"Hence the name… hot yoga," Marley teased.

"Fuck that. Can we do cold yoga?"

"Julius, please."

"Ok, let's get started." Remi clapped her hands. "We're going to start with some basic stretches. Please take your place on the mat. Feet together, hands at your sides, and take a deep breath."

Both Marley and Czar did as they were instructed.

"Slowly breathe in until I get to ten and then exhale while I count down," she softly spoke. "1...2...3...4...5...6...7...8... 9...10. Let it out. 5...4...3...2...1. Two more times." Remi walked around the room.

Czar stared at Marley while she tried to look everywhere but at him.

"Am I ugly or something? Why the fuck you keep looking over there?" he asked.

"Shouldn't you be focused on your breathing?" Marley whispered.

"54321," he counted down, making her laugh.

"Ok, we're going to go down into a downward dog." Remi cleared her throat.

"I'm straight," Czar waved her off. "Yall got this part."

"Come on. Get the full experience," Marley taunted.

"How about you take this whole dick?"

"Op," Remi snickered. "Ok, if you don't want to do that, just touch your toes."

"The fuck? That's the same shit."

"Julius! Touch your damn toes," Marley snapped.

"Aight damn and stop trying to boss me around."

"Then stop trying to take the easy way out and bend that ass over."

"Don't get fucked up in here," Czar warned, standing over her.

"Ok, ok, ok," Marley replied, coiling into his side.

Remi waited for them to stop bickering before she moved on. For an hour straight, they went through over fifteen poses and stretches. Czar swore he was in shape, but the way the yoga poses had him breathing told a different story. As soon as they were done, he was texting Romeo about getting back in the gym. Czar thought he was intrigued with Marely before, but after seeing her body twist and turn into uncomfortable positions he was obsessed.

"Alright, let's move into a couple of acro positions." Remi walked over to the speaker in the corner and started a playlist that Czar had provided prior to their arrival. *This Way* by Khalid and H.E.R. lowly played in the background while Remi pulled the strings on the blackout curtains. The only light in the room came from the strips that lined the floorboard.

"Ok, for this part we'll only need one mat. Czar, I want you to sit down with your legs open, and Marley, I want you to position yourself with your back against his chest," Remi instructed.

Marley's pulse quickened and the way Czar was staring at her didn't help. He was already on the floor with his arms stretched out, waiting to receive her. Marley's mind started to play tricks on her. She started to feel guilty for wanting to be in his arms, for wanting to connect with him.

"Aye," Czar interrupted the internal battle going on in her head. "Focus on me." He motioned for her to come to him.

Taking a deep breath, Marley walked into his arms and allowed him to guide her to the space between his legs. Czar slowly enveloped her in his arms, with her back against his chest.

"In this moment, I want you to focus on your breathing. Stay centered and breathe. Deeply inhale, softly exhale," Remi said just above a whisper. She might as well have been talking to a brick wall because Czar and Marley were both in a space where only they existed. His head was lowered, softly breathing on her neck, and Marley fought the urge to kiss the burn marks on his forearm. She never noticed them before, and now that she was so close to him, it pissed her off. Czar was breathtaking and she couldn't understand how someone could want to cause him harm.

"I don't know what it is about you, but I'm feeling the fuck outta you." Czar kissed her neck. "At first, I wanted to fuck you because you got a smart-ass mouth and I like that shit." He kissed her again. "Now I want to save you." Czar lightly sucked her ripped ear lobe. "I want to keep a smile on your pretty face."

"Julius," Marley moaned, trying to get up, but his hold was so tight and her weak attempt only lasted for a few seconds.

"Stop running from me." His hand lightly brushed over her nipples.

"Ok, Marley, I want you to turn around and wrap your arms and legs around Czar," Remi instructed. "Czar, hold her tight. The goal is to make her feel safe. Allow her to feel vulnerable in your arms."

This time, Marley didn't need to be told twice. Czar released her and she positioned herself in his lap, wrapping her body around his. Resting her head on her shoulder, Marley tried her best to control her breathing, but she was failing miserably.

"I want you to breathe. Try to match each other's rhythm so that you are breathing as one."

"Why your heart beating so fast?" Czar whispered in Marley's ear.

"B-because you are too close," she stuttered.

"Not shit talking Marley scared."

"Hush."

"Ok, Czar, I'm going to have you run your thumb down the center of her back. Apply as much pressure as she can take."

Czar ran his hand down Marley's back a couple of times before he found her spine. Using four fingers, he massaged her back while she held on tightly. Czar didn't have to ask if she felt good because he could smell her arousal. It was then he understood what Remi was talking about. They were both sweaty as hell, but there wasn't anything musty about Marley. In fact, the sweet scent that floated from between her thighs made his stomach growl. The entire session his dick had been a good boy, but the minute he caught a breeze of her sweet essence, it was a wrap.

Czar's lips found the side of Marley's neck. His kisses were soft, making her squirm in his arms. Her skin was a mixture of salty and sweet, and Czar liked it... a lot.

"LB, we gotta get up, baby, because if we stay like this any longer, I'm going to get blue balls." Czar released her.

"O-ok." She sadly swallowed, removing her arms from around him.

"I'll let you two get dressed and I'll meet you out front," Remi excused herself.

"You wanna go get something to eat?" Czar asked, turning his attention back to Marley. He wasn't ready for their day to end just yet either.

"Yea, that would be cool."

"Aight, where you wanna go?"

"Shouldn't you have a place in mind already?" she sassed.

"You eat like a hamster, so I figured we could go to Metro Park and eat roasted twigs."

"Boy, fuck you... we can go to the Trap Vegan."

"Is that a strip club?" He threw his arms over her shoulder. "I knew you was a freak."

"No, fool," Marley laughed, pushing him off her. "And you're paying."

"Fuck outta here. You got me in these gay ass Lululemon pants and I still didn't get no pussy. I'm not paying for shit and you better hope I drop you back off at your lil exterminator van."

"I hate you." Marley pushed him.

"You'll love me in due time," Czar promised with a wink.

∞∞∞

Once they were redressed, Czar led Marley to his truck and assisted her with climbing in the front seat. She didn't need help, but he used it as an excuse to grip her hips and lift her into the seat. Marley tried her hardest to keep her composure, but Czar was making it hard because he wouldn't keep his hands to himself.

"You comfortable?" he asked, hopping in the driver's seat.

"Yea, I'm good. You have a nice truck," she complimented, sinking into the soft cloth seats.

"You want one? We can gut out the back, stick a crib sized bed back there and you'll be all set." "You get on my nerves." Marley reached across the console and punched him in the arm. "Stop talking about my van."

"Spark this up." Czar handed her a pre-rolled blunt the size of his finger.

"The fuck?!" She took the blunt and stared at it. "Why is it so big?"

"Because I only smoke them little ass joints with yo ass. Matter fact, outside of my brothers, you're the only person I ever shared a blunt with."

"You don't smoke with your little Instagram hoe?"

"What hoe?"

"You know, the one you be fighting over."

"Fuck outta here, I'll never fight over a bitch."

"Hm," Marley smirked, lighting the tip of the blunt. "That's not what The Shaderoom says."

"The Shaderoom can suck my dick. They are a bunch of clout chasers."

"You probably should tell your little girlfriend that. Seems like they're getting the information from somewhere."

"If you wanna know, just ask me." Czar glanced at her out the side of his eye.

"What are you talking about?"

"You wanna know am I with Tati?"

"Not really. I don't have any interest in taking it further with you."

"That's a lie," he chortled. "You might not want to admit it, but you wanna fuck me."

"Excuse me?" Marley choked on the smoke in her mouth. Czar reached over and took the blunt from her before pointing to the bottle of water in the cup holder. After catching her breath, Marley turned in her seat to face him.

"I don't wanna fuck you," she reiterated.

"You do, and it's ok."

"You're so fucking cocky it's sick."

"It's the truth, but you have soul ties to a nigga that's pushing up daisies. You might let me touch you, kiss on you, do just enough so you can play with your pussy at night, but giving me the pussy will make you feel like you're betraying him, right?"

"You don't know what you're talking about." Marley's eyebrows dipped, displaying her annoyance at the direction the conversation was headed.

"Then why haven't you been with anyone else? You fine as fuck, mean, but nonetheless fine. You're smart from what I can tell, and any nigga would be happy to have you. Then again, you live in a van, which means you're not looking for anything stable. When you're not in biker shorts, you're wearing baggy clothes and you rarely do your hair. I'm guessing you don't wanna bring any attention your way because of the situation that happened to you. Am I right?" Czar peered over at her before hitting the blunt.

"First of all, stop trying to dig into my life like you know me."

"I'm trying to get to know you."

"You're not. You're trying to fuck me, but I know your type."

"Oh yea? What's my type?"

"You don't like emotional connections. You're never pictured with anyone outside of your family, so you probably have trust issues which I'm guessing stems from your childhood. You're always with different women, but you keep one on the side for backup. I'm guessing she's your comfort zone because she probably just lets you walk all over her. You come off rude as fuck, and I can almost bet people only deal with you because of who you are, not because they respect you," Marley continued. "You say I remind you of your mama. Is that why you feel so attached to me? Did she abandon you or something? Do you have mommy issues?"

"You don't know what the fuck you're talking about," Czar barked.

"Neither do you, so let's change the subject before I put

you out of your own truck."

"You swear you can whoop my ass." He cracked a smile. "I don't want no smoke, baby."

"That's what I thought." Marley snatched the blunt from him and sat back in her seat.

∞∞∞

Once they made it to the restaurant, Czar's fans bombarded them for pictures and autographs. Marley stood to the side while he did his thing. She secretly admired him for taking the time out to acknowledge the people who listened to his music. After nearly having a heart attack, the waiter led the duo to a booth in the back.

"Welcome to Trap Vegan, my name is Tasha. Can I start yall off with something to drink?" she asked, pulling an iPad from her apron.

"I'll take a lemon water," Marley ordered.

"And you?" Tasha turned to Czar.

"Let me get a sprite."

"Ok, I'll give you two a moment to look over the menu." She switched away with a little extra twist on top just in case Czar's eyes were on her. Marley laughed to herself. The last thing on Czar's mind was her stank booty walk. He was too busy trying to decipher the difference between plant-based patty and cauliflower wings.

"Man, what the fuck is a plant-based patty?" Czar frowned, looking over the menu. "The fuck you be getting from here?"

"I like the BBQ Jackfruit bowl with the side truffle fries. I have the munchies, so I'm going to get the Trap Sliders too."

"So they have no real chicken?"

"Nope."

"Order for me then because if my shit ain't clucking or mooing, I don't know what to get."

"Everything is good, you can't go wrong."

"You two ready?" Tasha returned, sitting their drinks on the table. This time her lips were super glossed and her perfume nearly choked them.

"Damn shorty, you smell like a Swap Meet. Back up a little bit." Czar shooed her. "Matter fact, we want one of everything, but have somebody else bring the food out. You gone ruin our fucking appetite smelling like that."

Embarrassed, Tasha hauled ass across the restaurant without another word. Marley picked up her drink and took a sip while shaking her head.

"What I do now?" Czar hunched his shoulders.

"You couldn't tell her she smelt bad in a nicer way?"

"That was nice and I'm even going to tip her ass. Hopefully, she go buy some perfume that don't smell like garlic and old bay."

"You are hell," Marley laughed.

"Have you ever been to one of my concerts?"

"No."

"Why the fuck not?" Czar's eyebrows wrinkled. "How you trying to be my girl and never been to my show?"

"I'm not trying to be your girl, fool. And to answer your question, I don't like big crowds. Since the shooting, I'm a little paranoid around a lot of people."

"That's understandable, but just know when you start coming to my concerts you don't have to worry about shit. I'll make sure you straight."

"How you gone do that and perform?"

"You gone be on stage twerking to my shit, duh. Wait, can you twerk?"

"I don't twerk, I two-step."

"Yea, ok. I'll see for myself."

"Anyway, back to my question. Is Tati your girlfriend?" Marley toyed with her straw.

"If she was, why would I be out here with you?" he countered.

"You could just be that type of guy."

"Is that the kind of guy your ex was?"

"Not at first, but money changed the person he was. He loved me, but he also loved the attention that came along with his line of work."

"And you stayed?"

"I did. I was young and dumb. I thought I earned a spot in his life, and I wasn't giving it up for no bitch. It didn't help that my mama encouraged me to forgive him over and over."

"Straight up? That's a first. You don't hear about too many parents willingly putting their kids in the lion's den."

"Yea. She wasn't the best person to take advice from," Marley sighed.

"I see, and to answer your question, no. Tati is just somebody I fuck. She was cool before she stepped into the industry, but now she's just like the rest of them. Fake as fuck."

"But you still get down with her?"

"I do. She can suck a mean dick."

"You gross."

"I'm honest." Czar shrugged.

"I've noticed." Marley rolled her eyes.

"I do like you though," he admitted. "I think you're cool as fuck."

"What makes me so cool, Czar?"

"Honestly, I think it's cause you be trying to go in on my ass. That doesn't happen often."

"Well, I'm still not giving up the coochie." She blew him a kiss.

"I'll get it one day," he smirked, causing a small grin to pull at the corner of her lips.

"Can I ask you something?"

"What's up?" Czar leaned forward, giving her his undivided attention.

"What happened to your arm? I've never seen the marks in any of your pictures."

"I'm black as fuck, you can barely see my tattoos from a distance," he snorted. "But when I was a lil nigga, somebody used it as a ashtray."

"Oh God!" Marley covered her mouth.

"It's cool, LB, the shit healed."

"You wanna talk about it?" She reached across the table, taking his hand in hers.

"Nah, but if you wanna kiss them, I might feel better."

"You wish." Marley slapped his hand as the owner brought over their food.

"If this shit nasty I'm going to have the health department shut this muthafucka down," Czar warned, suspiciously eyeing the plates of food.

"Sir, I assure you," the owner began explaining before Marley cut him off.

"Please ignore him, we're fine," she assured him before pushing a plate of BBQ cauliflower to Czar. "Eat and leave these people alone."

"Man, I can't get no pussy and I gotta eat fake chicken. This some bullshit," he complained, watching Marley stuff a piece in her mouth. "I bet your poots be funky as hell."

"Stick around long enough and you will see," she winked.

Chapter 10

"I think Jaxon is cheating on me," Harper blurted out after their customer walked away.

Marley turned to face her sister with raised eyebrows. The outburst took her by surprise, but instead of asking why, she started putting away the leftover bottles of tea on the table.

"What are you doing?" Harper frowned.

"We about to go find his ass and get some answers. The fuck. Why think when you can know for sure? I have my pepper spray in the van and a crowbar, which one do you want?" Marley asked, scooping the tea bags into a box.

"Stop, fool," Harper giggled but appreciated her willingness to set shit off.

It was Saturday afternoon, and the sisters were sitting on the Detroit Riverwalk along with twenty other vendors from the city selling their products. They had only been there an hour and the support was real. Harper paid a local designer to create their flyer, and when she posted it on social media, Czar shared it. His followers went wild and started reposting it, swearing that it was the best tea they had ever tasted. Not only did the *Sippin' Tea* website sell out for the third time, but it also crashed.

"You're just looking for an excuse to leave," Harper continued.

"You know me so well," Marley snickered, removing the tea from the box and putting them back on the table. "But what's going on? What Jaxon long head ass do?"

"Oh, now he's Jaxon. What happened to him being your brother?"

"His relationship with me is contingent upon your feelings for him. If you not fucking with him then neither am I."

"That's the realest shit I ever heard." Harper wiped her fake tears.

"But seriously, what he do? I thought things were good."

"And they are. He hasn't done anything per se, but his actions are questionable."

Before Marley could respond, they were rushed with a small crowd. They cleaned out the white raspberry tea, the honey citrus with mint and the honey lavender. A few women even asked to take pictures with them. Marley declined, but Harper did it and thanked them.

"I'm waiting." Marley stared at her sister.

"He's been coming home later, he doesn't answer the phone around me, and I went through his text thread and it was clear. Like there wasn't even shit from me in there."

"Did you ask him about it?"

"Yea, and he said something about his phone glitching."

"And that's hard to believe? You know iPhones are always fucking up."

"True, and I thought about that but his body language

was off. I've been with this man since grade school and I know when he's lying."

"How?"

"His dumb ass top lip curls."

"What?" Marley laughed.

"I'm serious. His top lip curls when he lies, and when I was asking him about the text messages, the muthafucka curled like it was running from his breath," Harper explained, making her sister giggle.

"Ok, so what do you wanna do?"

"I don't know. I do know I can't do this shit again. When we were kids and in high school, the back-and-forth shit was cute. The breakup to makeup was routine, but now we're married and have so much time and love invested in one another. If Jaxon is cheating it'll come out and I'll be gone like a thief in the night."

"You'll leave him?"

"The fuck?" Harper snaked her neck. "Bitch, I'll be on the first bus to *Dick Me Down Town*. I'll be the biggest hoe on the market. I need to make up for all the years I spent with his dog ass."

"Thought about it much?"

"Every woman who has been with a man for more than five years thought about what they'd do if they were single. It's like an escape plan."

"Well, I don't think he's cheating. I think you should talk to him. He's your husband, and if something is going on, maybe it's not what you think."

"Hm. We'll see." Harper twisted her lips. "But if he is cheating, I'm going to cry my ass all the way to the bank and then the airport."

"And what about Jax?"

"He can stay with his cheating ass daddy. I'm not about to be a single mother. I'll get him on every other weekend and every other holiday."

"I'm guessing you thought about that too?" Marley quipped.

"Sure did." She winked as a few customers walked up to their booth.

While Harper took orders and chatted with the giddy girls, Marley faded into the background, or at least she tried to until they started talking about Czar. According to them, Czar was on Live encouraging his fans to check out the pop-up shop. Shaking her head, Marley removed her phone from her pocket and logged into Instagram. Sure as shit, Czar's profile picture was at the top lit up with the word LIVE underneath it. Against her better judgment, Marley clicked on it.

"*When am I dropping new music*?" Czar squinted to read the comment and then leaned back in his chair. "*I'm working on some shit, but as to when it drops, I don't know. Until then, go stream my other shit.*"

Czar read a couple of more comments and when he saw *her* name tag, his eyes flickered with excitement. Marley's heart leaped out of her chest as recognition set in. He was happy to see her.

"*LB, the fuck you doing on my Live*?" He smirked into the camera. "*And I still don't see my picture on your page. We could've had Lululemon endorsements, but you playing. I knew I should've posted that shit myself instead of sending it to you.*"

Marley tucked her lip into her mouth and replied.

"I'm not posting the picture and thank you for today."

"*You welcome, does this mean we can do hot yoga again?*"

Czar grinned, reaching for his water.

"Nope," Marley typed while laughing to herself.

The comment section started questioning him, wondering who he was talking to, and since the comments were coming in so fast, Marley's reply got lost in the mix. Czar tapped the button to invite her to his Live, but of course, it was denied.

"I knew yo scary ass wasn't about that life," he laughed into the camera. *"Aye, if yall just tuning in, my homegirl Marley is the owner of Sippin' Tea and she's currently on the Detroit River Walk. Go show her some love. Make sure you post a picture of your purchase and I just might raffle off something."*

Marley sent him a middle finger for the scary comment and a smiley face for her appreciation. She waited to see if he'd see it, but a woman wearing a too small shirt popped into the camera's view and claimed a seat in his lap. She couldn't see her face, but the comment section started typing Tati's name. The woman started twerking to music on her phone, and people in the comments were hyping her up, but Czar appeared annoyed. Marley shook her head in disgust. Even if she had the body, she wouldn't be caught on Ashanti's internet shaking her ass for the world to see. It was tacky, and she didn't know why, but her feelings were hurt. They weren't together; hell, Marley didn't even know if they'd ever take it further than kissing, but seeing another woman all in his lap evoked an emotion she thought she'd never experience again. Marley exited the live and dropped her phone on the table.

∞∞∞

On the other end of the phone, Czar ended the Live without warning. Tati didn't even have time to get comfortable in his lap before her ass was touching the floor.

"Oh my god, did you just push me on the floor?" she asked, looking at the black screen on the phone then up at him.

"Not at all. I stood up and gravity did its thing. Nobody told you to sit yo ass on my lap and start bouncing. For someone that's supposed to be low key, you're doing a lot to be seen."

"I'm not hiding our relationship, Czar." Tati stood up, dusting off her sore ass.

"The fuck is you talking about right now? This-" he pointed between them, "Ain't no fucking relationship."

"I swear you are so wishy-washy. One minute you're commenting on my picture, and the next you acting like I did something to you. Why fuck with me if you're going to be an asshole?" she snapped, folding her arms across her chest.

"I dropped an eggplant under your picture, and you ran with the shit. I didn't call you, Tati. You called me," he reminded her.

"I called you because I missed you. Do you honestly not miss me when we aren't together?"

"Mannnn," Czar chortled, dragging his hands down his face. This was the shit he didn't have time for. "How can you say that shit with a straight face?"

"What?" She pouted, poking her lip out. "How can I say what?"

"That you miss me. You have a whole nigga, shouldn't you be missing him?"

"I dropped Yaro. He's too clingy for me," Tati lied, flinging her wrist in the air. It was actually the other way around. Yaro broke up with her after word got back that she was still messing around with Czar. His career couldn't take another hit, so he broke up with her while taking everything he bought her in the process. Tati wanted to show her ass on Twitter, but Yaro was the type to go back and forth with her, so going off on him was out of the question.

"Get the fuck outta here. You think I want to make you my woman after every nigga in the industry passed you around like a hot potato? You a hoe, Tati, and I'll never take you seriously. Had this been a conversation when we first started messing around, then yea, but shorty your head got so big that you couldn't walk through the door."

"Wow." Tati swallowed her tears. The reality of their situation slapped her in the face like a closed door. "I thought we were just doing us until the time was right."

"If you're waiting on the right time, you'll be waiting forever, and I hate that for you."

"Who raised you?" she asked, shaking her head.

"The worse kind of nigga," Czar coldly spat. "But I'm about to make a move, so you need to bounce."

"Is this about that girl?"

"What girl?"

"The basic bitch you keep flirting with online," Tati barked. "She looks like she shops in a Salvation Army bin and she tacky as fuck."

"You been on her page?" Czar chuckled in amusement.

Tati wanted to kick her own ass. She had no intentions of mentioning Marley, but Czar showing attention to someone she considered beneath her was a problem. Czar had never shown her any kind of love on social media, yet he commented on Marley's videos, shared her posts, and called her out in Lives. In Tati's opinion, they weren't on the same level. The bitch sold tea for god's sake.

"I have and the bitch don't have shit on me. That big

messy ass wig and knitted bullshit she be wearing. She makes fucking tea bags, Czar. Is that the kinda woman you want on your arm? I mean she don't even have an ass, so please tell me what that basic hoe have that I don't." Tati placed her hand on her thick hip.

Czar stood back and eyed her from head to toe. He wanted to laugh in her face, but he almost felt bad for her. Sure, her waist length weave was curled to perfection, and her toes, nails, lashes, and eyebrows were top-notch. Her body was curvy, and her thighs even matched her ass, but that was it. Everything else about her was superficial. Tati couldn't hold a conversation that didn't involve labels and money. She had no aspirations in life other than being the next Lori Harvey, but she fell short every time.

Social media had her head so big that she forgot her ass wasn't real, and without makeup she was below average. The name brand clothes she wore came from photoshoots, and she received free bundles and wigs. Tati was so out of touch with reality that she thought she was *that* girl, but the thing about *it girls* is they changed with the season. Not only did she nigga hop, but besides a few bands, she didn't demand anything from those men. No one wifed the pass around. Fake pumping for the Gram had her head clouded, and Czar was honored to bring her back down to earth.

"She has my attention." He burst her bubble.

"What?" Tati frowned. "I know your type and she's not it."

"Nah, you know how I like to fuck, how I like my dick sucked. That's what we started off doing and it's nothing wrong with that. Just don't try to switch shit up after you've handed out more pussy than Meals on Wheels."

"Czar, please. I guess she knows what you like," she scoffed, ignoring everything else that was said.

"I'm dead ass, but I know you're too shallow to think a woman like her could snatch me up when you been on your knees since we met and you can barely get a nut out of me."

"Fuck you, Czar! You're not all that. I know plenty of niggas with more money than your cheap ass, and if you think I'm about to let you flaunt that basic hoe in my face, you have another thing coming." Tati pushed past him. "Can't believe you're about to let a bum bitch play you. Then again, you need someone to knock your arrogant ass down from cloud nine."

"Yea, yea. Grab your shit and get out before I make yo dookie booty ass climb down the fire escape," Czar warned.

Snatching her clothes off the floor, she quickly got dressed and stormed to the front door. Czar had her fucked up and if he thought he was going to just play in her face with a bitch who dressed like a high school reject, then he didn't know her well at all. As soon as the elevator doors closed, Czar told security not to let her back up and he deleted her password to his elevators. He didn't trust her by a long shot, and since he hurt her pride he knew she was going to be on her best bullshit.

∞∞∞

After taking a quick shower, Czar drove straight to his parents' house. He really didn't want to face his mother, but since she was his accountant, their monthly meetings were mandatory. Not only did they go over all of his business finances, but they discussed other ways to generate revenue. Czar knew that everybody had a season, and while he was still in his, he wanted to make as much money as possible. Stocks, rental property, commercial property, silent investments, Czar had his hands in a little of everything.

"I saw your deposit to the women's homeless shelter. You do know we send them money once a month," Ada voiced, closing the folder in front of her. "You don't have to keep giving them money, C."

"I know I don't have to, but I feel like I owe them."

Ada walked into Shells Women's Homeless shelter with her hood pulled over her face. With Czar at her side, she limped to the front desk and placed her purse on the counter. She hated that they had to stay in a shelter, but staying in a hotel was out of the question. The little money she had, they'd need for food and personal hygiene supplies.

"Good evening, all of our beds are full tonight," the lady behind the counter spoke without looking up.

"Uh, ok," Ada's voice cracked.

"These young girls kill me coming in here after these no good niggas leave them," another woman muttered. "That's why I do what I do," she bragged. "Now she got that lil boy out here looking homeless because she picked the wrong man. I'm going to lunch. Send them away. We don't have any more beds."

Ada watched the lady switch off and she wanted to snatch her by her hair. Sure, she was in a messed up predicament, but who was she to judge her? The wide hipped lady didn't know what it took to leave, for her to be standing there begging for help. Leaving Cain was no easy task, and if it hadn't been for Czar stabbing him in the back, they wouldn't have made it out. The knife in Cain's back immobilized him enough for them to escape into thin air, and hearing they had no place to sleep for the night broke her. "Ok." Ada wiped the tears from her face.

"No, it's not ok." Czar stepped forward. Only then did the woman behind the counter look at them, and she gasped. Ada's eyes were black and nearly swollen shut, her nose was bloody, and her shirt was torn, almost shredded. Czar's nose was bloody and his cheek was bruised.

"Oh my god, are you ok?" The woman pushed up from her seat and rounded the counter. She knew what her manager said, but there was no way she could turn them away.

"Do it look like we ok?" Czar frowned, fed up with their bullshit.

"I-uh didn't know. I didn't look up. I'm sorry."

"It's ok," Ada sniffled. She wanted to snap on the lady, and had it been any other day, she would have, but this version of her was broken. At this point, Ada was ready to call it quits because rock bottom wasn't the correct phrase to describe her situation. She was trapped under guilt, wrong turns, and stupid decisions, making it impossible for her to breathe. It felt like bricks were sitting on her chest, and no matter how hard she pushed, Ada couldn't break free.

"It's not ok," Czar's seven-year-old voice roared, "Can we stay here or not?" he asked, becoming irritated with the stares of the staff. "We don't beg."

"You can stay. My name is Mary." She handed them a box of tissues. "But we need to do intake. Do you need a hospital?"

"Nah, we need tickets to the zoo," he grunted.

"Czar, be respectful," Ada hissed. "I just need to get cleaned up and a place to sleep."

"Ok, if you have a phone or anything that can be tracked, I need you to cut it off."

"Is this a shelter or a prison?" Czar quizzed, not wanting to give up his phone. He didn't have any minutes, but he could play games.

"It's a shelter, but in order to protect you, we need to collect anything that can be traced," Mary explained.

"Czar, give her the phone," Ada told him.

"Fine." He stubbornly handed it over to her.

"Thank you." Mary warmly smiled but didn't get one in return. "We have an in-house nurse and if it's ok with you, I'd like to have her take a look at you."

"Just my mama," Czar replied, touching Ada's back. "I'm good."

"Ok, well are you hungry?"

"A little." His stomach growled telling his truth.

"Ok, follow me to the cafe while we get your mother checked out. By the time you're done, we'll have a room set up for you," Mary assured them, looking from Czar to Ada. "Is that ok with you?"

"You gone be ok?" Czar asked, looking at his mother.

"I'll be fine," she promised.

"Ok, I'll save you some food."

"My baby." Ada raised her hand to stroke his cheek, but a sharp pain in her side made her wince.

"I can wait," Czar changed his mind. "Let's go check on my mama."

Ada tucked her swollen bottom lip into her mouth to keep from crying. Since birth, Czar had been a protector. It didn't matter that he was born into an unfortunate situation. Ada was his everything, and the older he got, the more he knew it was his job to protect her. Mary nodded her head, understanding that Czar wasn't leaving his mother's side. Instead of trying to convince him to go eat, Mary led them to the nurse's station.

Czar sat back and watched them. Each time his mother winced, silently cried, or jumped, a fire burned in the pit of his stomach. At that moment, Czar swore that he'd never let another man touch his mother.

"I'm sure they appreciate everything you're doing for them, but you don't owe anybody anything." Ada reached across the table and stroked his cheek, bringing him back from visions of their past. "You ok? Have you been sleeping?"

"I'm straight, Ma," Czar lied, not wanting to get into what he was really feeling. His truth, his feelings, and his thoughts all centered around their past, and although she was asking him *if he was ok*, she couldn't handle the truth.

"Has Cain tried to reach out to you?"

Before Czar could lie again, the office door was pushed open and Romeo walked in with a plate of spaghetti and fish. He was dressed in shorts and a tank, which meant he was probably in the gym playing basketball with Slim or Nova.

"What the hell is going on between the walls in my home," he sang out loud, making Ada giggle.

"I swear you dropped this nigga on his head," Czar chuckled, welcoming the distraction.

"Hold on, C, let me explain before you start to place the blame," Romeo continued singing while altering the words. He danced over to them while stuffing a piece of fish in his mouth.

"Boy, sit down before you drop food all over my office."

"Aye Ma, you think you could teach Sammy how to cook? She made me some pancakes yesterday and I swear I almost chipped a tooth."

"You ate 'em though," Nova revealed, moseying into the room and taking a seat on the end of the desk.

"Duh. Nigga, she been taking up taekwondo. The last thing I need for her is to try her new moves on me for insulting her food." Romeo bucked his eyes. "I just sprinkled a little water on them and they softened up a bit."

"You a simp. Ain't that much love in the world." Nova shook his head.

"I don't know about him and Sammy, but when you're in love, you do crazy things," Ada told them and Czar shifted in his seat. He never wanted the type of love in his life that she was describing. Love is supposed to be easy, not painful.

"I'm straight on all that, Ma. Point me to the sluts." Nova stroked his chin.

"That's a damn shame. I guess Ro and Sammy will be the first to give me grandkids."

"I don't know, C gotta lil friend," Romeo snitched.

"You're seeing someone?" Ada raised her eyebrows. "This is news to me."

"I'm not seeing anyone." Czar waved him off.

"So you gone sit up in here and act like LB don't have you all in your feelings." Nova twisted his lips.

"What the hell is a LB?"

"C's girl, that's what we call her. It's short for Lil Booty."

"Yall niggas need to get a life," Czar grunted. "Her name is Marley and she's cool people. We just friends." He didn't know how true the statement was because she wasn't answering his calls or text messages, and he could bet it had everything to do with Tati's big face ass.

"Friends that lip lock," Romeo snitched.

"Nigga you need to stop lip-locking with Sammy and stand up. Scary ass over there eating cement patties but all in my business, and you better not chip your tooth because dental isn't covered in your health plan."

"My mama is your accountant. I'll just go straight to the source."

"Don't nothing move without my say so." Czar winked, snatching a piece of fish from his plate. "Ma, you need anything else from me?"

"Well, I wanna finish our conversation." Ada glared at him.

"Aight, we'll finish," he swore... another lie.

Chapter 11

With everything going on in his life, Czar needed a distraction, so he had Romeo book him for club appearances out of state. Because his music was tearing up the charts, everybody wanted a piece of him, so Czar decided to capitalize on it. He was paid top dollar for his appearance and extra if they wanted him to perform a song.

"We in this bitch," Romeo slurred, throwing his arm around his brother's shoulder. "I don't tell you enough, but I'm proud of you nigga. My muthafuckin' brother."

Czar simply grinned; he was running on fumes, yet he wasn't ready to stop. He couldn't remember the last time he got a full night's sleep, and at this point, it was much needed. The club scene was draining as fuck, but it took his mind off his current situation. Every other night he was in a different city and spotted with a different woman. At this point, he was drinking and fucking to keep his thoughts at bay. Czar had even flown Honey to see him, but she started being clingy, so he sent her ass back to wherever she came from with a one-way ticket. Czar's plan was to reduce stress, but Honey was on some other shit as if she didn't have three niggas name tatted on her inner thigh.

As long as he stayed high, Czar didn't have to face the fact that somewhere out in the world there were pictures of his mother doing ungodly acts. He hadn't heard from Cain, but he knew better than to think he had just walked away. He was somewhere lurking, waiting, plotting his next move. Men like Cain didn't stop until they got what they wanted.

"We got Czar in the building," the DJ shouted into the microphone and then proceeded to drop one of his hits. "Bless these people with a verse C!"

Just like that, Czar's section went up! The beat dropped and the lights started flickering as if they were dancing to the beat. The walls and dance floor trembled from the bass system, leaving you with no choice but to move. Nova and Romeo stood beside Czar performing the song as if they had written it. Asses and titties bounced around him, each trying to outdo the next like they were trying to get chose.

"Ugh, call me Mr. Snatch her lace. Dick all in her stomach while her girl sits on her face," Czar rapped into the microphone. *"I'm with all that freaky shit, ride me on yo toes while ole girl lick yo clit."*

"Say that shit B-Law," Sammy sang, popping her booty on Romeo while he rapped in her ear. *"We don't love these hoes, we just fucking,"* she rapped. *"And when we done, we pass 'em. Ain't no cuffin'!"*

Czar didn't think he'd ever be happy to see a woman in his life, but when Sammy popped up at his penthouse cursing out the doorman, he started to hug her. Czar didn't know the details of what transpired because he ended up leaving when Romeo started all that pleading shit. The only thing that mattered was when he returned home after the gym all of Romeo's things were gone.

"That boy happy as fuck," Nova said, taking the space next to Czar, who was now trying to fade into the background.

"As long as he ain't in my face all sad and shit, I don't give a fuck."

"Aye, so I looked into the dude from the concert," Nova revealed, causing Czar's blood to run cold.

"I thought I told you to leave that shit alone." Czar's jaw twitched.

"You did, but you know me. I couldn't let it go. Had I been anybody else you would have fired me. Shit, you probably would have tried to beat my ass."

"You not anybody else. You my fucking brother, and if I said I got it, then trust me."

"Do you got it though?" Nova thumbed his nose, moving closer so no listening ears could hear them. "C you moving different. You always drinking and I've noticed that you're back to taking your pills, but it's a little excessive. We been in a club every night, and don't get me wrong because I love this shit, but-

"But what hardheaded ass nigga?" Czar snapped, cutting him off.

"Fuck outta here. I'm looking out for you. I'm doing the job you pay me to do," Nova barked and then lowered his voice. "Dude is a pimp or some shit, right? You buying pussy now?" he continued.

"Aye, shut the fuck up," Czar gritted. "You about to open a can of worms yo ass won't be able to digest," he warned. It was on the tip of his tongue to give Nova what he was asking for, but he couldn't bring himself to say it out loud.

Nova and Romeo weren't built like him. They didn't have to fight for anything because Slim made sure they had it all. They didn't know what pain felt like and they didn't know about their mother's past because Czar held the secrets as if he was her diary. Nova probably wanted the truth, just not that truth. The stories Czar knew would change his life.

"Muthafuckin' Tati and her crew in this bitch," the DJ announced, completely blowing Czar's high.

As if he wasn't already irritated, the club owner seated Tati in the section directly across from him. Czar was starting to think she had a GPS on his dick, but he had to remember that his moves were all on social media. Glancing in her direction, Czar couldn't deny she looked good in her crop motorsport jacket and leather skirt. Instead of wearing a shirt, she rocked a bra-like top and a pair of long black boots that stopped at mid-thigh. Czar licked his lips. Tati was fine, but he was straight on her.

"There go yo girl," Romeo slurred, leaning against the banister as people started to fill Tati's section.

"Fuck outta here, that cum bucket ain't my shit," Czar gritted, pulling his attention away from Tati. Peering down at his phone, Czar noticed he had an Instagram notification. He started to dismiss it, but when he saw that it was from Sippin' Tea, he opened the app. The music from the club drowned out the sound from the video, but he watched it anyway. The caption read *Come Meditate With Me.*

Lifting the phone closer to his face, Czar watched Marley unroll her yoga mat and place it near the shoreline. When a small wave hit the shore, she backed it up a bit so she wouldn't get wet. Removing a thermal, he watched her take a sip of the tea and give the camera a thumbs up. The video sped up as Marley stretched her hands to the sky and then touched her toes. A grin tugged at Czar's lips as he caught a full view of her lil booty in the biker shorts. The thought of fucking her on the yoga mat crossed his mind and made him shift on his feet. Once she was finished stretching, Marley sat on the mat and crossed her legs, placing her hands in her lap. After a few seconds, she closed her eyes and exhaled.

He exhaled. She was so peaceful that even if he wasn't in her space, he could feel it.

"Fuck you watching?" Romeo questioned, leaning over Czar's shoulder and making him exit the video. "Is that Lil Booty?"

"Don't worry about it. I'm ready to bounce."

"Good because ole girl over there showing out." Nova nodded toward the other section.

A few feet away, Tati was in her feelings and it was her own fault. She thought after she stormed out of his place that he'd come around, but nope. He blocked her from his pages and kept it moving. Tati was used to the radio silence, but this was different. Czar blocking her was new and the only thing that changed was his infatuation with the homely looking chick on Instagram.

Being the petty person she was, Tati made a burner page and trolled Sippin' Tea's page for two nights straight. She left bad reviews and fake hospital notes, claiming she got sick from their tea and all. Thus far, no one had replied, but it didn't matter because Tati wasn't finished. Czar and his tacky lil friend had her all the way fucked up. Although she knew he didn't want a relationship, it didn't stop her from craving more. At one point, Tati thought messing with different men would make him jealous, but it did the complete opposite. She thought allowing him to have his way with her displayed her willingness to please him, but again, she was wrong. Czar fucked her and went on about his day without another thought of her. Tati was simply a good time, nothing more.

Normally when they were in the same club, he sent her a bottle or invited her and her girls to join him, but not this time. He didn't acknowledge her when she walked past his section. Czar barely looked in her direction and it made her feel some type of way. Her weave was laid to perfection, her makeup was beat down and her outfit was bossy as fuck. The Shaderoom had even posted her and the comment section went wild. With all that, the only man she wanted to pay attention hadn't even batted his eyes in her direction.

"What he doing?" Tati asked her friend Nique while dancing with her back facing Czar.

"I think he about to come over here."

"That's what I thought. That nigga know what it is and ain't none of these hoes fucking him like I do." Tati rolled her tongue across her teeth. She was frontin' but that wasn't Nique's business.

"Period, bitch! You think his brother is single?" Nique questioned, pushing her breasts up. Tati could have Czar, she wanted Nova. The lil nigga was working with a python and after seeing his sex tape, she wanted parts. "Oh wait, he's leaving," she paused, poking her lips out.

"What?" Tati spun around in time to catch Czar about to walk past her section. Moving at the speed of light, she sauntered toward him while adjusting her skirt. "C!" she called out over the music, trying to move through the sea of people.

Czar heard her, but he kept walking until he felt a hand grip his arm.

"The fuck you grabbing on me for?" He snatched away from her, causing her to stumble a little.

"I'm saying you didn't see me?" She stood up, trying to press her body into him, but he moved back. Tati was doing too much for his liking. Czar could smell the liquor on her breath and knew where the source of her courage came from.

"You damn near ass naked. Everybody in this bitch saw you. Move."

"Are you mad at me or something?" Tati cocked her head to the side.

"Nah," Czar said while trying to keep moving. People were snapping pictures of them left and right and he knew by the morning there would be about twenty different narratives on every platform. The media would swear they were having a lovers' quarrel, and she wouldn't deny it because Tati fed off the clout their situation created. A fight with him would keep her relevant for another week or so. Every popular blogger would dissect their situation and fan pages would share it. The shit was a never-ending cycle.

"Read the room. He not fucking with you girl, so move around," Sammy spoke up. Tati was cutting in her dick time and from the way Romeo was leaning, that window was getting smaller by the second.

"Does this have anything to do with the guy that plays for the Ravens? It was just dinner," Tati promised, but Czar laughed in her face. "What's funny?" She squinted.

"Your ego." He stopped laughing. "Yo pussy don't smack loud enough for me to be pressed."

"Op!" Nique covered her mouth at the insult, and Sammy flat out laughed all in her face.

"Come on." Nova gently pushed Czar. It didn't take a rocket scientist to see things were about to take a turn for the worse. Tati's face turned different shades of red as embarrassment consumed her.

"Her shit don't smack, B-law?" Sammy instigated.

"Fuck nah," he snorted. "Shit like a lil whisper."

"Fuck you, Czar!" Tati screamed, grabbing the back of his shirt when he tried to walk away from her. Czar didn't hit women, but he wanted to knock the shit out of Tati. She had to be drunk because she knew he didn't play that touching shit. If she wasn't on her knees or bent over, there was no reason for her to ever touch him. "You just mad because a nigga like you could never lock a bitch like me down. I'm Lori Harvey to you niggas."

"Lori Harvey?" Nova frowned. Tati was cute, but not Lori

Harvey cute.

"You want me to handle that, B-Law?" Sammy asked, removing her earrings. Even if he didn't, her mind was already made up. Tati was too loud and bold for her liking. All she had to do was mind her business, and since she didn't... whatever happened, she deserved.

"Yea, humble that bitch," Czar commanded as Tati's friends tried to calm her down. Being that her back was to them, Tati couldn't see Sammy removing her jewelry, nor did she see the excitement in her eyes. Raised by her father and surrounded by all boys taught Sammy how to knock a bitch from Detroit to California, and thanks to her big mouth, Tati's lips were about to be knocked to another coast.

"And I want a Birkin!" Sammy added as she handed Romeo her purse.

"She bet not have a scratch on her," he warned Czar.

"The way she be whoopin' yo ass, I'm sure she'll be aight."

"Girl, calm down, that nigga ain't paying you no attention," Tati's friend Dena begged. She was pissed that her kid-free night was about to be ruined because Tati couldn't control her liquor.

"Fuck him!" she screamed. "He not about to front on me like he don't answer when I call. Like he don't eat my pu-

Whap!

The blow to the side of her face caused her to fall into Dena, who stood there shocked. The impact from the blow knocked Tati right out of her red bottoms. Sammy didn't even give her a chance to get up and defend herself. She hopped on Tati and started laying haymakers all upside her head. Sammy was a little woman, but the way she dragged Tati, you'd never know.

"Get this bitch off me," Tati cried, trying to swing but only connecting with the air.

"Nah, you get me off you hoe," Sammy taunted, ripping the glued lace from Tati's forehead.

Whap! Whap!

As bad as Tati's friends wanted to help her, they couldn't. The thought of being dragged on the internet for letting a leprechaun beat them up didn't sit right in their spirit, so they did the next best thing. They screamed for help while covering their faces with their purses.

"Aye, break this shit up." Security bombarded the section, picking up Sammy by her waist.

"Yall better let my girl go," Romeo demanded, sobering up real quick.

"My fault, bro, but she gotta go." The guard put her down.

"I'm good, that hoe don't want no smoke." Sammy took her purse from Romeo.

"We out." Czar took one last look at Tati, who was still lying between the couch and the table. Half of her wig was off, her skirt was above her waist and her face was bloody. He didn't even feel bad for her and he hoped she learned a valuable lesson about keeping her hands to herself.

"Yo, you up?" Nova tapped on the door, causing Czar to jolt from his sleep. Beads of sweat rolled down his face and his body was drenched. "Our flight leaves in two hours."

"Aight." He rubbed his eyes to adjust to the brightness in the room.

It was a little after ten in the morning and Czar felt like he just hit the pillow. His mouth was dry and his body was sticky. Peering to his left, he spotted two naked bodies on the edge of the bed and another one curled up at the foot. Empty condom wrappers and liquor bottles littered the floor along with articles of clothing and shoes.

"Fuck," Czar mumbled, climbing over the bodies to get to the floor. Stumbling to the bathroom, Czar shook his head as images from the night before flooded his mind.

After leaving the club, they went to the Waffle House and turned it into an after-hour. At some point during the night his fans found out he was still in town from his Instagram post and they were able to piece together his location. The manager at the Waffle House had to lock the doors because fans were turning the restaurant into a meet and greet.

"You want some company?" A soft voice asked from behind him.

Czar turned around and stared at the woman trying to remember her name, but he couldn't focus, and the fact that she didn't look the same as she did last night didn't help. Last night she had a long curly weave that touched her ass, an ass that was no longer attached to her body. She also had perky titties and a pretty smile. Standing there, it was clear that she wore a Wonderbra because her titties were just as flat as her ass.

"Aye, go get your ID," he barked, waking up the other women.

"Excuse me," the girl frowned. "I told you last night I was twenty-three."

"Yo age isn't in question."

"Huh?"

Instead of repeating himself, Czar walked over to the nightstand and removed his gun. Atlanta had him fucked up, and if the bitch standing in front of him was born a nigga, he was about to catch a murder charge.

"I said get your ID before shit gets real ugly in this bitch."

"Oh my god," the girls on the bed shrieked.

"Aye, shut the fuck up. Did yall know this nigga slipped in here last night?" He pointed the gun at them. "Yall trying to set me up?"

"That's my sister. She's not a man. She just took after my dad," one of the girls cried as the room door flew open.

"The fuck you doing nigga?" Nova rushed him, taking the gun out of his hand.

"Gimme my shit. Yall let me leave with a nigga?" Czar roared.

"Who a nigga?" Romeo quizzed, checking out the naked girls.

"I know you see this nigga standing here covering his chest like he got titties. I'm about to murk all you niggas!" Czar reached for his gun.

"I'll call my mama," the girl on the bed pleaded. "She'll tell you."

"Fuck calling. I want baby pictures, her birth certificate, and dental records."

"C, chill. She's a woman, bro. I ran all their IDs when they jumped in the back seat with you," Nova swore.

"All yall get the fuck out and tell Terri to take Atlanta off the list. I don't trust these muthafuckas. I go to sleep with a bad bitch and wake up with her brother." Czar stormed off. "When I come out of the bathroom yall better be gone." He slammed the bathroom door, knocking the paintings off the wall.

Inside the bathroom, Czar could hear the women frantically moving around the room like their life depended on it and it did. He knew they were going straight to Instagram with their near-death experience, but that didn't matter to him. If he opened the door and they were still standing there looking stupid, it was going to be a problem.

Lifting his phone from the counter, he sifted through his notifications. He was hoping to see something from Marley, but a text from an unsaved contact caught his eye. Czar opened the text, and just like that, his day got a little darker. His nose flared and he fought the urge to slam his fist into the wall.

Unknown: You ready to talk numbers or do I need to shop my pictures around for the highest bidder like I used to do our girl?

Just like that, the boogie man was back.

Chapter 12

Marley chewed on her bottom lip as she examined her outfit. She couldn't remember the last time she actually put effort into her appearance. From the reflection staring back at her, she still had it. Dressed in a black vegan leather skirt that stopped mid-thigh, Marley paired it with a red crop top, exposing her flat stomach. On her feet were a pair of black platform pumps she borrowed from Harper's closet. Since she was only going to wear them once, Marley decided there was no reason for her to buy her own. Her makeup was light and a black choker cuffed her neck.

"See! This is what the fuck I'm talking about!" Harper clapped her hands. "Bad bitch alert!"

"Harp, please." Marley coyly looked away.

"I'm just saying. My little sister been a bad bitch and I'm happy I get to show you off for the night."

"You a baddie ya self."

"You see me?" Harper spun around giving Marley a 360 of her outfit.

Taking after her mother, Harper had ass and titties for days. She rocked a pair of black leather shorts that cuffed her booty with a mesh short-sleeved body suit. Harper paired the outfit with black open-toe booties and a Mia Ray flap bag.

"You cute!" Marley complimented her. "Jaxon about to let you out the house like that?"

"Let me?" Harper frowned. "I put some melatonin in his liquor. In five minutes, him and his son is going to be knocked out."

"Not you drugging your man and son," Marley laughed.

"Did," she snickered. "Finish your hair. I'm about to go pour us a shot."

"Oh hell nah, I don't want your Bill Cosby ass making me shit."

"The only thing I'll give you is mushrooms. Have yo ass in the corner grinding on a plant." Harper winked before twirling out of the bathroom.

Laughing to herself, Marley started parting her hair and pinning pieces to the side. As confident as she seemed on the outside, deep down she was a nervous wreck. She hadn't been to a club in over three years and never without Benny. He shielded her from the hand grabbers and hating hoes. With him, all she had to do was sit pretty and he took care of everything else.

"I miss you," Marley whispered, wishing she could hear him say it back.

Buzzzzzz buzzzzzzz buzzzzzz

Marley's phone skipped around on the bathroom counter, snapping her out of the sadness that plagued her heart. Glancing at the number, a grin pulled at the corner of her lips. It had been over two weeks since she heard from him, and Marley hated how badly she anticipated his voice.

"What?" she answered, propping the phone against the mirror.

"The fuck you mean what? I been calling you," Czar snarled.

"Don't call me, call the Bratz looking bitch you be with."

"I don't wanna call her. Ain't shit she can do for me."

"Hm. What do you want, Julius?" Marley twisted her lips.

"I want you, but you be on your bad girl shit."

"You can't handle me."

"Yea aight, pop your shit. Who house you at?" he asked, looking in the camera.

"My sister's," she answered, carefully using the flat irons to straighten her hair. "We're about to go out."

"LB, who you going out with?" Romeo quizzed, leaning into the camera.

"Romeo don't get fucked up. Who are you talking to?" Sammy snatched the phone up.

"Aye, gimme my shit," Czar snapped.

"You wanna call me back?" Marley was amused at how frustrated he seemed.

Unbeknownst to her, he was detoxing from all the shit he had been putting in his body. The only thing he did was smoke, and even that wasn't enough, but he made it work.

"Nah, they about to dip."

"And go where?" Sammy gawked. "I thought we were about to get some food and play UNO."

"Baby, that's my sis. She the one who gave me the tips on saving our relationship," Romeo explained in the background.

"Don't geek her up. She haven't earned the *sis* title yet,"

Czar snorted.

"I never said I wanted it," Marley countered, glaring at him and then back in the mirror.

"This the girl that said I should have stabbed you?" Sammy spun around to see Marley laughing.

"I said I would've stabbed him. I wasn't suggesting you should," Marley corrected her.

"That's exactly what I'm going to do next time he wanna be out here taking body shots and thank you for talking some sense into his ass because I was about to be outta here."

"Out where?" Romeo grabbed her arm.

"Pause, you suggested she stab you?" Nova tilted his head, looking up from the game.

"I didn't suggest it, I was just letting her know I got advice from another woman."

"You a damn fool. So next time you fuck up she's going to chop yo slow ass up and put you out."

"Ain't gone be no next time, right baby?" Sammy grabbed his chin.

"Right," Romeo agreed, wrapping his arms around her neck.

"Yall both delusional as fuck." Nova shook his head.

"Maybe if you found love you'd be a little happier," Sammy suggested.

"I'm straight." He waved her off.

While they bickered, Czar checked out Marley's outfit. His eyes lingered on her cleavage and then went back to her lightly made-up face.

"You fake as fuck," he snorted.

"What I do?" Marley sat the flat irons down and stared

into the camera. His hooded eyes were low and the smoke lingering in the air told her why. "You look tired."

"I am but fuck all that. You get all dressed to go shake your ass for a bunch of strangers, but I get leggings, ripped sports bras, and Crocs."

"Boy, fuck you," Marley laughed out loud. "If I'm fine, then just say that."

"You gorgeous," Czar flirted, making her heart flutter. "Still fake as fuck though."

"Oh my god, B-law! You so sweet," Sammy cooed, standing over his shoulder.

"Nigga, get your girl." Czar pushed her a little.

"Yall funny," Marley giggled, "and I don't shake my ass. I actually sit down and sip, but if my song comes on, I might do a lil one, two step."

"Period," Sammy co-signed.

"Fuck is you saying period for like you wasn't just in Miami shaking your ass for the gram?" Nova said matter of factly.

"Nova, stop being a hater. Me and my man put all that shit behind us. We're on a clean slate."

"Where you going anyway?" Czar asked Marley. Before she could answer, Harper strolled back into the bathroom with two shot glasses, a bottle of 1738, and Marley's personal favorite, a joint.

"Jaxon is knocked out," she said, setting the glasses down to fill them. "I'm about to start putting that shit in their food and baked goods. Every time they piss me off, I'm going to give they ass a cookie. Jaxon walks his ass in the house after dinner... here's a cookie. Jax talking about clown school... here's a cookie."

"Bitch you going to jail."

"Remind me to never eat anything she cooks," Czar spoke up, causing Harper to cover her mouth.

"Oh my god, why wouldn't you tell me you were on the phone! Now this man knows I be drugging my family."

"I didn't think you were about to come in here bragging about it."

"And if your sister don't let me hit, I'm going straight to the police."

"Julius, please." Marley rolled her eyes.

"Aye, why you got my best friend dressed like she's on the prowl?"

"Cause she is!" Harper bucked her eyebrows. "My sister trying to get her back broke!"

"I wanna go with yall!" Sammy pouted.

"For what?! You don't even know them," Romeo barked. "You trying to get your back broke by some random nigga? Come here, let me talk to your hot ass."

"I didn't even do nothing," she whined but did as she was told.

"That's what you want?" Czar peered at Marley through his low slits. "You want your back broke? That lil pussy purring?"

"Don't listen to her." Marley swallowed, ignoring the throbbing between her thighs. His deep voice always made her want to jump his bones. Marley found the authority in his tone was sexy.

"I hear another voice." Nova pushed up from the couch and made his way to the phone.

Harper's back was to the camera, so he only got a view of her round ass.

"Damn girl, what's your name?" Nova inquired, licking

his lips.

"Death sentence," she replied, turning to face him. "My hubby is sleeping right now, but you better believe the blicky is tucked under the pillow. I promise these ain't the problems you want."

"Damn, all that behind some pussy?"

"No, all that behind his wife." She flashed the fat diamond in the camera.

"Respect," Nova nodded. "Lil Booty, what you wearing?"

"Clothes, and can yall stop calling me that?"

"Why?" Czar questioned. "You think you grown because you got dressed and did something to your hair." He licked his lips.

"Boy, fuck you. I am grown." Marley playfully rolled her eyes. Czar lustfully stared at her with his bottom lip tucked into his mouth.

"Yea, you grown. Go have fun and call me when you're leaving."

"I'll text you," she insisted.

"Did I say text me, *Marley*?" Czar's raspy voice rumbled. His eyes pierced her through the screen, causing a lump to form in her throat.

"*Marley,*" Harper mocked. "His voice got deep and everything. I'll make sure she calls you."

"You don't have to. She's going to do it because I said so."

"Bye Julius." Marley ended the call and proceeded to finish flat ironing her hair. She could feel Harper's stare but chose to ignore it.

"Oh no, bitch! I know you don't think you're about to bypass what just happened."

"What happened?"

"Play dumb if you want to. That was intense." Harper twisted her lip. "He always talk to you like that?"

"Like what?"

"Soooo, I don't know. Like you're the only person in the room."

"I guess so," Marley shrugged.

"You seemed real comfortable."

"I mean I am. I've been over to his place and he came to mine, so we're well acquainted with each other."

"Do you like him?"

"No." Marley sat the flat irons down. "I mean I don't *not* like him."

"Hmm. Ok, we'll get into this later. Let's take these shots and hit the road. Our Uber will be here in ten minutes."

"We not driving?"

"No. I'm trying to get white girl wasted, and I know you not about to drive. Plus, I have a feeling you're going to end the night in bed with a millionaire."

"Girl bye. I'm not about to dip off with him."

"We'll see." Harper twisted her lips and pushed the shot over to Marley. "Drink up. The night is young."

"Where are we going anyway?

"Don't worry about it. You'll see when we get there."

Thanks to staying up late and scrolling on TikTok, Harper came across the perfect outing for them. She knew Marley wasn't ready to go clubbing yet, but she also wanted her to have a little fun. The tickets for the event were eighty dollars and it came with free wine and snacks. The location wasn't revealed until a couple of hours before the event, and all phones were to be collected at the door. Harper knew Jaxon wouldn't let her go to such an event, so putting him to sleep was the only way.

"Oh bitch, you got a death wish because ain't no way you got us out here at some paint-a-dick bullshit." Marley covered her eyes. "Out of all the places in Michigan."

"It's not called paint a dick," Harper refuted. "It's like Painting With a Twist, but it's called Painting, Drinks and Tips."

Peeking through her fingers, Marley took in the unorthodox scene. The room was exquisitely decorated in shades of pink with hints of white and cream. Pretty pieces of art covered the walls and a soft floral scent floated through the room. Each table was set up with an easel, whiteboard, and a spread of different color paints. Men walked around the room with only a sock covering their dicks, pouring glasses of wine and feeding women pieces of fruit. Marley's eyes popped out of her head as she watched a man fuck a woman's mouth with a banana. The other women at the table seemed unfazed. In fact, they sat there waiting for their turns,

"I can't stay here," Marley quickly decided. "This is too much. They are violating fruit! I'll never look at bananas the same."

"Ladies, welcome. Can I get your names so that I can seat you?" A man wearing a tie around his neck and a black sock on his dick greeted them. "Something in your eye, pretty lady?" he asked, touching Marley's arm.

"There's a whole lot of something in my eye. Oh my god, is your dick touching me?" Marley asked, scared to look down.

"Ignore her," Harper insisted. "I'm Harper, and this is

Marley."

"Well, right this way," he stretched his arm out. "I'm Curve, and I'll be your waiter for this exhilarating experience."

"I don't even wanna know why they call you Curve." Marley held on to Harper's arm.

"If you open your eyes, you can see why," he whispered in her ear.

"Shake that ass for Drake (yup), now, shake that ass for me. Bend that ass over (baow), let that coochie breathe," Sexxy Red rapped over the speaker, causing a few women to bounce in their seats.

"This is some ghetto shit," Marley exclaimed, watching somebody's grandma pop her pussy in a chair. "I'm going to need you to stay off TikTok."

"Nope, this is dope as hell. Don't get me wrong, I love Jaxon's dick, but it's nice to see other dicks," She glanced around the room. "Even if they aren't that big."

"Right here, ladies." Curve stopped walking and pointed to the table closest to the stage.

"It's not no tables in the back?"

"Nope, I asked if we could sit right up front and they said yes," Harper boasted. "I also told them you were blind in one eye, so this is the handicap table."

"Harper!"

"Shut up and close one of your eyes."

"Oh my god, I hate you and if I catch anything in here, I swear I'm telling Jaxon."

"Girl, shut up and drink up. We about to draw some dicks and get lap dances."

"I don't want these niggas dancing on me."

"Too bad. I also told them you were a virgin," Harper whispered.

"Ladies," a man dressed in a robe addressed the room. "I'd like to thank you for coming out to support our annual-

"Annual?" Marley questioned loudly. "This is an ongoing thing? Like this isn't the first one?"

"Yes, this is the 10th anniversary and it's always successful," the robed man swore. "What's your name?"

"Why?"

"Cause," he moved closer to the edge of the stage, "I need to know what to call you when I have you on the tip of my tongue."

"Oop," the women in the room gasped.

"As I was saying. We're going to start with the painting portion. After that, the lights go out and things can get a little wild," Mr. Robe warned. "Fellas, take the stage."

On cue, the men walking around the room finished up what they were doing and headed to the front. Each one stood on a white block in a different pose. The women picked up their pencils and started to sketch a man of their choice.

"This is some real weird shit." Marley shook her head.

"Who are you drawing?" Harper ignored her.

"Curve. That nigga dick looks like an arm."

"I can't try that bad boy, but I can draw it," she snickered. "But I'm going to let you have mine. I can't take this home."

"You think it's real?" Marley cocked her head to the side.

"Probably not. You know dick pumps and honey packs are the new wave. All these lil niggas gone need blue pills when they grow up."

After a couple of glasses of wine and an edible, Marley's

shoulders dropped and she grew a little more relaxed. She even found herself chatting with other women at the table. It had been so long since she picked up a pencil to sketch something, and once she started, it came back like riding a bike. At some point, Marley stopped painting and simply rocked in her seat to the music. With her hands in the air, she swayed to Tems' *Free Mind*. Marley made a mental note to do something special for her sister because this outing was just what she needed.

Mr. Robe had made himself Marley's personal waiter because every time her glass was empty, he made it his business to refill it. Each time he picked up her glass, his fingers lingered a little longer than the last time. The more she drank, the more her kitty purred, reminding her that she hadn't played with her rose in quite some time. It was almost like Mr. Robe could sense it because he kept blowing her kisses, forcing her legs shut. Yet, no matter how fine he was or how strong his back looked, Marley couldn't see herself allowing him to touch her in any kind of way. Her pussy deserved more than a quick fuck by a man who probably sold his dick on Only Fans.

"It's not that bad, is it?" Harper asked, bumping Marley's shoulder.

"Nope, I'm happy you drugged your husband so we could come. I thought you were about to have me at a club, sitting at a bar looking all crazy, but this is cool. It's ratchet as hell, but it's cool."

"Hush and close one of your eyes. You're supposed to be blind and you over here winking at people."

"You got me fucked up. I'm not about to sit here looking like Forest Whitaker's lil sister," Marley replied, lifting her glass up. "Where ole boy at? My glass empty."

Harper opened her mouth to reply, but a loud commotion near the front of the venue caused everyone to peer over one another trying to get a look. Minding her own business, Marley took another sip of her drink. Smoking was her thing. She could smoke Snoop Dogg under a table, but when it came to drinking, it was the complete opposite. One glass of wine made her feel fuzzy, and anything more had her on tip.

"Sir, do you have a ticket?" The host asked a little more aggressively than the first time.

"Do it look liked I'd have a ticket to this gay shit?" A man's voice roared. "My wife's phone pinged to this location, and unless you want me to shoot everybody in this bitch, I suggest you tell Harper Wilkins to get her hot ass out here."

"Oh shit!" Marley covered her mouth, snapping from her drunken haze. "Is that-

"Shhh!" Harper elbowed her.

"Sir, we'll bring her out, but because of the discretion that is promised to our guests, I can't allow you to go back there," the host explained.

"You think I give a fuck about a bunch of old desperate ass bitches being felt up by these young niggas? Go get my wife before I shoot your dick off," Jaxon roared, making the man jump.

To Jaxon's dismay, he woke up in the middle of the night on the couch with a crook in his neck. Jax was on the floor with a pizza roll hanging from his mouth and Sponge Bob was dancing his happy ass around on the TV. Jaxon called out to Harper and when she didn't answer, he went to search for her. After twenty minutes and no results, he tracked her phone. Harper told him that she was taking Marley painting, but this was not what he expected.

"Is there a Harper Wilkins in here?" the host nervously asked, standing in the doorway.

"Bitch, go before he starts shooting," Marley hissed.

"Come with me," Harper pleaded.

"No, he not about to cuss me out because you wanted to come to this freaky shit."

"Sir, no-" The host tried to stop Jaxon but was punched in the face when he grabbed his forearm.

Stepping over him, Jaxon stalked inside the room and looked around. The men were covering themselves, some cowering behind walls and tables so they wouldn't be the next one lying on the ground.

"What kinda freaky ass shit is this?" Jaxon quizzed, checking out a few paintings. Stick figures with dicks were everywhere. "Harper, you got two seconds to get yo fast ass up here, or I'm going to start shooting these niggas." He removed the gun from his waist.

"She over there with her blind sister." Curve pointed to the table in the front.

"Damn, Curve, you really just snitched on us like that?" Marley tittered, standing to her feet.

"Hey baby, you up?" Harper nervously picked up her purse and walked toward him.

"What the fuck you wearing?" Jaxon grilled her, taking a double look as she approached him.

"Remember I told you I ordered some stuff from Pretty Little Things."

"And you showed me everything but this shit."

"She had it delivered to my house," Marley ratted, obviously buzzed. "I mean my van."

"Shut up," Harper hissed.

"I'mma fuck you up." He pushed her toward the exit. "You don't want me at strip clubs, but you wanna be out here in private buildings with niggas in G-strings."

"Socks," Marley corrected him. "All they had on were black tube socks."

"Shut yo nappy headed ass up," Jaxon snapped. "You know better, and you let my wife come to this shit."

"Wait, I-"

"I need my phone," Harper cut her off, knowing she was about to snitch.

"Hurry up! Got me outside tracking yo ass down and my son in the car sleep."

"I'm sorry," she declared, stopping at the front desk where the phones were held.

"Nah, you gone be sorry!" Jaxon snatched the phone out of her hands. "And what the fuck did you put in my drink! Henny ain't never knocked me on my ass like that."

"I told you this was a bad idea," Marley whispered, cutting her phone back on.

"Can I stay the night with you?"

"Hell nah. Take that punishment like a champ. I'm about to go chill with Czar."

"Oh, you about to do the nasty?" Harper whispered, causing Marley to giggle.

"The fuck yall back there laughing for. Harper get your hot ass in the front seat," Jaxon fussed, making them cover their mouth and do as they were told. While Harper sat in the front seat getting her ass handed to her, Marley pulled out her phone and made plans of her own.

Hey, you up?

Czar stood in front of the elevator doors waiting for them to open. It was a little after one in the morning and he had to be up at five for a photoshoot, but when she texted, he unconsciously responded. He'd never tell her, but even if she wanted to come over and make tea, he'd let her, but something about her text told him the last thing she wanted to do was talk.

Ding

The elevator doors opened, and Marley stepped off. Czar's jaw clenched as he stood there taking her in. She was so fucking pretty and it bothered him that she got dressed up to entertain other niggas. Niggas who couldn't possibly satisfy her in ways that he could. Ways that she secretly craved, ways her smart mouth ass needed. Czar wanted nothing more than to wipe the smug grin off her face with his dick, and from the daring look in her eyes, that's exactly what she wanted.

"Hey," she breathlessly greeted when his eyes finally made it to hers.

"What's up, Lil Booty," Czar grinned.

"So, I don't want a relationship," Marley began, stepping out of her heels.

"Me either." He finished the brown liquor in his glass before sitting it on the table.

"I don't-

"Aye, just shut up and take all that shit off. I'm not trying to marry you. I just want to fuck," Czar cut her off. "That's what you want, right? From me to stretch that lil pussy open?"

Marley clamped her mouth closed. There was no need for a smart reply because he was right. Pulling the crop top over her head, she exposed her hand full of breasts and pretty brown nipples. Reaching back, Marley unzipped her skirt and let it fall to the ground, leaving her standing there in a black thong.

"Mm." He bit his lip, eyeing the fat print between her thighs. "I didn't take you for a thong girl."

"What did you think I wore?"

"Granny panties."

"Shut up, can we smoke?" Marley asked, feeling the nerves begin to form in her stomach.

"Why?" Czar taunted, knowing damn well the confidence in her decision-making wavered the second she stepped off the elevator. Reaching out, he cupped her breast, then lightly pinched her nipple, causing her lips to part and a slight moan to slip from the cracks. "I know yo shit talking ass ain't nervous."

"It's been a while."

"Don't worry." Czar reached down and cuffed her pussy. "I'll start off gentle," he promised, guiding her toward the balcony.

"Wait, I can't go out there naked." Marley tried to pull away, but he caught her wrist.

"Baby girl, we are thousands of feet in the air. They'll hear you before they see you," Czar promised, tapping her on the ass. "And this lil muthafucka jiggle."

Instead of responding to his smart comment, Marley swallowed her nerves and stepped out onto the balcony in her thong. She started to ask what they were about to do, but the Jacuzzi in the corner caught her eye. It was tucked near the end of the balcony, but the blue LED lights made it impossible to miss.

"This is nice. I didn't see it last time," she complimented, walking toward the whirlpool. Sticking her hand in the water, she nodded in approval at the temperature.

"You can't see it from inside," Czar replied, walking up behind her. Pushing her hair to the side, he pressed his lips to the back of her neck. "You want me to eat your pussy first?"

"Just like that?" Marley's stomach flipped. "You offer to eat everybody's pussy?"

"Not at all." His hands found her breasts again. This time, her nipples were hard. "I need to relax you a little or you'll never be able to take this dick."

"Boy please, you ain't swinging like that," she twisted her lips.

Believing in the art of showing versus telling, Czar stepped back and dropped his pants. The way his dick sprung to action made her heart plummet. His thick, veiny length was at least nine inches, and it curved to the right.

"You can eat it first!" Marley blurted, wishing she could take back all the smart shit she ever said.

"Get yo scary ass in the water," Czar chuckled, holding his hand out so she could climb in the tub.

Carefully, Marley lowered her body into the water and nearly moaned. Between the warm water, the bubbles, and the pressure of the jets, she was in heaven. The further she moved toward the middle, the higher the water rose. Once it was to the center of her chest, she turned around, catching a glimpse of Czar slowly walking toward her with a bottle of champagne in his hand and lust in his eyes. Lifting the bottle to his mouth, he drunk it from the neck and then held it out for her.

"Open your mouth," he instructed.

Without hesitation, Marley opened her mouth and held her head back a little. Czar slowly poured the champagne into her mouth and then proceeded to drizzle it on her body. The cold, fizzing liquid made her body jerk, and she started to slap him, but his tongue connecting to her hard nipples made her freeze.

Marley closed her eyes and tucked her lips. Her pussy, mind, and heart started to battle, each pulling her in a different direction. For years, her body belonged to another and her pussy only marched to the beat of his drums, but there she was. Standing on top of the tallest building in the city while Czar brought her to an orgasm by sucking on her breasts. Her thoughts started to run wild, and while it felt good, Marley started feeling guilty.

"Aye." Czar bit her a little, bringing her attention back to him. "Stay with me."

"I thought I was ready but," Marley explained, feeling herself about to hyperventilate. "I thought-

"Just let me make you feel good," he pleaded. "Let me ease your mind shorty." Czar kissed her shoulder, surprising himself.

Normally, he wasn't so attentive. He didn't have time for shy pussy. In fact, he liked his women slutty and ready to fuck on demand. One on One wasn't his thing. Czar was more of a bring your friend type of nigga, but with Marley, he'd be the one catering to her needs.

"You gone let me eat this fat ass pussy?" He kissed her neck.

"Ok," Marley whispered.

"Sit on the top step," Czar ordered.

Doing as she was told, Marley slowly walked across the whirlpool and sat on the top step. Her heart thumped against her chest and the pulse between her legs intensified with each step.

"Can I kiss you?" Czar swam between her legs, positioning himself inches away from her lips.

"Uh huh," Marley nodded.

Closing the space between them, Czar pressed his lips to hers. Just like he remembered they were soft, and he needed more. Slipping his tongue in her mouth, he sucked the remnants of the sweet champagne off her tongue. Marley tried to keep up, but he was everywhere. One minute he was sucking her lips, and seconds later, his mouth was back on her nipples.

"Ohhh," Marley moaned, feeling his hand in her thong. His middle finger fumbled between her lips until he found her bud. Marley gasped.

"Just kiss me back," he told her, finding her mouth again.

Marley sucked his tongue while simultaneously grinding her hips against his fingers. She played with her pussy all the time, but it felt nothing like Czar's fingers. He worked her as if someone had slipped him the cheat codes to make her climb the walls.

"Lay back," his husky voice whispered against her mouth while still playing in her pussy.

The coldness from the step made Marley arch her back, and Czar used it to his advantage. Keeping his lower half in the water, he looped her legs around his arms and brought her pussy to his face. Pushing her thong to the side, he dove right in as if he had been waiting to taste her. As if her juices would quench a thirst he didn't know he had.

Marley thought his fingers were good, but they had nothing on his mouth. The way he skillfully massaged her clitoris and stroked her insides had Marley reaching for the sky. The wind lightly blew, causing her nipples to harden, and as if he could feel them, Czar reached up with his free hand and stroked them.

"Oh my," Marley cried, feeling her toes curl. The euphoric feeling silenced her. She couldn't find the words to describe what he was doing. Her stomach clenched and her legs tightened around his neck as he sucked her pussy.

"Wait." Marley tried to push him back, not recognizing the intense pressure between her thighs. Czar didn't let up. If anything, he went harder. He continued to suck and stroke her until Marley's body shook like she was having a seizure.

"Sweet ass pussy," Czar muttered, unwrapping her legs from around his neck. Marley didn't even try to move. She laid there panting like a fish out of water.

"You straight?" He asked, picking her limp body up and pulling her onto his lap. Lowering them into the water, Czar sat on the bench and played in her hair while she caught her breath.

"Yea, but I'll never be able to listen to your music again," Marley whispered, trying to control her trembling voice. She had never in her life cum so hard. Marley hated to compare them, but she couldn't help it. Benny was good in the bedroom and he used to make her cum back-to-back, but what Czar just did was unmatched, and that was just his mouth! If his dick was anything like his tongue, she was in trouble.

"Why?" He furrowed his eyebrows, confused by her confession.

"Because you really eat pussy the way you rap about it." Marley touched his face. "I mean lord, how many tongues do you have in there? Like you really out here on your Kevin Gates tip."

"What?"

"Bitch bend over, stand up on your toes," she rapped, making Czar laugh out loud.

"Girl gone," he laughed, leaning back to pick up the champagne. "I gotta eat your pussy to get you to loosen up?"

"Yep."

Marley took the opportunity to lean forward and kiss his neck. She felt drunk all over again. Although she wasn't ready to have sex, Marley still had the urge to put her mouth on him. Her tongue started at the nape of his neck and worked its way up to his chin. A low growl slipped from his mouth, encouraging her to suck a little harder.

"I think I'm going to like this friendship shit," Czar smirked.

"Sex isn't part of the deal." Marley pulled back. "I was having a moment."

"Fuck outta here. You just almost drowned me."

"I told you to wait," she snickered.

"I don't see shit funny. What was you gone tell my mama when they found me floating in this muthafucka?"

"That you were well mannered." Marley stroked his chin. "Can you do it again?" She leaned forward, kissing him again.

"Freak ass don't wanna gimme no pussy, but want me to eat it," Czar complained.

"Can you?" She leaned back and seductively licked her lips.

"Yea, let's go in the house."

Chapter 13

Marley walked into her sister's backyard struggling to contain her laughter. She wasn't sure what was worse, the fact that Harper was walking around wearing a red curly wig with a big fluffy polka dot dress or that her nephew convinced his parents to throw a clown-themed party for his birthday. It was cute, but way too many clowns. They were parking the cars, serving the food, and running around with the kids.

"You bet not say shit," Harper hissed, walking towards her.

Marley tucked her lips in an effort to suppress her laughter but failed miserably. The closer Harper came into view, the worse it got. Not only was she dressed like a clown, but her makeup matched.

"You couldn't convince him to have a Hot Wheels party?"

"I tried! I even told him I'd take him to the Nickelodeon Resort in Mexico, but Jaxon's petty ass told him he could have the party and the trip."

"You still in the doghouse?" Marley asked, pulling at the flower on her shirt, causing water to squirt in her face. "Oh, this the real deal," she laughed, wiping her face.

"Bitch, yes. I've been sucking so much dick that I started taking melatonin my damn self. By the time he comes home, I be knocked the fuck out."

"So now you drugging yourself?"

"Is! I can't take it anymore. You know I love to suck dick! Like, I'm with the shits when it comes to pleasing my man, but this shit is torture. My jaws are starting to squeak. I can't even put a straw to my mouth without flinching," she complained, making Marley laugh harder.

"Yall are funny as fuck."

"It's not, but I'm happy you're getting a kick out of this shit. I try to do something nice for you and it ends up backfiring."

"I didn't tell you to take me to a dick farm."

"Ugh. Don't even say the word dick, my mouth starts aching." Harper massaged her jaws. "Let me get back over here. Jaxon told me if I try to hide when you get here, he's going to add time to my sentence."

"He didn't!"

"He did! And FYI, yo mama here so behave."

"I'm straight, as long as she doesn't say anything to me."

"Well, you know she is. Just please don't beat her up at my baby's party. All his classmates are here."

"Harper, please," Marley laughed. "I feel too good to entertain yo mama."

"Wait." Harper gave her a once over. Her eyes scanned Marley's skater dress and Converse sneakers. She took in her pushed back ponytail and blemish-free face. Finally, Harper leaned forward and sniffed her. "You had sex?"

"Nope, but he ate me out all over his penthouse." Marley

grinned, running her fingers through her ponytail.

"Perioddddd!" Harper started twerking, drawing attention to them.

"Stop, fool!"

"Oh I need all the tea! Oh my god! You should have went in the bathroom after he finished and called me."

"Uh, how about no."

"So yall didn't do the nasty?" Harper thrusted her hips in a humping motion. "You didn't let him tear that thang out the frame?"

"Harper!" Jaxon called out.

"Ugh, party pooper." She rolled her eyes. "I'm about to go over here and see why these hoes all in Jaxon's face because even in a clown suit the nigga is not that funny. We're going to talk about this later because I need all the details."

"Don't beat up them people."

"Girl fuck these Stanford Wives. I'll mess around and shoot the PTA meeting up over that one," Harper tossed over her shoulder.

"Wait, come here." Marley waved her back over. She waited until Harper was standing in her face before she whispered, "How has Jaxon been acting?"

"Ok so far, but I've been keeping an eye on him. In the meantime, my passport is on standby."

"Well, that's good."

"For now," Harper smirked, walking away.

Marley sat her gift on the table with the others and made her way to the snack bar. She appreciated the spread. There was a variety of everything, including vegetarian options and a big fruit platter in the shape of a clown car. After speaking to a few people, Marley found an unoccupied table near the back of the party. She prayed no one tried to sit with her because her social meter was declining by the second. Removing her phone, she checked her notifications and smiled when she saw a text from Czar.

It had been a week since she left him wrapped in silk sheets stained with her juices. Marley didn't bother waking him up because she didn't want a weird goodbye or promises to link up again. As much as she enjoyed the feel of his California King bed, she slipped on one of his shirts, grabbed an apple from his counter, and left without a peep.

Julius: Aye, where your van parked at today? My lawyer needs to know where to send these papers.

Marley bit into her watermelon before responding to his text.

What papers? She asked, confused.

Julius: I'm taking your thieving ass to court. You stole my shirt, fruit, and tastebuds.

Marley nearly choked on the grapes in her mouth when she read his response.

Tastebuds? She replied, looking up from her phone just in time to see Pam walking toward her.

Julius: I can't taste shit but your sweet ass pussy and then you got the nerve to be gatekeeping.

"Well, what a surprise. I haven't seen you smile this hard in years," Pam said, taking a seat across from her. "Must be a new man."

Marley ignored her comment and sat her phone down. Pushing grapes around on her plate, Marley said a silent prayer. The last thing she wanted to do was lose her cool and embarrass her sister.

"You cute and I like your hair like that, but why do you have on gym shoes with that dress?"

"Because that's what I choose to wear, Ma."

"Marley, look, we both said some things last time, and I think we need to address them while we both have a clear head."

"No lies were told."

"So you really think I hurt you on purpose?"

"Ma, look, this is JJ's day and I'm not trying to argue with you."

"Good, me either. I know I haven't always been the best mother or role model, but I want to make things right. I think you should forgive me so we can move on."

"Forgive you for what, Ma? If you don't think you've done anything wrong, what is there to forgive?"

"Well, how about you forgive me for whatever you think I've done wrong?"

Marley stuck a grape in her mouth and cocked her head to the side. For once, she chose to keep her negative comments to herself.

"You know you're stubborn just like your father," Pam reminisced. "That man was just as stubborn and mean as he wanted to be. God rest his soul."

"Probably because he was married and you trapped him," Marley shot back.

"Girl, please. I didn't make that man do anything he didn't want to do. He chose to lay down with me knowing he had a wife at home. Am I the blame for that?"

"Yep. You knew he was married when you pushed yourself on him." Marley bucked her eyes. "But I don't care about all of that. I'm not some scared lil girl who's suffering from daddy issues. My problem solely lies with you."

"Why am I not surprised?" Pam snorted. "The ain't shit

ass daddies always get off easy, but the mothers that stay pay the price."

"Oh, you think because you *stayed* you get brownie points," Marley sarcastically said.

"Marley, please! I made sure you had a roof over your head. I made sure you had food in your stomach, and you went to school in clean clothes. You had the necessities and never had to worry about where your next meal was coming from. You talking about brownie points? I deserve the whole damn award." Pam slapped the table, drawing attention to them.

"An award for what? Staying and being a mother to the kids you made?" Marley scoffed.

"For dealing with your ungrateful ass. Tell me, what did I do that was so wrong?"

"Ma, like I said, this isn't the time or place."

"Whatever, Marley, you can't say shit because I did my best. The Lord forgives me, so your forgiveness isn't required.

"So, your best involved tearing us down and running up our credit? Maybe it was emotionally neglecting us, or perhaps it was sucking your daughter's boyfriend's dick when he was drunk?" Marley stated, causing Pam to choke on her words. She couldn't deny it if she wanted to because the truth was etched across her face. It was the reason Jaxon stopped coming around, and her bitterness toward the situation caused her to dislike him.

"Oh, let me guess, you thought your secret was safe?"

"Marley, you don't know what you're talking about." Pam sat up straight. "I suggest you get all the facts before you mess up a happy home."

"What happy home? You, the pastor, and his wife, or my sister's? See, you trying to push this false narrative like you've changed, but like I said, I know the real you, Ma." Marley popped another grape in her mouth. "Big church hats, fake smiles, and praising the Lord can't hide the real you."

"How did I know yo ass was back here hiding?" Jaxon strolled over to them, breaking the tension that brewed in the air. "Yall straight?" he asked, seeing the pale look on Pam's face.

"I- uh, I gotta go." She jumped up from her seat and ran to the exit like her ass was on fire.

"Damn, what you say to her?" Jaxon questioned. "Put me on so I can use it against her ass."

"The truth." Marley pursed her lips. "When you gone let my sister off the hook?"

"I'm not, and I got something for yo ass." He smirked and turned around. Marley followed his eyes and then glared at him.

"If you call him over here, I'm going to slash your tires."

"Go right ahead, I have enough money to buy some more." Jaxon smiled, waving Lucky toward them.

Marley tried to get up, but Jaxon put his hand on her shoulder, forcing her to stay put. Her purse was in the house, so pepper spraying him was out of the question. She inwardly groaned as Lucky bopped toward them.

Lucky wasn't ugly per se, and on the right day, he could be considered a snack. He just wasn't her type. His deep, silky waves were well tamed, and his facial hair was neatly trimmed. Marley could tell he had been hitting the gym because his stomach didn't stick out as much as it used to and the fat around his neck had melted. Lucky had even cleaned up nicely. He was rocking a pair of white Polo shorts with the matching shirt and gym forces. Still, he wasn't the man for her.

"What up doe nigga? Thanks for the invite." Lucky bopped toward them with a smile on his face.

"No doubt, I'm happy you could bring the little ones through." Jaxon gave him a brotherly hug. "You remember my sister Marley?"

"Hell yeah, I remember her fine ass. How you doing, sweetheart?" Lucky rounded the table.

"Not good, I just found out I have herpes," she sighed, making Jaxon spit out his drink.

"Oh shit, I uh-

"She lying. Marley stop playing," Jaxon warned her.

"Fine, I'm doing good. How are you?" She gave him a tight smile.

"Girl, you had me scared for a minute." Lucky grabbed his chest. "You mind if I sit with you?"

"Nah, she don't mind, right sis?" Jaxon gave her a knowing look. Marley wanted to tell him to suck a dick, but she thought about Harper and her jaws and decided to take one for the team.

"No, I don't mind." She stretched her arm out.

"Cool, I'll let yall kick it. Let me get back over here to the balloon show."

"So what's up?" Lucky questioned. "Why you not trying to give a nigga no play? I got my money up, my weight down, and I'm looking for a pretty lady to spend some time with," he stated as if he were auditioning for a dating show.

"I'm not sure what Jaxon told you, but I'm not-

"He didn't tell me nothing. I asked him about you a few weeks ago and wanted to know if you were dating. I'd love to take you out."

Buzzzzz Buzzzzz Buzzzzzz

"Sorry, give me one minute." Marley quickly snatched her phone off the table. She didn't bother checking the caller ID because it didn't matter if it was Sallie Mae. Marley was simply happy she was saved from the uncomfortable conversation. "Hello?"

"Where you at Houdini?" Czar's rough voice flowed through the line, causing the corners of Marley's lips to turn upward. Just the sound of his voice launched a replay of all the nasty things he did with his mouth.

"Do you ever say hello before you start questioning people's whereabouts?"

"I'm not a hello type of nigga. I'm more of a get yo ass over here and drop your draws type," he declared. "Where you at?"

"In my skin," Marley sassed.

"Keep fucking around like I won't tow your van to the east side and have that bad boy sitting on bricks."

"You better not touch my baby."

"Then stop acting like you don't know what's up. On some real shit though, why would yo lil booty ass leave me like that? You didn't say thanks for eating my pussy or nothing. Just let me suck on that fat muthafucka and dipped."

"I didn't know you wanted me to stay."

"I didn't tell you to leave," Czar rebutted, causing her heart to skip a beat. "You could have at least woke me up. My face was all sticky and shit."

"Well, I told you to stop," Marley snickered. Thinking about the number of times she tried to push his head from between her legs.

"I'mma go grab another drink, you want something?" Lucky asked, clearing his throat. It didn't take a rocket scientist to know she was on the phone with a nigga, and he felt slighted that she was grinning all in his face.

"Who the fuck is that?" Czar quizzed.

"Um, no, I'm ok. Thanks," Marley replied to Lucky while ignoring Czar.

"*Thanks,*" Czar mocked. "Fake ass, he gets a weak ass thanks and you told me to kiss your ass the first time we met," he ranted.

"Make sure you wrap that up too. I'm trying to kick it with you," Lucky shot over his shoulder before walking across the yard.

"Put me on speaker 'cause who the fuck he talking to?" Czar barked. "Matter fact, send me the addy. I'm about to pull up."

"Don't you have a video to record or a show to perform?" Marley asked. "You about the most non-rapping rapper I know."

"Fuck outta here. I do more than rap, and if you stop running and hanging up on a nigga you'd know that. I'm still working. I just have more free time to do what I want."

"And that includes harassing me?"

"Shut up, you like it. Come fuck with me."

"Where are you?" Marley questioned, tempted at the thought of seeing him.

"About to pull up to my people house. It's game night."

"Come get yo ass tapped in Taboo," Nova shouted out in the background.

"Mm, I'll pass."

"Why you gotta make this shit so difficult?" Czar sighed, running his hand down his face. Never in his twenty-nine years of living did he have to press a woman so hard to spend time with him.

"Boy, don't get loud with me, and difficult is my middle name."

"Stop playing with me and hop yo homeless ass in an Uber and get over here. I'll send you the address."

"Fine," Marley gave in without much convincing. "You paying for my Uber, and I'm on Nova's team."

"That's no problem, but you got me fucked up. You on my team, but we'll discuss that when you get here."

"I need a minute. I'm at my nephew's birthday party."

"Oh straight up, why you ain't tell me?"

"Tell you for what?"

"I sucked the electrolytes out of your pussy, we go together."

"Real bad," Nova cosigned.

"Bye, Julius. Send me the address and I'll be over there later." Marley ended the call just as Harper approached her. Instead of stopping at the table, Harper kept walking until she made it to the big tree in their yard.

"You brought some weed with you?" she whispered, hiding behind the tree, out of Jaxon's view.

"Yea, why?" Marley picked up her water. "I know you not trying to get high with all these PTA parents running around."

"Let's go in the house and smoke. If I have to listen to one more knock-knock joke, I'm going to pull my ears off," Harper whined. "I thought Jax was a bad joke teller, but his friends are worse."

"Come on, let's go before Lucky comes back over here. He lost a lil weight, but his titties are still bigger than mine." Marley shivered at the thought of him on top of her.

"Girl, he got lipo and hair plugs. You can't tell him shit,"

Harper revealed.

"You lying!"

"Nope, hubby told me."

"Yall stay gossiping."

"It's called pillow talk," Harper corrected her.

"Sure, let's make this quick. Czar invited me to come chill with him."

"Bitch, you ditching me to go get some dick?"

"Dick, no, but if he wanted to offer me lip service again, I'm with it." Marley chewed her bottom lip.

"Harper!" Jaxon called out. "They about to start the show and need a volunteer."

"Okkk," she replied through clenched teeth. "I'm over this shit! They can cut me in half for real at this point."

"Welp, looks like our smoke session is over before it even started. Gone on over there and join the show. Just one big ass clown family," Marley taunted.

"Just for that, I'm about to tell Lucky you're waiting on him."

"You better not. If his chunky ass comes over here, I'm running, and you know CeeLo can't catch me."

"Consider it done!" Harper held her hand up, marching away with her big wig bobbing with every step.

"Well, well, well. If I didn't push you out of my body, I wouldn't even believe I had a son named Julius," Ada chided the moment Czar and Nova crossed the threshold.

"I told him, Mama. I don't know why he keeps trying to

test your gangster. I say you slap him upside the head for old times' sake," Nova jeered, bumping into Czar to get to their mother. After placing a kiss on her cheek, Nova moved to the side so his mother could rip into his brother.

"I'm going to do more than slap him upside the head. Bending him over my knee doesn't sound too bad." She pursed her lips.

"And I'll hold him for you too. The bigger the nigga, the harder the fall."

"Shut up." Czar pushed his brother, making him stumble a bit. Catching his balance, Nova gave Czar the middle finger and went to find everybody else while Czar got his ass handed to him.

"What's going on, old lady?"

Giving his mother one of his boyish grins, Czar pulled her into his arms and placed a kiss on her forehead. Immediately, he felt bad for keeping his distance, but while he figured out what to do with the Cain situation, it was necessary. Ada could read him like a book and avoiding her was the only way he could keep the visit to himself.

"Don't what's up me," she snapped, swatting him across the chest. "What happened to you answering my calls?"

"My fault, Mama. I got kinda busy."

"Too busy for your own mother. Picture that."

"I'll do better," he swore.

"You can't sing that same song and expect a different tune. If something is on your mind, then you need to say it. We've always had an open, honest relationship. Just because you're grown, it doesn't need to change."

"I know, Ma." Czar scratched his head. "I had a lot on my mind."

"And now?" Ada quizzed, examining his face for any signs

of stress.

"Now I found a lil honey that's going to help me clear it," he grinned. Czar was low-key excited to see Marley.

Just the thought of her made his mouth water. Czar wasn't new to eating pussy, and everyone he fucked didn't get the treatment, but Marley was different. Once he started eating her, it was hard to stop. Her juices were naturally sweet and he couldn't wait to taste her again.

"Your sanity shouldn't be measured by temporary feelings for another person. What happens if you and this mystery girl don't work out? Then what? You're back at square one."

"Ma, I hear what you saying, but I'm good. Me and Marley are kicking it."

"Yall kicking it, but she's coming to my house. You never bring girls here."

"Don't think about it too much," Czar kissed her forehead, dismissing the conversation.

"I heard that Sammy beat the other girl up." Ada shook her head. "Tati."

"More like dog walked her, Ma. Sammy's little ass was on her like a piranha. I almost felt bad,"

Nova interjected.

"Nigga why you gossiping like a chick?" Czar snatched a wing off his plate.

"Cause I just know she be over there beating on Ro like that."

"Let me find out she over there putting her hands on my baby." Ada lowered her eyes.

"What you gone do?" Nova questioned, amused.

"Fuck around and find out." She arched her eyebrow. "And

who is this girl you've invited to my house?"

"LB. Remember we told you about her?" Nova answered. "She cool as hell, Ma. C thinks she reminds him of you."

"Oh really?"

"Bro, shut up," Czar snarled. "You doing too much talking. Go get the cards ready. I'm about to tear that ass up in UNO."

"You ain't said nothing but a word. We can do a band a game."

"Let's get it popping and tell your broke ass cousins don't come with that IOU shit. This time I'm taking shoes, veneers and all."

"Not they teeth," Nova cracked up.

"Collecting them boys like a tooth fairy," Czar stated, draping his arm around his mother's shoulder.

"Don't start your shit, Julius."

Together, the trio entered the living room where Slim, Romeo, Sammy, and a few of Slim's relatives were waiting. Czar wasn't surprised to see his mother had gone all out. Game night was one of her favorite pastimes and there was no half-stepping. Along the wall was a table filled with chicken wings, subs, chips, dips, and things to make tacos. The bar was stocked with every liquor you could think of and a tray of Jello shots. Music played in the background as everyone talked shit, gearing up for another crazy night.

"Bout time yall got back," Romeo said, shifting Sammy on his lap.

"Shut up." Czar shot him a bird. "What's up, Sammy?" He strolled over to her. "You straight, you talk to the lawyer?"

"Yea, I don't know what you said, but ole girl dropped the charges."

"Cause she don't want no smoke." He winked.

The day after she was dragged on the internet, Tati went to the police station to press charges. Her nose was broken in two places and her eye was swollen shut, but her pride took the biggest hit. Tati was trending in a way she never expected. Everyone was sharing the video of her getting dragged in the club. Her bare ass was a meme and the fact that Czar kept retweeting everything didn't help the situation. Tati didn't have any information on Sammy, so she called Czar, who told her to suck a dick. With the help of her friends, Tati was able to track down Sammy through her social media posts. The police caught her coming out of the nail salon and placed her under arrest for aggravated assault.

"She dumb," Slim's niece Pooh said as she snaked her neck. "The way you drug her ass all across that nasty ass club floor. Ain't no way."

"Well, that's the consequence of writing a check your ass can't cash." Sammy tooted her lips while throwing her leg across Romeo. "Plus, you worried about the wrong thing. You need to be worried about this ass whopping I'm about to lay on *you*."

"Oh hell no. I don't wanna play against her." Pooh shook her head. "Sammy too aggressive. I'm on C's team."

"No can do shorty. My home girl about to come through and she's on my team."

"Oh shit. Stop the press." Sammy sat up straight. "Lil Booty about to come through?"

"Why yall calling that girl Lil Booty?" Ada asked, returning to Slim's side.

"Because that thang little, Ma," Romeo answered and quickly dodged Sammy's hand. "I mean not that I be looking," he corrected himself making the men in the room holler out with laughter.

"Sammy keep your hands to yourself," Ada warned.

"Sorry, Mama, but he be trying me."

"Ok, ok. Yall know the rules." Slim stood up and passed a red bucket around. "For the next three hours, yall are on our time. No phones, no interruptions, and no bullshit. If you place a bet on a game, pay up." His eyes rolled over to his uncle Goose, who was sipping his drink.

"The fuck you looking at me for? Like I don't pay my debt," he snarled.

"You don't," the room sang in union.

"Fuck all yall. C and Loverboy can't be on the same team." Goose pointed his shaking finger between Czar and Nova.

"Don't be mad. Just say you wanna be on the winning team." Nova smirked.

"I do."

"Too bad. We don't want yo broke ass over here."

"Fuck you, Nova." Goose gave him the middle finger.

"Phones, iPads, all that shit. Drop it and yall can have them back when yall leave." Slim passed the box around. "If you are too drunk to leave, find a bedroom and call it a night. Any side bets are to be paid before you leave!"

"We know the rules, Pops." Romeo sucked his teeth. "Let's get this party started. My right hand itching."

"I don't know why. You gone be the first one crying about losing your money." Pooh sucked her teeth.

"Shut up and take them lashes off, you look sleepy as fuck."

"Watch your mouth," Ada scolded. "But Pooh you do look sleepy. Them thangs not bothering you?"

"No, I'm used to them." She playfully batted her lashes. "You should get some."

"Don't suggest that hoodrat shit to my mama." Nova

glared at her.

"Fake eyelashes, tattooed eyebrows, long weave, I mean do you have any hair that actually belongs to you?" Romeo goaded.

"Yea, in the crack of my ass. Wanna see?" Pooh snapped.

"I mean we do every time you bend over," Nova cracked.

"Boy fuck you and your henpecked brother." She gave them the middle finger.

"Not too much on my man." Sammy stroked Romeo's face.

"Girl bye, he went from Auntie Ada's titty to yours."

"Watch it." Ada tossed a napkin at her.

Chapter 14

Marley's stomach did somersaults as her Uber driver turned into the gated community filled with homes she'd only seen on TV or the internet. She was well aware Czar had money, but this was on another level. Every mansion was equipped with long driveways, beautiful fountains, sculpted trees, and hundred-thousand-dollar cars. The grass was green, the streets were perfectly paved, and from what she could see, it looked very peaceful.

"Got damn, whoever stay this way got money *money*," the Uber driver whistled, checking out the houses in amazement.

"Same thing I said," Marley mumbled, checking her phone. She was low key hoping Czar was going to text her and say something came up. Marley had even thought about standing him up and putting him on block.

Sister: ***I just want you to know that you ain't shit, but if you ask Czar to get me tickets to Coachella, I might forgive you.***

"And we are here," the Uber driver said.

"Thank you." Marley swallowed hard, taking in the big brick house.

"Oh shit, is that Czar?" he squealed, watching the tall man bop toward them. "And to think I wasn't going to Uber today. Aye, ask him if I can have a picture, a autograph, or one of his shoes."

"Are you high? I am not asking him that."

"If I ask, are you going to drop my rating?" He peered at her through the rearview mirror.

"If you ask this man for his shoes, I'm going to call Uber and have them fire yo crazy ass."

"You know what, that's a hit I'm willing to take." The Uber driver jumped out of the car as Czar approached them. "Bro, I'm your biggest fan!"

"Oh yea?" Czar bypassed him, heading toward the car where Marley was still sitting, trying to act like she didn't see him. Pulling the door open, Czar lowered his head. "How you gone be on my team if you won't get out of the car?"

"Who lives here?" Marley asked, peering up at him.

"My people. Get yo scary ass out of the car."

"When you say your people, do you mean like close friends or industry people?"

"I'll never put you in harm's way by bringing you into an unsafe situation." Czar helped her out of the car. "You look good." He licked his lips, pulling her in for a hug. "Smell even better."

"Thank you," Marley whispered breathlessly, allowing her lips to graze his neck.

"Soft ass lips." Czar released her. "Stop playing with me before I have that ass tooted up in the back of dude's car."

"Ay- uh, before yall start slobbing each other down, can I get an autograph?" The Uber driver cleared his throat.

"Yea, but don't mention shit about seeing me. Matter fact,

delete this ride and I'll tip you in cash."

"Say less!" He reached for his phone. It only took a couple of seconds for him to delete the ride from his history. "Done. You think I can have one of your shoes or your shirt?"

"The fuck? No." Czar pulled a couple of hundreds from his pocket.

"Oh shit! Thank you, bro. If you need me to pick her up, let me know. I'll be here with bells on. Matter fact, if you want me to stay here and wait, I can do that too."

"We straight," Czar dismissed him. "I bet not see shit about this on social media."

"Aye, I ain't gone say shit," he called after them. "If you wanted to hide a nigga in my trunk for safekeeping, I got you! If you was on some *Set It Off* type shit, I'm your man."

Instead of telling him to shut the fuck up, Czar led Marley into the house by the small of her back. As breathtaking as the outside was, the décor and structure of the interior had her in awe.

"Who was that nigga in your background?" Czar inquired as soon as they crossed the threshold.

"Why? You jealous?" Marley teased.

"You came when I called, I don't have a reason to be jealous."

"Not you talking big shit like you running me."

"I'm not?" he quizzed, stepping in her face.

Marley sharply inhaled before twirling around.

"Who lives here? This is a beautiful home," she marveled, peering around the foyer.

"This my mama's crib," Czar nonchalantly replied.

"I know you fucking lying. You brought me to your mama's house?" she stressed, feeling her anxiety shoot through the roof.

"Her and my pops host game night. Shit legit too. Come on, we were about to start a new UNO game." Czar tried to reach for her hand, but Marley stepped back. Her eyes bounced around the foyer and her hand found the back of her neck.

"Julius, wait. I told you-

"Don't think about it too much and stop trying to label what the fuck we doing. I like chilling with you, so I invited you over."

"The fuck taking yall so long?" Nova questioned, bopping around the corner. "Goose drunk ass trying to start a dice game and that's a quick lick if you catch my drift."

"I'm not fucking with Goose. Last time we played he gave me $200 in pennies," Czar sneered. "You coming, or you want me to call you a car?" he asked, looking back at Marley.

Marley chewed her bottom lip while looking down at her feet. Meeting Czar's family felt too personal. Had they been out at a bowling alley or some kind of backyard gathering, she would have been ok, but to be in his mother's house, it spoke volumes, and Marley didn't like it. She didn't want to get attached to him, but he was making it hard.

"Aye, come back to me." Czar lifted her head, forcing her to look at him. "You fucking with me or nah?"

"Ok," she exhaled.

"That's what I'm talking about." Nova grinned, carefully watching their interaction. "Come on, Lil Booty, let me introduce you to the crew." He threw his arm around her shoulder and led her to the living room.

"You a muthafuckin' lie!" Goose hollered. "I said draw four, the color is blue!"

"And then yo slow ass put down a green card!" Slim

barked. "Either learn your colors or stick to spades. Either way, you gotta take a shot and send twenty dollars to the house pot."

"Mannnn," he complained, picking up the shot glass. Placing it to his lips, Goose tilted his head back, unfazed by the lil shot. He took double pints of 5 O' Clock gin to the head all day.

"Daddy, you need to slow down." Pooh frowned.

"I told yo mama to slow down and did she listen?"

"How would I know that?"

"Cause if she had, you wouldn't be sitting here trying to tell me what to do."

"Ew," Pooh gagged. "You need to stop."

"Aight, let's get this party started," Nova announced, walking back into the living room with Marley at his side and Czar right behind them.

"Oh shit! Are my eyes deceiving me, or is there an angel amongst us?" Goose licked his lips and pushed his matted hair back. "You a little on the thin side, but you'll do."

"Unk chill, this C girl," Nova chuckled.

"Nephewwwwww," Goose sang, staggering over to them. "I'm used to seeing you with big booty women, let me take this one off your hand."

"You can try." Czar reclaimed his seat. "She a lil on the stubborn side and she feisty." If looks could kill, Czar would have croaked on the spot from the death stares Marley shot his way.

"It's ok. My first wife was stubborn, and boom, Pooh was born." He grinned. "All it took was a restraining order, couple of court cases, and then we were smooth sailing."

"I'm not even about to ask." Pooh shook her head.

"Lil Booty in the house." Romeo made his way over to her with Sammy on his heels.

"Oh my god, yall are embarrassing. Please stop calling me that," Marley simpered.

"Nope, it is what it is." Romeo shrugged. "It's all love though."

"Hey girl, it's nice to meet you. We spoke on the phone a while ago. I'm Sammy, but you can call me-

"Chihuahua," Nova finished her sentence and ducked when she swung.

"Sammy, what I tell you about your hands?" Ada questioned, walking up with her husband.

Marley turned to the soft voice and was met with the same eyes as Czar. The woman was petite with long hair and blemish-free, dark brown skin. She was a little on the taller side and reminded Marley of the late Kim Porter. The woman could have easily passed for the model's twin or cousin. She was very soft-spoken, but the authority in her tone was not to be missed.

"Julius, get over here and introduce me to your friend," Ada demanded.

"I just said this Lil-

"Casanova, call this girl Lil Booty one more time and I'm going to slap you. I know her mother didn't name her that."

"Aight, aight." He backed away as Czar took his place.

"Ma, this is Marley, my home girl. Marley, this is my mama and pops."

"Nice to meet you both. This is a beautiful home." Marley stuck her hand out. Ada glared at it and then back up at the pretty face it belonged to. Her eyes zoomed in on the scar on her neck before focusing on her big brown eyes.

"If he brought you home, we're family and we hug." Ada embraced her. Marley froze. She couldn't remember the last time she hugged her own mother, and to hug someone else's felt foreign, but it was hard to resist when Ada's perfume and warm touch embraced her.

"How you doing, baby girl?" Slim asked once his wife released her.

"Fine, thanks," Marley replied, hugging him as well.

"Aight, yall doing too much. All this hugging is weird." Czar pulled Marley into him. "That's Goose-

"I can introduce myself." Goose stepped in front of Marley, smoothing out his shirt and running his hand across the thick waves on the top of his head. "My name is Jerome, I'm an Aries, and I know nephew got a lil money, but if you let me put a car in your name, we can do an insurance job and be sitting on top of the world within a few months."

"Nice to meet you, Jerome." She stuck her hand out for him to shake. "My name is Marley, I'm a Taurus, and my mama already beat you to the punch."

"What about a house?" Goose bargained.

"Move!" Czar pushed Goose to the side. "Like I was saying, the girl with tree branches on her eyelids is Pooh, my cousin Jones over there in the corner with his baby mama Rose, and them niggas by the bar are the twins, Biggie and Shortie."

"Nice to meet you all," Marley waved.

"Let's get this shit started." Czar rubbed his hands together. "Aight look, so every game is twenty dollars and the money goes into the house pot. If you lose a game, you gotta pay the house twenty dollars and if you go out of turn or mess up, you have to take a shot. At the end of the night, whoever won the most games wins the pot," he explained. "Since I invited you, I'll pay your fees."

"No need." Marley went into her purse. "I have my own money." She passed him twenty dollars.

"Periodddddd," Sammy sang. "I like you!"

"Aight baller." Czar took her money and handed it to Slim.

For the first game, the group broke into two teams and battled each other in UNO until there were only two people standing. Ada and Marley went head-to-head until Marley ended it with a reverse, draw two, and finally, the wild card and color change ended the game. No remorse was shown as she crushed Czar's mother in the card game, stealing her unbroken record while popping big shit in the process. Bowing out gracefully, Ada dropped her twenty in the jar and gave Marley her UNO crown.

Between laughing at Sammy and dodging Goose's flirtatious gestures, Marley fit right in. Czar's family was flat out crazy and they said whatever came to mind. Ada was the ringleader, and it was easy to see where the boys got their sense of humor from. No longer was she nervous, and her witty comebacks returned. The drinks were endless, blunts flowed freely and the laughter was nonstop. Marley loved how they treated Czar like a regular person. Ada called on him when she needed something three feet away like any other mother, and his brothers teased him to no end about bringing a girl around the family.

Czar kept Marley at his side and when his hands weren't on the small of her back, they were clutching her waist. A few times, he found his head nuzzled in the crook of her neck, inhaling her skin.

"Pay up nigga!" Nova clapped his hands, causing Romeo to suck his teeth.

"Fuck that, they only fell over because you in my ear breathing all hard."

"Key words, they fell over." Nova pointed to the Jenga

blocks.

"Told yall he a crybaby," Pooh snickered.

"Shut up." Romeo dropped his twenty in the jar. "Let's play Taboo now."

"I'll keep time," Nova offered. "Everybody else get a partner."

"I'm on Marley team," Goose slurred, making her giggle.

"Don't play yourself." Czar frowned, pulling Marley under his arm. Ada raised her eyebrows but kept her comments at bay until they were alone.

"Aye sweetheart, I know this nigga the millionaire of the family, but around here he don't get no special treatment. If you wanna be on my team, just say the word."

"Um, I think I'll stick with him." Marley leaned into Czar's side.

"Can't blame me for trying." Goose shrugged, picking up his liquor off the table.

"First up Sammy and Ro." Nova grabbed the timer.

"Let's gooooo!" Romeo beat on his chest. "We do this shit."

"Baby, it's just a game." Sammy rubbed his back in an effort to calm him down.

"Bullshit, this ain't no game! You ready?" He pressed his forehead to hers.

"Readyyyyy go!" Nova flipped the timer and picked up the buzzer.

"Our first date," Romeo started.

"Poundtownnnn!" Sammy wagged her tongue, causing everybody but Romeo to laugh.

"Damn shame." Ada shook her head. She loved Sammy, but she was a wild girl.

"Stop playing with me."

"Ok, ok, ok, Applebee's." Sammy picked her nails.

"Cheap ass," Biggie chuckled.

"After that," Romeo waved them off.

"Movies."

"Right." He picked up a new card. "Aight, it's gold and you put it on your head."

"Buzzzz, can't say head," Nova stopped him.

"Fuck you." Romeo picked up another card. "Old Macdonald had one."

"Farm," Sammy yelled out.

"After I smoke I get..."

"Horny."

"No!"

"Hungry."

"And what else?" he urged, glancing at the timer.

"Pass."

"Time's up!" Nova pressed the buzzer.

"Thirsty!" Romeo held the card in her face.

"Oh dang." Sammy slapped her forehead.

"They only got two," Pooh snickered. "I'm happy I stuck with my daddy."

"Shut up, yo daddy can barely stand up straight. How is he going to read the cards?" Romeo flicked her off.

"Aight, Lil Booty and C," Nova announced.

"You ready?" Czar asked, pulling Marley to her feet.

"Are you as intense as him?" She tilted her head toward Romeo, who was now in a heated argument with Sammy.

"Nah, that nigga a sore loser and think too hard. The shit ain't that serious, don't think about it too much."

"Ok," Marley nodded. "I'm ready."

"Go!" Nova flipped the timer.

"It can be used as a catcall when a woman is walking by a group of niggas," Czar explained.

"Whistle," she guessed.

"Right, it's gold and iced out. I keep one on and the last time we were together it got caught in your nappy ass hair."

"Watch!" Marley yelped, followed by the middle finger.

"You being stingy and trying to put me in this zone."

"Friend," she giggled.

"You like to stare at them 'cause you weird as fuck."

"Stars."

"These muthafuckas just met!" Romeo sucked his teeth.

"Ray J only wanted one."

"Wish!" Marley blurted.

"Time's up!" Nova shouted. "C and Lil Booty take the lead with five."

"Nah, let me see the cards," Romeo snapped.

"Nigga, no!" Nova pushed him.

"How the fuck they get five?"

"Cause Sammy was singing pound town, that's how," Ada answered, ready for her turn.

While his brothers argued, Czar draped his arm around Marley, slowly pulling her away from the noise. He led her to a quiet corner and positioned her between his legs while his back rested on the wall.

"It wasn't that bad, was it?" he asked, holding onto her.

"What?" Marley replied, playing with the locs that hung over his shoulder.

"Stepping out your comfort zone."

"Only because your family is cool."

"They aight," Czar smirked. Reaching in his pocket, he removed a blunt and handed it to Marley. She knew what he wanted her to do. It didn't matter if the blunt was long enough for him to hold. His high was better when the smoke came from her mouth. Lighting the tip, Marley took a pull and reclined her head. Czar leaned forward, pressing his lips to hers. His hand found the nape of her neck as he inhaled the potent combination of good weed and lust.

"Again," Czar's husky voice demanded, bringing her body closer to his.

Blocking out the noise around them, Marley inhaled the smoke and playfully blew small circles in his face before catching them. Once her mouth was full, Marley grabbed Czar's chin and exhaled into his. Like a drug fiend, he inhaled the smoke and then slipped his tongue into her mouth. Czar sucked her tongue, catching the minty flavor from her lip gloss.

"Gotdamn, that's sexy as fuck," Goose coughed.

"Why everybody minding their own business but you?" Czar interrogated, releasing Marley from his grip.

"Cause I'm trying to see what that be like."

"Uh, where is the bathroom?" Marley ran her fingers through her hair, needing to get away from him before his family caught them doing ungodly acts.

"Come on." He stood up, pulling up his pants.

"Wait, is that code for something?" Nova questioned. "Are yall coming right back?"

"Why wouldn't we?" Marley side-eyed him.

"Cause this nigga been up your ass like you poot perfume," Biggie jested. "I been trying to get your attention all night and his ass blocking."

"Biggs, please. The only thing that has your attention is the snack table." Czar shot him a bird, leading Marley out of the living room. Romeo gave them a knowing look because he knew they weren't returning. It didn't bother him. In fact, he was happy because his chances of winning the house pot were that much better.

Holding her hand, Czar led Marley up the spiral staircase and down a long hall. He could have let her use the one on the first floor, but his mouth and dick had other plans.

"Aww, is this Romeo and Nova?" Marley asked as they bypassed a wall full of family pictures.

"Yea."

"Show me your baby pictures."

"I don't have any."

"None?"

"Nah, just these." Czar pointed at a portrait of Slim, Ada, Nova, Romeo, and him. They were all dressed in white and standing in front of a tree. Czar remembered not wanting to take the picture because he thought it was corny. Ada had to beg him because if he wouldn't participate neither would his brothers. With Czar being nine years older than them, they looked up to everything he did.

"And why didn't you smile in any of these pictures?"

"Wasn't shit to smile about." Czar shrugged.

"Aww, him was a grumpy baby?" Marley cooed, lightly pinching his cheek.

"Grumpy as fuck. The bathroom is the second door on your left."

"I didn't need to use it," Marley admitted. "I just needed a minute because you be trying to knock me off my square."

"How?" He cocked his head to the side and pulled at his beard.

"Touching all on me, kissing me, I mean it's a lot. You're going to give people the wrong idea."

"People?"

"Yea, your uncle and your cousin been giving me the eye and you're blocking," Marley teased. "What if I want to creep with Uncle Goose?" she continued. "Let him fuck up my already bad credit and drip Jheri curl juice on my pillows."

"Fuck outta here." Czar pulled at this goatee while running his tongue across his bottom lip. "You know what's up."

"I don't, so tell me." Marley playfully poked his chest.

"I can show you better than I can tell you." He caught her hand, pulling her toward him.

Czar trapped Marley between his body and the wall. Placing one hand above her head, the other one traced her small curves.

"I've always loved thick women," he expressed, gripping her hip. "But you." He kissed her lips. "These little ass titties, narrow hips, and little booty is fucking my head up."

Lifting her dress, Czar slipped his hand inside of her panties.

"Ain't shit little about this though." He kissed her again while cuffing her pussy. "This muthafucka so fat and juicy. You didn't miss me?"

"Nope." Marley clamped her eyes shut.

"You don't wanna be mine?" he questioned, sucking her neck.

"Noooo," she moaned as he massaged her clit. "I-I –I don't wanna be your anything."

"Then what do you want?" Czar's mouth moved to her chin.

"I just want you to fuck me. That's it." Marley slowly humped his fingers. "I want you to make me cum."

"You gone take this dick the right way?"

"Yesssss."

"Let's see." Czar removed his fingers and placed them in his mouth. "Fuck, I been dreaming about this sweet ass pussy. I'm about to fuck the shit out of you, LB."

"We're going back to your house?" She fixed her dress.

"Yes but let me get a little bit first." He grabbed her hand, pulling her down the hall and into the bathroom before she could protest.

Flicking on the light, Czar bent Marley over the bathroom sink and hiked up her dress. Marley held onto the counter, praying to God that he didn't split her into two or damage her organs with the pool stick he called a dick. Spreading her cheeks, he lustfully gazed at her pussy from the back. Czar's mouth watered, prompting him to bend down and quench his thirst.

"Oh God," she cried out when she felt his mouth cover her lips. "Julius," Marley moaned, shivering at the sound of him slurping her juices. Czar heard her cries, but his mouth was too full to respond. Nastily sucking her lips and massaging her clitoris with his finger before slipping one inside of her.

"Hm," he smacked. The more he sucked on her pussy, the more it creamed, and it drove him wild. If he ever had to overdose on anything, it would be the taste of her juices. Czar would happily drown in her pussy and beg the Lord for a redo.

Pushing his face deeper between her cheeks, Czar devoured her pussy like he had the munchies. When his tongue grazed her asshole, Marley flinched and damn near died when he doubled back and sucked it while feverishly thrusting his fingers in and out of her. Czar could feel her insides pulsate and her breathy moans bounced off the wall. Marley's legs started to shake and before she could escape his touch, she was crying and creaming all over his fingers.

"Oh shit, it's like that?" He kissed her cheek, dropping his pants. "Basic bitches squirt, I gotta shorty that cream," Czar rapped against her lips.

"Shut up." Marley wiped her face. "Keep going."

"Aight, but you gotta stop crying and shit."

"I'm good," she assured him.

Marley was anything but good. Her heart and throbbing pussy were battling again, but this time her pussy won. Even if it was just this once, she needed to feel him. Marley needed him to make her cum. Turning around, she sat on the sink and opened her legs, allowing him to step between them.

Czar didn't say anything. He simply watched her take his dick into her hands and massage it. A soft growl slipped from his lips as her tongue connected to his neck. Lightly, Marley traced the tattoos on his neck before she sank her teeth into his flesh. Czar's dick grew even harder.

"Put it in," he demanded, ignoring the consequences of running in her raw.

Marley scooted closer to the edge of the sink and placed his dick at her opening. Sensing her hesitation, Czar moved her hand to finish the job. Inserting the head, Czar closed his eyes as a euphoric warmth swallowed him. He couldn't believe it. There was no way her pussy was that tight, that warm, that wet. Yet, with every inch her tight walls suffocated him.

"Oh fuck." The words fell from his lips as his head dropped, connecting with hers. "I fucked up," he mumbled against her lips. Forehead to forehead, Czar thrusted inside of her while cursing her name.

"Julius," Marley panted. Just when she thought he was all the way in, his dick curved, hitting a wall she didn't know existed.

This was no normal stroke. Czar's moves were hypnotizing her, erasing every memory of another nigga. Czar fucked her like he was marking his territory, like he'd murk a nigga for staring at her for too long. With each stroke he poked her heart, causing the tears on her eyelids to fall. Instead of stopping, Czar kissed them away. His hand found her throat and forced her head back against the mirror.

"This creamy ass pussy," he grunted, speeding up the pace. Marley locked her legs around his waist, pulling him deeper into her. Their moans and juices smacking bounced off the walls as they feverishly fucked each other like it was the last time instead of the first. Czar was so deep in her pussy that he didn't know where his body ended and hers started.

"You gone cream on this dick?" He growled, feeling the tip of his dick swell up.

"Uh huh," Marley hurriedly agreed. Czar picked up both of her legs and placed them over his shoulders. With deep strokes, he fucked her long dick style until she started clawing at his shirt and cursing his name.

"Shit." Czar jumped back and released his nut on the counter.

"Oh my god." Marley's legs shook uncontrollably. "That felt so good."

"I see. You crying and shit."

"I can't go back down there. I don't even think I can stand up."

"You wasn't going back anyway." He kissed her lips. "I have a room here and I'm about to fuck a few more tears out of you. Can I do that?" He lovingly stroked her cheek.

"Uh huh," Marley nodded, completely gone. Czar could have asked her for a kidney and she would have laid on the table and allowed them to cut her open.

"Good." He dropped her legs. "Get yo freak ass off my mama sink so I can clean up this mess."

"Oh my God." Marley covered her face, coming down from her high. "I can't believe I fucked you in your mama's bathroom."

"You got me fucked up." He gazed at her through the mirror. "I fucked you, and as soon as I clean up in here, I'm going to do it again."

"Can I have something to eat first?"

"Yea. I'll go pick you a couple blades of grass."

"You're such an asshole," Marley replied.

"I'm fucking with you. I had my mama make you a salad and a couple of wraps."

"You didn't have to do that."

"Shut up with the polite shit and get ready to ride this dick." Czar swatted her on the ass and proceeded to clean the bathroom.

He hoped she could keep up because Czar planned on fucking her all night long.

Chapter 15

Marley woke up the next morning wrapped in Czar's arms. She didn't remember falling asleep and she hated how good it felt waking up next to him. It was probably one of the best nights of rest she had in a very long time. The sense of comfort she felt lying next to him scared her. He didn't just fuck her good, he talked her through every inch of dick, so not only did he leave an impression on her walls, but on her brain too.

Unwrapping herself from his embrace, Marley paused for a moment to take in his features. Using her finger, she lightly traced his lips, his nose, and soft eyebrows. Czar was perfect and he deserved someone equally yoked. Marley wasn't the girl for him. He didn't deserve her up and down moods. Czar didn't know it yet, but the minute she stepped outside Marley planned on blocking him. It was clear Czar wanted something she wasn't offering.

"Ouch," Marley whined, standing to her feet. The aching between her thighs was evidence that Czar put it down. Not only did he fuck her all over his room, but he also sucked her pussy until she started shaking. By the time he was done, all Marley could do was climb next to him and fall asleep from exhaustion. Carefully collecting her clothing, Marley slipped on her dress and sneakers. She draped her purse across her arm and clutched her phone to her chest. Taking one last glance at Czar, she sighed and quietly closed the door.

Slowly tiptoeing to the front door, Marley fidgeted with her phone, trying to get an Uber. Being that it was six in the morning, there was a twenty-minute wait. The thought of catching the bus crossed her mind, but she doubted she could even walk far enough to find a bus stop.

"Good morning," Ada greeted, seeing Marley bypass her.

"Good morning." Marley grabbed her chest. "I didn't see you sitting there."

"You're in a rush, I see."

"Just waiting for my Uber."

"Czar isn't taking you home?" Ada quizzed, skeptically eyeing her.

"I didn't wake him up," Marley replied.

"Oh, I see. Well, what time will your ride be here?"

"Fifteen minutes."

"Oh good, you have time for a quick conversation. We didn't get a chance to chat last night." Ada started walking away. "How do you like your coffee?"

"Black." Marley swallowed the lump in her throat.

"Oh." Ada arched her eyebrows, now even more intrigued by the woman who had her son breaking unspoken rules. All night, Ada watched how Czar handled Marley. His protective nature was at an all-time high. The way he smiled when she talked, how he possessively kept her in arms reach, how attentive he was to her needs. Ada was all too familiar with her son's nurturing side, but the vibes between Marley and Czar were way past nurturing.

"What?"

"Black coffee drinkers are independent, stubborn, but dependable and love hard."

"I didn't know that."

"How long have you known my son?" Ada asked, handing the cup of coffee to her.

"Almost three months. I met him at the start of the summer."

"And are yall dating, or do you spend the night with men of his stature all the time?"

"Men of his stature?" Marley's eyebrows furrowed, meeting in the middle of her forehead. "I know that this looks bad, me sneaking out of your home at 6 in the morning, but this is not something I do. Julius and I are friends. Nothing more."

"Friends, huh?" Ada reached out and softly turned Marley's head to the side, displaying the passion marks that cascaded down her neck. "I'm sure that's how it started, but you two are headed in a totally different direction."

"Ok, close friends."

"You sure about that? Last night, I saw something between you two and it wasn't friendship."

"I don't know what you think you saw, but-

"Listen, Czar is a stubborn man. Things weren't always easy for us. His hard exterior is a defense mechanism that developed at a young age. He loves hard and he's a protector. I love all three of my boys." She paused. "But Julius is my baby. He taught me the meaning of unconditional love. You might think you're friends, but the fact that you are standing here in my kitchen says otherwise. If you aren't ready for what he has to offer, then I suggest you run. It's going to come at you full force, and if that's not what you want, you need to decide

now. There is no in-between with him. He either loves you or doesn't give a fuck about you."

Marley nodded. The underlying message was clear.

"Um, my Uber is outside." She swallowed the lump in her throat. "Could you tell him I need some space?" Marley sat the mug on the table.

"I could, but I'm not doing your dirty work." Ada pursed her lips. "Enjoy the rest of your day."

The way Marley hauled ass out of the kitchen, you would've thought her ass was on fire. She thanked God the Uber was early because she didn't know how much longer she could stand in Czar's mother's kitchen with his nut seeping from between her thighs.

"Well, you don't say," the same Uber driver that dropped her off greeted her when she opened the door.

"Oh my God, did you sleep around the corner?" Marley slapped her forehead.

"Maybe." He shrugged. "Is Czar coming out?"

"No, you can leave."

"You sure? I don't mind waiting."

"Sir, put this car in drive before I pepper spray yo ass and take off," Marley gritted.

"Ok, damn girl." He smacked his teeth and pulled off. "You want some water? Gum? Plan B?"

"Just drive." She closed her eyes and laid her head on the headrest.

Czar's eyes slowly opened, adjusting to the sunlight that

peeked through the sheer curtains. He didn't need to look over to know that she was gone. Her wild hair wasn't all in his face, nor was her head on his chest. His plan was to wake up, eat her pussy, take her to get breakfast, and then lay up in her pussy, but because she dipped off like a thief in the night, his plans were ruined. Czar reached out for his phone to give her a piece of his mind but remembered that it was downstairs. Snatching the sheets off his body, he slipped on a pair of shorts and slides before storming out of the room. He had a few choice words for her nappy headed ass. Loud voices led him to the kitchen where his siblings were.

"Yall go to sleep arguing, yall wake up arguing. Shut the fuck up, damn," Nova complained, listening to Sammy and Romeo go at it. His head was throbbing and the last thing he wanted to do was hear them bickering.

After Czar and Marley disappeared, Nova, Goose, Biggie, Shortie, and Pooh played beer bong. The amount of beer they consumed left them spread around the house like dirty clothes. Biggie and Goose ended up wrestling and breaking one of Ada's end tables, Pooh fell asleep in the bathroom hugging the toilet, and Nova went on Live acting like Boosie. The number of women he had shaking their asses on the Gram broke the internet and got his page blocked.

"That's your brother still talking about last night." Sammy rolled her eyes. "Next month, I don't want to be on his team."

"Too damn bad." Romeo grabbed her by the arm. "If you just play the games the way I tell you to, we won't have any problems."

"Boy, fuck you. You're not Ike, and I'm not Tina. If you think about swinging on me or knocking me off the back of a couch, I'll slice your balls in my blender and pour it down your throat."

"Yall annoying," Czar grunted, strolling in the kitchen.

"Where the basket with the phones?"

"Aht aht," Sammy turned her nose up. "Who pissed in your cereal?"

"Real niggas don't eat cereal," he snorted, peering at Romeo, who had milk dripping down his chin.

"The fuck you trying to say?"

"Nigga it looks like someone busted on your chin," Czar cracked, causing Nova to chuckle.

"Where's Marley?" Sammy asked, looking behind him. Czar started patting his pockets and his chest.

"Grow up."

"Just saying, you don't see her in here so don't ask."

"Well, I like you better when she's around." Sammy snatched a water from the counter and stalked off toward the back of the house.

Czar ignored her and rounded the corner to grab his phone from the basket. Being that damn near everyone had an iPhone, finding his wasn't an easy task.

"You straight?" Nova asked, sensing his irritation.

"Yea," Czar lied. "Where the fuck is my phone?" He wondered out loud.

"Oh, I had it. I was scheduling your interview with Nesha Re and setting up a few meetings with the label and Terri. "Oh shit, what lil freak is this?" Romeo held up the phone and zoomed in. "This number been sending you nudes all morning."

"Come again?" Czar froze.

"Yea, look like some old porn type shit, but she got some pretty titties." Romeo held up the phone, showing them the woman lying on the bed holding her breasts in her hands. "And her pussy hairy. I didn't know you were into the 80's style porn. I might need to let Sammy grow her shit out because this isn't a bad look." He practically drooled over the nudes.

Czar tried to control his emotions, but a mixture of anger, disgust, and fear penetrated his veins. His stomach churned and the tip of his nose broke out in sweat. Czar tried to cover his mouth, but vomit shot out through his nose and fingers.

"Weak stomach ass," Nova chortled, reaching for the phone. "Let me see."

"Aye, gimme my phone." Czar coughed as Slim and Ada waltzed into the kitchen. Whatever Slim was whispering in her ear had Ada cheesing from ear to ear. The smiles on both of their faces fell flat when they saw Czar leaning over the sink throwing up.

"Oh hell no, yall gotta go." Slim left out the kitchen to grab a towel while Ada moved to Czar's side.

"Wait, nigga is this mama?" Nova frowned, zooming in on the woman's face. He studied the picture and then looked back towards his mother's face. His heart dropped and he felt as sick as Czar. She was much younger, but the ass naked woman was indeed their mother.

"Where?" Ada looked up confused. "And what's with you? You need some water?" she asked Czar, who was now dry heaving.

"What the fuck, Ma, this you?" Nova turned the phone around, shoving it in her face.

"Watch your mouth and what are you tal-" she paused when her eyes landed on the phone. Just like that, the skeletons she hid in the back of her closet came tumbling out. Ada's eyes filled with tears and her heart rapidly thumped against her chest. Her hands started to sweat, and her breathing became labored.

"Nigga, you foolin.'" Romeo frowned. "That's not Mama,"

he denied, trying to snatch the phone, but Nova slapped his hands down. “Right?” He glanced at his mother for reassurance.

“So this not you?” Nova swiped to the left and another picture filled the screen. This time Ada was on her stomach with her ass tooted in the air.

“Oh my god!” She snatched the phone from Nova, holding it to her chest. “Where-how-why do you have this?” she stuttered, feeling the tears fall from her eyes.

“Ask this weird ass nigga.” Nova charged Czar. “This why you fucking with ole girl? This what the fuck you was talking about when you said she remind you of Mama?”

“You got me fucked up.” Czar swung on Nova, knocking his head to the left. “Don’t ever disrespect me like that nigga.”

“Aye!” Slim ran into the kitchen trying to separate them.

“Nah, this a weird ass nigga. Walking around with naked pictures of my mama in his phone.” Nova swung.

Arrgggghh! Romeo threw up, not believing he was just lusting over his mama’s nudes.

“You don’t know what the fuck you talking about.” Czar pushed Nova, knocking him into the counter, but it didn’t stop him from running up again.

Nova was strong, but he was no match for his big brother or the years of pent-up aggression he possessed.

Whap!

Whap!

Czar punched Nova in the chest, nearly knocking the wind out of him.

Whap!

A blow to the face damn near crushed Nova’s eye socket, but it didn’t stop him from swinging.

"Enough!" Slim pulled them apart. "Y'all are fucking brothers! Blood brothers!"

"He sent those to you?" Ada's hands trembled nervously as she stared at Czar with tears streaming down her face.

"Who the fuck is he?" Nova roared, holding his bleeding face.

"Casanova, I know you have questions, but if you curse at my wife one more time, I'm going to beat yo ass all over this kitchen," Slim warned. "And you," he pointed to Czar, "Why didn't you say shit? How long has this been going on, and what does he want?"

"Who the fuck is he?" Nova repeated, catching Slim's right hand to the back of his head. "Ouch!" He rubbed his head.

"And take yo ass to the bathroom." Slim pointed at Romeo, who was still spitting up. "Throwing up on the floor like you crazy."

"Oh God," Ada called on The Most High to give her strength. Reliving her past was no easy ordeal and it pained her to open a door she'd sealed with concrete. Ada had somehow convinced herself that those pictures were destroyed and that her past was a dream. It was sort of an out-of-sight, out-of-mind situation. She hadn't thought about Cain in years and now he kept reappearing like a bad dream.

"I think we need to sit down," Slim suggested, rubbing his wife's shoulder.

"Nah, I thought you had people watching him. I guess he gets a pass, huh?" Czar questioned angrily.

"Julius," Ada warned.

"So they get to live in this world where shit smells like roses, but I have to walk around with the weight of our past on my shoulders?" He slapped his chest.

"You said you were fine," Ada cried.

"Because that's what you need to hear!" Czar roared. "Ain't shit ok and it never was. I say the shit to spare your feelings, to spare their feelings." He pointed to Romeo and Nova. "I'm walking through life with a blindfold on because seeing the world through my own eyes ain't worth living. I gotta take these dumb ass pills because I'm haunted by your decisions. Decisions I don't talk about because talking about the first eight years of my life is forbidden!"

"Czar." Ada grabbed her chest at his admittance.

"Then this Harriett the Spy ass nigga can't leave well enough alone," Czar ranted, glaring at Nova. "Yo nosy ass wanted to know who the niggas from the dressing room were, right? Well, he my fucking dead-beat ass father."

"Dressing room?" Ada squinted at Czar. His distance was starting to make sense and she couldn't believe she missed the signs. She should've known that Cain was going to find another way to get to her, and as always, he used Czar. "You saw him?"

"He's the reason you tore up that room?" Slim questioned, connecting the dots.

"Yea." Czar thumbed his nose.

"What does he want?" Ada whispered.

"You, Ma! He wants you and if I don't pay the nigga he's going to go the media on some scandal-type shit. He's going to sell those pictures."

"Oh my god." She grabbed her chest.

"Then pay the nigga. You got the money," Nova yelped. "My mama can't be all on the internet with her ass out."

Arrrgghh! Romeo bent over, throwing up again.

“Didn’t I tell you to go to the bathroom?” Slim pushed him.

“So this some disgruntled ex-boyfriend type shit?” Nova asked.

“Nah, it’s more than that. Cain was her- “Czar started but Slim cut him off.

“It’s not your story to tell!” Slim growled, ready to knock Czar's head off his shoulders, but little did he know, he’d be doing Czar a favor. Maybe it would stop the constant dreams and life-altering thoughts.

“Why not? Did I not suffer? Do I not have the scars embedded on my body and brain.” He stretched his arms out. “It’s my story just as much as it’s hers.”

“My parents had me in their late forties, so by the time I was a teenager, I was giving them a run for their money and there wasn’t much they could do. My dad had a bad heart, and my mom's focus was on him half of the time. They tried to keep me in the house, but I wanted freedom. I wanted to run the streets like my friends because they made it look so fun. I met Cain one night at a party. Although he was older than me, he saw me. He didn’t treat me like some annoying teenager.” She wiped her tears. “I was curious. He helped me explore my promiscuous nature and I lost control.”

“Aw, Mama.” Nova dropped his head, knowing where the story was headed.

“Cain started picking me up from school, buying me expensive clothes and jewelry. By the time my mom caught wind, I was far too gone.” Ada chuckled sadly, shaking her head at how stupid she was. “I ran away from home so much that my parents put me in a girl's home. I only stayed there for a month before Cain picked me up. I moved in with him, and for a while, it was good. He bought me gifts, took me on dates, and then one day he flipped. He lost all of his money in a card game and needed me to break even for him, so I did." Ada lowered her head, ashamed to let the words slip from her lips. "I used my body to pay off his debt, and that night he beat me, claiming I cheated on him."

"You don't have to go any further." Slim rubbed her back.

"I do," she sniffed, wiping the snot from her nose. "That night was the first of many. Cain realized that selling me to the highest bidder was a better profit than gambling. This became our routine for years. I was so brainwashed that I thought I could leave when I wanted, stop loving him when I wanted, but I couldn't. Cain owned my body, but most importantly, he owned my mind. Even if I wanted to go home, I couldn't. There wasn't a home to go to. My father died from a heart attack, and my mom passed away a few months later. I was alone in the world."

"When I got pregnant with Czar, I hid it for as long as I could because Cain didn't want kids. He knew deep down that having a baby would give me a different type of strength, and it did. It took many years, but Czar gave me the superpower that mothers have. I know it was selfish to have him, to keep him, but I needed something. I needed to know what love felt like again so I kept my secret until I couldn't. The day I gave birth to Czar was the best and the worst day of my life. Cain used Czar to control me. He knew that I'd do anything for my baby boy, and he used it to his advantage. For years, Czar was my best and only friend, and I did whatever I had to do to make sure he was good. I took the beatings and I snuck him food."

"Why didn't you just leave Ma?" Romeo asked, looking at her with pity.

"Leaving isn't always easy, but I did when he tried to kill your brother. We went to a shelter and stayed there for a year before your father found us."

"So what are we going to do?" Nova asked. "Are we

bodying this nigga?"

"I'll take care of it," Slim spoke up.

"The nigga should have been taken care of, but I guess because he's your brother, he keeps getting passes," Czar snorted.

"Brother?" Romeo and Nova repeated.

"Slim and Cain are brothers, so not only are we brothers, but we're also first cousins," Czar replied sarcastically. "How fucking ironic is that?"

"What's for breakfast family?" Goose asked, stumbling into the kitchen. When no one answered, he scanned the room and frowned. "The fuck happened in here?"

"Not right now," Slim told him.

"Well, make my plate and don't give me what yall gave Ro. He looks like he about to throw up," Goose mumbled and walked back out of the kitchen.

Chapter 16

"Wait, so the sex was good?" Harper inquired, lifting the glass of champagne to her lips.

"Good is an understatement." Marley sighed heavily. "It was phenomenal." She traced the rim of the glass with the tip of her finger. "He was so deep in me that I felt all of him. His pulse, his thoughts, his emotions, I felt it all." Marley paused, embarrassed by the next set of words that slipped from her lips. "He sexed me so good I cried."

"Bitch, you cried?"

"I did." She dropped her head and laughed a little. "I couldn't believe I was having sex again, and I felt guilty about how good it felt. That man was changing my whole life with his tongue, and I didn't know what else to do."

It had been a week since Marley ran out of Czar's parent's house and she hated to admit it, but she missed him. Blocking him was very immature, but now that it was done, she couldn't go groveling back. It wasn't in her character.

"So, what did he do when you started boohooing on the dick?" Harper sat up, fully invested in the story.

"He kissed my tears away." She sipped her drink. "And

then proceeded to fuck me like he lost his mind, like he was trying to make me lose my mind."

"Hot damn!" Harper kicked her feet, causing the lady doing her pedicure to jump and drop the tool in the water. "Oh shit, my bad."

"You stay still." The Korean woman frowned.

"Girllll, that's some hot shit." Harper ignored the woman and fanned herself. "So why did you block him again?"

"Becauseeeeeeee," Marley sang. "I don't want to be attached to anyone, and I know that just having sex isn't going to work."

"Work for you or him?"

"Shit, me! I can't continue to sex him knowing that he could possibly be sexing another woman the same way. He be all over the internet pictured with different women. You think I'm about to deal with that shit?"

"Then stop being stubborn and claim him! You already gone off the dick, might as well make the shit official," Harper all but yelled. The pedicurist mumbled something in her language and a woman across the shop responded. "Aht aht, talk in English." Harper snapped her fingers.

"My sister say you need to sit still," the woman told her.

"And my sister just broke her three-year celibacy. Excuse me if I'm a little excited. "

"Three years?!" The woman next to Harper gasped. "I don't mean to be all in yall conversation, but girl, I can't go three days. Three years without dick and I'd be delirious."

"And she is!" Harper insisted.

"Oh my god." Marley slapped her forehead. "Now you got strangers all in my business."

"Look, I know you loved Benny, but chasing his ghost is

going to keep you lonely, and I don't want that for you. I've already seen a change in you, and I like it. I think you should see how far this thing between yall can go. It's ok to miss your past and still live for your future. You just can't let it consume you."

"Yea, well-

"Excuse me," a guy in a jumpsuit said as he walked into the shop. Women turned to face the man, wondering who he belonged to.

"How can we help you?" The manager of the shop stepped forward.

"Yea, I have a van on my flatbed, and I wanted to leave the card in case the owner is in here. We're towing it to the shop on Michigan Ave."

"What kinda van?" Marley sat up, sitting her glass to the side. She couldn't remember being parked in a handicapped spot and her tags were up to date.

"I doubt it belongs to any of you beautiful ladies. It's an old piece of shit, the owner of the complex reported. It's leaving oil stains on the ground," he stated, handing the manager a card and hastily making his way to the exit.

"Oh hell no, is that your van?" Harper turned to Marley, who was already up and sliding across the floor with her soapy feet.

"It better not be!" she yelled over her shoulder, running out of the shop.

"Wait, you pay!" the manager yelled behind her.

"Lady, we gone pay." Harper removed her feet from the water and put on her Crocs. "I know you see my sister about to pepper spray that man." She pointed at the window. Harper didn't give the manager time to respond. She dashed right around her and out of the door.

"Sir, yo fat greasy ass have three seconds to remove my van from this tow truck, or I'm going to blind your corn chip smelling ass," Marley yelled, banging on the driver's door.

"Ma'am, contact Superstar Tow and we'll be more than happy to help you get this resolved." He rolled up the window.

"Fuck you bastard!" She banged on the window as he slowly pulled off. "Asshole!"

"Let's follow him in my car," Harper suggested.

"Come on because I'm going to run his big ass over when I get my baby back. Towing my fucking house," Marley snapped. "Where is yo car?"

"In the parking lot and don't yell at me. I told yo hardheaded ass to ride with me, but noooo, you wanna ride in that homely looking van like a freaking kidnapper."

"Shut up, and the next time you wanna hide your packages, don't ask!"

"And the next time I wake up and you park that oily shit in my driveway, I'm going to have Jaxon's brother steal that piece of shit." Harper popped the locks.

"Hey! You no pay!" the Korean owner yelled after them. "You can't come back!"

"And you got these people chasing me down. Call the tow company and see what you need to bring to get your van," Harper instructed. "I'm going to go pay before they put our picture up at the door."

"And get my purse and shoes."

"I should make yo unhinged ass go in there. Got soap all on these people floor."

"Give them a tip."

"Marley, I almost said fuck you and them." Harper

stomped away. “Talking about give them a tip. You give they annoying ass a tip.”

∞∞∞

Slim walked into the dimly lit bar and was immediately hit with a musky mildew odor that made his stomach churn. He hadn’t visited the establishment in years, but from its appearance, not much had changed. The same purple velvet couches lined the walls, only now he was sure that they were riddled with burn holes and DNA. The wallpaper was peeling, and the ceiling was missing tiles, leaving the wires and pipes exposed. The wooden barstools were tattered and barely standing, but that didn’t stop brave patrons from pulling them up to the bar.

The few people sprinkled throughout the bar didn’t seem to mind its shabby appearance. In fact, for them, it was paradise. There weren’t too many bars that opened at seven in the morning, but Dugs did.

Dugs catered to the lonely crowd, the desperate crowd, and the crowd that simply needed a drink at the crack of dawn. The building wasn’t in the best shape, but the liquor was cheap, and on the right night, they hired a couple of dancers to bring in the younger crowd.

“What can I get for you, big daddy?” the bartender flirted once Slim approached her.

“Nothing, I’m looking for somebody.”

“And who might that be sexy?” She leaned forward, giving him a glimpse of her cleavage. “My name is H-

“I got this one, baby girl. Go make sure the kitchen is stocked.” Cain cleared his throat.

“Stocked for what? These broke muthafuckas can barely

afford a beer. What makes you think they gone buy something to eat?"

"Bitch, just do it!" he barked, making her jump. Instead of talking back, the woman snatched her phone from the bar and stomped to the back. Cain's hand itched, and he had a good mind to go snatch her ass up, but she was his moneymaker for the moment, and niggas wasn't paying for pussy that was attached to a battered face.

"They don't make 'em like my baby no more." Cain shook his head. "How she doing?"

"Nigga, if you want your head to stay attached to your body, don't ask about my wife," Slim gritted.

"Ain't that some shit. You took *my* bitch and married her. That gotta be some kind of brother code violation."

"Keep playing with me."

"Oh shit, she put that million-dollar pussy on you, huh?" Cain grinned. "You don't even gotta tell me. I can smell it on you." He leaned forward and took a big whiff. "Ada has that effect on niggas. Her pussy gives niggas a newfound confidence. It'll have you walking like you own the planet. Trust me, I know firsthand."

Slim dropped his head and let out a low chuckle. He promised himself that he was going to be calm about the situation, but his wife's name coming out of Cain's mouth bothered him. Without warning, he reached across the bar and popped Cain right in the mouth. Instantly, blood squirted from his top lip and filled his mouth.

"See what I mean." He spat the blood out onto the floor. "The fuck you even mad for? I should be the one mad. You took my bitch, raised my punk ass son, and you around this bitch throwing punches!" Cain roared. "I should be the one around this bitch swinging."

"Why you fucking with Czar?" Slim questioned, ignoring

his rant.

"Cause the nigga owe me, that's why," he spat. "Don't act like you aren't reaping the benefits of his success. You walked in this bitch looking like new money," Cain grunted, griming his brother from the fitted Detroit hat on the top of his head to the Balenciaga sneakers on his feet.

"I'm not you nigga. I don't need to use women or blackmail my seed to get ahead. I worked for everything that I have."

"But I bet you don't turn down the handouts, do you?"

"Like I said, I don't need to use nobody to get ahead, but that's neither here nor there." Slim pulled an envelope out of his pocket and tossed it on the bar.

"The fuck is this?"

"You feel like somebody owes you something, right? Well, here it is. It's fifty thousand dollars in there, and I'll give you twenty-five more, but I want all the pictures and videos you have of Ada deleted, and I want you to leave Czar the fuck alone. Matter fact, I want you to move out of Michigan."

Cain picked up the envelope and opened it. The sight of the freshly printed one-hundred-dollar bills made his dick hard but knowing that there was a lot more where that came from made his knees weak.

"Nah." He tossed the money on the bar.

"Nah?" Slim frowned.

"Let me ask you something." Cain thumbed his nose and leaned in. "She listens, right?"

"What?" Slim eyebrows dipped in the middle of his forehead.

"Ada. She listens, she attentive to your needs, she cleans, she cooks, and she sucks dick better than a Hoover 3000." He paused, licking his lips. "You wanna know why? Because

I trained her. *Me*," he roared, pounding his fist on the bar. "I beat the disobedience out of her! I made her into the bitch that you so in love with, and if you think you about to give me some money my seed probably helped you get then you are dumber than I remember."

"See, like always, you got me fucked up. I know that it was you who put that shit in Ada's head to leave. I left you alone with her for a few hours and the bitch thought she could talk back to me like I was some nigga off the street."

"You tripping. Take the money because C isn't giving you shit."

"He don't have to because after I drag that nigga and his slut bucket mama through the mud, they'll hold hands and willingly jump into the Detroit River," Cain calmly said before a sinister smile spread across his face. "Now, with that being said, can I get you a drink or would you like to try out my new bitch? I know how you like to touch shit that don't belong to you."

"This shit ain't gone end the way you think it will." Slim picked up the money and stuffed it into his jacket pocket. "I'd hate to console Mama, knowing I'm the reason she's wearing a black dress."

"You'd kill me— your blood brother— over a ran-through bitch?" Cain asked, low key hurt.

"In a heartbeat," Slim promised him without missing a beat. "And it's half-brother. A nigga like you could never come from my daddy's sack.

The day Slim laid eyes on Ada it was a wrap. She was so beautiful and so broken that saving her was at the top of his list. He was fresh out of prison and didn't have a dime to his name but leaving her there with Cain wasn't an option. Slim never denied that his brother loved her, but he didn't deserve her.

"Cool, I see where we stand," Cain snorted, unmoved by the empty threat. "I don't really give a fuck how it ends. Just know this time I'm taking down everything in my path. Show yourself out."

∞∞∞

Pissed the fuck off couldn't even begin to describe the way Marley felt. Unbeknownst to her, Superstar towing had three locations and she had to visit all three just to discover her van was towed to their junkyard on the east side of the city. Marley was so mad that she couldn't even smoke when Harper handed her the joint. She dropped it on her lap and burned a hole in her favorite pants.

"If they tell me I gotta go to another place, you might as well get ready to bail me out because I promise you all these shops got me fucked up!"

"Just try to be nice because this is the last place I'm taking you. My free day has been spent driving you around. I didn't even get my toes painted."

"Well, let's just hope my shit is here because if it's not, I'm about to cut the fuck up." Marley slammed the car door and marched up the pebbled driveway.

Snatching the door open, Marley pushed her purse up on her shoulder and walked right up to the counter. The receptionist had her back to the window as she talked on her phone while watching reruns of *Love and Hip Hop*.

"Hello?" Marley tapped on the glass.

"Grab a clipboard, fill out the paper, and have your ID and insurance ready when your name is called," the receptionist instructed, without turning around. Marley pinched the brim of her nose and took a deep breath. She tried to bite her tongue, but her frustration got the best of her.

"Do this look like a fucking doctor's office?" she snapped. "I've been driving all over Detroit-" Marley paused. "Wait, I don't even know why I'm talking to you. Get your manager before I tear this waiting room the fuck up."

"Oop, you a lil feisty one, huh?" Pooh turned around, causing Marley's mouth to drop open.

"Oh my god. I am so sorry,"

"No you not, lil crazy. You was about to break this glass, huh?"

"Damn straight," Marley confirmed, still a bit confused. "I don't have time to keep running all over the world. Do you know who I can talk to about getting my van released?"

"Girl, nobody." Pooh reached into her desk drawer and removed Marley's keys. "C owns Superstar Towing Company and his petty ass had your van towed. It's in the lot to the left. I'll buzz you out."

"Oh my god! Tell your cousin I'm going to strangle him," Marley gritted.

"I'm pretty sure you'll see him before me." Pooh handed her the keys. "Your van is around the back and to the left."

"Thanks again. Sorry for snapping on you."

"Uh huh, sure. I can't wait to tell my aunt that Sammy might not be the only one beating on her son."

Marley laughed to herself while clutching the keys to her chest. A weight had been lifted off her shoulders, and now all she wanted to do was drive out of the city, find a quiet spot, and rest her mind. Marley stopped by Harper's car and told her everything was fine. She decided not to go into detail but made a mental note to fill her in later. The sisters hugged and promised to link up the next day for a redo, and of course, it was at Marley's expense.

Turning the corner to where her van was located, Marley sighed in relief. Her whole life was in that van, and the thought of starting over gave her a headache. As she drew closer, Marley could hear music coming from her van, but that had to be a mistake. She knew damn well Czar wasn't bold enough to steal her van *and* parlay in it.

"Oh, this nigga got me fucked up," she huffed, snatching the door open. "I know you fucking lying," Marley screeched at the top of her lungs, ready to charge him.

"Welcome home." Czar blew smoke out of his mouth and in her direction.

Shirtless, he was sitting in *her* bed with a pair of headphones on his head. A monitor she had never seen was sitting on her counter space, and a cup of freshly brewed tea was sitting on the shelf above her bed.

"Are you out of your fucking mind!" Marley screamed.

"Chill, I'm streaming on Twitch and I'm on Instagram Live." He pointed to the phone. "Relax."

"Don't tell me to relax and you stole my van!"

"Stole is such a harsh term. I *borrowed* it," Czar corrected her. "Would yall believe this girl blocked me?" he asked his Live and then leaned in to read the comments. "Yep, her mean ass blocked me, and now she's standing here all mad and shit. The nerve," he huffed.

"You have two seconds to get yo shit out of my van before I call the police."

"Not you threatening me like a Karen," Czar chortled. "I didn't take you for the snitching type, but then again, I really don't know shit about you since you keep fucking running from me like I have some kinda infectious disease." He glared at her and then at the phone. "And yall goofy muthafuckas better not twist what the fuck I just said. I know how yall be."

"Julius, I've had a long day and I'm not about to go back and forth with you. Get your shit and get out."

"Nah."

"Nah?" She cocked her head to the side.

"You not deaf shorty and I'm not about to keep repeating myself," Czar sternly stated. "Let me get back at yall later. I need to put this girl in her place." He winked before ending the Live and cutting off the stream.

"Put me in my place?" Marley arched her eyebrow. "Who do you think you are? Stealing my van, then got the nerve to be in my shit parlaying."

"You obviously got me fucked up." Czar slid off the bed and removed his headphones. "I don't know what kinda niggas you've been dealing with, but I'm not them. I don't chase women all over the city, invite them into my home, or steal their van...well, house," he chuckled. "By the way, if you're sleeping in this shit, you need a ring cam or something. I mean can you do that? Put a ring cam on a van?"

"You're such an asshole, and who asked you to do all that?" Marley yelled. "I told you I didn't want this."

"Yo, you getting on my fucking nerves and I don't even say that gay shit. Why you making it so hard? I like you, so what the fuck is the big deal?"

"I didn't ask you to like me! In fact, I warned you *not* to like me."

Czar sized her up. He took in her pouty lips, her low eyes, and her labored breathing. Licking his lips, he advanced toward her, never breaking eye contact. "I'm hooked like a muthafucka and I'm not coming up off that shit."

"Julius. I cannot," she stressed, gripping her forehead. "Were you even listening to me? You can't bully me into being with you."

"You know that nigga not coming back, right?"

"What are you talking about?"

"Your ex-nigga. He not coming back, so putting your life on hold like he's about to reappear is sad."

"Fuck you." Marley's voice broke. She didn't need him to tell her what she already knew. Of course it was sad, but how was she supposed to move on when everything about them was so unfinished? "This has nothing to do with him. It's you. You're a bully, and you think because you're this big ass rapper that I have to fall at your feet. I don't even like you for real."

"You got it wrong, my baby. I want to fall at your pretty ass feet."

"Julius, no."

"I hear what you're saying." Czar cocked his head to the side while intensely staring into her eyes, causing a shiver to slip down her spine. "But I don't give a fuck about none of that shit."

"Czar," Marley pleaded, backing up with nowhere to go.

"Shut up." He towered over her, careful not to hit his head. "You think I'm about to keep letting you fuck me and dip?" He lowered his head and bit down on her neck. "You don't like me?"

"No," she cried out, feeling his teeth sink into her flesh. "What do you want from me?!"

"I want your fucking soul, baby, isn't it obvious?" Czar grinned wickedly, wrapping one hand around her neck while the other handcuffed the gap between her legs. "I want to own everything from your smart ass mouth to this creamy ass pussy. Who pussy is this?"

Marley rolled her eyes because she hated that question. It was attached to her fucking body, wasn't it obvious who pussy it was? Sure, he fucked her good, made her cum back-to-back, and ate her pussy like he was in a pie eating contest, but it didn't give him rights over her body. Those rights belonged to another... even if he was long gone.

"Oh, you don't know?" Czar smirked, stepping away from her. "Let me remind you." He pulled at the string on his joggers. One tug and they fell to the ground, forcing her eyes downward.

Big crooked ass dick, Marley thought, eyeing the thick vessel. Still, she played hard, refusing to answer his question.

"Say it." He softly jabbed her in the middle of the chest, forcing her to fall on the bed.

"Turn over and toot that lil muthafucka up," he demanded, snatching his shirt over his head. His gold rope chain rested against his tatted chest, making Marley lick her lips. Her mouth watered at the sight of him standing there like a dreadhead god her ancestors prayed to.

"Turn over," Czar's voice dropped, making her clitoris thump.

Slowly doing as she was told, Marley rolled onto her stomach and arched her back low and her ass high.

"Who pussy is this, Marley?" he asked, using her real name to let her know wasn't shit sweet about the dick he was about to deliver.

"It's mine. What kinda question is that?"

Whap!

His large hand landed on her right ass cheek.

"Wrong fucking answer." He kissed the stinging cheek. "But don't worry. I know you like a nigga to work for it."

Climbing on the bed, Czar leaned down and placed wet kisses on the nape of her neck, shoulders, and spine. Marley tried to keep her composure but almost lost her shit when the coolness of his chain slid down the center of her back and then the crack of her ass.

"You might not want to admit it, but this pretty ass pussy knows who she belongs to," Czar taunted, running his finger down her slippery slit before inserting it deep inside of her. "Why you think she cream the way she do?" He massaged her insides. After placing a loving kiss on each ass cheek, Czar lowered his mouth and tickled her clitoris with the tip of his tongue.

"Julius," Marley cried out, arching her back, scooting her pussy closer to his face.

"Answer my question." He twirled his finger inside of her while simultaneously sucking her hard bud.

"It's mine." She rocked her hips in his face.

Whap!

"Wrong answer." Czar slapped her ass and pulled his finger out of her.

Without warning, he raised up, gripped her hips, and pulled her to the edge of the bed. With one foot on the floor and the other beside her, Czar placed his dick at her opening. When he heard her inhale, he slowly inched his dick inside of her, causing low whimpers to escape her mouth.

"You think I'm a fucking joke," Czar chastised while thrusting inside of her.

"C," Marley moaned.

"Shut up, if you ain't saying what I wanna hear, shut the fuck up." He popped her on the ass. Marley bit down on the pillow to keep from cussing him out.

Reaching around, Czar fumbled between her legs until he found her clitoris. With his thumb, he lightly stroked it while fucking her from the back. Marley didn't know what it was about the curve in his dick, but every time he was inside her, his dick explored a different part of her pussy.

"Say it." Czar popped her on the ass a little harder while stroking her a little faster.

The combination had Marley in tears. She didn't know if it was from the way he stretched her open or the way his dick tapped against her kidneys, but it always brought her to tears. Czar fucked her like his dick was made for her. Like the second he entered her, the stars and moon aligned, and everything was right in the universe.

"Focus on me, baby." Czar pulled out and flipped her around.

Marley didn't have time to think because he had her knees next to her ears, his dick in her stomach, and her titty in his mouth.

"Oh fuck," Marley cried.

This time there were tears. The pressure built up in her stomach, threatening to explode if he didn't stop. Czar ignored her cries. In fact, he released her breast from his mouth and licked her tears with a smile on his face.

"Say it," he whispered in her ear.

"I hate you sooo much," she lied, pulling his hair. Little did she know, that shit turned him on.

"Say it." Czar thrusted into her. "Say it for me, baby,"

"Ugh," Marley cried. "It's your pussy," she gave in, shaking as the orgasm coursed through her body.

"That's what the fuck I'm talking about." He kissed the side of her face, stroking her through one of the most intense orgasms she'd ever had. To make matters worse, he pulled out and proceeded to clean up the mess she made with his mouth. Harper said she was crazy about him, but she had it wrong. When it came to Czar and his abnormally shaped dick... she was fucking stupid.

"No more running." He kissed her lips while sliding back inside of her. "Do you hear me? No more fucking running."

Chapter 17

"Did you always want to rap?" Marley asked, lying on Czar's chest, tracing the tattoos that covered it.

"Nah," he answered, fingering her curls.

"So, what did you want to be when you grew up?"

"Alive."

"That's loaded."

"It's the truth. I didn't think I'd make it to sixteen, let alone be this fly ass nigga that's dicking you down."

"Can I ask why?" She gazed up at him.

"Why you trying to get all deep and shit with my nut leaking out of you?" Czar removed his hand from her hair and shifted her off him. Reaching for her ashtray, he picked up the clip and relit the joint that was attached to the end of it.

It was in the middle of the day, and they were ass naked sitting in Marley's van. Being in her presence gave him a serene feeling he'd never experienced. Czar swore her pussy was laced with mushrooms or some shit because every time he was inside her he lost his mind, and when he wasn't between her thighs he was tweaking. He had done a lot of wild shit in his life, but fucking in the middle of a field was at the top of the list. Czar couldn't believe she had him out there on some *Jason's Lyric* type shit. Marley had his head so gone that the thought of catching a Gross Indecency charge went right over his head. He'd happily tell the judge that Marley and her downward dog position set him up.

"Tell me your secrets and I'll tell you mine," she whispered in his ear before placing a kiss on his shoulder.

"I had a fucked-up childhood, shorty." He exhaled. "I was beaten, neglected, starved, and tortured. The burn marks on my arms came from the nigga that helped make me. I lived in a homeless shelter for a year and the shit still haunts me. The real Czar is broken and I don't think the world can handle that. It doesn't fit the image. With a microphone in my hand, I create my own story, which is far better than the one that was written for me."

"I take anti-depressants, I smoke, and I drink when the world gets heavy. Rapping allowed me to create my own narrative. Czar is an alter ego. I've been shot at, in jail, and a bunch of other shit." Czar blew smoke out of his mouth. "That's me in a nutshell, LB." He glanced back at her. "I'm possessive as fuck, and as long you hold me down, I'll do the same for you. So, if this shit too much for you, then now is the time to leave."

The phrase *"Don't judge a book by its cover"* hit Marley with force. From their first encounter, she thought Czar was just another arrogant ass rapper who did whatever he wanted whenever he wanted. He was so poised that his confidence greeted you before he opened his mouth, and she hated it— until she didn't.

"I'mma stay." She wrapped her arms around his shoulders and kissed his neck.

"Good, because I'm not chasing yo ass. Next time you run

you're going to need a mariachi band to get me back."

"I'm not going to lie, Julius, I'm scared."

"Of what?" He blew smoke out of his mouth.

"For starters, we've been together for a couple of days and *Twinkle Pussy* and *Head Hunter* have been calling you back-to-back."

Czar nodded and reached for his phone. He flipped his camera around and snapped a picture of them. Marley didn't have time to protest because he started tapping on the screen.

"What are you doing?" She frowned. Czar pressed a few more buttons and then showed her the phone. "JULIUS!" Marley shrieked. "My hair is all over the place." She examined the picture he posted and captioned: *If be my peace was a person.*

"So, I'm the reason it's all over the place." He took the phone from her.

"And I'm not some love-sick teen; posting a picture of me doesn't solidify a relationship."

"You're right, but there aren't any other women on my page. I just told the world that there's only one female getting the dick. That says a lot."

"And your little friends?"

"Twinkle Pussy and Head Hunter are two chicks I fuck when I need to relieve some stress."

"Well, while you were bullying me into a relationship, did you let them know you were off the market?"

"Nah, I just ignore their calls." He foolishly shrugged.

"That's not good enough, Julius. It doesn't matter how many calls you decline or how many text messages you ignore, if you don't outright say that it's a wrap, they're still going to have hope. Now if that's what we doing, giving out false hope, then let me know."

"Don't get fucked up, LB." Czar reached out and pinched her nipple. "You want me to call them?"

"*You want me to call them*?" Marley mocked. "Duh, nigga."

"Man, you better be lucky you got a pretty pussy because I don't take kindly to being bossed around."

"Whatever, less jaw jacking and more dialing."

"Oh shit, let me find out you a little jealous." Czar kissed her collarbone.

"Julius, you sucked my toes while fucking me from the back, and I ain't ever experienced no shit like that. Jealous ain't the word, my boy. I'm unhinged."

"You got it," he chuckled, knowing that he felt the same way about her. Without hesitation, he dialed Tati, and of course, she answered on the first ring.

"Hey," she purred.

"What up doe?"

"Why are you asking her what's up like you really wanna know? Get to the point, Julius." Marley pinched him.

"Alright, crazy ass girl."

"Um Czar, who is that?" Tati frowned at the phone. She knew damn well he wasn't calling her with another bitch in the background.

"That's my baby LB, but look, stop calling me. My shorty ain't with that sharing shit."

"Your shorty?"

"Yea. I have a girlfriend now," he said with a grin on his face, sending a chill down Marley's spine.

"Are you talking about the Salvation Army hoe?" Tati

squeaked.

"Salvation Army?" Marley squinted, looking at Czar for clarification.

"Oh yea, that's what she calls you. Don't worry though, baby. I'm going to boss you up on these hoes." He kissed her cheek.

"The Salvation Army be having some cute shit though, so I'm not offended."

"Off-brand hoe. You think this nigga about to take your nappy head ass serious?" Tati snapped.

"I don't know if he serious or not but being that the nigga sitting up here with the taste of my ass on his tongue, I'm sure it's quite serious. I mean has he ever ate your ass?"

"You got me fucked up bitch wa-

"So that's what we doing? You telling bitches my breath smell like ass?" Czar snatched the phone from her and ended the call.

"At least it's good ass. Call the next one." Marley snapped her fingers.

"Bossy ass," he growled, but like a lovesick puppy, he did as he was told. Honey didn't answer as quickly as Tati, but when she did, Marley rolled her eyes.

"You must've sensed me playing with my pussy," she moaned into the phone.

"Straight up?"

Whap! Whap!

Marley's quick hands popped Czar in the back of his head.

"Aye, don't call me no more." Czar ended the call before tossing his phone on the floor. Marley thought she was in the clear until Czar flipped her over and pinned her hands above her head.

"You happy now?" He kissed her lips.

"So it's that easy?"

"Easy as Sunday morning. I don't hold any emotional ties to either of them."

"I can't have kids," Marley blurted, causing Czar to pause and release her. "When I was shot in the stomach, the bullet was lodged in my uterus and caused it to rupture. My mama gave them consent to perform a hysterectomy. I still don't understand it, and at times, I hate her," Marley admitted. "I lost the love of my life, I lost our daughter, and then found out I could never reproduce all in the same week. I lost it. I snatched a pair of scissors from a tray when the doctors weren't looking, and I cut my throat from ear to ear. I ended up with over one hundred stitches, and my mama admitted me into a psych ward for six months. So, the real question is, do you still want me? I'm damaged goods and I'll never be able to give you kids. I'll randomly cry because thoughts of my past still plague me, I'll push you away even when I want to crawl inside your skin, and some days I'll disappear."

"As long as you fight for me, I'll fight for you." Czar kissed her lips again. "And when the time is right, we can adopt five kids if that's what you want."

"I want two." Marley wiped the tears from her eyes.

"Aight, let me know when you're ready and I got you." Czar hugged her. "Now, as fun as it's been chilling in the back of the magic school bus, I need to get back to the real world."

"Don't talk about my van."

"I'm fucking with you, shorty. I fucks with your shoebox, but since you're mine, we need to discuss living arrangements."

"Czar, I'm not about to move in with you."

"I'm not saying you have to, but you're not about to

continue living in this van. The world has too much access to you, and I wouldn't be able to sleep at night knowing that all someone has to do is wiggle the handle and lift the door to get inside."

"You play all day. I'll look for an apartment."

"Preferably in my building. You know what? I'll have my people handle it for you."

"Czar, no! I'm capable of looking for my own place. I don't need you spending your money on me."

"Shut up, I'll spend my money how I see fit. Now get up and show me the downward dog again. I need to stretch."

"Hush, you just wanna do it to me."

"That too." Czar licked his lips. "Bend over and let me eat that pussy from the back."

"Ok."

"Nasty ass," he chortled when she rolled over on her stomach.

"You like it." Marley tooted her ass in the air.

"Never said I didn't." Czar slapped her on the ass and began to feast.

∞∞∞

"Ooooweeeee!" Rah excitedly rubbed his hands together. "This shit right here is the anthem for the rest of the year." He bobbed his head to the beat. "*If you ain't talkin' paper, get the fuck on.*"

"*The way she throw it back, I swear my mind gone,*" Czar rapped, blowing smoke out of his mouth. He too was impressed with the project they'd been working on.

After weeks of comparing schedules, Czar and Southwest Rah finally made it to the studio. The moment they entered the booth, magic was created. The duo locked themselves in the studio for a little over a week and went to work. What was supposed to be a quick collaboration turned into six songs and a music video. The video was created in real time with minimal editing. It gave the fans an up-close glimpse of the rappers in their writing sessions, talking shit to one another, eating, napping, and everything else that made them human. One of the highlights of the video was Rah reading a bedtime story to his baby girl over FaceTime. The cameraman caught the moment, and it was pure genius.

Terri was ecstatic about the project and the wheels in his head were already turning, thinking about how he could maximize the collaboration so that it could benefit them all. The vibes were giving Drake and Future, Rick Ross and Meek, and Kanye and Jay-Z. Just from listening to the first couple of songs, he knew they struck gold. With their permission, he had the video touched up and dropped it, along with a song they called *Sleepwalker*.

Within twenty-four hours the Detroit rappers completely stopped the world. Taking a page from one of the greatest, Terri released the video and allowed the internet to do its thing. Like wildfire, *Sleepwalker* spread across every social media platform. Everybody wanted to be the first one to say they heard it first. Every YouTuber reacted to it, every TikToker stitched it, and black Twitter claimed it was the therapy song black men needed.

"Aye, can I ask you something personal?" Czar asked, cutting down the music.

"You bet not ask me shit about my wife." Rah glared at him.

"Nah, nothing like that... although I do wanna know if her a-

"Get fucked up in here if you want to."

"I'm fucking with you," Czar chortled. "You ever been blackmailed?"

"No. I'm kind of an open book and it really ain't shit somebody can hold over my head. I have a past, but I stand on all the shit I did. Why? You being blackmailed?"

"Maybe," Czar answered vaguely.

"Nah, nigga. You can't ask me something like that and don't tell me what's going on. A groupie trying to exploit you?"

"No." He shook his head, not sure if he could say it without throwing up.

"Then what? You about to get outted on someone P. Diddy shit?" Rah guessed, becoming impatient. "Bill Cosby? R Kelly? The fuck you do?"

"Fuck outta here." Czar waved him off. "I don't have to drug women to get the pussy. My charm does that all by itself," he boasted.

"Then what nigga?"

Czar exhaled loudly. He was conflicted. While he needed guidance about his situation, talking to a person outside his immediate family was something he didn't do. It was something he was taught not to do.

"Aight look, whatever it is, get in front of it," Rah started, not needing an explanation. "Don't allow another muthafucka to tell your story. If it's something that can harm your career, talk to Terri. He's your manager and he's equipped to handle all kinda shit."

"And if it's something that can harm the ones I love?"

"The good thing about love is that it's unconditional. It's supposed to be tested and strong enough to withstand the storm. That means good, bad, and ugly. If it's not no foul shit on your part, I'm pretty sure you'll come out on top, but whatever you decide to do, don't pay another person to keep your secrets. You'll be paying for the rest of your life and who wants to live like that?"

Czar took in everything Rah told him. When he opened his mouth to respond, the studio door opened. Both men turned to see Terri and his assistant walking in. Terri was on the phone, per usual, and Ebony was right on his heels.

"Ok, Ok, let me see what I can do." Terri walked around the room with a gigantic smile on his face.

"Aye sweetheart, who he talking to?" Czar asked Ebony, who was standing by the door holding her breath.

"Uh-I-he," she stuttered.

"Baby girl, you need to breathe before you pass out. This ugly nigga make you nervous?" Rah teased.

"No, I-uh," Ebony cleared her throat and took a deep breath. "He's talking to the CEO of the Detroit Pistons. They want to invite both of you to play in a charity game and want you to perform at halftime."

"Oh yea." Czar stroked his chin.

"Yes, and since they want to use both of your names to sell out the game, Terri is working on a deal," she whispered. "A big deal."

"I thought you said it's for charity," he questioned.

"The game, yes. The show, no."

"That's what I like to hear." Rah nodded.

"Ok, John, let me talk to my guys and I'll circle back to you," Terri said before ending the call. "And that's why I do what the fuck I do!" He fisted the air.

"Oh shit. Big T out here cursing and shit. This must be good," Czar noted.

"Good is an understatement, my friend. That was the coordinator of events for the Pistons. Both of you have been invited to attend Ball for the Kids."

Ball for the Kids was created by the Detroit Pistons and multiple non-profit organizations. The game raised awareness and money for homeless families across metro Detroit. With the money that was raised, they built homes, paid medical bills, sent teens to college, and made surviving a little easier for the less fortunate.

"Just attend?" Rah cocked his head to the side.

"Attend, take a couple of pictures with fans, play in the game, and perform *Sleepwalker* during the halftime show."

"What's the payout?"

"It's six figures! You'll be the highest paid performers... ever! They are hoping to sell out since your names will be attached, and I have no doubt that they will. The video that we posted is trending at number one across all platforms, and I have at least ten calls from rappers wanting to jump on the remix. City Girls included," he winked.

"Fuck nah, I wish the fuck I would hop on a track with their non-rapping ass," Rah snorted, and Czar agreed.

"No problem. I was thinking because they're hot right now, we could capitalize off the feature," Terri reasoned.

"I'd rather not. Hot isn't always better."

"So, about the game?" He switched gears, knowing how perverse both men were when it came to their art.

"I'm with it. Easy money." Czar shrugged. "How many tickets they giving us?"

"Eight floor seats, a suite, and if you need more, we can work it out," Terri explained.

"Cool. Let me talk to Esha. She is handling my scheduling and shit," Rah said, referring to his sister.

"How is she doing?" Terri asked.

"Don't worry about it." Rah frowned. "I'm out, C. Hit me later on Twitch. Be easy, Eb. Terri send the details and I'll hit you back."

"Will do." Czar gave him dap.

Terri waited until the door closed and took a seat across from Czar, who was engrossed in his phone. He was a little surprised to see that he was by himself. Normally, his brothers were around, and if not, at least security, but Czar was alone. Terri took notice of how tired Czar looked. It wasn't the tiredness from being burned out from work but from life. Life tiredness had a different look, a different feel. Had it been exhaustion from working, Czar could have easily slept it off, but this wasn't that.

"You by yourself?" Terri asked, tapping his phone against the palm of his hand.

Instead of answering, Czar patted his pockets, looked under the table and then back at Terri. Ebony snickered under her breath. She knew he was being an asshole.

"You could've just said yes."

"And you could've opened your eyes."

"Where is everyone? You do know that you're a millionaire. You can't be out here alone like you don't have enough money to change someone's life.

"I'm not worried about none of these muthafuckas." Czar shrugged, scrolling through his phone.

"You don't have to be, but you still need to be smart. *Move* smart. Is there anything I need to know?"

"Nah." He stood up. "Close up the studio on your way out."

"You know if there was ever something you needed done but didn't know how to do it, I could help," Terri stated lowly, stopping Czar in his tracks.

"What?" He spun around.

"I'm saying as an artist I know you need a clear mind to focus and create. You have situations with Tati, Yaro, I'm guessing your family being that you are out here solo. Is there anything I can help with?"

"Nah."

"I'm just letting you know that you're at a point in your career where you don't have to get your hands dirty. You don't have to stress about anything. My only goal is to make sure you have a successful career, and I can only do that if you're straight up with me."

"I'm good," Czar fibbed, letting the door close behind him.

Outside, Czar's heart started to beat radically against his rib cage. His vision became blurred, and his stomach churned. Visions of his childhood plagued his mind, sending his thoughts into overdrive. Patting his pocket, Czar removed his pill bottle and fumbled with the cap until he got it off. Dropping two pills in his hand, he quickly popped them into his mouth and crushed them with his back teeth. Slowly but surely, his breathing returned to normal, and he was able to see clearly.

"You got a medical condition, son?" Cain asked, moving from the side of the building like a snake. "You definitely got that shit from yo mama's side of the family... not that I know much about them," he chuckled. "They weren't big fans of my lifestyle."

"You think this shit a game?" Czar charged Cain, lifting him off the ground while pressing his forearm into his throat. "I don't know why the fuck you keep coming around like I'm not unhinged. Like you didn't beat any common sense out of me. Like I won't leave you slumped on the pavement like the trash ass nigga you always been," he gritted, watching the life drain from Cain's face. This discoloration in his face made Czar smile. To know that he was struggling to breathe warmed his heart. Right before Cain could lose consciousness, his body dropped to the ground.

"Bitch ass nigga," Czar sneered, thinking maybe the monster that used to scare him wasn't so big after all.

"Maybe you not soft." Cain chuckled in between trying to catch his breath.

"Nigga, I don't know what kinda crack you smoke, but you need to get the fuck on before you come up missing."

"Come on, son, don't threaten me like that."

"This isn't a threat." Czar thumbed his nose. "I'm promising you that if you don't get the fuck on, I'm going to bury yo bitch ass alive."

"Shit, you sound more like me than I do." Cain rubbed his throat, impressed. "I guess the apple doesn't fall too far from the tree."

"Czar, are you good?" Terri asked, approaching them with a skeptical look etched across his face.

"I'm straight, T. This just a snake that slithered his way out of the garden," Czar assured him.

"A snake, huh?" Cain responded, wiping the corners of his mouth. "You got it, son. I'll catch up to you soon. Real fucking soon," he promised before backing away.

Terri tried to call out to Czar, but seconds later he was in his car and wildly pulling out onto the street.

∞∞∞

"Alright, I'm sitting here with your favorite influencer, Tati," Nesha Re announced, followed by a little hooting and quick claps. Nesha Re wasn't a fan of Tati, but when her people called claiming they wanted to give an exclusive interview on the number one radio station in Detroit, Nesha Re had her producer set it up.

"Hey yall," Tati spoke into the microphone. "Thanks for having me," she smiled, running her fingers through her fresh weave.

The ass length lace was melted to perfection and her makeup was beat down and complimented her slim face. Tati's plump lips were shining, and thanks to her latest sponsor, the Chanel bag she sported matched her Fashion Nova 2-piece set. Not only did Tati look like that bitch, she felt like it.

"How you been? Detroit treating you right?" Nesha Re asked, trying to make small talk.

"Oh God, I can't get enough of this city. I love it here. I've actually been looking at condos and land. The city is on the come up and I'd love to be a part of the comeback."

"Detroit is one of a kind," Nesha Re smiled. "So you know I read up on my guests before they arrive, and I read something interesting. It was just published, so I'm sure many people don't know yet."

"Oh lord, what did you see?" Tati held her forehead as if she were shy.

"That you just signed a deal with Tubi. It'll be an original reality show, the first of its kind on the platform."

"I did!" Tati clapped her hands together in excitement. "*Life with Tati* begins filming in two months, and I can't wait to give the world a glimpse of my life.

Nesha Re wanted to tell her that everything about her life could be found on social media, but for the sake of her show, she kept her mouth closed.

"Congratulations!" Nesha Re clapped. "Now you're no stranger to being connected with famous men. Will any of them be a part of your show?"

"Welllllll, being that I'm pregnant, the father will be making a couple of appearances."

"Whoa! That's a bomb! Congratulations! Dare I ask who the father is?" Nesha Re asked, on the edge of her seat. Her phone lines were blowing up, and on the other side of the booth, her producer was giving her the thumbs up. They were expecting Tati to talk about her show, but this was gold!

"No one other than Detroit's bad boy himself, of course," Tati smirked, running her tongue across her teeth. "I'm having Czar's baby."

"Wait, I thought you and Yaro were a thing?" Nesha Re sat up in her seat.

"We were until we weren't. No love lost, but Czar has always been it for me."

"Girl, if this not some tea." Nesha Re palmed her head. "And this new girlfriend he keeps posting? They look like they're in love. Where will you and your baby fit in all of this?"

"Tuh. I don't know where her homely ass came from, but Czar and I know what it is." Tati rolled her eyes.

"Well, there you have it, folks. Tati and Detroit's bad boy are having a baby."

Chapter 18

Czar stepped off the elevator with a massive headache. If he ever wanted to slap the dog shit out of a woman, now would be the time. Not just a regular slap either, Czar wanted to pull his hand back so far that his body would twist and release it with Sonic the Hedgehog speed. He wanted to slap Tati so hard that her wisdom teeth lodged from her gums and she choked on them. Czar wanted to slap the bitch so hard that she disappeared into thin air like she was one of the Avengers.

Twitter and Instagram were in shambles, thanks to Tati and her big reveal. And in true Tati fashion, she was eating it up. It hadn't been a full 24 hours, and she was posting pictures of her flat stomach and pregnancy cravings. Czar wasn't surprised by her actions, nor was he worried about her being pregnant by him because he never fucked her raw. Tati lying on his dick was a different story, and if she thought he was going to appear on her crackhead show, she had another thing coming.

"The fuck." Czar frowned, seeing his brothers sitting on the couch smoking and playing the game like they were invited.

"Well, hello to you too," Romeo greeted. "Where yo ugly ass been?"

"Why yall in my shit?"

"Because I let them in," Marley sassed, walking past Czar with two plates of nachos in her hand. She reached over the couch and handed one to Romeo and the other to Nova.

"Good looking, LB," Nova thanked her. "Shit look good and it's all vegan?" he questioned, not bothering to address his brother.

"Yep."

"Well it smell good!" Romeo complimented, biting into a chip fill with chopped black beans, peppers, onions, and salsa. "Mm, shit got a kick to it," he coughed, reaching for his water.

"So I hear congratulations are in order." Marley leaned against the couch with her arms folded across her chest.

Instead of addressing the nonsense that spilled from her lips, Czar's eyes roamed her comfortable attire. Dressed in a pair of loose joggers, a Nike sports bra, and Crocs, Marley was applying pressure without trying. Her bushy hair was pulled away from her face and into a ball on the top of her head. Easily, his girl was putting all of the half-naked hoes on social media to shame without even trying.

"Hellooooo? Daddy to be, are you listening?" Marley waved her hand in his face.

"I mean I wanted a lil nephew or niece, but damn, that mean Tati hoe ass gone be connected to us for life." Romeo grimaced. "Bitch gone use that baby like a support animal."

"Stop playing. The only way that bitch pregnant is if my seeds are growing in her esophagus and she gone burp the muthafucka out," Czar retorted.

"She seems pretty adamant, and I'm not one to step on

the next bitch toes. If you on your family shit, let me know and I'll slide." Marley gestured toward the exit.

"Mannnn." Czar dragged his hands across his face. It simply wasn't his day. Pop-ups, surprise pregnancies, and now his peace was being disturbed. "Come here." He reached out to her, but Marley stubbornly stood her ground.

"Marley," Czar deep voice rumbled. Dropping her arms, she reluctantly entered his space. "Stop playing with me like I'm about to let you walk away from me. That bitch lying and it's something I don't need to clear up because time reveals everything."

"Mhm Hm." Marley chewed her bottom lip. "I hear you."

"Then gimme a kiss and make me some of those playdoh nachos, they look good as fuck." Czar cuffed the back of her neck and planted a kiss on her lips before she could reply. Unintentionally, Marley moaned in his mouth while hungrily sucking on his tongue. Czar's free hand found her waist, pulling her in closer to him as if he was trying to infuse their bodies.

"Well damn, she folded faster than two crackheads on

the 1st," Romeo chortled. "And bro, that was some smooth shit. You insulted her food and tongued her down. I tell Sammy her pancakes taste like cement and I don't get no pussy for weeks."

"Cause you ain't this smooth nigga." Czar winked, releasing Marley.

"You not that smooth, and if you say anything else about my food, the only thing you'll be eating is ass." She poked his nose.

"Don't threaten me with a good time." Czar licked her finger and she quickly snatched her hand away.

"Nasty ass," Marley snickered and walked away before she

found herself bent over the bathroom counter.

Czar wiped the corners of his mouth while rounding the couch to take a seat next to Romeo. Nova still hadn't spoken to Czar, nor did he make eye contact with him. When Nova reached for his water, Czar smacked it out of his hand, forcing Nova to look up.

"Grow the fuck up," Nova barked.

"You sitting in my shit, eating my food, and got the nerve to be mad at me." Czar leaned forward, clenching his jaw.

"Do you see my fucking eye?!"

"Can't miss the muthafucka," Romeo chuckled. "C got you out here looking like you stepped in the ring with Mayweather."

"You gotta lot of mouth for a nigga that got a hard-on from looking at his mama titties," Nova rebutted, snatching the smile from Romeo's face.

"That shit not funny."

"It is."

"Look, I didn't mean to hit you like that, but yo ass had it coming," Czar interrupted them. "You triggered the fuck out of me with all that hot shit you was talking. The fuck I look like walking around with some shit like that in my phone?"

"I'm saying, you couldn't tell us?"

"For what? To taint your view of her, to make you feel sorry for me?" Czar frowned. "It's fucked up, but it's our story and I don't need a fucking pity party."

"I hear you, but until my eye heal, I'm not fucking with you. You almost damaged my retina."

"How ironic is it that you're the head of security and you got dog-walked by the artist?" Romeo laughed out loud. "I mean nigga when he hit you in your chest, I saw tears fall from your eyes."

"And yo bitch ass ain't help me," Nova replied. "You ain't shit."

"You so fucking selfish. What makes you think I wanted to be walking around with matching black eyes?"

"Fuck you, bro. Real shit."

"Here, and you better not say nothing smart." Marley handed Czar a plate and stood back while he examined it.

"The fuck you watching me for?"

"To see your reaction." She bucked her eyes.

Czar lifted a chip to his nose and sniffed it. He liked vegetables and shit, but he was a carnivore, and eating nachos without meat was weird as fuck. Throwing caution to the wind, Czar put the chip in his mouth and chewed. His tastebuds fizzled as the different flavors mingled on his tongue, creating a spark in his eyes.

"It's aight," Czar lied, stuffing another chip into his mouth.

"Gimme my damn food back." Marley tried to take the plate from him, but Czar blocked her.

"I'm playing, girl, damn, it's fire."

"That's what I thought." She smiled, walking back into the kitchen to clean up her mess.

"Aye," Czar called after her. "Did you talk to the designer about your loft?"

"Loft?" Romeo butted in. "She moving out of the clown van?"

"Boy, fuck you." Marley gave him the finger. "And yes, but she doing too much. I don't need all that stuff."

"Chill and let her work."

"Why she getting her own place?" Nova questioned. "That's stupid."

"Same shit I said, but she on her independent shit so I'm rocking with it." Czar shrugged, knowing that the Loft was really a waste of money because there would never be a night where she wasn't by his side.

"For both of yall's information, I like having my own space." Marley popped her head back in the living room.

"Space?" Nova laughed. "You hear this shit, bro? Why she acting like she didn't give up her rights to life the day we met her at the park?"

"Fuck if I know. LB know what it is though." Czar stared at her.

"What is it?" Marley flirted, cocking her head to the side.

"You belong to me." He licked his lips and winked at her.

"Whew, yall be hot and heavy around this bitch. I need to call Sammy." Romeo fanned himself.

"So what we doing about this nigga?" Nova asked, sitting his plate down and bringing their attention back to the matter at hand.

"I thought you wasn't talking to me?" Czar taunted, biting into another chip.

"Nigga, I'm not, but this is some heavy shit. He blackmailing you?"

"Basically."

"And you didn't pay the nigga?" Romeo quizzed.

"I need to talk to Mama first, but he gets nothing," Czar gritted. "I'd donate all of my money to a third world country before I ever give that nigga a penny."

Ding

Czar's eyes shot over to the screen above the elevator.

He wasn't expecting anyone and the elevators didn't move without the proper code. Focusing on the screen, Czar watched his mother and Slim step on the elevator. Since he wasn't near it, he couldn't hear what they were saying, but it didn't take a rocket scientist to see Ada was pissed. Slim was trying to rub her shoulders to calm her down, but Ada was on ten. She hadn't heard from Czar since he stormed out of her house. Her calls were ignored, and as far as she knew, no one had heard from him.

"Man today is not my fucking day," Czar sighed, wiping his mouth and sitting his plate to the side.

"I'll be in the back." Marley backpedaled with a bottle of water in her hand.

"That's fucked up, you just gone leave me in here?"

"You got it, big dog." She chucked him the deuces. Marley had her own problems with her own mother, and she didn't need any with his.

"Oh shit. I forgot to tell you that Mama is looking for you and she's pissed," Romeo blurted.

Ding

"Baby, calm down," Slim pleaded.

"Don't tell me to fucking calm down when my disrespectful ass child is ignoring me," Ada yelled, pushing passed her husband and out of the elevator. "Julius!"

"Hey Ma," Romeo shakily greeted.

"Shut yo nappy headed ass up. I sent yall over here to check on him, and you in here eating and laughing," she snapped.

"I was about to tell him to call you Mama," Nova fibbed.

"You can shut yo raccoon looking ass up. He beat yo ass and you sitting in here breaking bread. You told him to call, but why didn't you call me when he walked in the door like

I told you to?" Ada asked, rounding the couch. Nova didn't have time to answer because Ada was still on her rant. "And you!" She pointed at Czar. "You really need to grow up. Not only am I your mother, the woman whose organs were rearranged while carrying you, but I'm also your accountant and partner in managing your businesses. If you aren't going to answer the phone for your mother, at least answer the phone when your accountant calls."

"Something happened?" Czar quizzed.

"*Something happened*?" Ada mocked him. "Yes, something happened, Julius. We had a fight, you beat up your brother, your dead-beat ass father popped back up, and you are nowhere to be found."

"My head is all over the place. I stepped back to gain a little clarity."

"And did you?"

"Yea, Ma," Czar answered, staring down at her.

"Ok, good. I also want to apologize," Ada sighed. "I was young, dumb, and selfish. I knew it was wrong for me to keep you in that situation as long as I did, and I'm sorry."

"It's cool, Ma. I'm sorry for how I snapped."

"It's not cool. I'll be the first to admit that parents don't always make the best decisions and the child ends up paying. This is your story too and I'll stand behind you 100%. Whatever you want to do."

Instead of replying, Czar stood up and pulled his mother into his arms. A simple apology and acknowledgment of his feelings broke years of trauma. Tears streamed down Ada's face as she consoled her big baby. Czar was born a protector, and he'd been doing it since he entered the world. Now it was her turn to protect him. Ada cleared her throat and pulled back.

"So what do you want to do?" she asked, looking up at him.

"Get in front of it," Czar responded. "I damn near choked the nigga out today, so I know he's pissed. I want to connect you to a publicist and a ghost writer. Write the story and we'll release it. Doing things this way, you'll get to control the narrative. He doesn't get to make money off you. From there, it'll open up doors for talk show appearances, movie deals, and more. The world loves a good comeback story."

"And what about you? Won't this affect your image?"

"I'm not worried about me, but I have a lil project I've been working on. You handle your end and I'll handle mine."

"How do you feel about this?" Ada asked, turning to face Slim.

"I stand behind you, and whatever you want, I want." He kissed her temple.

"Wait, so how did yall end up together?" Nova asked, still trying to put the pieces together.

"Cain invited your father over one night to be entertained. I was in the room with your brother, and Cain hated it when I made him wait, so he put a pillow over Czar's head. Slim stopped him, and that only pissed Cain off because when Slim left, he made sure I'd never take my time again. A few nights later, we ran away from Cain's house and went to a shelter. Your father came and got us a year later."

"Damn, that's crazy as hell." Nova shook his head.

"It is, but I think it's time I share my story." Ada smiled warmly. "And it smells good in here, who cooked?"

"LB." Romeo stuffed a chip into his mouth. "It's good too."

"LB." Ada arched her eyebrow. "She's still here?"

"She back there hiding," Czar snitched. "Baby, come out here for a quick second," he called out.

Seconds later, Marley walked down the hallway talking shit.

"That was quick. I was hoping your mama was going to kick your a-

"Ass," Ada finished her sentence. "I almost did."

"How are you, sweetheart?" Slim rounded his wife and hugged Marley. "It's nice to see you again."

"It's nice to see you too."

"By chance, is there any more food left?"

"Yes, I can make you a plate."

"Damn, so you offer this nigga a plate and I had to damn near beg," Czar scoffed. "Fake as fuck."

"I'm just surprised that she's here." Ada tooted her lips. "Last time I saw her she was running out of my kitchen talking about you weren't her boyfriend."

"You told my mama I wasn't your nigga?" Czar whipped his head around.

"You weren't," Marley gawked, not backing down.

"And now?" Ada asked, even though it was clear she was there to stay.

"And now-

"I be beating that thang out the frame," Czar cut Marley off.

"Oh my god." She covered her face.

"Hm. No need to act all shy, them hickies gone tell on you every time." Ada pointed to her neck.

"Whew," Romeo chuckled. "One big happy family again. Wait until she hears about the baby."

"What baby?" Ada and Slim squawked.

∞∞∞

A few days later, Marley stood in the middle of her empty living room with a smile on her face. The moment was bittersweet, but she wouldn't change it. Since Czar posted her in his story, the vultures on social media had been on her ass. Some liked her, vowing they were the cutest couple since Big Sean and Jhene Aiko. Others hated her, claiming she was breaking up a happy home, and Tati encouraged the negativity.

When a group of weird hoes found out Marley lived in a van, Czar stepped in. Marley wasn't ready to move, but she really didn't have a choice. For the first time in 3 years, she didn't feel safe in her van. A burner page posted a picture of her getting out of it at a store, and days later, she walked out of the yoga studio and her baby was on flat and had been egged. Mad wasn't even the word to describe the way she felt, but with the help of Harper, she was able to find a cute two-bedroom loft that overlooked the Detroit River. Czar approved because it was only five minutes away from him.

"Do you have any idea what kind of furniture you want?"

"No, but Czar's decorator is coming over this weekend."

"Must be nice," Harper smiled.

"It's not because I have my own money, and don't act like Jaxon don't be over there lacing you up."

"I never said he didn't. Jaxon has been taking care of home since I was a teen and hasn't stopped. You, on the other hand, need to let that man spend his hard-earned millions on you. All you should be doing is rubbing his back while he swipes his card."

"Eh no. With Benny, it was so easy for me to spend his

money, but I think I hold some kind of resentment towards it. Like he flashed his money all day every day, and in the end it cost him his life."

"Well, Czar isn't Benny. Czar has legal money and he has the protection to make sure nothing happens to you. Benny was reckless. He was content with being hood rich. His vision didn't go any further than the east side of Detroit."

"I guess," Marley sighed, removing her phone from her back pocket. "Speaking of the devil."

"Benny?" Harper held her chest.

"No, bitch, Czar."

"Oh, I was about to commit yo crazy ass myself."

"Shut up," Marley laughed. "Hello."

"Fuck is you doing?" Czar's deep voice asked over the music in his background.

"Why do you insist on greeting me like that?"

"Cause it makes your pussy wet," he smirked.

"The lies."

"You know what's up. How shit looking at the loft?"

"Empty," Marley snickered. "I'll probably get an air mattress tonight."

"Fuck outta here. You staying with me tonight. Honestly, I don't even know why you wasted your money because you're going to be at my place most of the time anyway, but if this helps you feel like an independent woman, I guess."

"First of all, shut up! I like my own space, and are you asking me or telling me?"

"Telling you because only weak niggas ask."

"Your way of thinking is all messed up."

"So I've been told."

"Where you at?"

"A video shoot with Rah. The label turning this album into something bigger than it was supposed to be."

"Go big or go home, right?"

"Something like that." Czar yawned.

"You tired?"

"Fuck yea. This shit has been nonstop. I'm about ready to dip on these niggas and lay up."

"Who you trying to lay up with?"

"This little booty chick that be trying to give me a run for my money."

"Julius, please. You know it's your world."

"Keep that energy but let me get back over here so we can wrap this shit up."

"Wait, were you calling me because you missed me?" Marley cooed, causing Czar to chuckle.

"I can show you better than I can tell you," he smirked. "Be at my place later."

"I'll see what I can do."

"Don't play with me. I'll pull the fire alarm and have your neighbors running outta there ass naked."

"You wouldn't," she gasped.

"You know I'm with the shit, so be at my crib later. I need you to come put that pussy on me."

"Ok." Marley played hard to get knowing she'd be over there with her freshly waxed pussy on his silk sheets. Czar ended the call.

"Y'all are too cute," Harper purred. "I really like this for you."

"Why?"

"You being with Czar is a sign that you're moving forward, and I like it. We hang out more, you smile more, and you're living in a freaking apartment. If this isn't growth, I don't know what is. I thought you'd never give up that predator looking ass van. I don't know if it's him or the dick. Either way, I got my sister back and I'm happy."

"Hush, you never lost me. I just needed time to get my mind right." Marley turned to face the window. "I do like Julius though... a lot."

"You know what I don't like though?" Harper frowned, looking down at her phone. "This big mouth bitch," she snarled.

Marley moved in to look at the screen and sucked her teeth. Tati was one of the most annoying people on the internet. If she wasn't complaining about her barely there stomach, she was promoting her ratchet ass show. Since Czar wouldn't give her the time of day, Tubi was on her ass about coming up with another storyline and it was stressing her out. They were threatening to pull the plug on her, and Tati wasn't having that.

"Ain't nobody thinking about her bird brain ass." Marley rolled her eyes. "That ball of cells in her stomach ain't even a baby yet and the crazy hoe made an Instagram for it."

"I'm not thinking about her either. I've never had internet beef, but her funny looking ass acting like she wants smoke. It's kinda exciting, honestly."

"Internet beef is exciting?" Marley frowned.

"Yep, and if she keep playing I'm going to drag her wannabe ass all over the Shaderoom."

"It's not worth it. I'm in my calm girl era and I don't have time for all the bullshit."

"Whatever." Harper flicked her wrist. "So, what are you going to do if the baby is his?"

"Nothing. That's his ball of cells and that's his problem. He said it's not his though."

"You believe him?"

"I believe that he thinks it's not his, but they had a sexual relationship. Condoms aren't 100%, so it can go either way."

"Well, for her sake, I hope that it's not his baby because I don't see that man coming up off you anytime soon. Baby or not, Ms. Tati will never be first."

Marley wrapped her arms around her waist and stared out of the window. As much as she liked Czar, there was no way she was dealing with a bunch of baby mama drama, so she hoped like hell he had all that shit under control.

∞∞∞

"Do I have anything in my teeth?" Tati opened her mouth wide and ran her tongue across her pearly white veneers.

"Nope, we're good to go," Moni, her new assistant, reassured her while hoisting the camera bag and Tati's purse on her shoulder.

"Alright, let's do this." She clapped her hands and exited the car.

The day after Tati left Czar's penthouse, she started throwing up. Chalking it up to food poisoning, she rested and drank a lot of fluids, and within three days she was back to her normal self. It wasn't until her friends made a joke about her being pregnant did the wheels started turning in her head. Tati wasn't on birth control, but she used condoms whenever she had sex with someone. The thought of being pregnant didn't cross her mind and she waved them off until she got home. The two pink lines on the plastic stick nearly gave her a heart attack. Tati wasn't ready to be a mother, and she damn sure wasn't ready to fuck up her body and go through all of the surgeries again.

In all honesty, Tati didn't know who her baby's father was, but since she was grabbing at straws, Czar was the winner, and because he was icing her out, Tati decided to take matters into her own hands. Thanks to his brothers posting their whereabouts on social media, she was able to pinpoint Czar's location, and from there, her plan was born. If Czar didn't want to acknowledge her and the baby growing in her stomach, she would bring the problem to his front door.

The video shoot was in full effect when Tati stepped out of her car. Dressed like the bad bitch she proclaimed to be, Tati rocked a pair of black cargo pants that clung to her waist, a white belly shirt with Chinese writing, and red Chanel booties with a red Chanel bag. Her long weave was laid to perfection as usual and the makeup she wore complimented her skin. Thus far, the pregnancy wasn't agreeing with her body because her face stayed in the toilet, but her hair, nails, and skin were soaking it up.

"Start filming," Tati instructed as she sashayed up the walkway.

"I'm about my riches. Money on my mind, don't give a fuck about these bitches," Czar rapped, standing on the top of a Hummer while two women danced behind him. His pants hung low and the chains on his chest jumped around as he dented the hood on the Hummer without a care in the world. Czar was in his zone. This is what he did. Perform, and put on a damn good show at that. It was work for the people around him, but for Czar it came easy.

"And I keep the tooly, watch what you say 'cause this ain't no fucking movie," Rah finished the lyric. Shirtless, he bopped around on the ground looking like a walking wet dream. Every woman wanted a piece of him, but they didn't have a chance. Rah's dream girl sat across from him beaming

proudly, and there wasn't a soul on God's green earth touching her.

Abruptly, the music stopped, and everyone stopped dancing. The lights popped on and groans could be heard as they tried to figure out what was going on. The vibe of the shoot was unmatched, so they didn't understand why someone interrupted the flow. Czar hopped off the truck and marched over to the video director, who was now in a heated argument with Tati. The moment Czar's eyes landed on her, the vein on the side of his temple started throbbing.

"Are you fucking stupid?" He snatched her by the arm, yanking her body toward him. Moni discreetly pointed the camera in their direction. She wasn't able to get a good focus before the camera was snatched from her hands and thrown to the ground. Moni turned around to go off but stopped when she stared into Nova's furious eyes. He too was pissed, and it was written all over his face.

"Let me go!" Tati snatched away from Czar, putting a little space between them. "This what I gotta do to get your attention."

"I swear you gotta be smoking dope because ain't no way you this fucking slow." He angrily chuckled.

"Well, what do you want me to do? I'm pregnant with your baby and-

"What seems to be the problem?" Rah asked, approaching the circle while everyone looked on.

"This doesn't have anything to do with you, so go back over there." Tati waved him off like he was the one in the wrong.

"Oh bitch, you got me fucked up." Taylor, Rah's wife, stepped in front of him. "First of all, watch your fucking mouth when talking to what belongs to me. You might be pregnant, but I'll pop you right in them big ass Tic-Tacs you call teeth. Second, this has everything to do with him. Time is money, hoe, and you fucking it up by bringing this bullshit to their video shoot. Move the fuck around before I drag your ass back to the cum bucket you popped out of."

Tati glanced around and wanted to smile. This was the type of drama she needed for her show. Discreetly, she glanced at Moni and saw that she was now recording on her phone.

"You wives kill me. You jumping to this nigga defense, but he was fucking on my friend last month," Tati lied, snaking her neck in Taylor's face, which proved to be a mistake.

Cocking back, Taylor slapped Tati so hard her body stumbled backwards, making her fall into Moni.

"Aw shit." Rah picked up his wife and carried her away while people laughed and cheered her on. They knew Taylor stayed out the way and was unproblematic until she was provoked. Fucking with her family earned you a one-way trip to stomp a hoe town. Taylor also knew the lie about Rah cheating on her was about to spread like wildfire and it pissed her off. In this industry, lies traveled faster than the speed of light and everyone had an opinion. People would swear they knew it, claiming niggas ain't shit. They'd swear Taylor was out of shape and couldn't keep her man, which was the furthest thing from the truth.

"Oh my god, I'm suing that bitch. Moni did you get that?" Tati asked, standing there holding her cheek.

"Ye-

"She ain't get shit." Nova smacked the phone to the ground, cracking the screen in the process.

"Wow, so yall condone the way he acting?" she screamed. "Yall helping him become a deadbeat ass father?"

"Girl, you five seconds pregnant and you fuck so many

niggas that could be the milkman's baby. Get the fuck on. We trying to shoot a video," a dancer smacked her lips.

"This how you let them talk to the mother of your child?" Tati swallowed, staring at Czar. He glared right back at her without feeling an ounce of sympathy. Whatever she was going through Tati brought it upon herself.

"Bitch, that's public ass," he spat, waving her off. "Get that nigga Rah back on the set and get cum stain out of here. She canceled."

"She canceleddddd. She canceleddddd. She canceleddddd," the crowd chanted, mortifying Tati as she ran away in tears. Her plan backfired, but she wasn't finished yet.

Chapter 19

"Oh, this is nice. Kinda small, but nice." Pam's nose pointed to the sky as she walked around the loft like she wasn't jealous. Like her toes didn't melt in the carpet like butter. Like the smell of lavender and vanilla didn't greet her the second she stepped inside the beautiful loft. Everything about the loft was breathtaking and it made her stomach turn. She was still stuck in the same tattered house and her youngest daughter was living in a loft that overlooked the Detroit River.

"I mean anything is better than that tacky looking van," Pam continued, running her hand over the mantel that housed a 60-inch flat screen.

As promised, Czar's designers came through and took Marley's loft to the next level. The cream and beige decor with splashes of mint green fit her perfectly. Mkono plants hung from the ceilings and expensive artwork clung to the brick wall. A state-of-the-art entertainment system stretched throughout the entire loft, along with everything else Czar thought Marley would need.

"Ma, don't hate. This place looks like something out of a magazine." Harper twisted her lips.

"It does, but is it hers or is this man going to use you, get mad, and put you out? That's one thing you can say about ya mama. I've always had my own."

"Anyway." Marley rolled her eyes. "Harp, there are three new flavors and I'm thinking about a fourth. Now that I have more kitchen space, I'd like to start testing out a few different things."

"That's what I'm talking about. Get inspired then! Jaxon is more than ready to get us a shop."

"Tuh, with what, his drug money?" Pam rolled her eyes.

"It's sure not a problem when your hand is out," Harper shot back.

"It really hurts, huh?" Marley stared at her mother with pity.

"What?"

"That your kids are living the life you wish you had. You still living in that raggedy ass government-assisted housing, driving the same broke down Honda Civic, and still gotta sleep with married men to fund your low-budget lifestyle."

"Oh shoot, look who's talking shit now that she's attached herself to some random rich man. Seems like the apple didn't fall too far from the tree."

"Big difference. Your roots are rotten, which is why your tree never grows."

"It'll only be a minute before this one is laid out on somebody cold ass table like the last one," Pam replied. "Let's just hope you aren't with him this time."

"Ma!" Harper yelped.

"So much for you being a changed church woman, huh?" Marley chortled.

"LB! Where you at?" Czar called out, walking through the

front door with bags of food in his hands. "It's looking good in here, baby."

It didn't take him long to find her, and when he entered the living room, Czar stopped in his tracks. He knew Harper was going to be there, but he had no idea who the second woman was, yet the closer he got, the more familiar she looked.

Pam's eyes roamed over to him and she was immediately taken aback at how handsome he was. If his masculine features didn't move her, the jewelry on his body made her purr. As if he was there for her, Pam fixed her posture and pushed her hair behind her ear.

"Hey," Marley spoke, clearly still bothered.

"You aight?" Czar asked, leaning down to kiss the side of her neck before giving Harper a head nod. Taking the bags from him, Marley sat them on the table and returned to Czar's side.

"Well now, introduce this handsome young man to yo mama," Pam insisted. The sound of her voice caused the hairs on the back of Czar's neck to stand up.

"This yo mama?"

"I am, and you should be a little nicer, being that you're dating my daughter." Pam stretched her hand out.

Instead of taking her hand, Czar stared at the manicured limb like it was covered in shit. He had been through a lot in his life, but he'd never forget the face of the woman that basically shitted on him and his mother when they left Cain's house. Ada was literally on her last leg, and instead of the woman being kind to them, she instructed her co-worker to put them out on the street.

"Why am I not surprised you're in a relationship with someone who is just as rude as the last one? You sure know how to pick them," Pam laughed to herself.

“You don’t remember me, do you?” Czar asked, pulling at his chin hair while sardonically staring at her.

“Can’t say that I do.” She licked her lips, thinking maybe he was an old flame from her past. Pam would love that. Her daughter's new boo being one of her old ones. “Did we date?”

“Argh,” Harper gagged at the thought.

“Hell nah,” Czar snarled, disgusted that she’d even suggested that. “Me and my mama tried to stay in a shelter you worked in years back.”

“I never worked at a shelter.” Pam frowned.

“You did. You were fired for stealing and selling people food stamps,” Marley said, snapping her fingers. She remembered that day clearly because the man that Pam sold the stamps to never returned with the money and they had to eat bologna sandwiches for almost two weeks.

“Like I said, I don’t remember you.” Pam bucked her eyes. “But if you went from a homeless shelter to putting my daughter up in this lil loft, then I’m guessing you turned out alright.”

“Yea, no thanks to yo rude ass,” Czar snapped.

“Excuse me?” Pam’s eyebrows dipped in the middle of her forehead. “This how you allow your lil boyfriend to talk to your mother?” She glanced over at Marley.

“I’m not even surprised you did something so inhumane. I mean have you ever done a good deed in your life?” Marley leaned into Czar.

“I didn’t abort your suicidal ass,” Pam gritted. “Now I said I don’t remember you,” she lied.

Pam knew exactly what he was talking about. She was pissed with her coworker for going behind her back and told their manager, who gave them the order in the first place. Pam could have left well enough alone, but she was pissed with her boyfriend at the time and took it out on everyone around her.

"Yea, aight," Czar nodded. He didn't feel the need to press the issue because they both knew the truth. Karma would have the last laugh.

"I don't, and I don't need to lie," Pam snapped. "Harper, take me home! She finds a nigga just as crazy as her and thinks she's done something. Tuh," she cursed, snatching her purse off the counter. One of the handles popped, and because it was unzipped, all of the contents fell to the ground. "Shit," she hissed, bending down to pick up her things.

In the midst of the madness, Pam's phone started ringing, and by mistake, she hit the speaker button.

"Aye, where you at? This the last time I'm doing this shit. I'm about ready to tell Harper my damn self."

Silence.

Harper's heart dropped to her stomach, and Marley covered her mouth. Pam sat there looking like a deer caught in headlights, and Czar scratched his head in confusion.

"Hello?" Jaxon barked. Pam scrambled to pick up her phone, but Harper stepped on her hand, beating her to the punch.

"Jaxon?" Harper uttered, swallowing the lump in her throat.

"Baby?"

"How long?"

"Harper?" Jaxon repeated.

"How fucking long have you been sleeping with my mama?" she shouted into the phone.

"Is that what she told you?" he questioned. "She a fucking

lie. She been blackmailing me!"

"Give me my phone." Pam stood up, adjusting her broken purse under her arm.

"The fuck going on?" Czar whispered in Marley's ear, but his question went ignored. Marley couldn't find the words to tell him some major shit was about to go down.

"How is she blackmailing you, Jaxon?" Harper all but yelled. Her question was directed at her husband, but her gaze was fixed upon her mother.

"Aight look, back when-

"He tried to sleep with me," Pam blurted, cutting Jaxon off. "Before yall moved out he tried to sleep with me and I turned him down, but he was persistent."

"Bitch, you played!" Jaxon yelled through the phone. "I tried to help your desperate ass and you played on that shit."

"Sure, lil dope dealer, like you haven't cheated on her before."

"Ma, stop." Marley came to Jaxon's rescue. "Harper, you had just found out you were pregnant with JJ, and me, mama, and Jaxon were drinking. I ended up leaving with Benny. When he dropped me back off, I walked in on Mama, and she had her face buried in Jaxon's lap."

"Liar!" Pam lunged at Marley, but Czar stepped in front of her.

"Wrong one," he warned.

"You slept with my husband?" Harper said above a whisper, still trying to wrap her head around what was happening.

"Girl, I knew you was the slow one. No! He tried to sleep with me," Pam yelled. "Why else would he be paying me off?"

Whap!

Harper lost every ounce of self-control as her hands went upside her mother's head. Like a dog off the street, Harper dragged her from one end of the kitchen to the other.

Whap! Whap!

"Get this fat-

Whap!

Harper popped Pam in the mouth, stopping her mid-sentence. Blood oozed from her split lip as she begged Marley for help, something she never thought she'd do.

"Marley!" Jaxon bellowed over the phone. "Get my wife!"

Snapping out of her daze, Marley jumped into action and tried grabbing Harper by the waist, but she was no match for her sister's rage.

"Czar, do something!"

"Hell nah," he refused. "Tag her ass one time for me," Czar encouraged, recording with his phone so he could show his mom. "And another one for my Mama."

"Julius!" Marley yelled at him when Harper started ripping their mother's braids from her scalp and tossing them next to her wig.

"Aight, damn," he grunted, sticking his phone in his pocket. With ease, he picked Harper up while Marley tried to pry her hands out of Pam's hair.

"Fuck this bitch!" Harper tossed a braid at her.

"No," Pam sniffed, fixing her stretched out shirt. "Fuck you and your loose dick husband. You automatically believe a nigga over the woman who gave birth to you!"

"No, I believe my sister."

"Like that's any better. This dumb ass girl don't know her head from her ass."

"Ma, get out of my house." Marley picked up her wig and

tossed it to her.

"I swear I gave birth to a couple of ungrateful bitches! Yall hate me so much, but I was good to you! I could have put you on the streets like my mama did, but I raised you," Pam fussed. "I was young, but I raised you."

"No, we raised each other!" Harper yelled back with so much force her throat burned. "Who do you think cleaned up your throw up on drunken nights? Who do you think cut the stove off when you got drunk and fell asleep? Who do you think stepped up when you let a nigga break your heart over and over and couldn't get out of the bed? We did! My sister and I were there for you even when you tried to compete with us! Dancing in front of our friends and allowing us to lay up because the same niggas that had their hands in our pants were the same niggas lacing your pockets."

"Y'all were going to do the shit anyway, so why not get a couple of dollars from the situation?"

"That wasn't parenting."

"It was! That's how I was raised. Your grandma didn't care what I did as long as I brought home a few dollars."

"So you passed down your fucked up family traumas to us! Instead of wanting us to be better than you, you wanted us to be just like you. Old, desperate, and miserable as fuck."

"Yea, and my only regret is that I didn't fuck Jaxon, and her boney ass didn't die on the pavement with that bum and his baby," Pam spat.

Whap!

Harper slapped Pam so hard her neck cracked.

"When it rains, I pray you can handle the storm," Marley hissed.

"I have God on my side and He doesn't judge me for my past," she returned. On her way out the door, Pam knocked over a vase, causing the glass to skate across the floor.

"Damn, yall mama a wild girl," Czar chortled, not knowing what else to say.

"Julius, could you please give me and my sister a minute," Marley requested, never taking her eyes off Harper.

"Yea, I'm about to catch up with my people. I'll be back later." He kissed her cheek. "Harp, I owe you a Birkin." Czar winked before bopping out of the kitchen. "Aw shit, let me pick up this damn glass. For yall to have raised her, she sure don't have no home training," he mumbled, picking up the big pieces of glass.

"Why didn't you say something?" Harper asked, staring over at her sister through glossy eyes.

"Because it would've caused more harm than anything. You were pregnant, and Jaxon was so remorseful when it wasn't even his fault. She got him drunk and tried to take advantage of him," Marley explained.

Harper felt stupid. Back then she noticed how her mother looked at both Jaxon and Benny, but she chalked it up as Pam being her normal promiscuous self. It's one thing to sleep behind your friends, but your family was a different story.

"It wasn't your decision to make, Marley. You should've told me."

"Then be mad at me because I wasn't putting you or my nephew at risk because your mama was being a THOT. Now if Jaxon would have been palming her head or alert that would have been a different story."

"Thanks for the visual," Harper scoffed, looking down at her ringing phone.

"Are you going to talk to him?"

"No. I mean I don't know, my head is all over the place," she sniffed. "Did you know he was paying her?"

"Hell no, but I'm not surprised. It's very Pam-like."

"This is crazy."

"I'm sorry." Marley hugged her sister, allowing her to fall apart in her arms. "Hey, look on the bright side."

"What's the bright side?" Harper wondered out loud. From where she was standing, there was nothing but darkness and anger. For months, she thought Jaxon was cheating on her. Hell, that pill might've been easier to swallow because the thought of her mama and him was sickening. Harper wanted to believe that she would've been mature enough to handle the situation when it happened, but she wasn't. JJ wouldn't have existed, and Pam and Jaxon both would have been a distant memory.

"When the ladies at the church jump her ass, we don't have to help."

"I wasn't helping her anyway, and I hope they beat her ass with tambourines up and down that aisle. From this moment forward, I'm done with her."

"And Jaxon?" Marley quizzed.

"I just need a minute to collect my thoughts. Can I stay here?"

"Of course."

Chapter 20

Three weeks later

Czar moved through the crowded stadium hand in hand with Marley while Harper, Nova, Romeo, and Sammy walked beside them. Shortie and Biggie brought up the rear with vicious mean mugs etched across their faces. The charity game was packed, and just as Terri predicted, it was a sold-out event. Czar wanted to bring in extra security for Marley's comfort, but she declined, not wanting to bring more attention to them. Little did she know, it was impossible. All eyes were on them. Up until that moment Czar had never publicly been linked to another woman besides Tati and the people were eating it up. Not only did Czar post random pictures of them, but when they weren't together, he was inviting her to join his Live. Marley was like the shiny new toy on the shelf and everyone wanted a piece of her. They complimented her hair, her skin, and outfits.

"You wanna sit on the floor or the box?" Czar whispered in Marley's ear as cameras flashed around them.

"The floor," she told him, clutching his hand like her life depended on it.

Marley didn't want to ruin his moment, but being

surrounded by so many people was triggering. The noise, the lights, the people were all too much, but she sucked it up to stand next to her man. Her man. Two words she never thought she'd say again, but there she was, looking like Pocahontas with her waist-length passion twists. The stylist Czar set her up with enhanced her style, dressing her in a pair of vintage wide leg jeans that hung dangerously low on her waist and a long sleeve Bob Marley crop top that stopped below her breasts. Since it was cold out, Marley rocked a floor-length, distressed jean jacket. Czar finished the look by placing a couple of gold chains around her neck and an iced-out Rolex on her wrist. As much as Marley fought him about spending that much money on her, she appreciated his efforts.

"Yo C, what can we expect tonight?" One of the commentators asked as he tried to bypass them. Czar stopped and peered over at the microphone that was inches away from his lips. He hated the lack of personal space and started to push the microphone out of his face, but Marley tickled his palm, making him think twice about his actions.

"A good ass game," Czar boasted. "I have my good luck charm tonight. Ain't no way I'm losing. Enjoy the game." He walked away.

"Good boy," Marley whispered.

"I almost blew that nigga shit out," Czar swore. "And don't think that tickling shit is going to work every time." He popped her on the ass.

"As long as it worked this time I'm good."

"Nigga, are we almost there?" Biggie quizzed. "All this walking got my back burning."

"Then buy a fucking waist trainer and stop eating everything in sight," Romeo jested.

"Fuck yo stick figure looking ass."

Marley giggled at their banter. She was learning that there was never a dull moment with them. All they did was talk shit to one another, smoke, and eat, but when shit got serious, there wasn't a grin in sight.

"Aight, yall right here." Czar led them to their seats. "If you need me, let me know. I'll stop the game and we'll dip," he assured Marley.

"Boy, she ok, gone on." Sammy waved him off.

"Worry about your nigga looking at them cheerleaders versus being all in my shit."

Romeo quickly turned his head, but it was too late. Sammy was all in his face asking which hoe he was staring at.

"I'm good, baby. Go tap some ass," Marley promised.

"Do I get an incentive?"

"Yes." She licked her lips and leaned in. "For every point you get, I'll turn them into minutes and let you fuck my throat until your time is up."

"Fucking freak." Czar gripped her ass and kissed her lips. "Drink some tea because I'm going for thirty." He winked before bopping away.

Marley loved the way Czar dressed, but tonight he was really on his boss shit. The NBA commissioner asked that the players dress up for the red carpet, and dressed up is what they did. Czar rocked a custom navy-blue Armani suit with a pair of Kobe 6 Dark Knights. His locs were neatly twisted into four barrel braids that hung down his back. Per usual, his lineup and facial hair were neatly tapered. With a watch on his wrist that matched Marley's and diamonds on his neck that danced under the lights, Czar understood the assignment.

"Whew, it's some fine ass niggas in here." Harper fanned herself. She wasn't half-stepping either in a jean jumpsuit that hugged her curves. The heels were killing her, but she loved how they complimented her outfit.

"You need to stop before Jaxon pulls up on your ass." Marley bumped her shoulder.

Harper had been on her best bullshit and was giving Jaxon a run for his money. She refused to go back home, and the only time she talked to him was when they needed to meet up to exchange JJ. Even then, Harper still gave him the cold shoulder. Jaxon tried to explain his reasoning behind not telling her, but Harper wasn't trying to hear it. The angel on her right shoulder was telling her to forgive him, but the hoe on her left was urging her to act the fuck up.

"Girl please, I'm not worried about him or no other nigga." She tooted her lips. "Do they serve drinks over here?"

"Yea, what you trying to drink?" Shortie flirted, standing next to her.

Harper was at least five inches taller than him, but she was a tree he wanted to climb. He had been eyeing her thick ass for a minute, but the wedding ring on her finger had him second-guessing. For a while, Shortie just watched her from afar, and from what he could tell, she was never with her husband and always down to party.

"Sir, no sir. You standing too close to me. I don't need none of these famous people thinking I'm with you. Back yo little ass up." Harper flicked her wrist.

"I might be short, but I have a couple of features that make up for my height." He licked his lips, eyeing her breasts. "What you tryna do?"

"Yea, Harp, what you tryna do?" Jaxon towered over Shortie, nearly making Harper jump out of her skin. "Let us both know so I can handle the situation how I see fit."

"Ah shit," Marley mumbled, feeling around in her purse for her pepper spray. She loved Jaxon, but she loved her sister more and didn't know what kind of time he was on.

"W-what are you doing here?" Harper stuttered. "How did you get down here?"

"I know people." His jaw clenched, taking her outfit in. While it was cute, he didn't appreciate her breasts being on display. "So tell this man what you trying to do," Jaxon insisted.

"Nothing, Jaxon," she pouted.

"That's what the fuck I thought. Get up and come holler at me."

"The game is about to start," Harper whined. She didn't even know how he got a floor seat ticket at the last minute, but when she made eye contact with Czar, it became clear. He was taking pictures with his team but shot a wink in her direction, prompting her to roll her eyes.

"Harper," Jaxon gritted, leaning down in her ear. "I haven't had no pussy in three weeks, I've been eating TV dinners, and the house is a fucking wreck. Get your hot ass up and come talk to me before I show the fuck out and embarrass all of us on national TV."

"Ugh. Fine, but we better be back by halftime," she hissed, stomping away with Jaxon on her heels.

"Damn cuz, you let that nigga punk you," Nova teased.

"He didn't punk shit. That's that man's wife. The fuck was I supposed to do?" Shortie waved him off.

"Stand on a chair and let the nigga know you mean business and his big ass can't help you because he trying to flag down the snack lady." Romeo glanced over at Biggie.

"Fuck you, I'm hungry and you lil niggas don't eat." Biggie flicked him off. "Aye, bring that tray of hotdogs over here," he motioned.

"Yall embarrassing." Sammy shook her head. Marley

silently agreed, but she enjoyed their company.

∞∞∞

On the court Czar chopped it up with his teammates, which consisted of a few more rappers from all over Michigan, including Yaro. Thus far, Yaro hadn't said anything to Czar and it was in his best interest. Terri had already warned Czar that Yaro would be there and he urged him to be on his best behavior. Czar already had a bad reputation for acting out in public, so Terri was hoping this event would shed light on a different side of him.

"Um, Czar, can I talk to you for a minute?" Yaro asked, shifting on his feet.

"Nah."

"C, talk to the lil nigga," Rahlo asserted, bypassing the duo standing in the middle of the court.

Czar looked over his shoulder and saw Terri nervously watching him. Matter fact, everyone was watching them, waiting to see how things would turn out.

"The fuck you want?" Czar frowned, stopping Yaro from walking away.

"Look, I'm not trying to beef with you. I was on some other shit and I'll admit I let the clout go to my head."

"No hard feelings."

"Cool, and the whole Tati thing-

"There is no Tati thing," Czar cut him off. "You gotta know that she's a pass around, so I hope you ain't in love with the bitch."

"I don't know what the fuck it was, but like I said," Yaro stretched his hand out, "I'm not trying to beef with you."

Car stared at his hand for a few seconds before balling up his fist. Yaro caught on, and they pounded, sending the stadium into loud applause.

"And that's what we need in the community," the commentator spoke over the microphone. "Fewer fights, gun battles, and prison sentences. With men like Southwest Rah, Czar, and Yaro Detroit just might be alright."

∞∞∞

After the players from both teams changed into their basketball gear, they were brought back out and the game began. This was Marley's first time at a basketball game and she couldn't lie, the atmosphere was a vibe. The cheerleaders stood off to the side shaking their pom poms while the commentators excitedly followed the game. The fans were going wild, holding up signs for their faves and hooting when they made a basket.

"And another three by Czar," they shouted over the speakers. "We're only twenty minutes into the game and this man is on fire!"

Marley giggled to herself when Czar shot her a wink. She'd never tell him, but every time he dunked, her pussy got a little wetter. Even if he didn't get thirty, she was going to bless him with sloppy toppy off GP.

"Nigga, you putting on a show?" Rah asked, dribbling the ball next to him. "The fuck you blushing for?"

"You see shorty over there next to my brothers?"

"The H.E.R. look alike?" Rah glanced over his shoulder.

"Yea. That's me, and she said if I score thirty, I'll get more than the game trophy." Czar grinned.

"Then let's make that shit happen for you, my boy."

Together, Czar and Rahlo controlled the first half of the game. They fed off each other's energy, shooting twos and threes without their team's assistance. When it was time for them to perform, they didn't even bother changing their clothes. Rahlo brought his daughter on the court and Nova and Romeo joined their brother. The lively crowd stood on their feet as Rahlo and Czar put on a halftime show that they'd never forget.

"Head spinning, can't tell my left from my right, on the road to riches, flow so tight I got 'em fighting for their life. Shorty sittin' pretty looking like my future wife," Czar rapped, winking at Marley, who was now blushing on the jumbotron. Harper and Jaxon walked back in just in time to see Marley shining, and they loved that for her.

By the end of the game, Czar scored thirty-five points, and Marley had her head in his lap the entire way home.

Ada pulled her hood down as she walked into the shabby bar. Her hands shook uncontrollably, so she kept them tucked in her pockets to hide her nervousness. The last thing she wanted to do was come off scared, but that was exactly what she was. It had been years since she came face to face with the demon in her dreams, and now that he was near, she couldn't control her breathing.

As bad as she wanted to write the book about her life, Ada couldn't do it. Constantly talking about her past was like reliving it, something she never wanted to do. Ada couldn't even get past the first chapter without calling it quits, so the next best thing was to go see Cain. She knew Slim would be against it, so she waited until he went to sleep and snuck out of the house.

"I knew you'd come." Cain slowly approached her, dropping his towel on the bar. "Mama bear to the fucking rescue. You look better than I remember." He licked his lips, making her skin crawl.

"I wish I could say the same. You look like shit," Ada snorted, finding her voice. It was a lie.

His dreads were neatly twisted, his beard was full, and the cream sweater he wore looked good against his dark skin. Cain's voice was deeper and his movements were more suave than she remembered, reminding her how easy it was for him to annihilate every relationship she had prior to him. Now, he did nothing for her. In fact, being in his presence repulsed her. "Ah, there she is. That smart ass mouth." He grinned.

"Cain, why are you bothering Czar? What do you want? Haven't you done enough?"

"Isn't it obvious? I want you. I miss you." He reached out to touch her, but Ada jumped back, pulling the gun out of her pocket.

"Don't touch me. You'll never touch me again! I have a restraining order."

"Come on now, A baby. You know damn well that lil piece of paper don't mean shit to me." He wickedly gazed at her. "Just give me one night."

"Excuse me?"

"That's what I want. One night alone with you. I mean it's the least you could do since you fucked my brother and had kids by the nigga. Then you let the nigga marry you. I should beat yo ass off GP."

"You gotta be out of your fucking mind. I'd jump into a tank full of piranhas before I lay down with you."

"Then say your goodbyes, baby, because that's the only

way I'm coming off that ass."

"Hey daddy, you want something to eat?" The voice caused Ada's head to snap in the other direction, and Cain snatched the gun out of her hand.

"Nah, Honey baby. I'm good. Let me wrap this up."

"Well, who is this?" Honey questioned, placing her hand on her thick hip. "She looks a little too old to be selling pussy."

"Bitch, go back in there," Cain snapped, making both Honey and Ada jump. "Here," he handed Ada her gun after removing the clip. "I want one night and then I'll leave you alone. You can go on about your life and I'll disappear."

"And you'll leave Czar alone?" Ada eyed him skeptically.

"Yea. You know I never liked the lil nigga anyway."

"He's your son."

"No," Cain barked. "He's your fucking son. All I wanted was you! You just had to get pregnant and keep the muthafucka. Everything that happened after that was your fault. You were supposed to love me, cater to me, but you started taking care of another nigga."

"He was a baby." Ada bucked her eyes.

"Yea, well I wish I would've stomped him out of you when I had the chance. Now, are you going to give me the one night or not?" Cain cocked his head to the side.

"And what about the pictures?"

"I'll get rid of them. Well, I'll keep a couple to remember you by, but I won't share them."

"If I'm going to do this, I want all the pictures."

"Ok, fuck it. You can have them all."

"Ok." Ada cleared her throat. "I'll do it."

"One night."

"My girl," he cheesed, taking a step forward. "And don't try no funny shit because I'm still the same nigga I've always been," Cain threatened, sending a chill down her spine. "Be ready when I call. Get the fuck outta here before I tie your ass up in the back and have my way with you for old time's sake."

Chapter 21

"What the fuck you getting me for my birthday?" Czar asked, snaking his fingers between Marley's toes.

"Why you always gotta cuss?" She giggled, melting into his touch.

It was Sunday evening and Marley and Czar were laid up in her loft, watching holiday movies and eating snacks in between their smoke sessions. Czar swore it was corny as fuck, but for her, he laid there watching *This Christmas* while she lusted over Chris Brown. Marley got a kick out of watching Czar act jealous and almost pissed on herself when he inboxed Chris Brown, challenging him to a dance battle.

"It lets muthafuckas know I mean business. Now stop deflecting and tell me what you plan on getting me. I'm expensive too, so don't come with no bullshit," Czar told her.

"You can't put a price tag on the gift I'm buying with my money."

"Yes the fuck I can. Walk yo ass in my party with one of them big fake ass Burlington watches if you want to, and I'm gone embarrass yo ass."

"Julius, what is a Burlington watch?" Marley asked,

unsure of what he was talking about.

"The watches at Burlington Coat Factory. Fake ass diamonds, hard ass bands, and dramatic face pieces."

"Somebody brought you a Burlington watch before?" She giggled, caressing his ankle.

"I bought it myself. I wore it to school in the 9th grade and that shit stopped working by third period. I was late for every class and half of the diamonds were missing."

"Oh my god." Marley laughed harder, holding her stomach. "You was faking it?"

"Fake it until you make it." Czar twisted the Patek on his wrist. His days of wearing fake jewelry were long gone. "Back to my question."

"I don't know, what do you want?"

"I want a *yes day*."

"What the hell is that?"

"You have to say yes to everything I ask for 24 hours."

"Uh, no. I'll get you a Target gift card." Marley shook her head. "Giving you a *yes day* is giving you too much power."

"Target?" he snorted. "Real niggas don't shop at Target."

"Well, that's what you're getting because I'm not about to say yes to you for 24 hours."

"You scared?"

"I think you should do it," Harper cosigned, coming from the back of the loft with her phone in her hand. "I'm on Live doing a Q&A session. Do yall mind?"

"Do ya thang sis," Czar said.

"Sir, I'm not talking to you." She rolled her eyes, making Marley giggle.

"The fuck you still mad for? I said sorry." He threw a

couch pillow at her.

"You know why." Harper squinted at him, catching the pillow with one hand and tossing it right back.

Thanks to Czar, Harper was now back at home sucking dick, cooking, and going to dumb ass PTA meetings. She was enjoying her single life, but Czar just had to invite Jaxon to the game, fucking up her whole vibe. Jaxon was making up like he really cheated on her. When he wasn't in the house, he was making sure she didn't need anything, and when she did, he dropped everything and ran home.

"And do yall separate? I mean damn, it's almost disgusting how cute yall are." Harper playfully rolled her eyes.

"That's him." Marley tried to move her foot, but Czar snatched it right back.

"Take yo ass home," he told Harper, who only gave him the middle finger before turning back to her Live.

Czar pinched Marley's big toe. "Come on. It'll be fun."

"Fine. I'll do it." Marley pulled her lip into her mouth and let her head fall back.

"Yall some real haters," Harper laughed, looking at her phone. Every time she got on Live, someone had something to say about her sister or their business. "See, my sister not the one to go back and forth with you hoes, but I have time." Harper stared in the camera. "Pop all that hot shit toward me. I want all the smoke from you internet hoes."

"Let them know what it is," Czar instigated.

"Stop being messy," Marley spoke up.

"I'm just saying," Harper said with a roll of her neck. "Imagine being pressed about a nigga and he over here playing in my sister's toe jam." She flipped the camera around to face Czar and Marley. They were both still laid out on opposite ends of the couch. Marley's feet were resting in Czar's lap while his fingers snaked through her toes.

"Bitch, I don't have toe jam!"

"I wasn't gone say shit, but-

"Julius, please, if I have toe jam, you wouldn't always have them in your mouth."

"Perioddddd!" Harper wagged her tongue. "Pop your shit, sister."

"Don't encourage her." Czar glared at the phone then back at Marley. "And stop telling people I suck your toes."

"You do though," Marley bucked. "Toes, fingers, pus-

"Czar, they asking why you not over there with your baby mama," Harper read one of the comments.

"That's not my shit, and don't bring her ass up. She like one of them annoying ass Facebook ads. As soon as you start talking about her, she popping up everywhere."

"Yall nosey." Harper shook her head. "Czar, they wanna know do you love Marley."

Lifting her head, Marley stared at him, wanting to know the same thing. She didn't know if what she felt could be defined as love, but it felt good. Czar was the first person who crossed her mind in the morning, and he was the last person she wanted to see when she closed her eyes. More than a lover, Czar was her friend. They spent countless hours talking about everything from their childhoods to places they wanted to travel. Czar made her feel safe and she saw herself being with him forever. Marley felt crazy, but she was learning that love didn't have a timeline. Just like grief, it hit you out of nowhere and could turn your world upside down.

"What's understood doesn't have to be explained," Czar voiced.

"Booooo!" Harper gave him a thumbs down. "That's such

a manly answer." She rolled her eyes.

"Awe shit, I done spoke up the devil. Your baby mama is requesting to be on my Live."

"Ignore that shit."

"Too late." Harper accepted the request.

In seconds, Tati's face appeared on the lower half of the screen.

"Where the fuck yo husband at? You need to go home," Czar grunted. "Why you accept that shit?"

"Cause famous people funny, and I'm tired of her little trolls all on my page, leaving us bad reviews and fucking with my sister. I think we just settle this once and for all." Harper shrugged, facing the camera.

"Girl, where did you even come from?" Tati laughed. "You bitches need to crawl back into the Goodwill bin yall crawled out of."

"Goodwill?" Harper raised her eyebrow. "Sis, you wearing a Fashion Nova jumpsuit. I know you don't think you shutting shit down because everybody and their mama got one of them dumb ass wrestler looking outfits."

"Damn. At this point, I'm wondering if you and your sister both fucking my baby daddy."

"Kick the hoe off yo Live," Czar demanded.

"Oh hey, baby daddy." Tati waved. "I see you still over there playing with your charity case. I hope you wrap this shit up because our baby will be here by summer."

"Tati, stop playing. You know damn well I didn't leak a drop of nut in your pussy."

"Whatever. Keep showing off for lil homeless." She rolled her neck. "I'm going to have the last laugh."

Up until this point, Marley was still sitting on the couch.

She had her fair share of going back and forth with bitches when Benny was out in the streets, so none of this was new to her, but the fact that Tati kept talking shit irritated her. Marley's plan was always to let Czar handle his situation, but enough was enough. Without warning, she got up and snatched the phone from Harper.

"Ah. There she is." Tati smiled, knowing that she got under her skin. "What happened to your lil van? I heard somebody slashed your tires."

"Awe shit, her thin lace ass in trouble now." Harper shook her head.

"LB, you don't have to respond to that hoe." Czar tried to take the phone, but Marley pushed him away.

"See, I was going to let you have your moment." She grimed Tati. "I was going to let you and that lil ball of cells live in this make-believe world you created since that's what bring you happiness."

"Ball of cells?" Tati frowned, not catching on. She glanced down at the comments and they were cracking up. Calling someone's unborn child a ball of cells was a different level of pettiness, and unfortunately for Tati, this was only the beginning of Marley's rant. If she could dish shit out to her mother, wasn't nobody safe.

"Yea, lil dumb bitch. Ball of cells, or did you drop out of school to be a toss-around?"

"Bi-

"Shut up. You wanted my attention, now you have it," Marley cut her off. "See, you so pressed over a nigga that's not even thinking about you. He had your name saved in his phone as Head Hunter. Like, come on, is this the kind of man you want to pin a baby on? A man who disrespects you at every turn? A man who had another woman drag your ass in the club and then made you drop the charges?"

"Damn LB, I didn't even do shit." Czar threw his hands up.

"It's not about you. I'm just trying to tell your little lover girl the difference between us. She got the shitty version of you. Meanwhile, I'm at family game nights and got you fucking me on a bed of flowers in the middle of nowhere while you suck my toes."

"Marley!" Harper screamed. "Bitch, not *Jason's Lyric*."

"I'm just saying. She keeps calling me Goodwill, but this man just dropped half a mil' to furnish a loft I rarely sleep in. You been fucking with him for what, two years, and what do you have to show for it besides a stretched-out pussy? Six months in and this man just bought me a fucking Rolex and a new wardrobe."

"So what does that prove?" Tati rolled her eyes. Deep down inside, she wanted to cry. Marley seemed so meek and she didn't think she'd go off like that. The comment section was going wild and the Live had over a million views. Tati was sure by morning it was going to go viral. "You can have all that shit because I'll have his firstborn, and that trumps a random bitch any day.

"Call us when your ball of cells forms a head. Right now, you and that lil sea horse can suck a dick." Marley blew her a kiss. "Just not Julius' dick." She ended the Live.

"Welp. I think I'm about to go home." Harper picked up her phone as Marley glared at Czar.

"I'm going to ride with you." Marley broke their eye contact.

"Wait. Where the fuck you going?" Czar asked, confused.

"To my sister's house. I suggest you go put that lil bitch in check because next time I'm going to catch a flight and beat her big mouth ass."

"Why though? I thought we were going to watch another

dumb ass Christmas movie." He grabbed her hand.

"And we were, but I'm not in the mood anymore."

"You switchin' up on me?"

"Are you going to switch up on me when little Miss Waffle pussy has your baby?" Marley snatched away from him.

"That's not my fucking baby."

"But it could be. Look, just give me a little space."

"So this you running?" Czar rubbed his jaw.

"No. This is me saving myself from heartache. Lock up when you leave."

This time Czar didn't stop her from leaving. He sat on the couch trying to figure out where they went wrong. Because he had never been in a relationship, Czar was genuinely confused and his head was starting to hurt. If Marley were any other female he would have told her to kick rocks, but she wasn't just anybody. As hard as she tried to be, she was sensitive as fuck, and now he had to fix some shit he didn't break.

Picking up his phone off the floor, Czar dialed Terri's number and waited for him to pick up.

"What did you do?" Terri asked, answering on the first ring.

"Why you act like I'm always in trouble," Czar scoffed.

"Because you are. Now, what did you do?"

"I need a doctor."

With nothing to do, Czar got dressed and went over to his parents' house. He wasn't surprised to see his brothers' cars there when he pulled up. Goose was over cooking chili, and as drunk as he was, his chili was top-notch. Prior to liquor taking over his life, Goose could've been a world-class chef. Before Czar could knock, the door was pulled open.

"Hey, I thought you were staying in." Ada smiled, moving to the side so he could step in.

"I was, but LB on some other shit," he vexed, removing his boots so he wouldn't track snow through the house.

"Damn nigga, you just got in a relationship. How you fucking up already?" Romeo questioned, as he walked into the living room where everyone was seated. Czar gave him the middle finger and spoke to everyone else. Stretching out on the floor in front of the fireplace, Czar noticed that his mother put out her Christmas decorations. In the first seven years of his life they didn't celebrate any holidays because Cain didn't want her spending *his* money on Czar. Ada usually waited until Cain passed out and then she gave Czar something small. Most of the time, it was a comic book or a Hot Wheels car.

"Lil Booty was on Live going in on Tati. Shit, she almost made me cry," Sammy snickered.

"Pooh said she has a little spark." Ada grinned, recalling the story Pooh shared with her.

"Little ain't the word. She called that girl baby a ball of cells. That was some creative shit right there."

"Wait, so why is she mad at you?" Nova asked, looking up from the TV.

"About the whole baby thing," Czar sighed.

"You told her it wasn't yours, right?"

"Duh, but she not trying to hear that shit."

"Neither would I," Ada voiced. "Dealing with a man with kids is one thing, but dealing with a man that has a newborn with a crazy hoe that's still in love with him is a different story. I'd run for the hills too."

"Ma, come on now. Tati is reaching. I wrapped my joint up when we got down."

"Ok and? Sex education tells us that no form of birth control is 100%." She perched her hand on her hip. "If that girl is having your baby, do you really want Marley to stick around while yall work out your situation?"

"Yea," Czar selfishly answered, causing them to laugh. "She stuck with me. If anything, I'll have her adopt the baby and it'll be ours."

"You're going mighty hard for a girlfriend." Ada eyed him.

"He cookie whipped, Ma," Romeo smirked. "Welcome to the club." He gripped Sammy's thigh.

"Aww hell. Please don't be like this nigga," Nova stressed.

Czar waved him off. He started to say something, but his eyes landed on his mama. She was fidgeting with her phone. Czar didn't know if his eyes were playing tricks on him, but she seemed nervous.

"Give me one minute yall.. This is the lady about the book," Ada muttered, scurrying out of the living room before any of them could respond. The conversation resumed, but Czar's eyes followed his mother out of the room.

"So what are you going to do?" Sammy asked. "I could beat her up again," she offered.

"Nah. I have something else in store for her ass," Czar mumbled, still looking at the doorway his mother walked out.

"Well, let me know."

"Yall ready to eat?" Goose stepped in the living room wearing Ada's apron.

"Yea, bring me a bowl," Romeo requested.

"Nigga, do I look like the psycho that's sitting on your lap?"

"Goose, don't play with me. I'll fight an old man," Sammy hissed, sliding out of Romeo's lap. She bypassed him, playfully bumping his shoulder in the process.

"And you like that manly shit." Goose peered over at Romeo, who was smiling like a fool in love.

"I do."

"Alright, so what are you going to do?" Ada asked, waltzing back into the room with Slim at her side.

"I don't know." Czar shrugged. "Slim, what do you do when Mama pissed off and you aren't the one that made her mad."

"I fix it." He shrugged.

"Why?"

"Because I'm not one of them pussy niggas that match vibes. We both not about to be stomping with attitudes, and I like to cuddle at night. Even if I didn't piss her off, I'm going to fix it because I like a happy home. These young niggas like to get mad and act more like bitches than they women do. The fuck I look like ignoring the woman that's cooking my food; that's a recipe for a disaster. The saying 'happy wife, happy life' is true. Since I've been with your mother, she's made sure I was straight at every turn. She takes care of home, and I take care of everything else," Slim expressed. Ada warmly smiled, ignoring the twinge of guilt she felt in the pit of her stomach.

"Nah, don't listen to this lovesick nigga nephew." Goose shook his head. "If I had your type of money, I wouldn't settle down with one woman. If she mad, get two, and if they get mad, damnit get a few." He clapped his hands together. "It would be like a pussy parade all the time."

"And then what? When your dick don't work anymore what are you doing to do?" Slim quizzed.

"Buy a new one, the fuck! If these hoes can trick us with new asses every five years, why can't I get a new dick?"

"You sick," Nova laughed.

"Nigggga, I'd get a new dick every three years. Each year it'll grow an inch."

"And you gone die lonely." Ada shook her head.

"Wrong," Goose smirked. "I'll die with a twelve-inch dick."

"This nigga," Romeo laughed as Sammy walked back into the room with a bowl of chili and crackers.

"Oh, this is good," Sammy cooed, scooping a spoon full of chili into her mouth.

"I know," Goose declared. "My cooking has been known to bring women to their knees."

"Um eww," she gagged. "So, did we decide what we're doing with Tati?"

"Yea." Czar glanced up from his phone. "Nova and Ro come ride with me."

"Don't go get into trouble," Ada warned.

"Never," he assured her, pushing up from the floor. "How's the book coming along?"

"I-uh, it's coming along great."

"I thought you took a break?" Slim side-eyed her.

"I did. I had writer's block, but it's ok now."

"So you're still writing it?" Czar stared at her.

"Uh huh," Ada nodded. "I'm going to make me a bowl of chili. It smells amazing."

"I know it do and while you're in there make me a drink," Goose called after her.

"Nigga don't get fucked up," Slim warned.

Tati's head bobbed up and down as she swallowed Yaro's dick whole. Being that he wasn't big in size, there wasn't a need to gag, but she did it to make him feel good. The five thousand dollars he sent to her cash app was an added bonus and encouraged her to go a little harder. As of lately, her checks were rolling in slower, and the jobs were almost nonexistent. After her last photoshoot, Tati was labeled a diva, and no one wanted to work with her. She was a pretty girl, but there was nothing special about her. In the world of social media, pretty girls were a dime a dozen. As easily as they found her, she was just as easily replaced.

"You a nasty bitch," Yaro grunted as she stuffed his balls in her mouth.

Tati rolled her eyes. She was used to his dirty talk, but tonight he was overly aggressive. His words were a little harsher and his hands were heavier. Every time he slapped her on the ass, Tati wanted to swing on him. When they were fucking, he rammed his dick into her without any foreplay and Tati was confused. Yaro usually ate her pussy from sunup to sundown, but this go round was different. He fucked her like he had a vengeance.

"Ah fuck." He removed his dick and spilled the contents on her face before giving it a swift slap. "Go clean up." Yaro nudged her chin.

Without a word, Tati picked up her clothes and walked to the bathroom feeling lower than low. In all the times they had fucked around, she had never felt so dirty. It was almost like Yaro was trying to purposely embarrass her. He kept calling her out of her name and made it a point to nut on her body. With his semen dripping down her face, Tati swore she would never mess around with him again.

"Yo Tati, you got company," Yaro hollered out from the bedroom.

"Huh?" She frowned, using a towel to dry her face.

Pulling the door open, Tati opened her mouth to ask him what he was talking about but clamped her mouth shut when she saw Czar, his brothers, and another man standing in the doorway. She turned to run back into the bathroom, but Yaro grabbed her by the arm, tossing her on the bed.

"Oh my god, please don't rape me," she cried.

"Rape you?" Czar frowned. "Stop playing. With the right amount of money, we could buy you." He thumbed his nose. "But that's not what this is."

"Then what's going on?"

"I need some blood work."

"What?" Her mouth went dry.

"This is Dr. Nixon and he's going to take your blood for a pregnancy test."

"You are out of your fucking mind. I could just pee on a stick," Tati suggested, hoping they couldn't hear her pounding heart.

"Nah, that's not going to work for me because I don't trust you. If you're pregnant, it'll show on this test. Come over here so we can get this shit started."

"Czar, you have really lost your mind. I don't know this man from a can of paint. You really think I'm about to let him stick a needle in my body."

"Bitch, please. You don't know half of the niggas you fuck,

but you let them stick their dick in you," Yaro snapped. "Get the fuck over here and take the test."

"Wait, are you seriously siding with this man after he embarrassed you on multiple occasions?"

"All that shit is in the past. Bros before hoes."

"He not your brother you Bart Simpson looking ass nigga," Nova snapped. "Can we please get this shit done?"

Czar's brothers weren't fond of Yaro helping them lure Tati to the hotel room. They swore it was a set up and had Shortie and Biggie camped outside. In their opinion, Yaro was a little too eager to help the man who almost ended his career. He handed Tati over with no problem, and while she was in the bathroom, he took her phone and sent back the money he gave her.

"I had an abortion!" Tati blurted, swatting Yaro's hands away.

"When?" Czar quizzed, cocking his head to the side.

"After I left your video shoot. I was so embarrassed, and you've been treating me like shit since you started messing with that basic bitch. I made the appointment and was able to get in on the same day."

"So why the fuck you keep bothering me?" he gritted.

"You chose a nobody over me!"

"Newsflash, you're a nobody," Romeo spat, tired of the back and forth. "I'll give it to you though, when you stepped on the scene you had potential, but you changed, wanting to blend in with everybody else because you weren't confident enough to stand on your own. You hollering LB is a nobody, but she snatched this nigga without even trying."

"I love him."

"She serious?" Nova laughed. "You was just in here fucking another nigga, but you love my brother?"

"Boy, fuck you. I don't have to prove anything to anyone. Yes, I was pregnant, but I aborted the baby because I don't have time for none of this shit."

While this was half true, Tati aborted the baby because she knew Czar wasn't stupid; he'd want a DNA test, and of course it would come back in his favor, leaving her to play *Blue's Clues*. Tati's plan was to say Czar and his girlfriend stressed her out so much she had a miscarriage. Not only would Czar get a lot of negative feedback, but she'd be the center of attention. People would feel bad for her, and Tati planned to run with the sympathy play until the well ran dry.

"Now if yall will excuse me." She tried to walk past them, but Nova and Romeo grabbed her by the arm, throwing her on the bed. Yaro put a pillow over her mouth to keep her from screaming.

"Aye nigga don't kill the girl," Czar barked.

"Oh right, right." Yaro removed the pillow from her face, but Romeo and Nova still held her down.

"I'm not comfortable with doing this if she's going to fight it." Doctor Nixon adjusted his glasses.

"Chill, Doc. You were requested to come out in a fucking snowstorm. I know you didn't think we were about to build a snowman." Czar glared at him and then his brothers. "Let her up. Tati, if you run, I'm going to clothesline yo dumb ass. All this shit could have been avoided if you didn't lie on my dick. Now my girl mad at me. This our first fight and it's about some shit I didn't even do."

"You sound like a bitch." Nova frowned. "I need to find other people to hang with because love is in the air and I don't wanna catch that shit."

As soon as Tati was free, she cocked back and slapped Yaro so hard her hand was printed on his cheek when she removed it. She hopped off the bed and tried to charge

Romeo, but he hit her on the head with a pillow, knocking her back on the bed.

"Aye, stop acting like you can fight niggas! Sit the fuck down and let this scary ass doctor do the fucking test so we can go," Czar roared.

"I just told you I'm not pregnant," Tati cried.

"Well, too bad I can't trust your word. Sit the fuck down and let this nigga take the test so I can go makeup with my girl."

"Fine, and after this you better not ever reach out to me."

"Bitch, you be fucking with me," Czar stressed, slapping his chest. Romeo and Nova chortled. They found it funny that he was having girl trouble at almost thirty years old. "And hurry yo scary ass up," he told the doctor. "I'mma fuck Terri up for sending me yo shaking ass. You gone fuck around and poke the girl artery."

With his portable kit, Dr. Nixon was able to draw Tati's blood and test it all within one hour. When the negative result came back, Czar wanted to throw the coffee maker at her for taking him through unnecessary bullshit. He knew there wasn't a chance in hell she was pregnant by him, but confirmation of knowing she wasn't made him breathe a little easier. For good measure, he made Dr. Nixon's scary ass print out a copy of the results. He couldn't wait to show Marley because she was going to be sucking dick and balls until he forgave her.

"That's crazy," Yaro said aloud as they walked to the elevator. "Now that we're passed that, what do you think about getting in the studio together?" he foolishly asked Czar.

"I don't."

The elevator doors opened, and Nova, Romeo and Czar stepped on. When the doctor tried to step on, Czar held his hand out.

"Yall can take the next one."

∞∞∞

Marley glanced down at her vibrating phone and rolled her eyes. She didn't even know why she was mad at him because, in reality, he did nothing wrong. Tati was before her, and as far as Marley knew, they weren't messing around. Still, the way her hormones were set up, she couldn't help but feel some kind of way. She liked Czar a lot and sharing him with a desperate bitch and her baby wasn't ideal.

"TT Marleyyyy," JJ sang, bouncing through the house.

"No, I don't wanna see a magic trick." She slid her phone under the couch pillow.

"Don't be a party pooper," he teased, sitting next to her.

"JJ, last time I let you show me a trick, I ended up in a relationship, so excuse me if I don't trust your judgment."

"Don't blame that on my baby," Harper snickered, taking a seat at the other end of the couch. "Has he tried to call you?"

"Yes, but I'm not talking to him," Marley responded childishly. "I don't know what the heck I was thinking."

"You were thinking with the little lady between your legs."

"You have a lady between your legs?" JJ's head shot in his aunt's direction. "I don't have nothing between my legs, just a ding-a-ling, and it's not even a big ding-a-ling like daddy."

"JJ," Harper shrieked.

"Boy, just show us the trick," Marley laughed.

"Ok, I'll be right back," he said, skipping away.

"Marley," Harper sighed, getting back to the topic at hand.

"You can't be mad at him."

"I know you not talking, Ms. I have an exit plan."

"Shut up. We're not talking about me. This is about your stubborn ass."

"Look, I know it's silly, but I'd rather cut ties while it's still fresh versus later down the line. That hoe is having his baby. That's something I'll never be able to give him." Marley dropped her head. "It's fun right now, but what's going to happen later when he decides he wants more kids, when I'm not enough? I feel so stupid even overthinking this. Our relationship is like a month old."

"It's natural to think about the future, and the fact that you are thinking long-term makes my heart smile. You don't have to worry about having babies, I'll have them for you. I'll pop out as many babies as you want."

"I'm serious, Harper."

"Bitch, so am I. You think I just go around offering to bust my pussy open for fun because I don't. When you're ready, I'll carry your babies for you," Harper promised. "Two max, anything after that you gotta adopt because I can't have droopy coochie lips."

"I really love you." Marley poked her bottom lip out.

"I love you too." Harper held up her wine glass for a toast. "Just know I want a mommy makeover, a baby moon, and 20 bands."

"Bitch," Marley laughed through her tears. She tapped her glass against her sister's.

"Just saying."

"Ok, I'm ready!" JJ ran back in the living holding a sheet. Marley and Harper turned to give him their full attention. "TT Marley, what kinda boyfriend do you want?"

"Aht aht, use ya mama for this trick." Marley shook her

head. "Messing around with you I might marry a frog for real."

"Stop it." Harper popped her. "Let my baby do his trick."

"Fine. Tall, handsome, smart, and someone to heal my broken heart."

"Ok, whisper it in your hand and put it in the sheet," JJ demanded, shaking it in front of her.

Playing along, Marley whispered in her hands and then wrapped it up in the sheets. JJ goofily grinned at her, while taking the sheet out of her hands. He mumbled a whole lot of gibberish and ran around in circles before throwing the sheet in the air.

"Now stand up and count to three," he requested.

"JJ."

"TT, stand upppp," he whined. "And close your eyes."

Marley passed Harper her glass and stood up. With her eyes closed, she slowly spun around three times. When she opened them JJ was standing next to the sheet, only this time there was a bulky figure under the sheet.

"Abracadabraaaaaaa," he yelled, snatching the sheet off Lucky. Harper spit her wine out, and Jaxon walked around the corner with a grin on his face. He didn't know why JJ asked to borrow Lucky, but now he understood, and he thought it was funny as hell.

"I found you a man." JJ pointed to a smiling Lucky.

"Your magic sucks!" Marley lowly growled. "I said tall."

"Get what you get and don't throw a fit!" He stuck his tongue out and ran around her.

"What's up, Marley," Lucky grinned, smiling harder than a Cheshire Cat.

"Nothing, how you been?" she asked, retaking her seat

next to Harper and snatching the wine glass out of her hand since she thought shit was so funny.

“Baby, come here for a minute,” Jaxon called out to his wife, and she happily jumped up, dodging her sister's hard stares.

“I’m straight. I see you out here dating celebrities and shit.” Lucky rubbed his sweaty hands down his pants.

“Something like that.”

“That’s what’s up, but if that nigga not acting right, let me know and I’ll beat that nigga ass.”

“Lucky, as nice as that is, I don’t involve other people in my situations.”

“Understandable.” He nodded, rubbing the back of his neck. “You mind if I kick it with you?”

“I’m really not on that kinda time.”

“I get it, but I really just wanted to tell you that I thought you were beautiful. Back when you were with that nigga Benny, I used to think you were too good for him.”

“Uh, thanks.” Marley shifted on the couch.

“I’m not trying to make you feel uncomfortable or no shit like that, just thought you should know that I'm happy you are moving on. You are shining and it’s a good look, I mean even if it’s not with me.”

“Thank you, Lucky. That was really sweet, and you’re a nice guy, but-

“No need to explain. Do you play spades?”

“I do.” Marley nodded.

“Aight, since I can’t have your pretty ass in my personal life, the least you can do is be my partner in spades.”

“I can do that,” she agreed. “And again, thank you, Lucky.” Marley stood up and stretched her arms out to hug him.

Lucky pushed up from the couch so fast he almost twisted his ankle. Taking her into his arms, he hugged her tight while taking a whiff of her hair.

"Fucking torture." He pulled away, making Marley laugh.

Harper returned and invited them both into the dining room where Jaxon had a deck of cards and a bottle of Hennessy waiting. Classic Jay-Z played in the background and there were a few snacks off to the side. Marley ditched her wine and was the first one to pick up a shot glass.

"Period, my sister said turn the fuck up!" Harper snapped her fingers, sitting her wine glass on the table. "Let's take a shot!"

"What we toasting to?" Lucky asked, following suit.

"To new fucking beginnings." Jaxon filled their glasses.

"I'll toast to that." Marley clinked glasses with everyone and tossed her shot to the back without flinching.

Between talking major shit and collecting books, Marley and Lucky tore Jaxon and Harper asses out of the frame. Every other hand, Marley got up and did a happy dance, sending them all into a fit of laughter. The more liquor she consumed, the more she showed out. When Harper switched the music and started playing Sexxy Red, the game was over. Together Marley and Harper danced around the living room using a brush and comb as microphones.

"Get it Marley, Get it Marley," Lucky chanted, discreetly recording her for his late-night beat session.

"Nigga, you know this song?" Jaxon frowned, getting up from the table.

"Yea, I make it a priority to listen to all the female rappers. Women love that shit," he gloated, pointing to Marley, who was now bent over, popping her ass.

"Where you going, bae?" Harper called after Jaxon. She

guessed the music was too loud because he kept walking with the phone pressed to his ear. Shrugging it off, she went back to hyping up her sister. It wasn't often that she got to see this side of Marley. She was usually so nonchalant and faded into the background, but tonight she was on one.

"Boy, you know this ass is super fat," Marley rapped.

"Nah, it's not, but I'll let you live, LB," Czar rounded the corner, interrupting her concert.

"Oop." Harper covered her mouth, finding the whole situation comical. If she had to guess, her husband sold her sister out. "She in trouble."

"Worry about how much trouble you're going to be in if you try that leaving shit again," Jaxon stated, causing Harper to redirect her focus.

"I thought we were over that."

"We're never going to be over it." He popped her on the ass.

Marley slowly turned around with a grin stretched across her lips. Despite the scowl on his face, she couldn't deny how good he looked. Czar always looked good and all she wanted to do was jump his bones.

"Oh shit!" Lucky squealed like a groupie, further proving why Marley would never take him seriously. "Bro, I love all your music."

"Oh yea?" Czar skirted around him with his eye on the prize. She hadn't acknowledged him, nor had she blinked since she heard his voice. "Why you playing with me?" He towered over her, pulling her toward him with the strings on her hoodie. The hood scrunched up around her face, temporarily blinding her.

"Stop." Marley slapped his hands away. "How did you find me?" she questioned, standing under his hard gaze.

"I never lost you." Czar tapped her nose. "You drunk?"

"Yep, and I don't even get drunk. I'd rather get high, but my scamming ass nephew is running around doing magic tricks so we can't smoke," she rambled, unconsciously leaning into him and placing her hand on his chest. His hand rested around her neck, keeping her close to him. "You know what I was thinking?"

"What?"

"That we were doomed from the start. How ironic is it that my shitty ass mama played in yall face? Like that evil ass lady tried to put yall out and I want to fight her."

"Baby, yo mama a big lady and I think she'll mangle your ass," Czar chuckled. "And then I'd have to pop her ass in the foot for fucking with my baby."

"You'd shoot my mama for me?"

"Calm down, Gypsy Rose."

"I'm serious, Julius. How do you even still want me?" Marley slurred. "I'm so blah, and you have your pickings of-

"Czar, do you want a shot?" Harper asked, holding up the bottle of liquor.

"Yea, I'll take one," he replied, never taking his eyes off Marley. "Let me tell you this one time." He placed his hand under her chin. "The reasons I want you have nothing to do with the outside world. You bring me a sense of peace that I want to live in forever. These bitches don't hold a candle to you. They never did. Tati, yo mama, and nobody else can dictate how I feel about you. I want you now." Czar kissed her lips. "And I want you tomorrow."

"You mad at me?" she whispered against his mouth.

"Nah, I'm irritated though."

"Why?"

"Because it's after midnight and you got me out here when I have shit to do tomorrow." He pulled back a little.

"You didn't have to come get me."

"Sleeping without you wasn't an option." Czar kissed her forehead, making her heart melt. "Did you get your shit off? You feeling better?"

"Here you go." Harper handed him and Marley a shot.

"A little, but it doesn't change anything. I don't want to be caught up in the middle of your baby mama drama."

"We'll talk about the rest later, you ready to leave?" He lifted his shot glass to her lips. Like a good girl, Marley tilted her head back and Czar emptied the liquor into her mouth. Before she could swallow it, his lips were on hers, and the warm liquor danced between their mouths until it evenly slipped down their throats.

"Bae! Give me a shot like that!" Harper belted, catching the intimate moment out the side of her eye.

"Fuck nah, I don't even know how they kept the liquor in their mouth without it spilling." Jaxon waved her off.

"I'm ready." Marley wiped the corner of his lips.

"Come on." He took the last shot from her and downed it before setting the glasses on the table. "Good looking, Jaxon. I owe you."

"We even." Jaxon stuck his hand out for a pound.

"Y'all have a good night." Czar wrapped his arm around Marley.

"Good nighttttttt," she sang, falling into stride with him.

"Call me when you get home," Harper called out.

"She'll call you tomorrow," Czar butted in, not giving Marley a chance to answer. If he had it his way, Marley's mouth was going to be full of nuts.

Once they were in the car, Czar reached in the back seat and handed Marley a folder and a small gift bag. She took it from him but rolled her eyes. This was how it always started and she wasn't feeling it. Drunk and all, Czar was going to hear her mouth because throwing his money at a situation wouldn't make it go away. As far as she was concerned, Tati was still a problem she wasn't willing to deal with.

"I don't want this." Marley pushed the gifts back into his hands.

"You don't even know what it is."

"And I don't want to know. You know what, Julius? I had some time to think, and I don't think I wanna do this relationship thing. You can take me to my Loft and leave me the keys," Marley slurred.

"Shut up and open the folder."

"What, you bought me some stocks and bonds?"

"LB, stop fucking with me and open the fucking folder," Czar fussed as he gripped the steering wheel.

"Fine." Marley snatched it back. She cut on the lights and slowly read over the papers. By the time she got to the end, she was smiling, but Czar's face still held a mean mug.

"Get the bag," he demanded. This time Marley didn't say anything; she picked up the bag. Reaching inside, she pulled out a small spray bottle and frowned.

"Numbing spray?" She squinted.

"You had me running around breaking laws and tracking your phone all for some shit I didn't have any control over."

"Julius-

"Shut up," he cut her off. "If this shit gone work then you gotta trust me. I'm in an industry where a bitch can say I fucked her, and if you believe that hoe over me, I'mma have

Sammy beat both of yall asses."

"I'mma pepper spray the shit outta her wild ass. I'm sorry I left," Marley pouted.

"Yea yea. Come eat this dick and I might forgive you."

Removing her seatbelt, Marley crawled over the console and unbuckled his pants. Removing his semi-hard dick, she looked into his eyes and licked her lips.

"I don't need that spray shit," she cooed, lowering her head.

"That's what the fuck I'm talking about," Czar growled, relighting his blunt. Pressing play on the steering wheel, he sat back as *All We Do* by Young Jeezy played at a low volume.

Chapter 22

A couple of weeks later, Marley woke up with a long to-do list. Czar's birthday party was later that evening and she still needed to find something to wear and get her nails and toes done. She had to pick up his gift from the jeweler and then make it back in time to get ready for the dinner that started at seven. Marley prayed that everything worked out the way it was supposed to because time was never on her side. Rolling out of the bed, she slipped on a pair of Czar's slides and went into the ensuite bathroom.

Flicking on the light, Marley glanced at her reflection in the mirror. Her wild mane was all over her head and the sleep caked in the corners of her eyes was evidence of how hard she slept. Hanging in the studio with Czar until the wee hours of the morning was starting to catch up to her. While it was fun and she enjoyed watching him in his element, she was losing out on her beauty sleep. Czar wasn't trying to hear it though. He swore he worked better when she was by his side.

Opening the cabinet, Marley reached for her toothbrush but spotted a post-it note on the shelf instead right next to it.

"The hell?" she mumbled, squinting at the tiny writing.

Today starts my yes day. Go get your phone and wish a nigga happy birthday since you were snoring like a grizzly bear when I left.

Marley laughed to herself and balled up the note before continuing her morning routine. She washed her face, brushed her teeth, and combed her messy hair. Slathering some coconut oil on her face and lips, Marley went back into the bedroom and picked up her phone. Instead of calling Czar, she clicked the icon to FaceTime him.

"You hardheaded." His deep voice flowed through the phone as soon as he picked up. "I told you to call me first."

"Happy Birthday, Julius," Marley cooed. "Why didn't you wake me up before you left?"

"Thank you, LB, and you sounded like you need the rest."

"I did," she agreed. "Where are you?"

"On my way to the barbershop to get a lineup."

"I'll never understand how you're so rich, but so normal. You couldn't have your barber come to the house?"

"I could have, but I have some shit planned for you and you're going to need the space. My chef is coming to make you breakfast."

"Wait, it's your birthday, why are you getting me a chef? I actually wanted to cook for you."

"I'm straight. You can make me carrot bacon and mud patties next time. I need to make sure you stay fueled because I'm going to wear your ass out tonight."

"You are ignorant," Marley giggled. "I don't eat carrot bacon asshole."

"Yea, yea, the Chef will be there in thirty minutes. Call your sister and have her chill with you. After breakfast a stylist is going to come through and match our outfits, and she'll also bring a few pieces of jewelry,"

"Julius, I don't need you to spend your money on me. I have something to wear," she sighed, but her comment fell on deaf ears. Czar was serious about her shittin' on haters, aka Tati and her band of followers. Daily they were in Marley's DM's calling her all sorts of names, commenting on everything she posted, and comparing her to Tati. The body shame was the worst. Marley wasn't insecure about her body, and she thanked God for that, but the internet bullies were relentless. If they weren't judging her natural puffy hair, they were talking about her slender frame, swearing she needed a BBL and breast implants. It was as if having a real body was frowned upon.

Marley wasn't materialistic, and she loved her knitted outfits, leggings, and sweatshirts, but Czar wasn't having it. In one weekend, he filled her closet with everything from Fendi, Prada, and Chanel to Glamaholic, House of Ki, and more. Marley had more purses and shoes than she knew what to do with.

"Shut up. It's my birthday, and if I want to trick on you, then let me do me."

"You're right, and since you're trickin,' I want matching iced-out chains," Marley joked.

"It's nothing."

"I'm kidding, Julius! You better not get me a damn chain."

"Hm hm." Czar ignored her while he texted his jeweler. "I'll see you, LB. I'm about to ice you the fuck out!"

"Bye."

After stuffing their faces and working with the stylist, Marley and Harper were out of the house with Biggie in tow. Security- another thing Czar implemented. Marley was no longer able to leave the house by herself, and it was for her own safety. He didn't trust people, and now that her tea website was getting way more traction, that came with an increased number of haters. Harper was also feeling it because Jaxon stayed on her ass about up and leaving without him.

"What do you think?" Marley asked, holding the pendant up for Biggie to look at it.

The iced-out microphone diamond-encrusted pendant was breathtaking. It wasn't over the top or outrageously big. She hoped he liked it because it was one of the biggest purchases she'd ever bought, but Czar deserved it. He was so giving, and all she wanted to do was pour right back into him. He swore her presence was enough, but Marley wanted to put a little extra on top.

"He's going to love that shit." Biggie nodded in approval.

"That's what I said," Harper cosigned, popping a bite-sized donut into her mouth.

"Gimme one." Biggie reached over, taking the bag from her without waiting for an answer.

"My God, you're like a damn toddler, always want a damn snack." She dusted the cinnamon off her hands. "And ain't security supposed to be like five steps back? You all in the mix."

"Leave Biggie alone," Marley snickered. "He's fine."

"She only saying that shit because I be letting her test out them tea masks on my face."

"I hope you don't be trying to eat them."

"I'll eat you," Biggie quipped with a wink.

"Anyway, why Mama been trying to reach out to me," Harper grunted. "I've blocked her on every device in the house and she still calling private."

"Well, you know you did a lot for her. I'm sure she realizes that she needs you," Marley guessed. "You were helping her with bills and driving her around like an Uber."

"I thought I was playing my part in the cycle of life. We all have to get old and I don't want bad karma because I shitted on my mama."

"And in another situation, I might agree with you, but Mama has *been* a manipulative, shady ass person. I used to think it was because she was lonely and had low self-esteem, but that has nothing to do with it. She's naturally a hater and never wants anyone else doing better than her, including her own daughters. She's a user and I've given her too many passes. She wishes death on me at every turn, and parent or not, I don't need that kind of energy around me."

"I guess I was hoping she'd change," Harper sighed.

"And I get that, but Mama is who she is, and while we want her to change, she's always shown us who she really is."

"Mm. Well, I don't have anything to say to her. She better lean on her church folks for help. We've greased that collection plate a few times. She better ask for a little of that back."

"You stupid," Marley snickered. She almost felt bad for her sister. Harper really loved their mama and it showed. While she was pissed off with her, deep down Harper hoped it wasn't anything too serious going on. Whereas Marley blocked her and hadn't thought about her since the day she walked out of her loft.

"Things between you and Czar are going well." Harper bumped her shoulder.

"They are." Marley smiled coyly. "He's crazy as hell, but he's fun and being with him is like a breath of fresh air."

"I love it. I was scrolling on Instagram yesterday and I saw a picture of yall pop up. I think it was a repost from Czar's page. You were in the bed knocked out and he was sitting next to you playing the game and smoking."

"He always posting pictures of me."

"It was cute though. I was like look at my little sister all in love and shit."

"Hm... love?" Marley cocked her head to the side.

"I mean that's what it looks like to me... shit, to the world. You took him to meet Billie. That's major."

Marley tucked her lip into her mouth. Taking Czar to visit Billie's grave wasn't planned. In fact, she tried to leave while he was at the studio, but unbeknownst to Marley, he left his phone at the house. When he returned, Marley was coming down the elevator crying. She tried to dry her face, but it was too late. Czar ended up driving her to the cemetery. He planned to stay in the car, but Marley asked him to come with her. It was cold as hell, but he sat there while she cried, and laughed while updating her daughter on everything going on in her life.

"I-

"Oh shit, Mars," a deep voice called out across the mall, causing Marley to halt her steps. The hairs on the back of her neck stood up. She hadn't heard that name in years and only people who were associated with Benny called her that.

"It's me, Tech." He tried to walk up on her, but Biggie stuck his hand out, preventing him from getting too close. "Nigga don't touch me," Tech barked.

"Then back the fuck up before I toss yo ass over the banister," Biggie barked.

"Damn, Mars, you got secret service now?" he joked, backing up.

"Uh, hey Tech," she forced out with a small smile.

"Damn girl, you look good." Tech eyes roamed over her, checking out the ice on her wrist and neck. "Lookin' like you hit a lick," he joked.

"I uh- I haven't seen you in years. Since uh-

"Yea, I moved to Ohio after all that shit went down. The streets were hot and shit didn't feel right without my boy."

"Oh, ok."

"What's up, Harper? You looking good." Tech's eyes roamed over to her. "Still thick as fuck."

"And you still look like you don't wash your hands," she snapped. "Marley, come on, we have things to do."

"You still funny," Tech laughed out loud.

"Um, Tech, I'll see you around. I have to go." Marley started walking away.

"Yea, you'll see me," he promised, bopping away.

Marley didn't know what that comment meant, but she wasn't feeling it. All of a sudden, she felt uneasy and was ready to go home. Anxiety was already kicking her ass, and she didn't know how she was supposed to get through the party when she couldn't even survive a trip to the mall.

When Biggie dropped Marley off at Czar's place, he was sitting at the bar, shirtless with a blunt hanging from his lips. Marley's eyes openly roamed over his body, taking in his smooth dark skin, chiseled chest, and sleepy-like eyes. The gold Cuban link chain complimented his skin while the diamonds twinkled under the dim lights. Marley didn't know how she resisted him for so long because now whenever they were in the same room, she folded.

"You gone stand over there being a creep or come catch this smoke?" Czar asked, running his tongue across his bottom lip. Kicking off her shoes, Marley placed his gift on the couch and made her way over to him. Czar filled his mouth with smoke and Marley lightly grabbed his chin, pulling his mouth to hers, catching all the smoke.

"What's up, LB?" Czar licked his lips, tasting her minty gloss.

"Nothing, happy to be back here," she sighed, climbing on the counter in front of him.

"You good?"

"I'm ok."

"Who was the nigga at the mall?" he asked, taking in her energy. It was off and that bothered him. He couldn't be peaceful if she wasn't.

"Damn, Biggie called you in the car?"

"Don't worry about it, answer my question."

"He was Benny's friend."

"And why was he in your face?"

"It was my first time seeing him since everything happened. Benny's family buried him while I was still in the hospital, and I haven't seen any of them in years. It's like they all fell off the side of the earth when he died and now I've been randomly seeing them. Like I saw his aunt a couple of months ago. It's just weird."

"It bothered you?" Czar rubbed her thighs.

"Yes, a lot, and I can't shake the way he was looking at me."

"How the fuck was he looking at you?"

"Like he knew something I didn't. It just made me feel

uncomfortable." Marley shivered as if she could still feel his eyes on her.

"You want me to take care of him?"

"You better stop offering to knock people off for me. We'll be on the run messing around with me."

"Just say the word."

"No." Marley shook her head. "I want you to take care of me. I feel stressed and I need to release or it's going to be a long night. I'd normally flick the bean, but I figured since I'm in a relationship, you could do the honors."

"Oh yea?" Czar grinned, ashing the blunt. "What do you want?"

"I want you to jump my bones." She grinned.

"I can do that." He stood up, swooping her off the counter.

∞∞∞

After sucking and fucking each other to sleep, Marley and Czar woke up refreshed and ready to party. Pregaming with friends was one thing, but pregaming with your man was a whole vibe and Marley enjoyed it. While they got dressed, Czar's music played in the background and every so often he'd rap to her while feeding her shots. It was like having her very own concert and she loved it.

"Aye, come here for a minute," Czar called out from the living room.

Dressed in a black thong and matching mesh bra, Marley checked her hair one last time before heading to the front of the apartment. To her surprise, he had three black gift bags lined up on the counter. From the grin on his face, Marley knew he was on bullshit, and because she agreed to his dumb ass *yes day,* she had to roll with the punches.

"What's this?" She defensively folded her arms across her chest.

"Vibrating panties, an anal plug, and Ben Wa Balls."

"I'm not putting any of that on or *in* me."

"Come on now, LB. You promised me a *yes day*,'" he grinned. "Pick a number between one and three."

"Julius, you can't be serious. What if I pick the freaking butt plug, how am I supposed to sit down with that thing up my ass?"

"Fuck if I know. Stand up all night. Pick a number."

"I can't believe I agreed to this."

"This is the easy part. Wait until tonight… I'm going to enjoy you."

"You've been enjoying me since I gave in to you," she mumbled.

"And I'm going to keep enjoying you. Stop deflecting and pick a number."

"Ugh," Marley groaned, stepping closer to inspect the bags, but nothing stood out. "Two."

"Pick it up," Czar instructed.

Skeptically, Marley picked up the bag and shook it. Still, she couldn't figure out what it was, so she dumped out the contents and immediately started shaking her head.

"Julius, you got me fucked up if you think you're about to put that dog toy shit up my ass."

"Those are Ben Wa Balls. I got the one attached to a string and there are only two balls," Czar recited as if he was doing her a favor. "Bend over."

"Wait!" Marley snapped. "I have questions. Where do they

go?"

"In your pussy."

"And how do they stay there?"

"You have to clinch. Keep them in place. I'll set a timer and pull them out after four hours."

"Yea," she laughed uncontrollably. "If I didn't know before, I know now. You got me fucked up if you think I'm about to walk around with a chew toy in my pussy. Not only do I have to walk around with it, but you want me to squeeze it to keep it in place, what the fuck! Give me the panties."

"Too late. We'll save that for a later date. You're thinking about it too much, just bend over."

"Julius, I swear to God if these things get lost inside my coochie, I'm going to kill you," Marley hissed, bending over.

Czar removed the Ben Wa Balls from the package and went to rinse them off. When he returned, Marley was bent over the couch with her thong pushed to the side. The sight of her fat pussy from the back made his mouth water and Czar couldn't help himself. He got on his knees and buried his face between her cheeks. Sucking and slurping, Czar munched on her pussy like it was the sweetest thing he ever tasted.

"You ready?" he asked, rubbing the cool balls down her slit.

"Yes," Marley moaned.

"You gone be my little freak bitch?" Czar kissed her ass cheek.

"Yessss."

"Say it."

"I'm going to be your little freak bitch," she purred as he pushed the first ball into her and then the second. For good measure, Czar sucked her pussy a little more and then popped her on the ass.

"Stand up."

"I'm scared."

"Come on, they won't fall. We gotta finish getting ready. Everyone is waiting."

"Don't act like it's my fault when you're the one up here sticking foreign shit up my ass," she sassed, getting up.

"Shut up." Czar slapped her on the ass.

"Ah," Marley whined, feeling the balls shift.

"This shit about to be fun as fuck." He moved around her to finish getting dressed.

Twenty minutes later Czar was ready, sitting at the bar waiting for Marley. She swore she was almost done, but every time he went into the room she was bent over panting. The slightest movement caused the balls to shift and Marley was on the brink of cumming. She didn't how she was supposed to last four hours when walking around the bedroom was a challenge.

To kill time, Czar propped his phone up on the stand while he talked to his followers on Instagram. At their request, Czar popped the top to his liquor and took a couple of shots with them while answering a couple of questions.

"My predictions for the Super Bowl?" Czar squinted, reading the screen and then sat back. "Shit, I'm hoping the Lions do what the fuck they were supposed to last season. They owe the city a win," he answered.

"Marley is in the room," Czar replied to someone asking where she was at. "Get the fuck outta here. She getting dressed, why would I take the phone in there? Yall niggas weird and I'm convinced yall be on some Peeping Tom type shit."

"I'm ready," Marley announced, slowly walking down the hallway.

Czar turned to check her out and was caught off guard. He knew Marley could dress her ass off when she wanted to, but the beauty before him took his breath away. Gliding toward him in a pair of four-inch heels, Marley's slender legs appeared longer than normal. The black dress hugged her body and stopped above her knees. There was a cute, oval cut around the stomach, exposing her navel and belly ring. Marley's hair was slicked back into a big curly ponytail and her edges swooped and framed her face. The makeup she wore was light but noticeable.

"What do you think?" Marley asked, spinning around to show off the back of the dress.

"LB," Czar bit his lip, "The fuck you trying to do because I'll get a jet and take you all around the world if that's what you want."

"I'm guessing you like it?" She giggled.

"What the fuck they be saying on TikTok?" he asked his Live, picking up the phone to show off his girl. "Can we get a little commotion for the dress? Give them a 360 baby."

Slowly doing as she was told, Marley spun around. The backless dress dipped and stopped right about her butt crack. Czar thought his eyes were playing tricks on him when he saw the silver charms on her thong spell out his name.

"I'm about to cancel all this shit," he said as he grabbed his dick.

"Nope, we're going out. Goodbye Julius' Live." Marley walked toward him and ended the video.

"You look good as fuck, baby." He kissed her glossy lips.

"Thank you."

"Oh wait. I have a gift for you." She tried to run back to the room, but the balls shifted. Making her gasp for air. "Oh my god," Marley moaned.

"You good?" Czar chortled.

"Fuck you," she mumbled, standing up straight.

Seconds later, Marley returned with a gift bag and handed it to him.

"This don't feel like a Target gift card." He shook the bag.

"Boy, it's not, open the gift." Marley rolled her eyes. She didn't know why she was so nervous, but she was. Butterflies swarmed around in her stomach as he pulled out the Diamond's Vault box.

"Straight up?" He smirked at her.

"Stop being extra." She waved him off.

Czar opened the box and a smile as long as the Nile River stretched across his face. Removing the pendant, he held it in his hand. It was the perfect size.

"How many bags of tea you sell for this?"

"A lot."

"Come here." He pulled her into his arms. "This shit is hard, LB. Thank you." He kissed her lips. "I fucking love it. I love you," Czar confessed, surprised that the words slipped from his lips with ease. Marley was stunned and the only thing she could do was kiss him back.

"Aye, I got something for you too." Czar released her, jogging back to the kitchen. He reached behind the bar and grabbed a neatly wrapped gift box.

"If that's another sex toy, I'm going to flip out," Marley promised, watching him approach her.

"Chill." He handed her the bag. "That lil pussy safe for now."

Marley took the box and gently pulled the ribbon off.

She didn't know what to expect. Czar was full of surprises, and with him, she was learning to tread lightly. His freaky ass would have her hanging from the ceiling while he masturbated on her toes.

"Seriously?" Her eyes watered at the rose gold 14ct Cuban link necklace.

"Seriously." Czar removed it from the box and carefully placed it on her neck.

"But it's your birthday."

"And you're the best gift I ever had. Gimme a kiss and say thank you Julius."

"Thank you, Julius," Marley purred, leaning in to kiss him. "It's beautiful."

"I know. Let's go stunt on muthafuckas, LB."

Czar's birthday dinner party was a private event that Ada took the honor of planning. It was located in Novi at a newly remodeled banquet hall. The guest list included a few of Czar's labelmates, Terri, his brothers, Biggie, Shortie, Sammy, Pooh, Jaxon, Harper, and Marley. Ada hired Carniece, one of the best event planners in Detroit to decorate the space, and a chef she found on Instagram. The cream and gold decor was fit for a king, and the food was even better. They feasted on lobster tails, steak, potatoes, pasta salad, and more. Ada also made sure there were plenty of options available for Marley since she didn't eat anything on the original menu. A variety of music played in the background, but it was drowned out by loud chatter and laughter.

"Aight, shut up." Nova stood up, clinking his glass, trying to get everyone's attention.

“Nigga, this ain’t no fucking wedding,” Romeo jested, causing the room to laugh.

“Fuck outta here, I just got something to say, and I’d rather say it while my brother still kicking versus standing at a podium expressing my feelings to a corpse.”

“Ain’t nobody dying today,” Ada refuted.

“I mean we don’t know that for sure. Tomorrow isn’t promised,” Nova reasoned, turning to face Czar. “Bro, I don’t know if you know this, but I look up to you and been doing it since I was a kid. You do a lot of shit that people aren’t aware of, from donating money to homeless shelters to putting your whole family on. You’ve put us in situations where we’ll make money for years to come. Bro, you created an empire. You didn’t just give us shit, you taught us how to make money that makes money. I see the shit you do around the community. You’re creating a legacy that will be talked about for years to come. You are one of the most loyal people I know, and I’m happy as fuck the stars aligned and put us in the same universe at the same time. I love you nigga, now and tomorrow.”

“Aww,” the room cooed, watching Czar get up and pull his brother into a hug.

“I love you too, bro,” Czar patted his back.

“Here’s my gift.” Nova dropped a set of keys in his palm. “You don’t like having a lot of cars, so I bought you a different type of toy.”

“A four-wheeler?” Czar grinned, holding up the key chain.

“A four fuckin’ wheeler! We all got one and when the weather breaks, we out this bitch! Happy Birthday, bro.”

Nova giving out his gift opened the door for everyone else to start giving him theirs. Czar received everything from cash to jewelry and a couple of paid vacations. The label had gone all out and bought him a Corvette, which Romeo called dibs on. The dinner was perfect, but Czar couldn't help but watch his Mama. She was sitting next to Slim and they were talking, but she seemed out of it. Like her body was there, but her mind was elsewhere. Czar had even seen her texting on her phone. When she noticed he was looking, she smiled and put her phone away. He didn't know what kind of shit she was up to, but something told him it wasn't good.

"Aight, the party bus is outside. Let's take this party to the club!" Nova voiced, ready to turn the fuck up!

"You good?" Czar whispered in Marley's ear, noticing that she was twisting the bracelet on her wrist.

"I haven't been to a club in years and I'm kinda nervous," she admitted, gazing down at her hands.

"Aye." He placed his finger underneath her chin, prompting Marley to lift her head and stare into his eyes. "I'll never put you in a position where you have to question your safety. You trust me?"

"A lil bit," she teased.

"Keep playing and I'll put your pretty ass out of my shit."

"Don't threaten me with a good time. I live for canceled plans."

"So you not trying to live it up with yo nigga?"

"I am." Her heart skipped a beat.

"Then let's do it." He grabbed her hand and stood up.

Marley had been to the club plenty of times. It was nothing for Benny to rent out a section and buy a couple of bottles for his squad. She was used to being in the back of the club standing on the couch popping her ass to the music while Benny posted up next to her, daring a nigga to step out of line. She was familiar with the hateful glares from jealous hoes and hating ass niggas. With all that being said, this was different.

The second they exited the party bus, Marley felt presidential. Everyone was calling their names for pictures, people who couldn't get in wanted autographs, and others simply watched on in awe. Czar stopped and posed for a couple of pictures with Marley at his side. She was always the center of his focus. Knowing how she felt about crowds, Czar made sure to keep her close.

"Aight, that's enough." He ended their photoshoot. With his hand on Marley's lower back, Czar guided her through the door.

"Walk slow," she moaned.

"How yo pussy feel?"

"Like I'm ready to go home so you can fuck me with your chains on."

"Stop saying shit like that." Czar adjusted his dick as they entered the club.

"Surpriseeeeeeeee," the crowd shouted out when the DJ announced his arrival.

"Fuck outta here. Y'all posted this shit on Twitter." He waved the crowd off, causing them to laugh.

Czar knew when he put his brothers in charge of his party that the idea of having something small went out the window. For them, that's what the dinner was for. Nova rented out Eastwood and paid Bone, a very well-known party promoter, to host. The theme was *Harlem Nights* and the decorator understood the assignment. Gold and black balloons were spread throughout the room, along with fake Tommy guns, feathers, and pearls. Czar's three-tier cake sat on a table surrounded by all kinds of goodies, including edibles. There were at least three photo booths and a 360 booth that had a line. Finger foods like wings, small sandwiches, and vegetables covered one table, while another one had strictly vegan items.

"Happy Birthday muthafucka!" Bone shouted. "Get this man a bottle, pass him the smoke!"

Czar was already fucked up from pregaming and the dinner, but it was his birthday and turning down a bottle wasn't something he planned on doing. Marley tried to fall into the background, but Czar wouldn't let her. If she wasn't talking to Harper and Sammy, she was sitting right under him. It was his birthday, but he catered to her. Czar poured her drinks and passed her blunts that only they shared. Everything around them was moving fast, but they were so wrapped up in one another that nothing else mattered. Czar planted himself behind Marley and draped his arm around her neck. Time had flew by, and before either of them knew it, two hours had passed.

"I'm fucked up," Czar whispered in Marley's ear while his hand clutched her waist.

"You wanna leave?" she asked, ready to cut out early.

"Nah." He kissed her neck. "Did I tell you how good you look?"

"Nope." Marley shook her head.

"You a damn lie, but if you wanna hear it again, I think you're gorgeous. I think your lil mean ass is the baddest, and I'm feeling the fuck outta you." He kissed her jawline.

"Julius, please. You're drunk." She blushed, unraveling with every drunken word that slipped from his lips.

"You want a grand gesture?" He stepped back as *Lovers and Friends* started playing in the club. "I'mma sing to the pussy. That's what you want, baby?"

"Got me feenin' like Jodeci, girl I can't leave you alone," Czar cooed.

"You need to stop." Marley turned her head to hide the grin that threatened to stretch across her face with every word he sang. To her surprise, he sounded good. Panty dropping good.

"VIP done got way too crowded, I'm about to end up calling it a night," Czar loudly sang, extending his hand in her direction.

"Sing that shit, B-law," Sammy cheered while Romeo recorded the moment. This was a first for them. They knew their brother was feeling Marley, but public affection was something they'd never seen. Czar was letting the world know what it was. Harper stood amongst the crowd, gazing at her sister. This was not the same woman from six months ago. This version of her sister was happy.

"Cause once you get inside you can't change your mind, don't mean to sound impatient, but you gotta promise baby." Czar pulled Marley to him and buried his head in the crook of her neck while the entire club watched them in awe. Czar was so in the zone that he didn't know every woman in a ten-mile radius was swooning and clutching their chest. Marley tried to act unfazed, but she was all in. Czar had her on cloud nine and she never wanted to come down.

"You think you're soooo smooth," Marley said, staring into his low eyes.

"Something like that. You ready to get outta here?"

"See, now you're speaking my love language. I need to use the bathroom and then I'll be ready."

"Come on, I'll take you down." Czar grabbed her hand.

"No, I'll take my sister. Say bye to your guests and I'll meet you at the bar in ten." Marley pecked his lips.

"Gimme another one," he demanded, holding her hand.

Doing as she was told, Marley wrapped her hands around Czar's neck. She playfully puckered her lips before pressing them to his. Czar pulled her bottom lip between his teeth and lightly bit down on it before slipping his tongue in her mouth.

"Hurry up." He popped her on the ass, reminding her about the life-changing balls moving around inside of her. "And you better not take them out."

"Don't rush me," Marley sassed, twisting away from him. "Come to the bathroom with me." She grabbed her sister's hand.

"Where yall going?" Jaxon asked, standing up to go with them.

"We're fine, love, just going to the bathroom," Harper called over her shoulder.

The bathroom on the VIP level had a line that wrapped around the section, and there was no way Marley was standing in it, so she led them out of the section. Downstairs, the club was way more packed, and it had Marley second-guessing her decision. When she tried to turn around, something wet spilled on her dress.

"What the fuck?" She jumped back.

"Oh my bad." Tati held her chest. "Did I mess up your little thrift store dress?"

"I swear yo dumb ass got me fucked up," Harper snapped, but Marley stopped her from swinging.

"You're like a fucking roach. Where the fuck do you be coming from?" she asked Tati.

"I guess because Czar spent a lil money on you, you think you all that," Tati scoffed.

"Not at all because I'm all that in Crocs and biker shorts,

but you know that."

"I can't wait until he plays your dumb ass. Industry niggas don't commit."

"Nah," Marley disagreed. "They don't commit to you… and lil baby, we are not the same."

"Aye." Biggie stepped between them. "Let's go." He touched Marley's shoulder. "C said go to the bar."

"Damn, and you got his security running to your rescue. You must be fucking them all." Tati threw her head back in laughter. Before either of them saw it coming, Marley slipped around Biggie and punched Tati in the throat. Her laughing turned to choking, and Marley used the opportunity to step over her, delivering a quick kick to her coochie.

"Bitch, you better be lucky I got these Ben Wa Balls up my ass, or I'd drag your desperate ass all around this fucking club," Marley snapped, watching security carry out a crying Tati.

"You got what?" Harper gawked, and Biggie started choking on his salvia.

"Julius and his stupid ass *yes day*," Marley scoffed, heading back to the section, but Czar was stalking toward her. He didn't know how Tati got in, but he had something for her ass because he was done with all the extra shit.

"We leaving?" Marley asked.

"Yea, you aight?"

"I'm great," she promised. "My body is so confused. It don't know whether to cum or fight."

"Bring yo ass on then. It's time to take them out and you down here about to fight." Czar popped her on the ass, causing the balls to jump.

"Stopppp," Marley moaned. "I hope I cracked the hoe windpipe."

"Fuck that girl, I don't even know how she got in here. I'm ready to fuck the shit out of you," Czar whispered in her ear.

"No," Marley spun around and wrapped her arms around his neck. "It's your birthday. You're going to sit back and allow me to put this pussy on you."

"No shy shit tonight?" He cocked his head to the side.

"Nope, I'm going to be your lil freak bitch," she cooed and licked his lips.

Chapter 23

"LB." Czar tapped Marley's thigh. "Get up, baby."

"Julius, no, I'm sore and my mouth hurts," she whined, pulling the cover over her head.

"Aww, my lil baby can't take the dick?" Czar teased.

It was two days after his birthday party and Marley was still feeling the effects of his *yes day*. Just like she knew he would, Czar took advantage of having his way with her. They fucked all over his place, including in the jacuzzi while it snowed. Marley's titties felt like icicles as she bounced on his dick, but she didn't stop. The only time he left her side was to get some food, and Marley thanked God for the small break. She was almost tempted to tell Harper to bring her some melatonin to put his ass to sleep because her body needed a break.

"The dick isn't the problem. It's the extra shit. I've never in my life had so many objects in me at once."

"Chill," Czar chuckled. "I didn't even put the butt plug all the way in because you kept whining. *Julius, it's too big. Wait, I have to poop, Julius, you're going to make me shit on your dick.*"

"Whatever, what time is it? I thought you had a flight," Marley snickered.

"I do, so get up so we can get this shit started."

"Wait, I'm not going with you. I told you I don't do concerts."

"And I told you that I got you, LB. You're safe with me. It's ok to let your guard down and live a little. Let me show you some superstar shit." He snatched the covers off of her. "Plus, it's not that kind of concert. Some rich ass nigga hired me to perform at his son's sweet sixteen in The Maldives."

"Shut up!" Marley set up, grabbing her chest. "Like as in Asia, the country?"

"Not the lil spot on the corner of 8 Mile that sells fish dinners," he joked.

"Julius."

"Yea girl, Asia. Get up so we can go. They're sending a jet and it'll be at the Detroit City Airport in two hours."

"Two hours?" Marley gasped. "I don't have a passport though," she slouched. The thought of traveling to another country sounded good, but without a passport, it was just that, a thought.

"You do." Czar reached in his back pocket and pulled out the book. "I had Harper take care of it a couple of weeks ago. It was delivered yesterday, but if it wasn't on time, I would've packed your ass in my carry-on."

"But how did she do it? Didn't I need to be there?"

"Sweetheart, you can buy a kidney off the internet. You don't think getting someone a passport is just as easy?"

"So I'm going to Asia?"

"Yea, as soon as you get up and handle yo business. Morning breath is real." He covered his nose.

"Oh my God!" Marley crawled to the edge of the bed and jumped into his arms. "I-

"You what?" Czar pulled her close to him. "You love me?"

The question caused her heart rate to speed up and the nervousness was displayed across her face. At a loss for words, Marley's gaze fell to the floor.

"I-I'm going to go take a shower so we can get this show on the road," she murmured.

"You do that. Don't pack shit though because we'll get new everything."

"How long will we be gone?"

"A week. We'll stop twice but only to refuel."

"Is this real?"

"It will be as soon as you get up and brush your gums." Czar tapped her chin.

"My breath stank for real?" Marley backed away from him.

"Nah, I'm fucking with you. Go get ready." He popped her on the ass before bopping out of the room.

Marley fell backwards on the pillows and screamed in the blanket. She couldn't believe it. Their first trip together wasn't going to be the typical Miami, Las Vegas, or Atlanta. The man was taking her to Asia. The Maldives! Sliding out of the bed, Marley danced her way to the bathroom, anticipating all the fun that was sure to come.

"Oh, fuck no. Nigga, I said you could come, not her." Czar frowned, getting out of the truck. He reached back to help Marley, who was looking at the private jet in awe. It wasn't as big as a regular plane, but she could tell from the design on the wings that it was luxurious.

"I told him," Nova snorted, heading to the stairs. "You never take sand to the beach."

"And did." Sammy popped her lips, switching up the stairs while Romeo struggled to carry their bags. She was dressed in a long mink fur with the matching earmuffs and thigh-high boots. As far as she was concerned, she was too fabulous to carry her own bags. "I'm the sand, the beach, and the fucking concession stand. Come on, LB, let's get on this jet and enjoy our flight on some rich bitch shit. You be acting scared to spend C's money, but I'mma savage with Ro's money."

"Nigga, you ok with that shit?" Nova inquired, looking at his brother for answers. Romeo shrugged because Sammy had access to his accounts and moved money around frequently.

"And is," Sammy answered for him, stepping on the jet. "His job is to make sure I'm happy, and mine is to make sure I'm everything these streets aren't."

"Let 'em know, baby." Romeo stepped in behind her, handing his luggage to the flight attendant.

"Yesss," she cooed, checking out the jet. "Nova, take my picture."

"No, tell yo nigga to take it." He bypassed her.

"Funny looking ass," Sammy spat.

"Bro, if they put her ass out the country, you on your own," Czar warned Romeo as he guided Marley up the steps.

"B-law, please. I know how to behave, thank you very much. LB, let's sit up front."

"Nah, she straight."

"Ew, why can't she sit with me?"

"Because you're not supposed to even be on this muthafucka," Czar returned.

"If you don't want me to go, just say that." Sammy pushed her mink to the side and placed her hand on her hip.

"I don't want you to go," Nova and Czar said in unison and then burst out laughing, along with Marley and Romeo.

"Too bad. Yall going to The Maldives. I'm in that thang." She stuck her tongue out. Sammy didn't take offense to their response. She had been around long enough to know they loved her, whether they wanted to admit it or not.

"I'm about to go talk to the pilot. We're in the back." Czar touched Marley's hip, pointing at the two big seats in the back.

"Ok." She nodded, moving through the cabin to take her seat.

Pulling out her phone, Marley snapped a few pictures of the interior that almost looked too pretty to touch. The cream and peanut butter leather seats were soft and reclined into twin-size beds. Each seat was equipped with a blanket, pillow, sleeping mask, socks, and sleepy-time tea. There was only one TV in the front that extended from the ceiling, along with a DVD player and tons of movies.

Marley sent her sister a couple of pictures before sitting back in her seat. Seconds later, her phone vibrated, and of course, it was a text message from Harper.

Sister: I'm gagging! You're about to go mingle with rich people and I'm at JJ's school talking about this dumb ass Christmas play. Everybody wants their kid to be Santa and all I want to do is go to the car and hit my joint.

Marley laughed out loud and replied.

Just wanted to say thank you for what you did. I love you and please don't get kicked off school property for smoking.

Sister: You're welcome! Have fun and bring me back a gift. Oh and I can't make any promises. This bitch Holly talking about her son wanna be Santa and because she donated to the school library it shouldn't be a problem. Like bitch your son eats paper. Stop fucking the pool boy and get his lil ass some help. Anyway, text me when you land.

Marley didn't have time to respond because Nova came and took the seat next to her.

"This situation with you and my brother, is it real?" he asked, staring at her intensely.

"What do you mean?" Marley shifted on her seat.

"Like this relationship shit. Is it real?"

"Yea, I mean as far as I know."

"I'm asking because C doing shit he's never done, and I need to make sure it's not in vain. I'm not saying that he's weak by a long shot, but he doesn't fall in love easy. He loves you, and I know that you have your own shit, but if you aren't ready for the type of love he's bestowing on you, then you need to speak up."

"You sound like your mom," Marley warmly smiled.

"Then you should know how serious this is."

"I get it and my intentions are never to hurt him, but I can't make you a promise saying it won't happen. We're human beings and sometimes we make mistakes. I'll never put myself on a pedestal and tell you that I'm perfect because I'm not. What I can say is that whatever is happening between us isn't one-sided."

"Respect." Nova stuck his fist out to dap her.

"Get up, nigga. The fuck you all in her face for?" Czar walked toward them.

"We was talking, nigga. She my friend too."

"No the fuck she not. You straight?" He looked at Marley.

"I'm great," she promised.

"Aight, well let's buckle up. We about to take off. Nova, yo seat over there next to Biggie."

"When he get here?" Nova questioned, turning to see Biggie asking for a drink.

"He been here. He was in the bathroom."

"Come up here with us, No." Sammy waved him over. "We about to play Tonk."

"I'm straight. I don't have time for your nigga to be crying and shit when I whoop his ass."

"Fuck you." Romeo gave him the finger.

Czar pulled both of his phones out of his pocket and placed them in Airplane mode. He removed his shoes and reclined the seat back. Once he was comfortable, he patted his lap for Marley to climb in his seat with him.

"Don't we need to wait until take off?" she inquired.

"What I tell you at the house?"

"That I'm safe with you."

"Right. That applies here too, so come over here. I want you to listen to a couple of beats with me."

"I'd love to." Marley placed her phone next to him and curled up on his side. Czar threw the blanket over them and handed her a new pair of AirPods. Picking up the iPad off the tray in front of him, Czar hit the share audio button and music filled their ears. Marley laid back on his chest and closed her eyes.

For the first five hours of the flight, the couple went through multiple beats, sorting through which ones were acceptable and deleted the ones that weren't. In their own little bubble, Marley and Czar joked and vibed with one another, turning the 26-hour flight into one of the best experiences they'd had thus far.

∞∞∞

When the jet landed, a driver was waiting for them at the airstrip. He was instructed to take them to a couple of shopping malls before they headed to the island. Because they were going to be in the middle of the water, getting the essentials would take a little time, so Marley made a list so they wouldn't forget anything.

At the mall, Czar spared no expense. He made sure Marley had everything she needed for the trip and more. He had even allowed her to shop for him, matching their outfits while he stood back and recorded everything. After shopping, the driver took them to get some food at Biggie's request, and then they headed to the boat that would take them to their resort.

"Oh my god!" Marley exclaimed, taking in the crystal blue water and tropical fish. "This is amazing."

"Aye, where the life jackets at?" Czar asked, ignoring her excitement. It was cool and all, but he couldn't swim, and being surrounded by some much water made him uncomfortable.

"We don't have any on this boat but we're almost there," the captain assured him.

"I'll save you," Marley promised.

"Fuck outta here. I seen *Titanic* and I'm sure Rose selfish ass said the same thing before she watched my nigga Jack freeze to death."

"Julius, please," she laughed. "Jack should've pushed her ass over, but he was so love-sick that he died trying to make sure she was safe."

"Tuh." Nova shook his head. "And yall want me to fall in love. Fuck that. I would've dunked Rose in the water with the quickness and pedaled away while she tried to get the salt water out of her eyes."

"You ain't shit," Marley laughed out loud. "Yall watched *Titanic* together?"

"Yea, it's my mama's favorite movie and she made us watch it with her a couple of times," Czar answered.

"A couple of times?" Sammy gawked. "Mama Ada fried as hell because that movie longer than Pooh lashes and she wear windshield wipers."

"You play all day," Marley giggled, but she had to agree. Pooh's lashes were long as hell and she batted them uncontrollably all day.

"And we're here," the captain acknowledged. "Welcome to the Maldives."

For a minute, no one said anything. They stood there taking in the beautiful island. Fro, the guy who hired Czar for the event, put them up in an all-inclusive resort where everything they need was at their fingertips. Fro paid for three Villas, leaving Biggie and Nova to share one, but that wasn't a problem because they were both on demon time. They knew it would only be a matter of time before they ran into a couple of exotic women and booked a room of their own.

"I've been instructed to give you these." He handed Czar three sets of keys. "Enjoy your stay and I'll be around if you need to go anywhere. Mr. Fro is at the bar waiting to meet with you."

"Good looking." Czar handed him a couple hundred dollar bills. He didn't care about none of the shit he was saying. His main focus was to get off the boat.

“Thank you, sir. My son loves your music and can’t wait to see you perform tomorrow night.”

“Make sure you bring him by so we can take a picture.”

“I will!” He nodded.

Marley stood next to him with a goofy grin on her face.

“Shut up,” Czar mushed her.

“Just saying. I might be rubbing off on you. That was nice.”

“I’m a nice nigga.”

“Hm.” She twisted her lips before snatching a key out of his hand. “Bring the bags, I need to use the bathroom.”

“The fuck,” Nova laughed. “She done turned your rich ass into a bellman like this nigga.”

“Cause that’s what boss bitches do,” Sammy smirked, snatching a key as well. “Romeo, come on, let’s go check out this room and see what kinda liquor they have. I’m ready to get my drink on.”

“I’m right behind you, baby.”

“*I’m right behind you, baby*,” Nova mocked, taking the last key from Czar. “Come on, Biggie, grab the bags.”

“Fuck you.” Biggie kicked the bags while bypassing him. “And I’m sleeping in the bed.” He snatched the key out of his hand. “Aye,” he looked back at Czar, “You need me to go to the bar with you to meet the Fro nigga?”

“Nah, I'm straight. Go do your thing and I'll meet yall for dinner tonight.”

“Cool.”

“Man, this some bullshit,” Nova grunted, picking up his bags, following behind Biggie.

∞∞∞

Instead of going to his room, Czar took the paved path that led to the main area of the resort. A few people recognized him, some waving while others snapped pictures, eager to report they were staying in the same resort as a famous person. Either way Czar didn't mind. He was in Asia and still had fans pining after him. That was a different type of success, and it brought a different kind of feeling.

"There he goes!" Fro clapped his hands as Czar bopped toward him.

"What up doe?" Czar greeted, sticking out his hand to offer Fro dap, which he accepted.

Fro Rodriguez was a Dominican tycoon who gained his riches from Bitcoin and YouTube. With his first million, he flipped it and started buying commercial businesses which he gutted and rebranded, turning it into a multi-million-dollar shipping company. Fro had ships, planes, buses, and anything else customers needed. His money was long, so when his son said he wanted Czar to fly in and perform at his party, Fro brought out his checkbook and made his son's dreams come true.

"I'm happy you made it safely. Was everything up to your standards?" Fro asked.

"Fuck yea. I need to get me a fucking jet. That shit was smooth."

"Until you do, mine is at your disposal. Here, take a seat." He stepped back, offering Czar one of the barstools. "My son is excited we were able to book you on such short notice."

"Yea, me too. This shit straight." Czar accepted the glass from the bartender. Fro picked up his glass and they toasted before getting down to business.

"I take it the check cleared."

"Of course. I wouldn't have boarded the jet if it didn't."

"Respect," Fro chortled, appreciating Czar's brashness. "My son is excited. We're flying him and his friends here tomorrow morning, so don't be surprised when you see a bunch of teenagers running around the resorts."

"It's cool," Czar yawned.

"Did you bring anyone one with you? My wife has a few friends on the island that wouldn't mind keeping you company," he offered.

"Nah, I'm straight. I brought my girl with me and she's not into that kinda shit. I'll be shark food fucking with her."

"Respect," Fro chuckled. "My wife is the same even while under the weather."

"Tell her to drink some tea. That shit works wonders."

"We've tried every natural remedy under the sun and it's not working. I'm not a man of medicine, but we might need to take it a step further."

"I understand." Czar nodded. "My lady specializes in natural tea, I could slip you a couple of bags for your wife. I drink that shit like water, and I love it."

"I'll take some," Fro said, standing up. "At this point, I'm sure my wife would try dope if it made her feel better," he laughed at his own joke. "I'll let you go, my friend. Just wanted to touch base to make sure everything was good. We'll see you tomorrow evening, and if you need anything, you know how to reach me." Fro stood up but paused. "Oh, wait, here. I was told you'd want this." He discreetly handed Czar a bag.

Czar didn't have to open the bag to know what it was. The musky aroma said it all. Nodding, he took the bag and tucked it under his arm.

"Good looking." Czar pushed back from the bar and left as smoothly as he came.

Back in the room, Marley was now laid out in the middle of the bed. Her hair was all over the place and light snores slipped from between her lips. He could tell she was fresh out of the shower because her coconut bodywash lit up the room. A white sheet was thrown across the lower part of her body and her arms were tucked under the pillow. Czar started to wake her up, but instead, he pulled out his phone and snapped a picture of her. Posting the picture to his story, he captioned it: *Jetlag is kicking LB ass.*

Czar stripped out of his clothes and opted to use the shower on the private patio versus the one in the room. He had never in his life felt so free. The sun was shining down on him and the sounds of the waves crashing against the villa relaxed him. Czar's eyes were closed when he felt her behind him.

"I was trying to wait for you," Marley purred, running her hands down his toned abs.

"Why?"

"Cause I wanted to thank you."

"Oh yea?" Czar's husky voice deepened and his dick hardened.

"Yea," Marley cooed, now standing in front of him. Dropping to her knees, she wrapped her mouth around his dick and thanked him by swallowing every ounce of nut in his sack.

Chapter 24

"Look, I can't touch my toes. I know you see this stomach in the way," Biggie complained.

"Then go as low as you can," Marley giggled, standing to her feet. "I'm still trying to figure out what you are doing out here anyway. It's six in the morning, shouldn't you be sleeping?"

"What I look like sleeping the day away and I'm in a place I thought I'd never see," he explained. "Niggas ain't even heard of the Maldives, and I'm out here surrounded by crystal blue water, watching the sunrise and doing yoga. I know niggas who don't even know what a passport is, so I consider myself lucky. Sleeping this experience away is not an option."

"I get it." She stood up, understanding his reasoning. "I feel the same way, but I'm an early bird anyway."

"Plus, C said this yoga shit relaxed him."

"It's very relaxing," she agreed. "Let's try something easier. Let's sit down."

"Aight, smooth." Biggie pulled up his shorts and sat down.

"Straighten your back and put your feet together," Marley instructed, doing the same. "Now breathe."

"Oh yea, see, I can do this shit." He grinned and inhaled the fresh air.

"Deep breath and hold it. 5, 4, 3-"

"The fuck yall doing?" Nova grumbled, taking a seat across from them.

"Good morning to you too," Marley sassily greeted.

"Fuck that. You might be having a good morning, but I'm not. This nigga snored all night!" He glared at Biggie, who still had his eyes closed, focusing on his breathing. "I got up to piss in the middle of the night and fell in the fucking pond bullshit in the middle of the floor. I pissed on myself, and the fucking water turned black. Housekeeping looking at me all crazy and shit, talking about I killed the fish."

"Wait," Marley giggled. "You fell in the pond?"

"That shit ain't funny. I started panicking because I had water in my eyes and this Big Worm looking nigga farted and told me to keep it down."

"You was fucking up my beauty sleep." Biggie shrugged.

"Say one more thing to me and I'm going to push yo ass in the water," Nova gritted.

"Come do some yoga with us," Marley suggested. "It'll help reset your day."

"I'm not about to do this gay shit."

"Yoga isn't gay, fool." She stretched her hand out. "Come on, sit on the edge and practice your breathing."

"Fuck it." Nova stood up. "Might as well since I can't smoke."

"Who says you can't smoke?" Marley removed a joint from the waistband of her shorts. She passed it to him along with a lighter.

"See." He grinned, taking the joint. "This is why I fuck with you." Nova lit the joint and inhaled.

Soon, the trio was buzzing while lying on the ground in the Cobra pose. The top halves of their bodies pointed toward the blazing sun while the tip of their feet dug into the ground. Biggie and Nova listened to Marley count them down and got lost in the softness of her voice.

"I'mma fuck you up," Czar gritted, stalking over to them.

"Did everybody wake up on the wrong side of the bed?" Marley frowned.

"We didn't," Sammy chirped. "Oh yall doing yoga? That's my shit. Come on, Ro, stretch me out."

"I did that last night." He slapped her on the ass.

"You could've kept that to yourself," Nova groaned. "Y'all fucking up my mojo. What's next, LB?"

"Ain't shit next." Czar swooped Marley up by the waist. "And you gave these niggas my weed. I'mma fuck you up." He popped her on the ass.

"Waitttttt," she laughed as he carried her away. "I wasn't finished."

"Nigga, put her back. You see we out here doing some limber shit," Biggie called after them.

"Yo fat ass ain't been limber since you were a sperm cell floating down the stream with your siblings," Romeo jested.

"Fuck you, lover boy. Help me up."

"Nah, you limber right? Roll yo ass over and stand up. They serving breakfast."

"Oh hell yea," Biggie cheered. Now they were speaking his love language.

∞∞∞

In their room, Czar had Marley in the middle of the bed with his head between her legs. His plan was to wake her up like that, but when he rolled over, she wasn't in bed and that irritated him. It was going to be a long day and Czar needed his fix before going to hang out with a bunch of teenagers.

"Oh fuck," Marley moaned, trying to roll over to alleviate the intense pressure between her thighs, but Czar wouldn't let up. With his mouth wrapped around her bud, he simultaneously worked two fingers into her pussy and another one in her ass. Marley swore she'd never let a man play in her ass, but now she couldn't get enough of it. If it wasn't his fingers, it was his tongue, and she was hooked.

"You gone let me fatten this lil muthafucka up?" he asked, lightly rubbing her clitoris between his fingers.

"Noooo." Marley tried to scoot away from him. "It's too big." She could take his fingers all day, but his yam-sized dick was out of the question.

"Holes are made to be stretched." He lightly bit her thigh.

"Czar, noooo. My booty gone be loose for weeks."

"I'll be gentle."

"You promise?"

"Yea." He released her. "Come wet it up."

Doing as she was told, Marley crawled between his legs and took his dick in her hands. Czar watched as she tooted her ass in the air, giving him a view of her perfect downward dog. Biting down on his lip, Czar took in the sight as she breathed heavily on his dick. Normally he didn't like that slow shit, but the way Marley sucked his dick was an art, and you never tell an artist how to create.

Starting at the base of his shaft, Marley ran her tongue alongside the thick vein on his dick and moaned. She took her time, placing wet kisses all over it while looking in his eyes. Those big sad eyes had him in a chokehold like vice grips.

"LB," Czar gritted, not liking the goosebumps that appeared on his arms. "Put your mouth on it."

"Don't rush me, nigga." Marley grinned, taking the head of his dick into her mouth. Like a skilled pro, she effortlessly swallowed him with her tongue hanging out of her mouth. When he felt it swipe across his balls, Czar lost his shit. His hands found the back of her head, holding it down until he felt the back of her throat. His ass clenched, slightly lifting every time he thrusted into her mouth.

"I swear I love the fuck outta yo ass," he confessed, fucking her mouth. At this point, she didn't have to say it back because the way she sucked his dick said it all.

"Is it wet enough?" Marley asked, puckering her wet lips.

"Fuck yea, turn over." Czar stroked his dick. "Put two pillows under your stomach," he instructed.

"Go slow," she whined, grabbing the pillows.

"I got you, baby. I wouldn't do anything to hurt you." He kissed the back of her neck.

Czar picked up the baby oil off the nightstand and drizzled it on both of her ass cheeks. He took his time massaging the oil into her skin and then placed kisses on both cheeks before giving her a slap. Marley's breath hitched. She braced herself, knowing that he never played around back there without licking on her. Just as she thought, he bent down and buried his face in her ass. Maneuvering between sucking her hole and fingering her pussy, Czar had her creaming on his face in no time.

Not giving her time to recover from the orgasm that

could've easily put her to sleep, Czar caressed the head of his dick, inching toward her hole.

"Relax, baby," his husky voice coached. "You trust me?"

"Y-Yes," Marley moaned, feeling him at her rim. She was waiting for the good part because at this moment she had to shit and wasn't nothing good about that. Czar reached around and stroked her clitoris while sinking deeper into her.

"Oh fuck," he grunted, trying to hold his composure.

Somewhere between him slapping her ass and stroking her pussy, Marley started to enjoy it a little more. She loosened up and before long she was throwing her ass back, matching his thrusts. Czar grinned, watching her take the dick like a good girl… like a freak bitch. When he couldn't take it anymore, Czar released in her ass, sending them both into a universe where couples like The Joker, Harley Quinn, and Bonnie and Clyde resided.

After taking a long shower, Marley and Czar got dressed and sat on the patio for breakfast. They could've joined everyone else, but Czar liked the idea of having her all to himself. While they ate he checked his text messages, and Marley conducted business on her laptop. There were a few restaurants wanting to do business with Sippin' Tea, but Marley was a little leery, whereas Harper was like 'Show me the money.'

"What's your favorite holiday?" Marley randomly asked, turning in her seat.

"I don't have one." Czar peeked over his phone. "Your skin looks good as fuck in this sun."

"Thank you. It's a new tea mask I made. I put one on while

you were sleeping."

"You selling it on your site?"

"Not yet. I've been testing it out. I'm surprised Biggie didn't tell you I did one on him the other day. I made a TikTok and everything."

"That big nigga let you put that shit on his face?" Czar laughed, not surprised. Marley had his brothers eating vegan food on the regular and now his security was getting facials and doing yoga.

"Yep. I'mma give you one."

"I don't mind," he grinned. "You can sit your pussy on my chest while you do it."

"You so fucking nasty," Marley laughed.

"Nah, for real though, I'm proud of you."

"For what? Giving Biggie a facial?"

"Nah, because you doing your thing. You could've easily put your business to the side when I sucked you into my world, but you didn't. We be in the studio till five in the morning, and you still come home, check your emails, make your content videos and all. I admire that shit because everybody ain't able."

"Thank you, Julius." Marley stirred in her seat. "Plus, my sister be on my head."

"That's a good thing."

"Now back to my question, what's your favorite holiday?"

"That wasn't a thing when I was little. My mama tried to do the shit on the low, but the nigga Cain didn't allow her to spend unnecessary money, and buying gifts for a kid he didn't want was unnecessary. We didn't get a Christmas tree until I was eight, and by then I didn't believe in none of that shit."

"Is he still around?"

"Who Cain?"

"Yea, because I'd love to pop his ass."

"You'd kill that nigga for me?" Czar grinned.

"Yep. I'd un-alive that nigga so quick for fucking up your childhood."

"Not saying shit like un-alive you won't," he chuckled. "I'm straight though, shorty. I came out on top."

"You did, and I'm happy that your past didn't turn you into a monster."

"Whattttt, I thought I was a bully?"

"That was before I got a chance to know you." Marley rolled her eyes.

"And now?"

"Now I think you a fine ass nigga with a big dick that's talented, loving, and rich as fuck."

"Saying shit like that gone get you fucked." Czar gazed at her. "We'll never leave this room."

"I take yams up the ass, so gimme what you got."

"You silly as fuck," he laughed, reaching for her hand. Placing it to his lips, Czar kissed it, making her heart melt.

"Just a little," she agreed. "Can you see yourself living out here?"

"Asia? Fuck nah, but I like the idea of traveling to a lot of different countries. When I retire from rapping, that's the goal."

"I love that for you."

"Play your cards right and I might bring you with me," he winked.

"Might?"

"Yea, this shit new. I gotta see if you can go the long haul."

"Oh whatever, Czar."

"I'm Czar now?"

"When you start being cocky, hell yea."

"You like that cocky shit though," he flirted, scooting closer to her.

Being that she didn't have on any panties, Czar easily slid his fingers between her thighs. Slipping two fingers inside her, he used his thumb to slowly stroke her bud.

"Julius," Marley moaned.

"I swear I love playing in this gushy ass pussy." He kissed her lips. "Cum on my fingers one more time. Can you do that for me?"

"Yes."

"That's my girl." Czar grinned, stroking her until his fingers were coated in her cream. "Mmm." He sat back, allowing her to catch her breath. Like the freak he was, Czar sucked his fingers clean.

"Keep your hands out of my coochie." Marley adjusted her shorts and did a quick scan to make sure no one saw them.

"Never," he promised.

"Whatever, but when we get back home, we're going to Wyoming and The Lodge to get you a tree."

"I'm not about to buy no fucking tree."

"You are. We're going to create some new memories."

"Oh yea?"

"Yea." Marley smiled, sitting back in her seat. Czar nodded his head and picked up his apple juice. Whatever Marley wanted, Marley got.

∞∞∞

Later that evening, Czar put on the concert of a lifetime. With Marley sitting in the front row, he showed out like she was the only one in the audience. Her hair was pulled on the top of her head and the strapless dress she wore showed off her neckline perfectly. She tried to play shy, but rapped the lyrics to his song like she wrote them. Czar glided across the stage in an all-white linen outfit looking like somebody's uncle at a barbecue. The Cuban link chains on his neck glistened under the night light while clinking together whenever he made a sudden movement.

The stage Fro set up for Czar was better than some of the arenas he had performed at. Fro's son and his friends bounced around on the stage next to Czar while rapping the lyrics and recording on their Snapchat. Nova and Romeo were both going Live, allowing people from all over to watch the performance. Marley swore there had to be over 200 hundred people present, but she felt safe with Biggie right next to her. Even when he was entertaining women, he never left her side. The birthday concert was the first event of their week and certainly not the last. Between doing crazy ass excursions, eating, vibing, and simply living life, Czar and his clan made memories that would last a lifetime.

Chapter 25

Christmas was a week away and Marley was battling a nasty cold. She guessed it was from the change in temperature, but whatever the reason was, she felt like she was dying. For days, her head had been spinning and her body ached. She had hot flashes, diarrhea, and was throwing up. Czar was running around like a chicken with his head cut off. Not only was he involved in a few local charity events, but Rah put together a coat drive and asked him to perform along with a couple of other rappers from Detroit.

"Bitch, if I didn't know any better, I'd think you was pregnant." Harper side-eyed her sister through the camera.

"Gotta have a uterus to get pregnant," Marley sniffled. "But keep going, I'm listening."

"So I think we're ready for a storefront. Nothing big, but a small shop with enough space for a few people to dine in. We can hire a local chef or a student right out of culinary school to cook small plates."

"I like the idea."

"At this point, it's more than an idea. I want to go look at spaces... well after you get better."

"That's fine and I was thinking about a mobile truck. We could do pop up shops and set up tables and lights. Something cute for the summer and fall."

"I love that!"

"Ok," Marley agreed. "Hold on, this is Julius on the other end."

"Just call me later," Harper insisted. "Love you sickly."

"I love you too." She clicked over. "Hello."

"Aye nigga, put my girl on the phone," Czar joked.

"Stop playing, Julius. Where are you? I want my soup," Marley whined.

"Calm down, girl. I'm leaving my mama's house. I'll be there in five minutes."

"And did you get me another lemon for my tea?"

"Yea, LB, I got you another lemon."

"Oh yay!" Marley cheered into the phone. "Thank you for taking care of me."

"Thank you," Czar mocked, sounding just as congested as her. "I'll see you in a few minutes." He ended the call.

Deciding to make herself another cup of tea, Marley crawled off the couch and went into the kitchen. She prayed like hell she didn't have COVID because, according to the news, it was back and worse than ever. With a long shirt on, knee-high socks, and a scarf, Marley dragged herself around the kitchen.

Knock knock!

The sound of someone knocking on the door made Marley groan out loud. She slowly walked to the door, hoping Czar would use his key, but the knocking persisted.

"What the heck did you do, fly over here?" Marley joked, pulling the door open.

"Something like that." Benny grinned, rubbing his hands together.

The mug in Marley's hand slipped through her fingers, causing the glass to shatter on the floor. She didn't know if her mind was playing tricks on her, so she skeptically reached out and touched his face. Marley gasped when her fingers collided with his cheek. He was very much warm and alive.

"It's me, baby." He took her hand and kissed her palms.

Like a recurring dream, Benny stood there in the flesh. He'd lost a few pounds, and his facial hair had filled in, making him look a few years older, but it was him. The dent in his cheek was evidence of the bullet that changed their life, and she was sure his teeth were fake. Marley never remembered them being so straight and white.

"Benny," she gasped. Tears fell from her eyes as she rapidly blinked to clear them.

"Come here girl." He pulled her into his chest, hugging her so tight that it hurt, but she didn't complain just in case it was a dream, just in case she opened her eyes and he wasn't there. Benny smothered her face with kisses as she cried her eyes out, holding on to him for dear life.

"Fuck I missed you," Benny whispered in her hair.

"I-I missed you too," she cried, kissing him back. "I missed you so much. How are you here? I-I thought-" Marley choked on her words. "I thought you were dead."

"It's a long story, but fuck, you look good man. Tech wasn't lying,"

"Tech?" She slightly leaned back, more confused than she'd ever been.

"I'mma need you to release my girl before I stomp holes in your fucking face," Czar's deep voice boomed. Like someone threw water on her, Marley jumped out of Benny's arms and wiped her face.

"The fuck is this?" he asked, griming Benny from head to toe.

"He's-

"Her nigga." Benny stood up straight, squaring his shoulders. He was still cocky as ever, challenging Czar as if he wasn't the bigger man. As if he wasn't touching something that no longer belonged to him.

"Fuck outta here. LB, dismiss this nigga before things take a turn for the worse," Czar snorted, protectively stepping in front of Marley.

"So what it is?" Benny raised his shirt, snatching the gun from his waistband. Tech had warned him about Marley's security, so he came prepared for whatever. Leaving without his girl wasn't an option. He did it once and couldn't see himself doing it again.

"I'm on whatever." Czar dropped their food to the ground and removed the Glock from his back.

"Wait a minute!" Marley panicked, moving from behind Czar. She stretched her arms between her present and her past. "Julius, this is my uh- this is Benny."

"Nigga don't look dead to me, but that's some shit we can make possible."

"Ole rapping ass nigga ain't no shooter."

"Check my credentials, bitch nigga, ain't no pussy in my blood."

"Please put the guns down," she begged, unraveling as she was caught in the crossfire once again.

"I will as soon as you tell this nigga to go on about his business. Daddy's home and we don't do that friends bullshit." Benny cocked his gun. "My name tatted on that pussy."

"Silly ass nigga," Czar chuckled angrily, wiping the corners of his mouth. "And I've been spending months tatting mine on her soul, now what?"

"You straight, C?" Biggie rounded the corner with his gun aimed at Benny's head.

"I'm straight," he snorted. "LB being haunted by ghosts and shit. Dismiss this nigga so I can feed you this fucking soup," Czar demanded, picking up the bag from the ground.

"Benny, can I talk to you later?"

"The fuck you asking for?" Czar roared, making her jump. "Go the fuck in the house."

He didn't know why, but his chest felt tight. The nape of his neck itched and he felt himself breaking out in a sweat. Fear. Something he hadn't felt in years. Questions swirled around in his head as he stared at Marley like he was trying to read her. *Did she want the nigga back?*

"It's aight, Mars baby. Call me tomorrow and not a day later." Benny stole one more look at her before bopping down the hall like his presence didn't snatch the rug from under her feet.

In a total twilight zone, Marley pulled herself away from the door, careful not to step on the pieces of glass. She didn't have to turn around to know Czar was staring at her. She was sure he wanted answers, but she was just as clueless as him.

"On my mama you better start talking!" Czar thumbed his nose. He couldn't even pretend he wasn't bothered.

"I-I don't know what you want me to say," Marley mumbled.

"Was the nigga ever dead?"

"Of course! I wouldn't lie about that?"

"So you saw the nigga in a casket?"

"No. His body was shipped down south, or at least that's what they told me."

"Shit ain't adding up, LB. So what, the Uncle Fester ass nigga just popped up like *The Walking Dead*?"

"Julius, you asking me questions I can't answer. The only person that can answer them just left," Marley stated the obvious.

"So what, you about to go back to him?" Czar quizzed, staring at her like his eyes could penetrate her soul.

"W-what? I'm not even thinking about that right now." Marley's eyebrows furrowed.

Czar took a step back and let out a low chuckle. He was entering new territory, and he didn't like it. The foreign feelings had him ready to punch a hole in the wall or worse. Czar didn't think he was capable of putting his hands on a woman, but he felt like shaking the fuck out of Marley. He wasn't the type to chase a bitch, but for her, he chased her, courted, sucked and fucked on every part of her body, and she still seemed confused about what they were. What he meant to her. For a brief second, Czar forgot who he was. He was so wrapped up in Marley that he forgot he was still that nigga who could snap his fingers and have three different bitches on their knees.

"Right now?" He rubbed his jaw. "Yea, I'mma head out."

"Why are you leaving?"

"Because obviously shit ain't mutual between us. I'm in love with yo confused ass, and you've been in love with a ghost who just so happened to pop up."

"Julius, I-

"You what, Marley?" He bellowed. "Don't say you fucking love me. I said that dumb shit and you kissed me like I'm a bitch. I don't-

"You don't know what I feel."

"Get the fuck outta here. You walk around this bitch with fifty emotions at once. You don't even know what the fuck you feel."

"Fuck you, Julius! You're jumping to conclusions. I never said I was going back to him, but a conversation needs to be had."

"The fuck is there to talk about? If the nigga was so concerned, he would have came back when you were mourning the loss of your child, *yall* fucking child."

"Fuck you, don't mention my baby."

"Fuck yo sad ass too," Czar spat, leaving her standing in the middle of the living room with her heart in her hands while his bled on his sleeve. He didn't even make it to the car before he sent a text to get his mind right.

Twinkle Pussy: You in town?

Czar planned to fuck Marley and those sad ass eyes out of his system. He'd never chase a bitch.

∞∞∞

It was hours after Czar left and Marley was still confused. She didn't want him to leave, but on the other hand, she appreciated the space his absence provided. Marley needed time to think, to make sense of the cruel joke the universe played on her. Benny was supposed to be dead. She cried for him, she mourned him, she prayed to God he'd come back, and now that she'd moved on, God granted her wish. How fucking ironic.

"So what are you going to do?" Harper asked, sitting at

the other end of the couch.

"I don't know," Marley sighed. That was the million-dollar question and she had been thinking about it for hours and hadn't gotten anything but a headache.

"Girl, this is some *General Hospital* soap opera type shit. Dead niggas popping back up. They could've sent 2Pac back and kept that nigga."

"Harper!"

"Ok, ok, it's not the time for jokes, but I can't help it. If we don't laugh, we're going to cry. I knew seeing Tech dirty ass was a bad thing. This nigga popped up grinning and shit. I wonder how he knew where you lived. Like I thought the building was secured for that very reason."

"I don't know." Marley shook her head. "I didn't even get to ask any of that. I was so shocked."

"Well, what are you going to tell Czar?" Harper asked.

Marley sighed.

"He knows already."

"Oh bitch, you should've led with that. What did he say? Wait, is that why you in here crying?"

"Julius left."

"Like left to go to the store, at a concert, interview? What do you mean left?"

"He asked me was I going to go back to him and I said I wasn't thinking about that right now."

"Oh hell no!" Harper jumped up from the couch. "What does that mean? Are you thinking about going back to him?" She questioned, knowing damn well her sister wasn't that stupid. Czar wasn't perfect, but Benny was bottom of the barrel, and Marley could do a lot better.

"No, I mean I don't know." Marley closed her eyes,

hoping it would stop her world from spinning. "Everything happened so fast. One minute I'm making tea and the next Benny is at the door like he wasn't supposed to be lying in a grave somewhere down south."

"I'm trying to figure out what is there to think about." Harper glared at her. "Benny is trash and should've stayed where he was at. He's been gone for three years, almost four, and now that you moved on, now that you're happy, he's back like some creepy ass zombie with his trash ass friends. There isn't a choice. Benny is not an option."

"I'm happy that you have it all sorted out," Marley snorted.

"Wait. Are you really thinking about giving Benny a chance?"

"You don't understand."

"Oh bitch, you stupid," Harper spat, clearly offending her sister, but she didn't give a flying fuck.

"Excuse me?"

"I didn't stutter. You are stupid. It's mighty funny how Benny is back after you move on... with Czar no less. You know what, let me go because you about to piss me off. Some things should just be left in the past."

"You didn't lose JJ or Jaxon. You've never had to wonder what life would have been like without them. So I might be stupid to you, but like I said, I need time to think," Marley said, feeling herself become choked up.

"Whatever. You go ahead and think about the could have beens while I get your nephew to concoct a spell that'll help your ditzy ass."

"Bye Harper."

"Bye Marley."

Seconds later, Marley heard the door slam for the second

time that day.

“Ughhh,” she groaned, kicking the cover to the floor. The thought of getting in her van and driving away crossed her mind, but her van was locked up at one of Czar’s towing shops. “Fuck,” she cursed, feeling trapped. Getting a car hadn’t crossed her mind because Czar or Biggie drove her around. Now that she wanted to run away from the world, she didn’t have any transportation or anywhere to go. The vibrating of her phone put an end to her sulking.

513-349-2093: Aye, I’m not gone wait too long. Wrap that shit up and come see me or I’ll be back.

“Fuck my life.” Marley threw the cover back over her head.

Chapter 26

Czar stood against the balcony with a stack of money in one hand and a bottle in the other. The dark lensed buffs covered his eyes, shielding him from thousands of questions. With the combination of pills, weed, and liquor in his system, Czar was a loose cannon waiting to explode. Nova was already looking at him sideways, but every time he opened his mouth to ask what was wrong, Czar motioned for a dancer to come occupy his time.

"I'm just stuntin' on my ex-bitch, diamonds got the flu, try not to catch it," Czar rapped along with Future as Honey popped her ass against him. Honey thanked God that he called. She was bored as hell and ready to get out of the house. When she asked him about his girlfriend, Czar snapped, and she took that as a hint to mind her business.

"Hol' up, you done made me wake up my savage," he rapped, throwing a hand full of twenties in the air and watching them rain. Cameras flashed around them and Czar gave no fucks. In fact, he hoped Marley watched the video and choked.

"Fuck that bitch," he muttered, turning the bottle up to

his lips.

"Period. I got you, Daddy." Honey bent over, exposing her round ass cheeks to the world. Czar didn't know why she didn't have on any panties in the short skirt and he honestly didn't care. If she wanted the world to see her pussy, who was he to stop her?

"Don't call me that shit." He slapped her ass and Honey purred.

"I'm about to dip," Romeo yelled over the music. "You riding with me or Nova?"

"Nigga I don't need no fucking ride. I drove my own car," Czar barked. Taken aback by his tone, Romeo glanced at Nova. "The fuck you looking at this nigga for?"

"You good, Ro. I'mma stick around for a minute," Nova assured him.

"Instead of watching me, yall need to be watching yall fuckin' mama. You wanna be Secret Service so bad, but have you noticed the changes in the woman that birthed you?" Czar asked, jabbing his finger in Nova's chest. "It's only one nigga that have her so fucking jumpy and it's not yo fucking daddy."

"What?" Nova frowned.

"Just sayin," Czar chuckled. "You wanted to know the real her, well put tabs on her ass because when that nigga call she's going to run."

"Nigga, you drunk. Take yo ass home before I call LB and have her come get you," Romeo kidded, trying to lighten the mood. Nova didn't see shit funny, and if Czar were anyone else, he would have pistol-whooped him, but they were blood, twice over at that.

"Fuck that bitch, you ready?" He roughly grabbed Honey's exposed ass cheek.

"I stay ready," she giggled.

"I'm out." Czar pushed past his brothers with Honey on his arm. Nova sent Shortie a text, telling him to come inside and keep an eye on Czar because he was leaving.

"Where we going?" Honey asked, noticing that he was pulling in the direction of the bathroom.

"To fuck." He popped her on the ass.

The second they entered the bathroom Honey was all over Czar. He didn't have to unbutton his pants because she was on the job. Once his thick dick was free, Honey stroked it until it hardened, making her mouth water. Thus far Czar had the biggest dick she'd ever had and she couldn't get enough of it.

"The fuck you still holding it for, eat this muthafucka," his husky voice demanded.

Honey didn't need to be told twice. She sat her phone on the counter, along with her purse. Leaning down, she inhaled the sandalwood body wash scent that flowed from his balls. Taking his dick into her hand, Honey wrapped her big lips around his meaty head and exhaled. Czar's dick tasted better than it smelled. Honey glided her tongue across the smooth flesh, allowing excess saliva to drip onto his balls.

"Ah fuck." Czar closed his eyes and thrusted into her mouth. Honey's phone vibrated on the sink, but Czar didn't care. She wasn't his bitch and he didn't give a fuck about who was waiting on the end of the phone. Instead, he enjoyed the feeling of his dick tapping her tonsils, and it was good until his mind did the gayest shit… it wandered.

"What do you think about this beat?" Czar asked Marley.

"It's fire, let me rap," she giggled.

"Do your thing." He pressed record on the switchboard.

"Uh," Marley grunted with the microphone in her hand.

"They call me the vegan rapper, don't need no meat, I'm like the veggie trapper."

"Man," Czar laughed out loud. "Gimme my shit back."

"You know you like my style."

"Nah," he said and pulled her into his arms. "I love that shit." Czar kissed her lips.

"Everything alright?" Honey asked, holding his limp dick in her hands.

"Move." Czar pushed her, pulling up his pants.

"What happened?"

"Nothing. Answer your fucking phone and tell that nigga to chill."

"Huh?" Honey frowned.

"Your phone, it's ringing."

"Oh, uh, I'll get it later."

"Nah, you can get it now. I'm about to dip."

"Am I coming?"

"Nah." Czar zipped his pants, leaving her standing there with his dick on her breath.

∞∞∞

On Christmas Day, Marley's Uber pulled up to the address Benny sent her and she frowned. She was supposed to be on her way to Harper's house for Christmas dinner, but Benny wouldn't stop calling her. He begged for her to hear him out, claiming things weren't as they seemed. Almost a week had passed since he popped up at her place on some 'Honey, I'm home' type shit, and she still felt she was dreaming. To put them both out of their misery, she agreed to stop at his place.

"Alright, we're here." The Uber driver cleared his throat, ready for her to exit because the neighborhood was sketchy.

Marley tried not to pass judgment, but she was no longer accustomed to certain things. Thanks to Czar, she no longer had a closet full of knitted clothing or hand-me-downs from the Salvation Army. He had upgraded her life in a major way, and she felt out of place getting out of her Uber in Givenchy boots with a Moose Knuckle coat.

"Uh, thanks." Marley exited the car.

She looked around, thinking Benny was going to come out, but he didn't. Swallowing her nerves, Marley walked up the snow-filled driveway, praying she didn't fall. Then again, she thought maybe she needed to fall and bump her head. Maybe she needed clarity.

"Who the fuck you here to see?" The door was yanked open by a heavy-set man wearing a too small shirt. If she weren't caught off guard, Marley would have told him to get his Winnie the Pooh looking ass out of her face. "Hello?" He waved his hand in her face. "Aye, who deaf bitch is this?" he called out.

"Who the fuck your big corn chip smelling ass talking to?" Marley snapped out of her daze.

"B-

"Aye, chill cuz. This Mars." Benny trotted through the house. "Baby, why you ain't call me?"

"Why weren't you outside waiting on me or looking through the window? You knew I was coming." She walked into the house, fighting the urge to turn her nose up. Old pizza boxes and liquor bottles littered the table, along with cigarette butts and water bottles.

"Entitled much?" Corn chip snorted, backing away from the door. "Do this look like a five-star resort with a valet service? Better get the fuck out the car and walk."

"Sir, I'd advise you to shut the fuck up before I pepper spray your big ass. I promise these are not the problems you want," Marley snapped before turning her attention back to Benny. "Is this where you live?"

"Yea, for now. Can I get a hug?" He held his hands out. Marley walked into his arms and she couldn't help but notice how wrong it felt. "How you doing?" He leaned in for a kiss, but Marley turned her head, giving him her cheek.

"We need to talk." She pulled away from him.

"Yea. I know," Benny ran his hand down his unkempt hair. "Come on," He took her hand, leading her to his bedroom.

Marley followed him, taking in the scene along the way. She could hear music the closer they got to the back of the house and the smell of cheap weed invaded her nose. Marley considered herself a marijuana connoisseur and cheap shit made her nose itch. Once they made it to his room, Benny closed the door.

While he cleared off the bed, Marley noticed all the shoe boxes stacked against the wall. A fifty-inch TV hung above the dresser, and from what she could see, the closet was full of clothes. Marley chewed on her lip as her mind ran a mile per minute. The nigga looked like he had been there for months. Hell, years maybe, and she couldn't figure out why it took him so long to reach out.

"You can sit on the bed," he suggested, walking over to the dresser. When she didn't move, Benny looked back at her and chuckled. "I thought yo ass was stuck up before; now you on a different level," he laughed. "Sit down, baby."

"Benny, I'm not trying to be rude, but this is crazy to me. You're offering me a seat when I need an explanation. I-" Marley paused, giving herself time to gather her composure. "I've been grieving you for three years, so excuse me if I'm a little shocked to see you breathing."

"Aye, that shit wasn't on me," Benny explained. "I woke up in Ohio with tubes and shit all in my nose and mouth. My people moved me when I was stable. They were scared whoever jacked us was going to come back."

"And it took you three years to recover?"

"Nah, a few months, but I tried to call you. Yo mama hoe ass cussed me out and told me I was better off dead, so I said fuck it. She said the baby was gone and that you were in some kinda crazy house bullshit, and if I came back, she was going to make sure you stayed there."

"She said that?" Marley squinted. "And you listened?"

"I did because what the fuck was I going to do?"

"Be there with me!" she screamed. "We could have healed together! We could have mourned the loss of our baby together, but you left me like I wasn't shit. Like you weren't the reason that shit happened."

"You blame me?" Benny palmed his chest.

"Duh, nigga! I begged you to slow down and I paid the price. My fucking unborn child paid the price. I didn't even get to hold her, to see her, and you asking me if you're to blame. Yes! You are to fucking blame!" Marley angrily spat. All those years of pent-up frustration escaped, causing tears to rapidly fall down her cheeks.

"I was shot the fuck up. My trap houses were robbed, and I didn't have shit to give you. What the fuck was I supposed to do? How was I supposed to fix your pain?"

"Be there," she cried. "You should have been there because I needed you." Her shoulders shook. "I slept in a fucking van to feel close to you. I fucking needed you."

"Come here, Mars baby." He tried to pull her in his arms.

"No," she punched him. "You did this to us and then left

me to face all that shit by myself."

"Take it out on me." Benny bit back tears of his own. "I fucked up. I should've came back, but I couldn't do it."

"You left me!" She punched him in the chest. "I hate you!" She clawed at his neck. "My babyyyyy," she whimpered, pulling at his shirt.

"I'm so fucking sorry." Benny grabbed Marley's arms, giving her a bear hug. "I fucked up and I'll spend the rest of my life making it up to you. I'm sorry, baby. I'm so fucking sorry. Just give me one more chance," he begged, kissing her forehead. "One more chance."

Breaking down in his arms, Marley buried her head in his chest and cried. He was her first love. They had history. This is what she prayed for, so who was she to turn her back on him? On them and their history?

∞∞∞

Czar watched Ada float through the living room with an infectious smile on her face. She had every reason to be grateful and thanked the man above for coming through for her like he always did. There were days she questioned her faith, but she learned that God didn't come when you wanted, but he was always on time. Her survival was a testimony of her strength, and Czar couldn't figure out why she was moving backwards.

As usual, Ada hosted Christmas, and just like every year, she went all out. She hired a chef to assemble a beautiful seafood dinner that consisted of just about every edible sea creature in the ocean. The chef also prepared crab cakes, Cajun pasta, corn on the cob, broccoli, potatoes, and more desserts than they knew what to do with. By the time it was time to give out gifts, everyone was full and ready to smoke, but Ada wanted to exchange gifts first.

Czar wasn't the shopping for a gift kinda nigga, so he simply put money in everyone's card and called it a day. The only person he went shopping for was Marley. Buying her exclusive shit made his dick hard. He knew she stayed on her independent kick, but his money looked good on her.

"Sad ass," Czar mumbled.

"You straight?" Nova quizzed, taking a seat next to him.

"I'm good," he lied, lifting the glass to his lips.

It was Christmas day. He should've been fucking his girl under a mistletoe every chance he got, instead he was drowning his sorrows in brown liquor while trying not to sulk. Six days. It had been six fucking days since he'd last seen or heard from her and Czar was low key losing his marbles. Waking up to an empty bed never bothered him before, but it bothered him now. He was still fucking Honey and a couple of random women, but they didn't do it for him. He didn't feel at peace between their legs and for this reason he was on edge.

"LB with her people? I got her a gift." Nova asked, bring Czar back to the festive event.

"Then mail the shit to her, nigga. She ain't coming."

"She still tripping about that Tati shit?"

"Nah and stop asking me questions."

"You a old grouchy ass nigga. Turned thirty and you started acting like one of them old muthafuckas that get mad at people for stepping on their grass."

"Fuck you." Czar cracked a smile. "About the other night-

"It's aight, but I listened."

"And?"

"And she been normal." Nova shrugged, looking at their

mother. "I went through her phone log, hacked into her bank accounts, social media pages, and I didn't see shit out of the ordinary."

"Maybe I'm just fucking paranoid." Czar pulled at a couple of his dreads before tossing them to the side. "And stop hacking people shit. I told you to watch her, not be a fucking stalker."

"I'm topflight security, nigga. It's my job to see all that shit. I keep telling you that. Oh, and I can't find shit on ya girl Honey."

"She not my girl."

"You been fucking with her heavy all week, so she something."

"A distraction, nothing more."

"The point is I can't find shit on her and I don't like it. Everybody gotta past and she just appeared out of thin air."

Czar heard him, but Ada discreetly walking toward the back of the house caught his attention. He noticed that her phone was clutched to her side and her eyes nervously bounced around to make sure no one was paying attention to her.

"Lean wit' it, rock wit' it," Goose rapped, snapping his fingers. "Nephew, where lil sexy at?" he asked, peering over at Czar. "I bet she know this dance." Goose rocked from side to side with not an ounce of rhythm.

"In her skin, nigga."

"I think they broke up," Sammy reported. "I was on Instagram and I saw pictures of him coming out the bathroom with some big booty bitch and I know that wasn't LB."

"Let me see." Pooh leaned over the couch.

"So you broke up with our girl?" Goose asked, still stuck

on that part. "I really liked her."

"Me too," Sammy continued. "I love you, B-law, but your new lil boo ain't it." She tooted her lips. "She cute in a whorish kinda way."

"Did I ask you if you like her?" Czar gawked. "And she not my girl."

"What's LB number?" Goose asked. "You rich niggas always fucking it up for the broke ones."

Czar took another sip of his drink and shook his head. If only they knew she was the one that left him. His pride was too big to let the shit slip from his mouth, so he ignored their rants.

"You aight, son?" Slim asked, noticing that something was off.

"I wish yall would stop asking me that shit," he snapped, slamming his glass down and storming out of the living room.

"Oh, I guess he mad," Goose snorted. "I'm the one that should be mad."

∞∞∞

Moving down the hallway, Czar fumbled with the top of his pill bottle. Since the blow-up with Marley, he had started popping them like Tic-Tacs. They made him feel like a zombie, but he appreciated the disconnect that it created. Dropping two in his mouth, Czar crushed them with his back teeth and swallowed. After a few seconds, he turned to head back to the living room, but low whispers caught his attention.

"You have to stop calling me," Ada whispered into the phone, stepping into the guest room. She tried to close the door, but Czar's foot stopped it from closing completely. When she noticed him behind her, her eyes doubled in size and she immediately hung up the phone and straightened her posture.

"Boy, you scared me." Ada grabbed her chest, giving him a phony laugh.

"Just checking on you, Ma," he said, taking a seat on the bed.

"My big baby." She stroked his chin. "Always checking up on your mama. I'm good."

"How's the book coming along?"

"Good," Ada lied. "I'm back at it. The ghostwriter is very patient and-

"That's fucked up," Czar chuckled, shaking his head. "We lie to each other now?" he mocked, using her own words against her.

"Julius, I'm not one of your little friends, so I suggest you watch who you're talking to. It's Christmas, go get a plate and sing a Christmas carol."

"Ma, I know you stopped writing the book two weeks after you started. You asked her not to say anything, but you keep forgetting that it's my name that goes on the checks. I called to touch base and imagine my surprise when I found out you put a stop to the whole project, yet you're lying to us. So which is it? Are you still writing the book or did you stop?"

Ada let out a soft laugh and shook her head. She should've known that he would find out. Whether Ada wanted to admit it or not, Czar was just like his father in that manner. They watched her, studied her, and knew everything there was to know about her before she ever uttered a word.

"You think you know everything," Her eyes filled with tears. "But let me tell you a few things. Yea, I stopped writing

the damn book because it was like reliving the past. All of those sleepless nights, hungry nights, fucking beatings." Ada quickly wiped the tear that slid down her face.

"Ma, I was there. I lived that shit with you."

"Well, then you should know that this is my life. I thought I could do it, but I can't. Don't worry about it. He's not going to show the pictures."

"You've been talking to him?" Czar questioned, already knowing the answer.

"I have, but only to get the pictures."

"Wow," he said in disbelief. "What did you promise him?"

"Excuse me?"

"Ma, I wasn't born yesterday and that nigga not giving up them pictures for free. He probably don't even want money so what did you promise him?"

"It's none of your business, Czar. I said I'd handle it, and when I'm done I'll have the pictures and Cain will be out of our hair."

"You can't be that naive."

Whap!

"You better watch your mouth!" Ada slapped him. "I'm not one of your friends or the hoes that switch around your video shoot like a groupie. I am your mother. I gave you life."

"You gave me a shit load of problems," he barked. "You ever think about why the first woman I fell in love with needs to be saved? What you gave me is a fucked up hero complex."

"So your relationship problems are my fault? You're thirty years old, Czar. Grow up," Ada scoffed.

"You got it. You want to handle that nigga by yourself, then do it. I'm done." Czar walked out of the room.

"You don't get to turn your back on me!" she yelled after

him. "It's not your job to judge me."

"And it's damn sure not my job to watch you self-sabotage. This time I can walk away." Czar didn't bother telling his brothers he was leaving and Ada didn't feel the need to stop him. She picked up her glass of spiked eggnog and went back into the living room.

∞∞∞

Marley watched JJ eagerly rip the wrapping paper off the gift she bought him. He knew exactly what it was because she always got him whatever he asked for, but that didn't stop the excitement from running through his little hands. Being that he was the only child, JJ's Christmases, birthdays, and Easters all looked the same. He was spoiled to no end, and he knew it. The lineup of Jordans, Nike dunks, Nike Tech outfits, game systems, and action figures testified to that fact. JJ had so many clothes and shoes that Harper had to clean out the guest room's closet to make space for all his new things.

"Aw man. How did you know?" JJ cooed, holding up the Nintendo Switch game system he requested.

"I'm a good guesser." Marley smiled, knowing that was the furthest thing from the truth. JJ sent her screenshots from his iPad. He placed Target ads in her purse and reminded her every time she came over.

"Spoiled ass." Harper switched into the living room, taking a seat across from her sister. "My damn feet hurt," she whined.

"You almost done?"

"Girl, yea. Jaxon took the last of the ribs outside, and I just mixed the green salad."

"What time are his parents coming?"

"They should be on their way." Harper rolled her eyes. She wasn't a fan of Jaxon's mother, Tina, but his father, Jason, and brother, Jeff, were cool people. Tina swore Harper trapped her son when, actually, it was the other way around. Jaxon knew the only way to sit her down was to put a baby in her, and that's what he did.

"Don't be like that," Marley snickered.

"Girl, fuck Mrs. Poch." Harper flicked her wrist. "She better hope I don't put melatonin in her coffee. Have that ass knocked out before dinner start. Fucking with me her wig will be marinating in those lil vodka tonics she loves so much."

"You better not drug that lady."

"Then she better not come in here talking shit and acting funny." Harper popped her lips. "What's up with you though? I've been calling you."

"I know. I just needed a minute to get my mind right," Marley sighed.

"And is it right?"

"No. I still haven't talked to Czar. Benny and I-

"Ah shit. I need something stronger than wine because you're about to piss me off all over again." Harper rolled her eyes. "You and Benny what? Ugh, just saying that shit pisses me off."

"Look, if it's going to have you acting funny, then why are you asking about my personal life?" Marley snapped.

"Bitch, because you don't have no fucking friends, and as bad as I wanna slap some sense into your ass, I have to listen and be an objective ear, but that doesn't mean I have to like it. I'm team you, even when you're acting like you don't know what's right for you. Now go ahead, you and Benny what? Did he tell you why he played dead?"

"According to him, Mama told him not to come around anymore. She told him about what I did and blamed him."

"And he listened to her?"

"That's what I said and then I started crying."

"And?"

"We're going to work it out," Marley sighed, tracing the rim of her glass with her fingertip.

"And that's what you want? You don't think you are jumping into this kinda fast?"

"I think... I mean don't I owe it to us to see what we could've been?"

"Girl, spare me with all that we could've been bullshit." Harper sat her glass down. "You already know what yall could've been and it didn't end well. You keep asking God to grant you a peace of mind and He did. You were moving on. You were happy, and here comes the devil, turning your world upside down. I mean how does this even work?"

"How does what work?" Marley furrowed her eyebrows.

"Mars and Benny 2.0. How does it work? Are you moving in with him? Does he work? Are we still going to open up a shop, or are you about to go back to being his passenger princess?"

"Ouch, that's what you thought of me back then?"

"I thought that you deserved much better than what he was giving you."

"Oh ok, because Jaxon was perfect."

"I never said that, so get out of your feelings. Jaxon was on bullshit back then, but he kept me away from his street business. He took care of home and never shitted where he ate. Benny wanted you to be his trap queen and you were worth more than that. You deserved more than that." Harper sat her glass down and reached for Marley's hand. "I can understand that you have history and Benny was the first boy you ever fell in love with, so you had nothing to compare him to, but now that you've been with someone else you really need to sit back and compare the two. You might find that some things are meant to be left in the past."

"I hear you."

"And what about Czar?"

"I haven't talked to him and it might be for the best. I'm so confused. I feel like I'm having an out-of-body experience. Like I'm having one of those dreams where you're sleeping but you're awake at the same time. My life is moving but I can't control anything around me. I feel like I lost control."

"Whew. This shit is crazy."

"It is, but Julius will be alright. I saw his story on Instagram and he went right back to his single life. He doesn't need me." Marley rolled her eyes. She couldn't deny that seeing Czar on Instagram at the strip club acting a damn fool rubbed her the wrong way, but she had no right to judge him.

"Somebody at the doorrrrrrr," JJ sang, rolling through the house on his new scooter.

"I got it." Harper released her sister and got up from the couch. "I know this Mrs. Poch."

"Why you call her by their last name?" Marley snickered.

"Because it annoys her."

"Because she petty as fuck," Jaxon said, popping his wife on the ass.

"Stop before I leave your mama and them dry ass turkey wings outside."

"Don't talk about my mama's food."

"Boy bye." Harper tooted her lips. "You know damn well your mama can't cook. She fry chicken in fish grease. That says it all." She pulled the door open with a tight smile on her face, which instantly melted away when her eyes landed on her own mother.

"Merry Christmas." Pam smiled nervously like she was invited.

"Lord, not today, Satan." Harper shook her head. "What are you doing here?"

"It's Christmas. I spend every Christmas with yall."

"Yea, before I knew you tried to take my man on your throat goat tour."

"Oh my lord." Tina held her chest, walking up behind Pam. "Is this how you talk to your mother?"

"Merry Christmas, Mrs. Poch. And to answer your question, yes. I found out she not only tried to play sucky sucky with my husband but she's been blackmailing him."

"Harper," Jaxon hissed when his mother started choking. "Come inside, Ma." He held his hand out to take the pan of turkey wings from her. "Where's Pop?"

"He went to play his lottery," she uttered, eyeing Pam like she wanted to knock her wig loose.

"Don't even worry about it," Harper told her, recognizing the look in her eyes. "I already snatched her lace."

"Oh my lord." Tina grabbed her chest, quickly moving around Harper.

"Make this quick. JJ is ready to open up the rest of his gifts," Jaxon said as he backed into the house.

"I got this. You take care of those birds." Harper pointed to the table. "I don't want to see that on my table."

"Please don't beat up yo mama on Christmas." He kissed

her lips and went inside the house.

Harper turned her attention back to Pam, who was still standing there holding a gift bag. The coat she wore barely zipped up, nor did it look strong enough to endure Michigan weather. Pam's head was covered in a POLO skull cap, and Harper could bet it was because her hair wasn't done. Glancing down, she looked at her chipped nail polish and then back up at her missing lashes. Harper let out a loud grunt.

"I guess now that you have to pay your own bills, you can't keep up your lavish lifestyle."

"Harper don't be rude. Aren't you going to invite me in?" Pam tried to push past the door, but Harper blocked her.

"Ma, I've loved you through a lot of shit, but what you did is unforgivable and I can't allow you in my house. In my life."

"Don't be dramatic."

"I'm being real. You might as well be a bitch off the street because ain't no way I'd ever allow you back around my husband."

"So you forgave him, but not me," Pam scoffed. "I swear your sister is rubbing off on you. That slow shit kills me every time."

"Yea, well let me take my slow ass in the house. I hope you don't run out of gas on the way down the hill." Harper backed away from the door.

"Wait!" Pam panicked. "Look, I need help. The lights are about to get cut off and I don't have any food."

"What happened to your yellowed tailed Pastor?"

"Him and his wife worked things out."

"Are you still going to church?"

"No," Pam sighed. "They kinda banned me, and because

of all the volunteering I was doing, my job let me go."

"Wait," Harper chuckled, getting a kick out of how fast karma came back around. "You lost your job because you were volunteering at the church where you were sleeping with the Pastor. The Pastor told you he was leaving his wife, and you fell for it. Yall got caught, they kicked you out of the church, and now you are jobless."

"Don't kick me while I'm down."

"How much money did my husband give you?"

"Why does that matter, Harper? I said sorry!"

"How much?"

"Twenty-five hundred every two weeks," Pam mumbled, looking down at the snow. "What does it matter? It was drug money anyway. Yall spend that in a toy store."

"But it's ours to spend!" Harper snapped. "You know I've always looked out for you. I never turned my back on you even when I should have."

"Ok. Yes, you were there, but now is the time when I really need you. You shouldn't turn your back on me when I need you the most."

"Ain't that what you do to my sister at every turn?"

"Yea, well I can't be too much of a bad person. I gave Benny her number when he came back sniffing around."

"You did what?" Harper squinted as things started to become a little clearer.

"I gave him her phone number and address."

"Oh my god! You are so evil."

"Excuse me," Pam said with scrunched eyebrows.

"You knew all this time that he was alive and you watched her suffer. He didn't come sniffing around, you called him because she moved on. You're so fucking jealous of your own flesh and blood that you welcomed Benny's lowlife ass back into her life to cause havoc."

"How he got here shouldn't be a concern. I mean she wanted him back so bad. She should be thanking me."

"You know what, let me go in this house before I knock your front teeth loose. You hungry? Take yo ass to the soup kitchen because I have nothing for you." Harper stepped back and closed the door in her mother's face.

Marley and JJ were playing Saber Beats on the VR when Harper returned. She thought about telling her about the bug their mother dropped in her ear, but Marley was laughing. She hadn't laughed all day, and for once, she looked like she was having a good time, so Harper went into the kitchen, refilled her glass, and put Mrs. Poch's dry ass turkey wings in the drawer under the oven.

With a blunt between his lips, Czar sat on the couch staring at the dumb ass tree Marley persuaded him to buy. She swore it would look good in his living room and had even decorated it with her nappy headed ass. Marley had even talked him into getting stockings and filling them with grown-up goodies like lube, honey packs, fruit roll-ups, and double shots of Hennessy. The tree was filled with boxes from Chanel, Prada, Gucci, and Pandora. For her, he had gone all out, and now his money was wasted. The more he glared at all the shit he bought for her, the more pissed off he became. It was Christmas and she had him sitting on the couch in his feelings.

"Fuck that bitch," he mumbled, jumping up from the couch. "Got me in this bitch feeling like Angela Basset."

Dropping his blunt in the ashtray, Czar pushed up from

the couch and started snatching the boxes from under the tree until his hands were full. Stalking over to the balcony, he used his foot to push the door open, and without a second thought, he tossed the boxes over the balcony. Watching all her shit fall to the ground didn't make him feel any better. It didn't give him any closure, so he grabbed their stockings and dropped them next. Still not satisfied, Czar dragged the tree across the floor and flung it over the railing without a care in the world. The loud thud made his heart smile, and only then did he shut the door and relight his blunt. Seated back on the couch, Czar picked up his phone and dialed her number.

"Hello?" Marley whispered, glancing over her shoulder to make sure Benny was still asleep. He was drunk as hell, and she doubted he'd wake up, but as a precaution, Marley slid out of the bed.

"The fuck you whispering for?" Czar gritted. "You laid up with the dead nigga?"

"Julius-

"That was quick. Yo nasty ass gone get worms laying up with Zombies and shit."

"You drunk?"

"Yea, I'm fucked up," Czar sighed, hating that her voice still calmed his soul. "I guess I needed to talk."

"And you called me?"

"Yea, to tell you that you not shit."

"I know." Marley closed her eyes as they started to fill with tears.

"Good." He ended the call.

Chapter 27

Benny pressed the phone to his ear, listening to the caller rant about all the things he wasn't doing. Since being back in the city, Benny's focus has been solely on getting his girl back. He hadn't thought out the logistics of their living situation, but if he had it his way, Marley would be packing up her life and going back to Ohio with him.

"Aye chill. I said I'll be back soon." Benny raised his voice in hopes of getting his point across.

"Soon isn't an answer! I asked what are you going to do when you come back! How will she fit into our life?" Toya nagged. She had no idea when she told Benny she wanted to buy some tea from a couple of Detroit girls that it would be his ex. Now Toya wished she could go back because since Benny saw Marley's face he had been on one. What was supposed to be a quick trip to Detroit had turned three weeks, and Toya was pissed.

When Toya showed him Sippin' Tea's Instagram page, the last people Benny was expecting to see were Marley and Harper. He nearly choked when Toya told him Marley was dating Czar. Benny fell down a rabbit hole, going through her pictures, reading comments and all. Marley was still as beautiful as ever, and Benny felt cheated. When Pam reached out to him, he took that as a sign to make a trip to Detroit.

"I told you what it was," he gritted, tired of repeating the same thing.

Benny appreciated Toya. She stuck by him for two years, helping when he didn't have a pot to piss in. When certain family members got tired of him being in their house Toya opened her doors. It was her who connected him to the who's who in Ohio. Toya handed him her check weekly, and as promised Benny flipped it, giving her back double what she gave him. It was her who held him down and Toya was having a hard time understanding why he cared what his ex was doing when it was clear he moved on.

"Whatever, Benny. You just better hope I don't link up with one of my exes."

"Do what you please, just better not have my-

Beep beep beep

The call ended, making him chuckle. Benny's patience was running thin. If he wasn't trying to convince Marley to hang with him, he was on the phone trying to keep Toya at bay. At any given moment, she was ready to hop in her car and drag his ass home.

"Hey." Marley pulled the car door open and slid inside the front seat.

"What's up Mars?" Benny leaned over to kiss her, but his lips landed on her cheek.

"Sorry, I-uh-

"It's cool, we'll get there."

When Benny asked her to ride with him, she was apprehensive but sucked up her fears and climbed into his car. The couple was still trying to find their footing, but this

time around, something was off. Marley tried to smile, she tried to be happy because she was living in a miracle. Her first love came back from death, and that wasn't something that happened every day.

"Are we going to see Billie?" Marley asked, cutting down the radio.

"Nah, not today. I need to get my mind right before I go there," Benny explained.

"Oh ok, so where we going?"

"Shooter crib."

"No, I'm good. You can drop me back off." Marley instantly copped an attitude.

"Why you tripping? We can chill with them for a minute and then stop over at my aunt's house."

"You mean our house? I could have sworn she's staying in the place that was once ours."

"Mars baby, I need you to let all that shit go. It's in the past and we're trying to move forward."

"Look. I don't wanna go over to your aunt's house. You've been with Tech and Shooter all week. Do you think I want to sit in some trap house while yall do only God knows what?" Marley snapped. "I thought we were going to visit our daughter. Aren't you the least bit curious about what her headstone looks like? Where she's buried at?"

"I am, but you can't make me be ready for something I'm not."

"And you're not ready to meet our daughter?"

"It's not that, but seeing her headstone makes it real and I'm not ready for all that."

"The fact that she's not in the back seat asking for McDonald's makes it real, but whatever, Benny." Marley waved him off.

Fifteen minutes later, Benny pulled up on the East side of Detroit. Marley tried her hardest to keep her calm, but it was damn near impossible. The more she thought about their situation, the more pissed off she became. She didn't expect him to feel what she felt for their daughter, but to keep putting it off didn't sit right with her.

"Welcome back, sis!" Tech greeted as Benny and Marley walked into the house.

"Don't give me that fake shit." Marley rolled her eyes. "Why you ain't tell me what was up when I saw you at the mall?"

"Wasn't my place." He defensively held his hands in the air. "You still looking good though, and what's up with your sister? She still with that nigga Jaxon?

"Boy, fuck you." Marley waved him off. "And don't worry about my sister. You don't wash your hands and you have lint balls in your hair. You could never."

"Ahh," Shooter and Benny laughed, watching Tech rake his hand over his unkempt hair.

"Nigga, you on her shit list just like Ruben. She can't stand that big nigga," Benny laughed, referring to his cousin who Marley called corn chip.

"My nigga went got his girl!" Shooter smirked, eyeing the couple as they moved further into the living room. "I don't remember you being this mean, but I like it." He stuck his fist out to dap her.

"It's fuck you too." She glared at his hand. "Yall all fake as fuck, and as far as I'm concerned, yall never were my family because my family wouldn't let me go through all that shit knowing this nigga was living four hours away. Y'all was quick to call me lil sis, but that shit was for show. None of yall called me, checked on me, or nothing, so take that fake ass fist and shove it up your ass."

"Damn Mars, give these niggas some grace." Benny rubbed her back.

"I'm out of grace to give," she spat.

"Whew. You sure you want her back? Sis back with a vengeance," Tech chuckled as if the harshness of her words hadn't affected him. He did love her like a little sister, but when the chips fell, he had to make a choice.

"Of course. A rapping nigga could never take my bitch," he boasted.

"Swear, we was about to run through that muthafucka and get shit popping. Ain't no rich nigga taking nothing from us," Tech said, causing the men in the living room to agree. Marley on the other hand chewed on the inside of her jaw. The thought of them bringing harm to Czar made her insides twist.

"Anyway, these niggas are rude. I'm Gloss, and this my home girl Mel. You want something to drink or you gone curse me out too?" Gloss joked, holding out a bottle of Hennessy.

"No, I'm ok. Thanks though." Marley warmly smiled at her.

"Ok, well this Shooter place and there's some chicken and pork chops on the stove."

"Nah, I think she like a vegan or something like that. She don't eat shit but salad," Shooter joked.

"Shut up." Marley gave him the middle finger. "And he's right. I'm vegan, but I ate before I left the house."

"Oh ok. Girl, you strong. I couldn't give up chicken." Mel shook her head.

"You don't miss it after a while."

"I don't know about all that," Gloss laughed.

While Benny talked to Tech and Shooter, Marley's eyes roamed around the living room. Being with Czar had her accustomed to a certain lifestyle and standing in the living room wearing over 25K on her neck made her feel uncomfortable. The paint on the walls was chipped, and the stone fireplace was filled with bags of clothes as if it were a storage. The leather couch was peeling, and the floors creaked whenever someone moved. Marley felt like a fish out of water.

Back when they were younger, sitting in trap houses all day was normal. They'd smoke, drink, and then go home to fuck like rabbits. Being around a bunch of random people and talking shit was their routine. Back then she felt protected with him. Marley never had a problem with it before, but now all she wanted to do was go back to her apartment, the apartment she hadn't stepped foot in since Christmas.

"You smoke?" Gloss asked, noticing that Marley was still standing in the same spot looking lost.

"Uh yea," Marley cleared her throat. "I have a couple of pre-rolls." She pulled the Ziplock bag out of her purse. They were cool and all, but she wasn't smoking just anything. Her weed was top notch and she'd never disrespect her lungs by smoking some random bullshit.

"Aight, girl. I was running out of shit to ask you. Come over and sit down." She waved her hand. "Girl, you smell good!" Mel said, catching a whiff of her perfume. "What's that?"

"Good Girl."

"Oh! Is that a new scent from Bath and Body Works?" Gloss asked, leaning over to get another whiff.

"No, I got this from Macy's."

"Some expensive shit," Tech joked, still trying to get

Marley to warm up to him.

"Boy, fuck you." Gloss gave him the finger. "Like I was saying, that smells good. I might need to pay them a visit with my lil blue bag," she snickered, reaching her hand out to give Mel a five.

"Baby, you good? I need to make a run," Benny said, looking up from his phone.

"Make a run?" Marley frowned.

"Yea. Chill with the ladies, get to know them so when we go back to Ohio you'll know someone."

"I never said I was moving to Ohio. What are you talking about?"

"It's a conversation for a different day, but you know what's up. I came for what's mine, and you know I play for keeps." Benny winked.

"Benny-

"Chill out. Let me make this run. I can't afford to lose out on this money."

"Fine, Benny." Marley rolled her eyes. "But we need to talk later."

"I'll be right back." He bent down to kiss her cheek before pressing the phone back to his ear. "I'm on my way," Benny spoke into the phone and ended the call. "Yall order my girl a salad or something."

"I'm fine, just go."

Taking one last look at her, Benny pulled up his pants and bopped out of the door with Tech and Shooter behind him. Marley tried to shift her focus, but she couldn't. She hated to admit it, but they were foolish to think they could pick up where they left off at. If Benny disappearing taught her one thing, it taught her that his friends weren't her friends, that his family was *his* family alone, and to never put all her eggs in one basket.

“You alright, girl?” Gloss asked, seeing the distant look in Marley’s eyes.

“Yea,” she lied, placing the joint to her lips.

“So how long have you and Benny been together because I thought he was-” Mel started, but Gloss bumped her leg.

“You thought what?” Marley furrowed her eyebrows.

“Nothing girl, I’m high.” She laughed it off, but from the shift in energy told Marley she was missing something.

“So, do yall live in Ohio too?”

“Yep, born and raised,” Gloss boasted.

“How did yall meet Benny?” Marley casually picked their brains.

“Girl, them niggas came to Ohio and started taking over shit.” Mel clapped her hands together. “Shooter is my cousin and he needed a plug, so a friend of mine hooked him up,” she popped her loose lips. “One call and them niggas was on.”

Marley simply shook her head. Benny was still just as reckless as ever. He acted like being gunned down hadn’t affected him one bit.

“And they been driving me crazy since,” Gloss laughed it off, but Marley found some truth in her joke. “Anyway, on to more pressing shit. How the heck did you pull Czar’s fine ass?” Gloss interrogated. “Ain’t no way I would have left him to come back to the slums.”

“Swear!” Mel agreed. “Czar is rich as fuck, fine as fuck, and I know he got a big dick. Benny cool people, but he not Czar. I would not have doubled back on that one.”

“Right,” Gloss laughed, clapping hands with Mel.

While they lusted over Czar, Marley sat back and allowed Mary Jane to invade her system. She couldn’t even be mad at them. Czar was everything they thought and more. He was fine, he had money and the dick. Lord. The dick had Marley waking up in cold sweats because she needed it. No, she craved it.

"Anyway, what do you do?" Gloss asked, snapping her from her daze.

"I have a company that sells tea."

"Oh, that's dope. I was thinking about doing something like that. Well, not tea, but some kind of business. I love Shooter, but running behind him is getting old. I'm almost thirty and this nigga still got me doing shit my old ass has no business doing."

"Gloss, please." Mel rolled her eyes. "Shooter takes care of you. If you want a side hustle, just say that because hood niggas is life." She wagged her tongue. "I love me a hood nigga."

"Well, I still want to start a business."

"What kinda business though? What do you know how to do besides cook crack?"

"I could learn how to run a business. I'm sure they have classes," Gloss said above a whisper, hating that she even shared her dream with a small-minded person. Women like Mel loved the hustle and bustle of the streets, and Gloss did too, but now she wanted to try something different.

"Yea, hood niggas life until you're staring down the barrel of a gun," Marley uttered. "I say take the classes and start the business because when it all falls down, who's going to have your back? Certainly not him or his family."

Mel wanted to comment, but she kept it to herself. She was sure if she said the wrong thing, Marley would bite her head off too.

"I can even give you the information for the business

classes my sister and I took," Marley added.

"For real?" Gloss side-eyed her, not knowing what real support looked like.

"Yea, put your number in my phone."

"Thanks, girl, I appreciate it."

"I'mma take another shot," Mel announced, but neither Gloss nor Marley replied as they started conversating about something she had no interest in.

∞∞∞

A few mornings later, Marley woke up to loud banging from the front of the house. At first, she thought she was dreaming, but the banging became louder as the person on the other side of the door grew impatient. Marley's heart wildly beat in her chest, wondering if it was the police. The night Benny left her at his people's house, he didn't come back until almost three in the morning, and he wasn't wearing the same clothes. When she mentioned it, he brushed it off, leading her to believe he was up to no good.

"Benny." Marley shook him out of his sleep. "I think somebody at the door."

"So, let 'em knock," he mumbled, rolling over.

"Benny, get the freaking door." She pushed him. Only then did he see the fear in her eyes.

Rolling out of the bed, Benny picked up his joggers off the floor and removed the gun from under the mattress. Marley's eyes nearly bugged out of her head as he stuffed it in the front of his pants. She had no idea they had been sleeping on top of a loaded gun.

"Stay here, aight," Benny demanded, even though he

didn't have to. Marley didn't plan on going anywhere.

"Ok," she whispered, clutching the blanket to her chest.

From where she was sitting, Marley could hear loud voices and laughter. She sighed, realizing that the coast was clear. It wasn't out of the ordinary for people to show up at the crack of dawn, but she was over it. Since Benny shared a place with his cousins, there were always people over and she was almost positive they were dealing in Detroit City limits. Benny hadn't come right out and said it, but Marley wasn't stupid. She remembered their nonverbal signals and code talk.

When the bedroom door opened, Benny stepped inside, shutting the door behind him. Without offering any explanation, he picked up his phone, tapped on the screen a couple of times and put it back on the nightstand. Marley swung her feet around the side of the bed and stretched her arms to the ceiling. Benny caught a peak of her flat stomach and underboob.

"Come here." He slid back on the bed and touched his hard dick.

Marley's eyes cast down to the print and then back up at the hunger in his eyes. For a week now they slept in the same bed, and he tried to touch her, to hold her, but Marley always scooted away. Benny tried to be patient, but he wasn't used to this version of her. The girl he fell in love with was a freak and would suck his dick behind the bleachers. This version acted like his touch repulsed her.

"Who was that?" Marley asked, ignoring his advances. Benny chortled and scratched the top of his head.

"Tech, he wants me to shoot a move with him."

Marley stared at him blankly. In all honesty, she wanted to laugh because there was no way this was her life. It had to be a sick joke because God wouldn't put her in a time loop like the one she was currently experiencing. There was no way after everything that happened Benny was still doing the same dumb shit. Then again, was it her who was the dumb one for thinking maybe he'd give her the happily ever after he promised?

"Why don't you go back to your place, and I'll meet you there tonight," he suggested. "I'm sure we'll have more privacy there. These niggas be wildin'."

"Umm, no, that's not going to work."

"Why?"

"For one, I thought we were going to visit our daughter, and two, it's not a good idea for you to be chilling at the loft. Julius paid for everything there and I wouldn't feel right parading around with another man."

"Another man." Benny stroked his chin. "That's what I am? Another man?"

"Well, yea." Marley frowned.

"Wasn't that nigga laid up in my fucking van? He still got my shit in his possession, the fuck is you talking about right now?"

"You can't do that." Marley shook her head. "I thought you were dead."

"You thought I was dead, so you love that nigga?" Benny cocked his head to the side. "Is that why I can't get a hug, a kiss, because you missing that rapping nigga?"

"Don't ask me a question you don't want the answer to."

"So why the fuck you even here?" he barked, making her jump.

"Excuse me?"

"I'm saying if you're in love with another nigga, then why the fuck am I even trying?"

"Trying?" Marley scoffed. "The only thing we've done is lay in this room and hang at what I'm sure was a trap house. You left me there until the wee hours of the morning and didn't even offer an explanation."

"Since when do I have to explain shit to you? I've never done it before."

"And you've never died and came back either! You haven't taken me out, we barely talk, and you're still running the streets, so tell me when you tried?"

"How the fuck can I try when talking to you is like talking to a brick wall!" Benny yelled, becoming frustrated with the entire situation. He knew coming back wasn't going to be easy, but this was more than he bargained for. Marley was nothing like the vibrant, funny, sassy ass girl he remembered. She was now cold and distant. It almost felt like he was forcing her to be there.

"I don't know what the fuck I'm doing here," Marley mumbled, holding her temples.

"What?" Benny frowned. "What the fuck that's supposed to mean?"

"I think we jumped into this way too fast. I don't even know if you were seeing someone else."

"Cause that shit don't matter. I'm where I wanna be. I've always been about you and I'm still about you."

"So that's a yes?"

"It was a situation that required no thought."

"What kind of situation?" Marley probed. "My relationship with Julius is public knowledge. Who were you shacked up with all this time?"

"It's not important and we're getting off topic."

"Fuck that topic! What bitch were you laid up with while you were pretending to be dead?"

"Aye chill. I wasn't pretending to be shit."

"Right. You let my mama run you off."

"Mars let's not do this. If it's dates you want, I can do that." He touched her arm. "You've changed, so teach me how to love this version of you. You know I still love you like a fat kid loves cake." He knicked her chin, trying to get a smile out of her.

"Yo nigga, come on!" Tech beat on the door, making Marley jump.

"Gimme a minute," Benny yelled back, and seconds later heard Tech mumbling as he walked away.

"Go ahead, handle your business. I'm going to see Harper."

"Aight, call me when you're on your way back. I'll get us something to eat and we can watch a movie, maybe talk a little."

"Ok." Marley nodded, needing the space.

"Can I get a kiss?" Benny playfully puckered his lips.

"Of course." She leaned forward and pecked his lips.

Czar sat in the studio with his hands locked behind his head. He'd been listening to the same beat on repeat for almost an hour. Writer's block was kicking his ass, and he could bet it had something to do with the women in his life. Marley and her disappearing act, his mother and her dumb decisions, Honey blowing up his phone for dick, and Tati posting about a baby she aborted. Czar was so tired of muthafuckas tagging him in her fake sympathy posts that he almost made a story time video.

"Look, how about we go to the booty club, get some drinks and chill? You need to take a load off," Romeo suggested.

"For a nigga in a relationship, you love being surrounded by other bitches," Nova commented. "Where the fuck is your girl?"

"Mad."

"And that's an excuse for you to be a hoe?"

"Yep!" Romeo grinned, prompting Czar to shake his head. He wasn't even mad at his brother's thinking. He honestly was on the same tip, but he wouldn't have to worry about going home to someone bickering in his ear. Relationships and all that extra shit was for the birds, and Czar would never do it again.

"Aye, C." Biggie popped his head in the door. "LB at the door. You want me to let her in?"

"Duh, nigga, that's sis." Romeo frowned, not sure what was going on. Biggie didn't budge. They were family, but at the end of the day, Czar signed his checks. "Am I missing something?"

"Nah, don't let her ass back here. I'm trying to work." Czar turned back around. He didn't have shit to say to her.

"Too late." Marley's voice made him close his eyes.

"The fuck is really going on around this bitch? How yall go from game night champs to being awkward as shit?"

"Aye, clear the room," Czar roared. "And I'm about to start firing you niggas. I told yall not to let her ass back here."

"Nigga, you see how little she is." Biggie frowned. "She slid under my arm. The fuck you gone fire me for?"

"For being fat!" Nova poked his stomach.

"Fuck yall."

They continued to argue as they filed out of the studio, and any other time it would have been funny, but now probably wasn't the best time to laugh. Marley didn't know why, but all of a sudden, she was nervous. Going to see Czar seemed like a good idea after his call on Christmas, but now that she was in his presence, the butterflies in her stomach were going wild. The way he glared at her made her think that she should've just taken her ass to Harper's house like she was supposed to.

"Julius-

"You done playing house with that dead nigga?" he asked, cutting right to the chase. "Or are you here to officially break up with me?" Czar stood up from his chair.

"I could've sworn you were the one who walked out on me." Marley gawked.

"Because you were standing there acting fucking stupid."

"Julius-

"Aye." He gripped the brim of his nose. "Stop calling my fucking name."

"Look, I only came to talk."

"I haven't seen you in a fucking week! Do you think I wanna stand here and talk to your confused ass? So, what you about to finish being a down ass bitch for a nigga that left you for dead?"

"That's not fair, he didn't know." Marley shook her head, willing herself not to cry.

"Fuck outta here!" Czar roared. "That nigga put you in harm's way every time yall left out the house and he failed to protect you. He's the reason you've been walking around all sad and shit. He's the reason you lost your kid."

"Don't!"

"Don't what, Marley?" He stepped in her face. "Don't tell

you the truth?"

"You don't understand. We have history," she tried to explain, becoming choked up by the tears in the back of her throat.

"And what the fuck are we?" Czar scoffed. "What the fuck was this?" He closed the space between them, wrapping her in his cologne. "You made me fall in love with your indecisive ass and now you want to leave me because Casper the friendly ghost popped back up."

"That's not fair. I told you not to fall in love with me."

"You told me?" He angrily chuckled. Lightly gripping her neck, Czar forced her to look him in the eye. "Well I did, now what?" he questioned, inches away from her lips. "What about my feelings, huh?" He kissed her lips. "You're going to deprive me of what's been keeping me sane?"

"Czar, please," Marley cried, visibly breaking down.

"Please what?" He used his free hand to unbuckle his pants. "You been fucking that nigga?" He yanked her leggings down and swiftly ripped her panties off. "Did you give that bum my pussy?" He licked his fingers before sticking them inside of her.

"You let that bum touch you?" Czar slowly stroked her. "You let him touch you like this?"

Czar picked Marley up off the floor and slid her down onto his dick. She wrapped her legs tightly around his waist, trying her best to hump him back, but she was no match for his angry thrusts. With her back pressed against the door, he feverishly fucked her. Cries and moans escaped her lips while tears ran down her cheeks. Angrily, Czar bit down on her shoulder, causing her to cry out in pain.

"Ah!" Marley tried to hit him, but Czar caught her hands and pinned them above her head. Pressing his forehead to hers, he took his anger out on her pussy. He was mad at her for choosing another nigga over him, and he was even madder he couldn't make her stay.

"I asked you a question." He dug her out.

"Nooooo," Marley answered.

"You wanna know why you can't fuck that bum?" Czar licked her lips. "Cause this my pussy."

"I'm sor-" she moaned, but he bit her lip. "Ju-

"Shut. The. Fuck. Up." He thrusted deeper inside of her with every word.

Doing as she was told, Marley closed her eyes and relished in the feeling of his dick assaulting her in a way that only he could. The thought of never feeling him again caused tears to fall from her eyes.

"Don't cry. You want that nigga, right?" Czar kissed her tears.

"I- I- want youuuu," Marley moaned in his ear, further pissing him off.

"Liar." He bit her cheek.

For ten minutes, Czar fucked her against the door, making sure she'd never forget him. He lodged his dick so deep inside of her that whenever she walked, laughed, or went to the bathroom, she'd feel him. He disrespectfully busted her pussy open so when she decided to let Benny hit, he'd recognize that her pussy was no longer his home.

"Fuck," Czar grunted, releasing inside of her.

Slowly, he let her down and pulled back. Marley wiped her face and straightened out her clothes. Awkwardly she stood there waiting for him to say something, but he never did. Czar went back to the board and took a seat.

"Julius, can we please talk?"

"Are you going back to that nigga?" He lit his blunt,

blowing smoke in her direction.

"What would you do? If you were in this situation and you were him, what would you do?"

"You can't ask me that because I'm not that goofy ass nigga. Niggas protect what they value and you shouldn't have been in a situation where you could be touched. If I had beef in the street, you'd be locked up until I handle that shit. Your safety would've been my number one priority."

"I just need time to sort all of this out."

"And that's something I don't have to give. Get yo sad ass out of my fucking studio."

Dropping her head, Marley wiped the tears from her eyes. She wanted to plead for his forgiveness and friendship, but Czar wasn't the type of man you befriended. He was the type you fell in love with, the type that protected you from the world. Czar was the type of man you didn't let go of because as hard as he loved, he needed it in return.

"Aye," he stopped her.

With hope in her eyes, Marley turned around to face him.

"I got my clothes and shit from the loft. It's yours. The lease is paid up for a year." He tossed two keys to her. "Oh, and I put new tires on your ice cream truck. It's parked at the loft. Find something to do with it because if it lands in my tow yard again, I'm sending it through the smasher. Have a nice life, trap queen," Czar dismissed her.

Chapter 28

New Years Eve

Marley chewed on the corner of her lip while she waited for her website to update. Just like she thought, the tea facemask was a hit. Whenever she restocked, the product sold out in less than an hour. Harper swore it was a gold mine, and Marley had to agree. *Sippin' Tea* was doing better than ever, and Marley couldn't be prouder. She couldn't see it at the time, but Harper gave her something to occupy her time. *Sippin' Tea* was the perfect distraction. It was the one thing going good in her life, whereas everything else was in shambles.

"This tea shit legit?" Benny asked, looking over her shoulder.

"Yea." Marley nodded, closing her laptop. "It's my baby. When we first started I wasn't into it. Harper had to force me to do events and keep the page updated, but now it's something I enjoy doing."

"That's what's up. I didn't think you were into that kinda shit." He sat on the bed next to her. "Or at least you never expressed it to me."

"What do you mean?"

"When we were together you never showed interest in stuff like that. You used to draw in that notebook you carried around, but I didn't know you were into this." He pointed to her open notebook and invoices. "We could've started a business if that's what you wanted to do. I had the money then."

"You serious?" Marley peered. "Do you know how many times I asked you to slow down and invest your money? You told me that hustling was in your blood and your way out of the hood."

"You make it sound like I was some knucklehead," he chuckled. "I listened to you."

"You never listened to me, Benny, but I get it. Neither of us had the space to be creative and act on our dreams. You were raised in a fatherless household, and I had a mama who was for the streets. The cards were stacked against us, so we gravitated to what we knew best. I fell in love with a hustler who was in love with the streets."

"And after all this happened you decided you wanted to start a business?"

"No. I was only making tea because it made me feel good. It helped keep my mind off you and Billie. I was struggling to live, to keep pushing, but the smell of the different herbs and spices brought me back to life. Plus, they tasted good. If it weren't for Harper, I don't know where I'd be."

Benny wiped the corners of his mouth and watched Marley fiddle around on her phone. She was right on so many levels and his mind couldn't help but drift. He started to wonder if he was holding her back because it seemed like, without him, she had flourished. Marley was a grown ass woman, and it showed in the way she walked, talked, and took care of business. He always knew she was talented and hated that he didn't encourage her to follow her dreams instead of being a passenger in his.

"Well, I can invest now. I still have money put up and we can expand," Benny offered, and as nice as it was, Marley couldn't accept his offer.

"Um, no thanks. This is me and Harper's thing, but I can show you where to start."

"Nah, I'm straight. I was trying to be supportive but fuck it."

"Why are you getting mad?"

"Because I keep hitting all these dead ends with you. I been back almost three weeks and we still haven't fucked. I can't even get you to bring the New Year in with me.

"I'm not ready for sex, and you should understand that," Marley stressed. "And I don't do clubs anymore, we can stay here."

"Me and my niggas got a section, so staying in the house like old people not gone work for me. You free to do you though. I know me and my niggas not your speed anymore."

"Is that a bad thing?"

"Yea, when you act like you're better than us. I feel like I'm chasing you harder now than I did back then," Benny stressed. "It's almost like you don't trust a nigga no more."

"I don't," Marley belted. "From what I can see, you're still the same reckless ass person you were back then. I'm sure now you think you're untouchable. You wear those bullet holes as a badge of toughness; meanwhile, mine are a reminder of everything I lost."

"You tripping right now, Mars, but I'm about to dip.

Benny slid off the bed and was about to leave the room, but her phone rang, causing him to pause to see if she'd answer it. Thus far, if she wasn't talking to her sister, she didn't talk to anyone. When he asked her if she still talked to Czar's people, she said no, which wasn't a lie because she hadn't heard from them since their trip to the Maldives. Well, with the exception of Biggie. He checked in on her frequently.

"Hello."

"Happy New Year, bihhhhh!" Sammy sang into the phone. "Please tell me you're coming out with us tonight."

"Happy New Year, crazy girl! And no, I'm not coming with yall." Marley smiled, genuinely happy to hear from her.

"Boooo, you should. C got like two sections and a party bus. You remember the last time we went out, we turned the club out."

"That was a one-time thing. What are yall doing now?"

"Girl, nothing, at Mama Ada's house pregaming before we go turn the fuck up. Goose wanted me to call you. This nigga swear you was his girl. I think he moping harder than C."

"Oh God. Tell him I said hey!"

"His crazy ass can hear you." Sammy spun the camera around and Goose was standing in the middle of the floor two stepping. "This nigga swear he can dance. He dripping that hair gel shit everywhere."

"Hey, Uncle Goose," Marley giggled, knowing it would bother him.

"Oh nah, sweetheart, don't call me that shit. I'm trying to be Daddy." Goose stumbled toward the camera.

"I know you ain't talking to my girl," Romeo barked, stepping into the camera's view.

"You the only one that want the Bride of Chucky." Goose waved him off. "I'm talking to my boo." He pointed to the camera.

"Bae, he talking about LB," Sammy snickered.

"Where sis at?" Romeo turned around, seeing the phone in her hand. "Sis, what the fuck is good?" He cheesed. "We miss you."

"Hey Ro," Marley laughed. "I miss you too."

"You don't miss us enough. I heard you back with the nigga that faked his death."

"Ole *Weekends at Bernie* ass nigga." Nova popped into the camera. "Sup sis, or can I still call you that being that you left my brother for lil ugly?"

"Ole invasion of the zombies ass nigga," Romeo taunted.

"Ah," Goose laughed in the background. "Tag me in, nephew. I got one!" He held his hand out and Romeo slapped his palm. "Frankenstein ass boy."

"I hate yall," Sammy giggled. "Don't talk about her boyfriend like that."

"Fuck that nigga," Nova, Romeo, and Goose spat.

"Yall gotta chill." Marley tried her hardest to suppress her laughter because Benny was looking upside her head, waiting for her to defend him. Deciding it was best to end the call, Marley cleared her throat. Before she could bid them goodbye, she heard his voice.

"How the fuck yall leave me to bring all that shit in the house?" Czar barked in the background.

"You rich but yo hands ain't broke," Goose countered. "Ain't no special service around here."

"We talking to LB," Sammy messily announced. "Say hi."

"Hang up on her confused ass." Czar bopped over to the camera, snatching the phone from Sammy. Marley's heart skipped a beat once his handsome face appeared on the screen. Per usual, his locs were freshly retwisted and hung freely over his shoulders. She could tell from the picture that he smelled like fresh soap and sandalwood.

"Aye, hang that shit up!" Benny glared at Marley,

watching her hopelessly stare at the screen.

"Tell lil walking dead to chill," Czar chortled. He could've hung up or walked away, but the pettiness in his heart wasn't having it. "He taking care of you this time or are you ready to come to daddy?"

"Period, B-law!" Sammy clapped her hands. "Bring that ass home, LB! We miss you."

"She'll be back because I'm imprinted on that pussy, brain, and soul. Ain't that right, baby?" He licked his lips, making her pussy thump.

"I- uh gotta go," Marley stuttered.

"Aight but come see me when you need me to stretch that pussy out again." Czar cockily winked, ending the call before she had a chance to say anything.

"Again?" Benny barked, stepping in her face. "When was the last time you fucked that nigga?"

"You can't be serious." Marley stood up.

"Aye, don't play with my mind." He grabbed her arm.

"Benny. You better let me go before I stab you with this pencil. I don't know what kinda time you on, but you need to get your mind right."

"Let me get the fuck outta here because I swear you got me fucked up." Benny released her. "I think you should stay at your crib tonight."

"I was going to do that anyway." Marley rolled her eyes.

Without another word, Benny backed out of the room. He was starting to think Marley was right. His coming back might've been a mistake because they weren't the same people as three years ago. This version of them didn't belong together, but he couldn't see himself walking away from her.

∞∞∞

Czar didn't know whose idea it was to play basketball before they went out, but he was thankful. His lungs worked overtime to keep up and his knees felt like giving out, but it felt good to blow off some steam. Running up and down the court while dribbling the ball between his legs, Czar effortlessly pushed the ball to the other end of the court. He was playing what was supposed to be a friendly game with Shortie, Nova, and Romeo while Biggie recorded them. They were on their third game, and everybody was wheezing, but this was the tiebreaker. The losing team had to buy everybody Jordans and a Nike Tech outfit.

"Come the fuck on, nigga! Check him," Romeo yelled across the court at Nova.

"Fuck, how did I get the crybaby on my team?" he griped, reaching for the ball. Czar stepped back and passed the ball to Shortie, who ran around Romeo and scored. "And you let a midget get down on you."

"Fuck you." Romeo gave him the finger. "Ball up." He held his hands out.

"Yall can argue on yall way to the Nike store," Czar quipped. "Set me up for a dunk, Shortie," he instructed.

"Niggas play at Little Caesars and think they doing something," Nova balled up his mouth, dribbling the ball down the court.

"Don't be a fucking hater all your life." Shortie reached for the ball, stepping on his foot.

"Foul!" Romeo called out.

"Nigga, he fouled your teammate, not you," Biggie hackled from the sidelines.

"Shut your big ass up before I throw the ball at you."

"Fuck outta here. I'm fat but I got hands bitch."

Czar ignored their rant, keeping his eyes on Shortie. In a matter of seconds, Shortie snatched the ball from Nova and passed it to Czar, who dunked on Romeo's head.

"Foul!" Romeo hollered, falling to the ground.

"Ain't no foul, nigga. We won."

"Yall cheated."

"Nova, get your brother, and I want my Tech fit in navy blue."

"I'm not about to go shopping for another nigga, I'll send you the money." Nova waved him off, walking to the bleachers.

"I'm not buying shit! I want a rematch," Romeo hollered, dribbling the ball.

"Play by your damn self," Shortie bumped his shoulder, going to have a seat.

Czar picked up his water and guzzled half of the bottle before picking up his phone. He had a few missed calls from Honey and swiped to clear them. Czar didn't know what kinda time she was on, but Honey was becoming annoying. Fucking her while she was in town was cool, but it seemed like she was always in town and always wanted to link. He didn't want her feeling entitled or to think there was more to them other than fucking because that wasn't the case.

"I don't know how the fuck I be attracting the neediest bitches," Czar voiced, sliding his phone in his shorts.

"It's that mystery shit you got going on. Hoes be thinking they're going to be the first to crack the code," Romeo speculated.

"Who?" Nova asked. "The Honey chick?"

"Yea."

"I thought she lived out of state. How the fuck she always here?"

"Fuck if I know, but I'm about to block her annoying ass," Czar sneered. "I'm about to be celibate in a minute because this shit is getting out of hand."

"Have you talked to LB?" Biggie quizzed.

"The lil exchange today, but nothing serious."

"That's crazy," he sighed.

"What's crazy?" Czar glanced at him.

"That you let another nigga take your girl."

"Swear!" Romeo agreed. "I wasn't gone say shit because I know how sensitive you can be, but ain't no way. I'd go gun blazing to get my bitch back. Sammy annoying as hell, but she's mine, and dead or alive, ain't no nigga taking her from me."

"Yea, I'm not gone lie. LB cool as fuck and it's rare to find a woman yo whole family vibe with," Shortie cosigned. He didn't spend a lot of time with Marley, but his twin loved her, and that said a lot.

"Yall vibe with Sammy," Romeo reminded him.

"No, nigga, you vibe with her crazy ass and we just go with the flow because she crazy as fuck."

"Yall stupid." Czar stood up. "The fuck was I supposed to do when she wanted to go back to that nigga?"

"I don't know, but I do know that if she was mine, I wouldn't have gave her up so quick," Biggie imparted. "There are a million bad bitches with fake asses and long weave, but chicks like LB don't come around often. Her ex-nigga popped back up after she thought the nigga was dead. I'm sure that shit is confusing as fuck, and yo ass probably went off on her, making the choice easy."

"Fuck all that." Czar waved him off. "I'm not about to chase no bitch that's running after another nigga."

"I don't think it has anything to do with him honestly. I think it's more of the trauma that binds them. Their story is open-ended, and I don't know if she plans on staying with dude, but I'm pretty sure she's there looking for a different outcome for their situation," Biggie concluded, leaving them all speechless.

"Where the fuck that shit come from?" Nova questioned. "You been reading one of them Steve Harvey books?"

"Nah. LB gave me a facial and we talked about a lot of shit. She's cool people and I still check on her."

"The fuck, you still talk to her?" Czar squinted.

"Yea, nigga. You put me with her for months, we're friends."

"Yea, well like I said, I don't have shit to say to her."

"And I get it because I'm sure you've never felt those type of feelings, but running isn't going to make it any better. Love isn't something you can turn on and off."

"And the shit's not supposed to be hard."

"Nigga you fell in love with a broken heart," Biggie uttered. "That shit requires work. I know you didn't think it was going to be easy."

"I don't know what you been watching but change the channel. I'm straight on shorty and that's the end," Czar swore. "And stop talking to her."

"Aye, since we talking about relationships," Romeo started but everyone quickly walked away, leaving him sitting on the bleachers. "Fuck yall too," he called after them. Biggie had said a mouth full leaving Czar with a lot to think about.

∞∞∞

"I know you fucking lying!" Harper gawked, sticking her head out of the front door. "Get that shit out of my driveway. You bringing niggas and vans back from the dead. I need to sage."

"That's not funny." Marley frowned. "I just need somewhere to store it until I can figure out what I wanna do with it."

"You can take that shit to the junkyard for all I care." She blocked the doorway, preventing Marley from coming in. "Stop before I tell your husband you sent some packages to my loft."

"You wouldn't." Harper squinted.

"I would so open the door and let me in. My feet are cold."

"I should let you freeze after what you did to my brother-in-law."

"Harper, please." Marley pushed passed her. "He's not your brother-in-law because I'm not married to him."

"But you could've been! I had faith in you. We had a plan! I was going to carry yall baby and get a new body."

"Where is your husband? Because it's way too early for you to be drunk and harassing me."

"He's at his mama house with JJ. She's having a New Year's party and I acted sick. I have the house to myself; well I did until you showed up."

"I came to spill some tea, but I can hop back in my van and leave."

"You're boring, you don't have any tea."

"I cheated on Benny," Marley blurted.

"Oh shit! Well, step into this room." Harper extended her hand.

"You're an asshole."

"I'm just saying. This is some tea and I'm here for it." She pulled a bottle of wine off the rack on the wall. "Spill."

Marley sighed and started from the beginning. "So on Christmas Julius called me and told me I wasn't shit."

"Rightfully."

"Haha, very funny. Anyway, I was going to come over here a couple of days ago to clear my head, but I started thinking about him-

"Him or the dick?"

"Him. As much as I love his dick, I admire the person it's attached to. I miss him. Like a lot."

"Then be with him!" Harper stressed. "You don't owe Benny shit, and if I'm being honest, now that you know he's alive, it should be easier for you to move on. That nigga was safe and sound. You had a whole life before he came back. I mean has he said anything about who he was dealing with?"

"Girl, no. He claims it was easy to let it go."

"So he didn't give you a name or nothing?"

"Nope."

"Hm. Kinda fishy." Harper tooted her lips. "Well, we can look into it ourselves." She pulled out her phone.

"I'm pretty sure his street ass don't have a Facebook." Marley tooted her lips.

"You right, but this a different day and era. These niggas love flexing on the Gram. If he don't have one, I'm sure somebody he hangs with does. Oh!" Harper exclaimed. "What are those girls name again?"

"Gloss and Mel. Do Mel, she got a big mouth and she looks

like she post shit she shouldn't." Marley rounded the corner, standing next to her sister.

"Let's see." Harper typed Mel's name into the search bar and strolled down as the profiles started to populate. "That's a common name. What's the other one?"

"Gloss."

"Ok." She typed Gloss's name into the search bar. There were still a lot of names, just not as many Mel. "Tell me when you see here," Harper said, slowly scrolling down.

"Right there!" Marley exclaimed. "I think that's her with the blonde hair."

"Oh yea, they from Ohio. Them weak hoes lace fronts touch their eyebrows. Let's see what she got on here."

Quietly, the sisters scrolled on Gloss's Instagram page, not sure what they were looking for. Marley noticed that she posted a lot of fashion pictures, which made sense being that she wanted to start her own business. There were a few of Shooter, but his face was always covered. Marley knew it was him because of the tattoos on his arm.

"Bingo." Harper stopped.

There was a picture of Gloss, Mel, a few other girls, Tech, Shooter, and Benny's not so dead ass. Harper read the comments and clicked the profile of a girl who proclaimed Benny was bae. Marley didn't know why but her stomach started to twist.

"Mm," Harper grunted. "Ok, lil Ms. Ohio, you cute." She nodded, exploring the girl's page. "Oh shit!"

"What?"

"Nothing." Harper clicked the side button, cutting off the phone.

"What?" Marley asked again, this time placing her glass down.

"Nothing. That was stupid. You right, I'm drunk."

"Harper, stop playing with me." She reached for the phone. "What did you see?"

"Nothing, um, I think I'm about to go to bed. Let yourself out."

"I'll slap you. Give me the damn phone," Marley gritted.

"Ok, just wait one second."

Reluctantly, Harper handed her phone over. She grabbed the wine and put the cork on it before breaking out the heavy shit. Retrieving two shot glasses from the cabinet, she sat them on the counter and took a deep break.

"Go ahead."

"You so extra," Marley mumbled, cutting the phone back on. She entered Harper's password and the picture was still on the screen. Not believing her eyes, Marley shook her head and went to the next picture. Her eyes filled with tears as she swiped to the next picture.

"Oh my god!" Marley gasped, holding her chest as a video played.

The sound of a crying baby pierced her ears and tortured her heart. Benny rocked the newborn to his bare chest while cooing in her ear. The pink hat let Marley know it was a girl and somehow that made it ten times worse. Not only did he forget about her, but he went and started a whole new family.

"Here." Harper handed her a shot glass.

"This muthafucka." Marley laughed through the tears that streamed down her face. "I was over this nigga! I fucking moved on!"

"I know."

"And he got another bitch pregnant!" She continued to examine each picture.

With each video and picture, Marley's heart constricted a little more. According to Instagram, Benny was the father of the year; meanwhile, he hadn't visited their daughter's gravesite yet. He hadn't asked her any details concerning their baby girl, yet he was on the fucking internet loving on a child that didn't come from her womb.

"Marley, did he tell you how he found you?" Harper softly asked.

"No." She wiped her nose.

"Um, on Christmas when Mama came over, she told me that she contacted Benny and gave him your number and address. She said it was a good deed, but I know she had an ulterior motive. I'm sure seeing Tech was just a coincidence, but I do think he was coming to find you."

"Why though?" Marley wiped her nose. "Why the fuck would he come disturb my peace and he has a whole fucking family?"

"Because niggas are selfish, Marley. I can almost bet when he saw you trending he lost his mind. You elevated without him in your life."

"Oh my God. I'm so fucking stupid."

"Maybe a little, but we all play the fool."

"I couldn't even admit that I loved Julius because I was still mourning him, because I felt like giving my heart to someone else was betraying him, and a year after being shot the fuck up, this nigga started a new family?" Marley rhetorically asked, slapping her chest. Picking up the shot glass, Marley tossed it back and reached for the bottle. "Ugh! I'm going to kill him."

"And I'm going to bury his funky ass body," Harper toasted.

Chapter 29

Marley didn't wake up until almost three in the afternoon the next day. Her head was spinning, but the anger in her bloodstream outweighed the hangover she was suffering from. All night she went through Toya's page, watching videos of her and Benny's life together. Half of the time, Benny didn't know she was recording, and by the time he found out, it was too late. They looked happy, and Marley couldn't figure out why he came back. Why would he leave his family to uproot her life? Why wouldn't he tell her that he had a daughter with someone else? The questions she had could only be answered by him.

"You're up." Jaxon startled her, stepping into the living room with a cup of black coffee in his hand. Marley sat up and he extended it to her.

"Yea," she grumbled. "I don't even know how I made it to the couch."

"Yall were passed out on the kitchen floor. I brought you in here and took Harper upstairs. She kept ranting about fighting some Ohio bitch. The fuck yall do last night? My wife been throwing up for three hours straight."

"I'm pretty sure we have alcohol poisoning." Marley shook her head. She was pretty sure she cussed out Benny, drunk called Czar, and sent the Toya bitch a DM. "Oh my God." She held her head.

"Wanna talk about it?" Jaxon sat across from her.

"Not really," Marley mumbled, feeling stupid.

"Yall drunk all my 1938 and polished off the rest of the Henny. Something is on your mind."

"I messed up... bad." she sniffled, overcome with emotion. "I've been sad for so long and I thought Benny was the cure to my pain, to my sadness. When he showed up, I thought I was getting a second chance, so it was a no-brainer."

"And now?"

"And now I'm in love with someone else, and this nigga has a whole familyyyyyy," Marley cried.

"Awe, sis." Jaxon moved closer to her, removing the coffee from her hand.

"I fucked up and now Julius hates me."

"That nigga don't hate you. His pride hurt. No man wants to be someone's second option. As men, we pride ourselves on knowing that our women can't be touched, and I'm sure for him, this was a humbling experience. As for Benny, that nigga on some slime shit. I'm sure he saw you out here shining and thought he could come through and reclaim some shit."

"Would you have come back for Harper?"

"I would've never left her, but honestly, if three years had passed, I'd let her live her life. As much as I love your sister, I'd want her to be happy, and if she thought I was dead and found happiness in another nigga, then that's just what it is. On the flip side," Jaxon rubbed his beard, "Your sister is my whole life. There's no way I could claim to love her as much as

I do and let her think I was dead."

"Oh my God, I'm stupid." Marley's head fell into her hands.

"Nah, you just made a mistake and sometimes they can be corrected. You know what you need to do."

"Um, Daddy," JJ whispered, rounding the corner with his hands behind his back.

"Yes, son."

"I made Mommy a magic drink to make her feel better and she's puking in your bed."

"You what?" Jaxon jumped up.

"I gave her orange juice, pickle juice, and a little hot sauce." He shrugged as if he hadn't just mixed a bunch of bullshit that was going to have his mama on the toilet for the next few hours.

"JJ!"

"It's a magic potion I learned from clownspellsrus.com," JJ defended. "I was trying to help Mommy because she kept running to the bathroom."

"Stay out of the damn kitchen, boy," Jaxon fussed as he bypassed him.

Taking a seat on the couch, JJ and Marley shared a look before a small grin stretched across his little lips.

"Do you-

"Don't even try it." Marley mushed him. "I'm about to take a shower. Go have a seat and don't touch anything until your dad comes back down here."

"Man, that's cold," JJ pouted. "I wanted to make Mommy feel better and I get in trouble."

"You're not in trouble, but I didn't know clowns made magic potions."

"I'm a clown that does it all," he cheesed.

"Oh yea, can you turn back the hands of time and make me smarter?" Marley joked.

"No, but if you want to fly, I think I can make you a bird."

"I'll pass." She kissed his forehead. "Stay out of the kitchen."

"Ok." JJ sat back on the couch and folded his arms.

Marley picked up her phone off the floor and staggered to the bathroom. The thought of lying back down crossed her mind, but she couldn't go another minute without giving Benny a piece of her mind. She wasn't the same immature girl she was years ago. She wasn't about to battle a bitch for his love, love that she had outgrown at that.

∞∞∞

Hours later, Benny was laid out in the middle of his bed. His first New Year's back in Detroit hadn't been anything short of perfection. He popped out showing niggas he was still untouchable. His clique was loud and proud, boasting in the middle of the club like niggas weren't still wanting their heads. Benny bought the bar and had nothing but bad bitches in their section. Benny felt good. While he partied, he ignored calls from Toya and Marley. They were both blowing up his phone, but Benny's hands were full of ass, and at that moment, he didn't give a fuck what they were talking about.

"Yo, Benny." Ruben tapped on his bedroom door. "Mars just hopped out of a Uber and she look mad as hell."

"What?" Benny mumbled, turning over.

"Nigga, she beating on the door."

"Let her in, the fuck?" He sat up, rubbing his eyes.

Benny reached for his phone and saw all the missed calls and texts from Toya. Marley's name was sprinkled in the mix, but Toya was going hard. She was threatening to put his shit out and flush his drugs if he didn't return her call. Quickly clicking on one of the texts, he read the message and almost shit on himself.

Toy: Um I don't know what you're telling ole girl but keep her ass out of my inbox.

"Hm. Same look I had when I discovered you had a fucking baby." Marley pushed into the room. The door flung back so hard that the knob created a hole in the wall.

"Aye, I can explain." Benny stood up.

"Do you or don't you have a baby with some bowlegged bitch from Ohio?"

"I do, but-

"There is no but, Benny!" Marley yelled at the top of her lungs, causing the vein in her neck to make an appearance. "You left me for fucking dead and then have the nerve to come back for me after you made a family for yourself? In what fucking world does that make sense?"

"It don't, but I saw you and I couldn't let it go, aight? You were always supposed to be mine."

"But you put us in a situation and it caused you to lose me, nigga!" Marley shouted, swinging at him. Benny jumped back and fell into all the shoe boxes that lined the wall.

"Fuck," he grumbled as she started throwing bottles of cologne at him. "Chill the fuck out!"

"Nigga, fuck you!" Marley charged him.

"Aye, one of yall come get this girl off me," Benny hollered, feeling like he was being attacked by a raccoon. Marley's hands were little, but she packed a mean punch. Her nails dug into his arms as if she was trying to skin him alive.

She showed no mercy as she fought him through her tears.

"Aight, come on, lil mama." Ruben picked her up, which proved to be a mistake. Marley wiggled out of his arms and reached into her pocket. In one swift motion, she removed her pepper spray and tapped the nozzle.

"Ah fuck!" Ruben hollered, falling against the TV and knocking it off the wall. With him blinded, Marley jumped on Benny, digging her nails into his eyes.

"Aye, yall know the front door open?" Shooter skeptically asked, walking to the back of the house with Gloss on his heels. "What the fuck!" His eyes doubled in size, watching Marley try to snatch Benny's hair out of his scalp.

"Aye, bro, get her off me," Benny breathlessly demanded. He knew Marley was mad, and he was trying his damnedest not to hit her back, but she was fighting him like a bitch off the street.

"Sis, sis, chill," Shooter pleaded, trying to pry Marley's fingers from Benny's hair. She had a grip on his shit tighter than African braiding shops pulling someone's edges.

"Don't call me sis, you fake ass nigga!" Marley released Benny. "You knew this nigga had a family in Ohio and you couldn't warn me? The same sis that used to cook you meals, that gave you a listening ear and advice when this nigga was treating you like a peasant? The same sis that beat up hoes for you even when you were in the wrong? You niggas got money and forgot about the sis that had your fucking back since grade school. I wasn't just there for this nigga. I was there for all yall, so spare me that sis shit. Benny, drop dead, and this time I won't shed a fucking tear!"

Turning on her heels, Marley started snatching her things from Benny's room and stomped through the house, knocking over everything in her path. Before Benny could get a word out, the tattered front door was kicked off the hinges.

Like a deer caught in headlights, Marley froze as masked men ran into the house pointing guns at them.

"Get the fuck on the floor!" One of the intruders pushed Marley to the ground.

Ruben came from the back with his gun drawn, but his stinging eyes caused him to lose focus, and he was popped in the back of the head with a gun, knocking him out cold.

"Do yall niggas know who yall robbing?" Gloss screamed.

"Ask me do I give a fuck?" Another intruder responded, slapping her upside the head with the butt of his gun.

Marley wanted to make a run for it, but she was stuck. Her life started to flash before her eyes and it scared her that with Benny there was no future. It took him coming back for Marley to realize that God didn't make mistakes. While she wanted Benny in her life, the man upstairs had his own plans. By her veering off from those plans, it changed the course of her life, putting her back at square one. This time she understood, and instead of asking God why this was happening to her, she silently repented, swearing she'd follow His lead if He got her out of this situation alive.

"Let's go, you niggas know the drill." The masked man pointed a gun at Benny, who wanted to kick his own ass for getting caught up. "You niggas was stuntin' last night. Where the dope, where the money?"

"Ain't shit in here, man." Shooter scowled with his hands in the air.

"Then we about to air this bitch out." The intruder pressed the gun to the back of Marley's head. "Aye bitch, run all that shit."

"P-p-please don't kill me." She frantically shook her head.

"Shut the fuck up and take this shit off."

With shaking hands, Marley removed her necklace and

watch.

"Oh shit, jackpot." He held it up to the light. "This bitch got diamonds on her neck in this fucking neighborhood. What else you got?" He dug the gun into her back, roughly patting her down. Snatching the purse from her shoulder, he tossed the contents on the floor, keeping her bank card and a few dollars.

"Aight, aight, let her go. Everything yall want is in the garage," Benny gave in, knowing the dope in the garage wasn't shit compared to what he had at home in Ohio.

"Then let's go nigga," the first intruder demanded, pushing him and Shooter out of the door while his counterpart stayed put with his gun trained on Gloss and Marley.

"Just don't hurt her, aight," Benny requested but was hit upside the head with the gun.

"Worry about your damn self." The intruder popped him upside the head again.

Marley didn't know how much time had passed, but when Benny returned, he was bloody, Shooter's eye was swollen shut, and the masked men were gone. As if a tornado had touched down, the house was a complete disaster. In their pursuit to find money and dope, the masked men cut up the couch cushions, flipped over tables, and completely destroyed the bedrooms. They left out with boxes of shoes, name brand clothing, and belts.

Marley was still lying on the floor, completely shook. She could hear the commotion going on around her, but her mind had checked out of the situation. She was supposed to be somewhere laid with up Czar, not on a dirty ass floor inhaling all kinds of debris. Benny laid beside her, trying to bring her back, but his pleas for her to get up went ignored.

"Call her sister," Shooter suggested.

"Nigga, no. Mars just almost blinded Ruben dumb ass with the fucking pepper spray. What do you think her crazy ass sister is going to do when she finds out she was held at gunpoint again?" Benny harshly whispered. "Mars, come on baby, get up, let me take care of you."

Take care of you. He was always supposed to take care of her but fell short every time. As if something snapped inside her, Marley jerked away from him. She didn't need him to comfort her when he was the source of her pain. Standing to her feet, Marley picked up her bag and went to lock herself in the bathroom.

∞∞∞

Czar listened to Marley's drunken messages for what seemed like the 20th time. The shit was corny, but Marley and Harper had zero sense, and he was tempted to use the voicemail as an intro for a song. One minute she was crying and begging him to come save her from herself, and the next she was cursing him out for something she saw on social media.

"It's his voicemail," Marley slurred. "I told you his mean ass wasn't going to answer. He don't love me no moreeeeee," she whined before they both burst out laughing.

"Bitch, stop! He not gone take us seriously," Harper hissed.

"Ok, ok." Marley cleared her throat. "Julius, I'm sorry. I made the dumbest decision in the world. I miss you and I want you."

"And?" Harper coached.

"And you better not be fucking nobody like you fuck me, or I promise I'll beat you and that bitch up."

"And I'mma help her."

-beep-

"You need to hear the beat again?" the producer asked, glancing at Czar, who had totally checked out of the session.

"Nah," he said without looking up. "I don't like it. Shit sounds demonic as fuck, like I'm about to turn in Doja Cat or some shit."

"Aye, I was thinking the same thing," Biggie agreed, shifting on the couch. "Like you about to start calling out to the dead homies," he joked, removing his phone from his joggers. Hitting the speaker button, Marley's sniffles filled the room, sucking the life out of Czar. In two seconds, he was across the room, snatching the phone from Biggie before he could ask her what was going on.

"LB," he questioned.

"Can I please talk to Biggie?"

"Nah, talk to me. What's wrong?"

"Can you tell him to come get me?" Her voice broke.

"Where you at?" Czar grabbed his keys from the table and practically ran out of the studio. Biggie pulled out his second phone and started making calls.

"At Benny's house in southwest. I was leaving and the house was robbed. They took m-my necklace and watch and pointed a gun at my head," she cried into the phone.

"Cut on your location," Czar told her, hopping in the passenger seat of his truck.

"Mmm uh," Marley moaned. "I'm so sorry, Julius."

"We'll talk about all that shit later," he told her as Biggie wildly pulled into traffic. "Where are you in the house?"

"I locked myself in the bathroom."

"Aight, sit tight. I need to make a call. I'll be there soon."

"Ok." Marley nodded, ending the call.

"I swear to God if these niggas touched my baby, I'm about to be out for blood," Czar ranted.

"She straight, let's just get her and move around. I don't trust niggas who fake their death." Biggie gripped the steering wheel, pushing the truck to the limit.

∞∞∞

"Mars!" Benny beat on the bathroom door. "Open the door for me, baby," he pleaded. "We need to leave."

Yanking the door open, Marley flew at Benny with her fists balled up.

"I fucking hate you!" she screamed. "You keep doing this to me!"

"I'm so fucking sorry. I'm going to find them niggas."

"Fuck them, Benny! This is your fault. You did this because I keep trusting you to protect me."

"I fucked up." He pulled her into his arms.

"That's the problem." Marley pushed against him. "You keep fucking up and I keep paying the price. I'll never make the mistake of thinking you can protect me when you can't even protect yourself. Go back to Ohio and leave me the fuck alone."

"Aye, it's a truck full of niggas out here," Tech announced, standing in the hallway. "I think it's that rapping nigga."

"You called him?" Benny beseeched, staring at Marley in disbelief.

"You thought I wouldn't," Marley snapped, wiping her face. With Czar nearby, she found a new sense of confidence.

"Good, then you can see me murk this fake Future wanna-be ass nigga." He spun around and marched out the door with Marley on his heels.

Once they made it to the front door, the passenger door on the truck opened and Czar stepped out in all black. A ski mask covered his face, but Marley knew it was him. His dark orbs bounced around the scene until they landed on her, and only then did they soften.

"Let's go, LB," his deep voice demanded.

"Nah, she straight." Benny grabbed Marley by the back of her shirt. "You think you about to come to my hood and take my bitch?!"

"I can't take what's already mine. Now my nigga we can do this shit the easy way or the hard way. Either way, she leaving."

"You wanna bet?" Benny cocked his gun, putting a bullet in the chamber.

Unfazed, Czar glanced behind him, and all the truck doors opened. Nova, Romeo, Shortie, Biggie and a few more men Marley had never seen hopped out of the trucks holding guns the length of their arms.

"You don't have enough money to bet me nigga, and you don't have enough lives to outrun me," Czar promised. "LB, let this bum know what it is so we can get the fuck from around here."

"Like I said," Benny raised his gun with one arm and gripped Marley's shirt with the other, "She not going nowhere."

"Do you think this is fair?" Marley yanked away from him. "I don't know what your thought process was behind all of this, and I don't care. You decided not to come back because of the guilt you felt. It had nothing to do with what my mama said. You simply couldn't look me in the face every day knowing all the pain you caused. If you ever loved me, you need to let me go, and this time don't come back."

"So that's it?" Benny balled up his face.

"That's it." Marley turned on her heels and walked toward Czar. Her heart was wildly thumping against her chest, but Biggie gave her a reassuring smile. She had nothing to be afraid of because they had her back.

Not one to take rejection lightly, Benny raised his gun, aiming it at her back. His finger shakily rubbed against the trigger, but he hesitated to pull it. Benny didn't know if he could kill his first love, but he also couldn't see her walk away from him.

"Nigga, chill, let her go." Shooter stepped in front of the line of fire as Marley climbed into the back seat of the truck.

"So let them take my girl?" Benny roared with spit flying from his mouth.

"Wake the fuck up. She's not your girl anymore, nigga. You need to let that shit go. It's the least you can do."

"The fuck you saying?"

"That she deserves better than this," Shooter reasoned, turning around just in time to see the trucks pulling off. "Let's go, Gloss. I'll see you back in Ohio." There was nothing left for him in Detroit.

∞∞∞

Marley sat in the back seat curled into Czar's side. She didn't know what to say, but it felt good being in his arms, so she savored the moment. Czar hadn't said anything to her, nor had he released his grip on her waist. Quiet as it was kept, the frantic call from Marley scared him. The entire way to her, he contemplated ways to make Benny disappear.

"You eat?" Czar asked staring down at her, breaking the silence.

"I can stop somewhere," Biggie quickly answered. He had been in the studio all day with Czar and eating didn't sound like a bad idea. He needed something fat and greasy to soak up the liquor from the night before. Their New Year party went off without a hitch. They smoked and passed around bottles of liquor all night, and Czar still woke up inspired. Biggie loved his dedication to his craft, but he was hungry as fuck.

"Nigga, you need to start carrying around a box of Lunchables or a fanny pack full of snacks," Czar shot.

"Fuck you, skinny boy." Biggie gave him the finger through the rearview mirror but made a mental note to get some car snacks.

"I'm not hungry. I just wanna go to bed," Marley sighed, running her hands across her face. She was in need of a shower, a cup of tea, and a warm bed.

"Aight, I'mma drop you off at the loft."

"Wait," Marley panicked. "You're not staying?"

"Nah. I just wanted to make sure you were safe. I'm still not fucking with you like that."

"Julius, I'm sorry," she pouted.

"I don't know if I believe that. What happens if another dead ex pops up and you decide you want to try to relive the past with him? I'm supposed to trust that you won't do that hoe ass shit again?"

"That's not fair."

"Life's not fair, my baby. And I'd believe you if your moods didn't shift with the wind, and I don't have time for that shit."

"Then why come get me? I called Biggie." Marley pushed off him. "I didn't even call you!"

"See what I'm saying. Shifty ass." Czar thumbed his nose.

"And check this out," he scooted closer to her, "I came and got you because I fucking love your hardheaded ass, and as bothered as I am about the entire situation, I would have bodied that nigga if something happened to you."

"Then come home with me," she pouted. "Come cuddle with me."

"Nah, I'm straight. Go upstairs and lock the doors. Call me if you need me." He hit the locks, and only then did Marley realize they were in front of her loft.

Chapter 30

One week later

It was three in the afternoon, and instead of getting ready for his interview with Nesha Re, Czar found himself waiting for his mama to emerge from the nail salon. Slim was supposed to pick her up, but he volunteered to do it. Czar could have bad blood with anybody in the world, but when it came to his favorite girl, it didn't sit right in his spirit to be at odds with her. Just when he thought about calling her, Ada exited the shop with her phone pressed to her ear. Czar watched her, wondering if she was on the phone with Cain. The thought instantly pissed him off, causing him to blow the horn. Ada nearly jumped out of her skin. Pushing her purse on her shoulder, she stalked over to him.

"I'mma slap the shit out of you, Julius," she snapped when she slid in the front seat. "I almost pissed on myself."

"Don't blame your weak bladder on me," he chortled.

"I am. You and your brothers. I can't even cough without clenching."

"That's messed up."

"Yea, well that's what happens when you alter your body to bring life into this world." Ada twisted her lips. "Weak bladder, stretch marks, saggy breasts, and a million other things, buts it's all in the name of love. When you have kids of your own, you'll understand. Being a parent is one of the most selfless things a person could ever do."

"I hear you." Czar pulled away from the curb.

For a moment, the car was quiet as they both sat, listening to The Isley Brothers and overthinking. Ada didn't know where to begin. She was caught in a space where she was tired of apologizing for her past but felt the need to explain her reasoning for handling the situation as she saw fit.

"I know you're mad at me," Ada sighed, breaking the silence. "I'm not going back to him. I'm just going to get the pictures and we'll be free."

"Why put yourself in that position though?"

"Julius, I don't have to keep explaining myself to you. I'm the parent, you're my child, not the other way around."

"I think my earliest memory of my childhood was Cain dragging you across the kitchen floor. He was mad because you fed me first, so he threw my plate away and made me go to bed. You tried to hug me goodnight, and of course, that pissed the nigga off, and he started his bullshit."

"I remember that." Ada tucked her lips. There were still burn marks on her back from being dragged across the floor.

"Even then, I knew he didn't deserve you. He was nothing like the men on TV. He didn't come home and kiss you, he didn't play with me, and honestly, I didn't even want him to. The only thing I ever wanted was for you to be free. I used to think that if you didn't have me, he wouldn't be so mean to you, that you wouldn't cry so much."

"It wasn't you."

"I know that now, but as a kid, that kind of shit messed with my head. I started to wonder if I would grow up to be like him, but I loved you too much to ever be anything like him, but I didn't want to be like you either. So nah, Ma, I'm not mad. I'm disappointed." Czar wiped the tears from his face. "We escaped hell, and there are thousands of people who don't, so the thought of you negotiating with that man fucks with my head, Ma."

Ada silently cried, tucking her lip into her mouth. Czar normally didn't go into detail about the horrible encounters they experienced. She thought he blocked them out, but to hear him recall something that happened when he was only five broke her heart.

"Me saying this was not to make you cry or dig at old wounds, but don't sell me a dream. You can't tell me that you stand behind me, then go behind my back and talk to the same nigga that drove us into the ground. You don't have to write the book but don't fall back down the rabbit hole chasing your tail. I'll pay the nigga off, and we can go on about our life. I need you to let me handle it."

"I don't know what I did to deserve you."

"God knew you needed a real nigga in your life, so he sent you a son," he smirked. "I gotta go to my interview, but I'll be by later so we can talk. This lil booty girl stressing me out," Czar chuckled, trying to lighten the mood.

"That's good. It's about time you found someone to stress you out," Ada chuckled. "Is she ok?"

"Why you ask that?"

"Because you said the first girl you fell in love with needed to be saved. Who does she need saving from?"

"Ma, I-

"It's ok, Czar. I'm aware that my situation left you with some unsolved problems but don't allow my past to affect your future. Is she worth saving?"

"She is."

"Then that's all that matters," Ada smiled. "Now hurry up and get me home before I pee all in these comfortable seats."

"That's why yo sons act like heathens."

"Boy, hush, all my children are well-mannered."

Feeling a little lighter, Czar sat back in his seat and headed to his parents' house. He was running late for his interview, but he was now able to walk in with a clear head, and that was good news for everybody involved.

∞∞∞

"What's up, Detroit? I'm here with Detroit's favorite bad boy, the one and only Czar," Nesha Re hooted in the microphone.

"What up doe Re." Czar coyly smiled, giving her the proper Detroit greeting.

"What up doe." She shifted in her seat, understanding why women fell at his feet. His enticing scent had her ready to jump across the table. It didn't help that he had a beautiful smile and a deep voice. "Listen yall, I've been trying to get this man on my show for months now. I was on his team's ass, like this man promised me a show and I want that shit now."

"My fault. I know about the rescheduling, but life be doing its thing, and we all know how that goes."

"No need to explain. We all need time to take care of ourselves." She nodded, completely understanding. "We're going to start with a quick icebreaker, you down?"

"Let's go." Czar rubbed his hands together.

"As you know, I switched platforms and this is my shit," Nesha Re boasted. "There are no rules, and you can be as free as you want."

"So you telling me to act up?" He grinned, pulling his bottom lip into his mouth.

"Do whatever feels natural," Nesha Re flirted like she wasn't a married woman. "Liquor, brown or light?"

"Brown."

"Favorite football team?"

"The Lions, the fuck?"

"Should've known. You're a diehard Detroit fan. Favorite food?"

"Pizza."

"Favorite color?"

"Black."

"Favorite thing about a woman?"

"Oh, that's a good one." Czar leaned back and his mind immediately shifted to Marley. His favorite thing about her was everything. Her voice, her smile, her lips, her narrow waist, and her hand full of ass. "That's hard to say." He stroked his chin. "When I'm into a woman, everything about her is my favorite thing."

"And this new little lady that's all over your page is someone you're into?" Nesha Re probed.

"Aw shit." Czar leaned back into his chair. "Ro, pour me a shot."

Romeo chuckled and removed a bottle of Hennessy from his backpack. They were all aware that Czar wasn't a fan of interviews and he hated talking about his life even more, but Nesha Re was right. She had been trying to get him in for months, and he canceled every time.

"Ro, pour us all a shot." Nesha Re danced in her seat. "And you a lil cutie." She winked.

"Sweetheart, don't do it. I'll have you sitting in divorce court begging that man to let you keep your last name."

"Oh, and I don't need those problems," she laughed. "These are your brothers, right?"

"Yea, but they are more than that. Romeo is my walking PalmPilot. He schedules everything from shows to coordinating with the venues to make sure shit is right when I arrive. He takes care of my flights, travel arrangements and all. I'd be lost without him. Nova is the head of security and takes his job seriously as hell. He vets everybody I come into contact with, and it can be overwhelming, but he be on my ass. Shortie and his brother Biggie are my shadows. They travel with me everywhere I go, and besides my brothers, they are the only ones I trust with my life."

"A family business, I love that. They're young, so I'm guessing after they graduated high school they started working for you."

"Nah. They don't work for me; they work with me, but they went to college after high school. It was a requirement before they joined my team. They need to be able to sit in a boardroom and properly articulate so nothing goes over their heads. They all have degrees and businesses of their own," Czar revealed.

"Really?"

"Hell yea. Nova has a degree in Homeland Security, and Romeo has two in Business Administration and Accounting. Shorty and Biggie have degrees in Computer Science. Our playing field is leveled."

"Now that is taking care of your family on a whole different level." Nesha Re clapped her hands. "Shoot, let me get some act right in the presence of all this talent."

"You straight," Czar chuckled.

"Ok, so the home front seems straight, let's get into some messy stuff. What's going on with you and Ms. Tati?"

"Oh hell nah," Nova snorted. "Give him another shot."

"I take it you don't like her," Nesha Re laughed.

"It's not that I don't like her; I don't like her ways. This industry has a way of turning the good girls bad. The Tati that you see today isn't the Tati we met a couple of years ago."

"And you agree?" She glanced at Czar.

"Yea but change the subject. That girl is like Beetle Juice, say her name too many times and she'll pop up."

"So let me ask you this and I'll change the subject. She's been getting a lot of sympathy because of the loss of her baby. Do you check on her?"

"For what? That wasn't my kid, and if miscarriages and abortions are the same thing, let me know something."

"Oh shit!" Nesha Re covered her mouth. "Are you saying she aborted the baby?"

"I'm saying that everything isn't always as it seems. Muthafuckas be supporting a cause that they don't know shit about."

"Preach to these people! Since we're on the topic, how do you feel about social media?"

"Social media is a fucking façade. We live in the day and age where a person can get on Twitter, post a couple of stolen quotes, pictures, and backgrounds, and all of a sudden, they're an influencer and can pass judgment on other muthafuckas."

"I agree, and you know what? That's why I like you. You've remained the same since I first met you."

"I am who I am." Czar shrugged.

"The fuck?" Nova said aloud, causing Czar to turn around.

"What?"

"We gotta go." He headed to the door. With no questions asked, Czar followed suit. Nesha Re stood up trying to figure out what was happening. She didn't make it out the door before the phone lines in the studio were blowing up. Her cell phone started going off with notifications from every social network.

"Oh my god!" She covered her mouth.

∞∞∞

"You want her? Come get her. I'll be in touch and don't tell your bitch ass uncle daddy or I'll send her fingers in the mail."

Fire flooded Czar's bloodstream as he listened to the voicemail. His heart ached and the unsettled agony in the pit of his stomach had him ready to vomit at any minute. Each time he heard Cain's voice, his heart grew a little colder. His eyes grew darker, and the devil positioned on his shoulder told him exactly what he needed to hear. There was no compromising. Cain violated him in the worst way and there was only one way to make amends.

"You want her? Come get her."

Fear, embarrassment, and a tremendous amount of anxiety tortured his being as wild thoughts penetrated his mind. Naked pictures of Ada spread through social media like California wildfires, and there was nothing he could do to stop it. It didn't matter that she was underage at the time or that she was high out of her mind. People captioned them for laughs, not caring about the pain it caused. The Internet therapists started to dissect his family as if the pictures were the answers to Czar's behavior. People were tagging him, while others jumped in his DMs to check on him. Czar's phone was going off with calls from the label's PR team, Terri, and Honey. Czar was sure by now Terri was doing damage control and needed him to clarify a few things, but he didn't have the mental capacity to clear shit up for him.

"What the fuck we gone do?" Romeo asked, pacing. They knew one day the pictures would surface, but not like this. They were blindsided and unprepared.

"I have people looking for her," Slim sighed. He too was fucked up and couldn't believe Cain not only released the pictures but snatched Ada up as well.

"The same people you had watching the nigga?" Czar snorted, glaring up from his phone with raised nostrils. His eyes were bloodshot red and his fingers drummed against his thigh. "See how that shit turned out," he scoffed.

"You got something you need to get off your chest?" Slim peered in his direction. "Are you blaming me for this shit?"

"Nah," Czar denied. "Just stating facts, but I understand your hesitation. He's your brother, and the thought of bringing harm to him might not sit well with you, but no worries, I got it."

"C, I don't think-

"I really don't give a fuck what you think because it's your job to protect her. The minute you came to pick us up from that shitty ass homeless shelter, you assumed responsibility for her. You're supposed to protect her from the world. It's your job as her husband and father of her fucking kids, but you failed," Czar roared. "I guess that's what you and your brother got in common because yall both keep fumbling her trust."

Slim flew across the living room and snatched Czar up by the collar of his shirt. He raised his fist to hit him but stopped when a small smile appeared on Czar's face. It was as if he was daring him to hit him.

"What, you gone beat me like that nigga too?" He chuckled.

"Fuck you, Czar. I'm not like him," Slim growled. "I love my wife and I love your knuckle headed ass."

"Then you should've put a bullet in that nigga instead of offering him money." Czar yanked away from him. "I'm out." He headed to the front door. "And I don't need none of you niggas following me. I'll bring her home myself."

∞∞∞

Marley was dead to the world when she felt someone staring at her. The TV offered a small light, but not enough to see the figure's face. She knew falling asleep on the couch was a bad idea, but she didn't like the thought of lying in that big bed by herself. She prayed Benny hadn't broken into her house, but then again, she didn't put it pass him. Benny had been calling her phone nonstop begging her to let him explain. As far as she was concerned, Marley didn't have anything to say to him. He might as well chalk their situation up as a lesson learned because she did. Jumping up, she grabbed the pepper spray from under her pillow and aimed it into the dark.

"What I tell you about that lil shit," Czar spoke, causing her to sigh in relief. "You gone fuck around and spray that shit in your own eyes one day."

"I'm not because I can feel the nozzle. Why are you being a creep?"

"Because you snoring and shit. I guess after shacking up in the trap you needed to catch up on your rest."

"I wasn't shacking up." Marley sat the pepper spray next to her.

"I don't know what the fuck you were doing since you decided to break up with me," Czar growled.

"I already apologized, what else do you want?"

"Figure it out," he snapped.

"What are you doing here, Julius? I thought you gave me back my key."

"That was just one copy. I was hoping to catch that nigga in here. I was going to fuck him and you up." He glared at her.

"I wouldn't do that," Marley said just above a whisper. "I never brought him here."

"I'm fucked up." Czar dropped his head, locking his fingers behind his neck. "You're the only person I feel like being under and I hate that shit."

Marley pushed the covers off her body and slid off the couch. She walked over to him, positioning herself between his legs. Czar removed his hands and wrapped them around her waist. Burying his head in her stomach, he exhaled.

"For as long as I've remembered, my past is something I didn't talk about. It's like this dark ass secret I've held onto. I'm good at burying that shit, but now," he sighed. "I can't get away from it. No amount of money can erase it or the emptiness I feel." Czar sat back and chuckled. "The crazy thing is I don't think about that shit when I'm with you. When I'm next to you my mind be so fucking clear and I love that shit."

"Julius-

"You ain't gotta say shit. That's just some intrusive thoughts I needed to get out. I just need a minute to clear my head," he sighed.

Czar didn't have to mention the pictures because Marley saw them every time she opened Instagram. It got so bad that Marley deleted the app. She liked Ada and couldn't continue to see her like that. Even when some of the pictures were flagged, people moved them over to Twitter and made collages.

"You want some tea?"

"Yea."

"Ok." Marley released him.

Slipping on her Crocs, Marley went into the kitchen to prepare Czar a cup of chamomile tea with honey infused CBD. While the water boiled, she sliced fresh lemons and oranges to add a hint of citrus. After rolling a couple of joints, she returned with a tray that contained two cups of tea, a lighter, and her bedazzled clip.

"I'm still not fucking with you like that," Czar reminded her, taking the cup of tea from her hands. "Ain't shit changed."

"I know." She slowly blew her tea while he lit the joint. Reaching for her phone, Marley tapped on the screen until Russ's *Losin Control* started to play, filling the quiet space.

She's fallin' in love now, losin' control now.

Fightin' the truth tryin' to hide, but I think it's alright girl.

Silently, they sat in the dark, sippin' tea, smoking, and listening to music.

∞∞∞

Czar didn't know when they moved from the living room to the bedroom, but when he opened his eyes, Marley was lying across his chest and his arms were tightly wrapped around her. Shifting her weight, Czar patted his pockets until he retrieved his vibrating phone. Thinking it was Cain, he answered without looking at the name on the screen.

"Yo?" he answered.

"Can you come get me?" The soft voice whispered.

"Ma?"

"It's Honey."

"The fuck? No. Do I look like your nigga?" Czar snapped, slipping out of the bed.

"Czar, I don't have anyone else to call and I really need help."

"Then hang up and call 911." He hung up on her. Marley sat up and flicked on the lamp next to her bed. She watched Czar pull his hoodie over his head before he glanced back at her.

"You leaving?" she asked, clutching the pillow to her chest.

"Yea. I got some shit to handle."

"You think we can talk later?"

"Nah. I think we both have too much baggage to make this situation work. I don't have time to wonder are you here for me or am I a placeholder until the next supposedly dead nigga returns."

"Julius, please don't do this."

"You did this when you went back to that nigga and tried to play house in the hood. I'll see you around." Czar headed toward the front of the loft.

"Really, Julius? So you about to go back to fucking random bitches?" She grabbed the back of his shirt.

"You damn right. At least I don't have to worry about

them running some sad ass game on me until the next nigga comes along." He snatched away from her. Picking up the car keys from her end table, Czar bopped out of the front door without looking back. Marley locked the door and went back to her bed, where she planned to sleep the day away.

∞∞∞

It was a little after three in the morning when Czar picked up Honey. He hadn't heard from Cain, and all of Slim's connects kept coming up empty. It was as if Cain had disappeared, taking Ada along with him. Czar was so on edge that every little notification had him reaching for his phone.

"Hey," Honey whispered, sliding into Czar's front seat. Honey tried to keep her head turned to the side, but Czar caught a glimpse of the ring around her eye. Reaching over, he lifted her face to get a better look at the bruises on her cheek. Honey was too pretty to let a nigga beat on her, but if that's what she liked, he wasn't going to stop her. His captain save-a-hoe cape was already split between two women and he couldn't take on another.

"Why the fuck you keep calling me? Shouldn't you be sitting in a fucking doctor's office?" Czar let her go. "And how the fuck you supposed to suck my dick and your lips look like inner tubes?"

"I need to tell you something." Honey pulled at the sleeves of her coat.

"Don't come at me with that *I'm pregnant* shit because at this point you hoes got me ready to snip my sack," Czar scoffed, popping the locks to his truck for her to exit.

"I'm not pregnant," she blurted.

"Then what the fuck are you talking about? It's almost

midnight and I don't have time to be sitting here listening to your Lifetime sobs. If the nigga beating your ass, fight back or duck. That's my tip."

"Can you please just listen?"

"You ain't saying shit!" Czar barked.

"Umm, years ago a couple of my friends started this thing where we talk to men that are locked up, sorta like pen pals. The men would pay for our time, and we'd take their phone calls, visit them. I even have a couple of friends that got married to their pen pals when they were released."

"Aight, so yall ran a whorehouse through letters. The fuck you telling me this shit for?"

"I started talking to this guy who had a couple of months left. He was so sweet and promised me this lavish lifestyle when he was released. I believed him. From behind bars, he taught me all the right things to say to have men eating out the palm of my hand. With his help, I was able to move from my shitty apartment and into a nice loft on the west side of Detroit. I kept his books stacked, and in return, he taught me something new."

"The fuck? You live in Detroit?" Czar glared at her.

"I do, and my real name is Justine. He nicknamed me Honey," she paused.

Czar rubbed his jaw, replaying the conversation he had with Nova about Honey not having a history and now he knew why. The bitch was made up.

"Aye," he removed the gun from under his seat and sat it on his lap, "You have five seconds to wrap this long ass story time bullshit up before I shoot you in the fucking knee and have you hopping around this bitch with a nub."

"Czar, please, I swear- don't be mad. I really didn't know," she cried.

"The fuck is you talking about?" he roared, making her jump.

"Cain! He started having me go to all these industry parties and mess with different men to get closer to you. He wanted me to get you comfortable and make you trust me. And at first, I was doing that. I was supposed to drug you and send him our location, but you never let me pour your drinks, and your brothers are always watching us."

"Bitch, what?" Czar lost his cool, placing the gun to her head.

"Oh my God, please," she cried. "I'm so sorry, please don't shoot me. He beats me and makes me do things with men that I don't want to. I tried to leave, but he owns everything, and my family doesn't talk to me, and-

"Aye, shut the fuck up!"

"I fell in love with you, Czar, and I'm sorrrrrryyyy," Honey cried uncontrollably.

Whap!

Czar slapped her with the butt of the gun. He had no sympathy for her tears. She was trying to set him up, and as far as he was concerned, she was the enemy. Honey tried to get out of the car, but Czar snatched her by the hair, slamming her head against the window.

"Your mom!" she screeched. "Cain plans on hurting her really bad."

"What?" Czar released her.

"He made me leave tonight to keep you occupied until he was ready. When he calls, I'm supposed to bring you to him."

Whap!

"Bitch, and here I was thinking you was trying to get some dick," Czar snorted, pissed off. "Where the fuck are you supposed to take me?"

"To the bar he works at."

"Give me the address," he demanded.

"I think you should-

"I'm not a woman beater, and I'm trying not to hit you because I know that nigga be going upside your head, but if you don't give me the address, I'm going to call my sister-in-law and have her drag your ass."

"Ok." Honey rapidly nodded, wiping her face. "We're going to Southwest."

∞∞∞

Czar pulled up to the bar and frowned. The windows were boarded up and there was a big sign on the door forbidding anyone from going inside. It was clear the city had shut the bar down, making it the perfect place for Cain to hide. Pulling a ski mask over his face, Czar allowed Honey to lead him through the pitch-black alley. She didn't have to look back to know his gun was still trained on her and Honey didn't blame him. For the part she played, she deserved it. She had allowed Cain to sell her a dream with a fake dollar and promises of them building a legacy. He promised her the world, but she soon found out it was a lie. Cain's only goal was to get his ex and their son in the same place at the same time, and with her help, he did it.

"Where the fuck my mama at?" Czar grilled as they walked through the dimly lit bar.

"I tied her up in the bathroom in the back," Honey shamefully whispered.

Whap!

"You what?" Czar popped her on the back of the head. "Where he at?"

"I-I don't know. He's probably in the back," Honey stuttered.

"Call the nigga." He jabbed the gun in her side.

"CAINNNNN," she whimpered. "Czar, please let me go. I'll say whatever you need me to say, please."

"Call him again."

"Cai-

"Ah, there he is." Cain maliciously grinned, strolling from the back of the bar. "I knew you'd come to save her. That's what you were born to do, right? Protect the woman that gave birth to you from monsters like me," he laughed sarcastically, recalling one of the many bedtime stories Ada used to make up. In her stories, it was always the prince who saved the queen from the wicked king.

"So you back to kidnapping folks," Czar seethed, folding his arms.

"Kidnap?" Cain scoffed. "Nah, your mama willingly entered my world, she happily sold her body and brought the money home to me."

"Nah, you sold her a dream, and she was foolish enough to believe the wolf in sheep's clothing, much like Honey, huh? You still recruiting young dumb ass girls to do your dirty work?"

"Come here, Honey," Cain barked, making her jump three inches off the floor. Tucking her hair behind her ear, Honey walked into his arms. "It doesn't take much to get a weak-minded bitch to follow your command." Cain softly caressed her arm. "See, most niggas think that dick controls their bitch, but it's the furthest thing from the truth." His hand traveled from Honey's arm to her shoulders, then her chin. "Anybody can give a bitch dick, but fucking her mind is the real goal. You pierce the layers of her brain and that bitch will do anything you say." Cain tapped Honey's temple. "Go get her."

Without a word, she scurried around him, leaving the father and son in a heated stare-off. Czar removed his ski mask and aimed his gun at Cain, who seemed unbothered.

"You wanna know something?" Cain asked, rubbing his chin. "Yo mama not as slick as she thinks. I knew she was pregnant because pregnant pussy feels different. That shit sold for top dollar, and I allowed her to keep her lil secret because the money was top-notch. I'm talking back-to-back niggas,." he reminisced. "Shit, so many niggas poked the top of your head, it's no wonder you have mental problems."

"Fuck you." Czar charged him, knocking Cain into the barstools.

Whap! Whap! Whap!

The gun slammed across Cain's face, splitting his eye in the process. The satisfaction from seeing blood cover his face willed Czar to keep going. Cain used a broken leg from the barstool and clocked Czar upside the head, but it wasn't enough to immobilize him.

"Julius!" Ada cried out when her eyes landed on him viciously beating the fuck out of his father. She tried to limp toward him, but Honey kept a grip on her forearm. On any other day, Ada would've chopped her ass in the throat, but she had been sitting on the floor so long that her ass was numb and her back ached.

Czar paused at the sound of her voice, and Cain used the opportunity to push Czar to the side. Crawling around the bar, Cain hit the lights and the room went dark.

"Czar, run!" Honey warned before shots rang out.

"Ma, get down!" Czar roared. "Ah fuck," he groaned, feeling the hot metal pierce his side. Lifting his gun, Czar shot in the direction of the gunshots. Glass shattered around them as Honey and Ada screamed at the top of their lungs.

Bottles of liquor exploded, sending broken fragments of glass and liquor into the air. The tattered bar chipped from the impact of the bullets, launching pieces of wood around the room.

"Shit," Cain groaned, falling against the bar. With the confirmation that he'd been hit, Czar shot two more times until he heard a loud thud.

"Ahh shit. I think you might've shot the wrong person," Cain laughed out loud, flicking on the lights.

"Ma." Czar swallowed, seeing her lying across from him.

"*Ma*," Cain mocked, limping around the bar, stepping over Honey's dead body. Seeing her face split into two didn't bother him one bit. It was exactly what she deserved for trying to warn Czar.

"Ma, get up." Czar pulled her body into his arms.

"I-I'm ok," she promised with blood leaking from the side of her mouth as she fought to catch her breath.

"You gave birth to this lil nigga and he shot you." Cain shook his head, watching her bleed out. "You should've aborted him. None of this would have happened. This wasn't supposed to be our story, but maybe we can try again next lifetime." Cain pressed his gun to the back of Czar's head and pulled the trigger. The gun clicked, indicating that there weren't any more bullets.

"Learn how to count, bitch nigga," Czar taunted. Cain's eyes doubled in size as Czar aimed the gun at him, sending a bullet right between his eyes that exited through the back of his skull.

Chapter 31

Marley stood over Billie's headstone with her arms wrapped around her waist. Although the ground was covered in snow, the sun was shining, giving her the energy to get out of bed and back to life. Marley was supposed to be meeting with Harper, but she needed to see her baby girl first. It had been far too long, and she felt like shit.

"Hey baby," Marley cooed, using her hand to brush the snow from the top of Billie's headstone. "I miss you," she sighed, tucking her bottom lip into her mouth. "I hope you're up there living your best three-year-old life with all the toys and cake you can eat. Mommy is down here making a mess and I don't know how to fix it. Maybe you can put in a word for me with the Big Guy. Tell Him I'm sorry for questioning His direction and-" She paused. "Oh lord, not me asking my deceased three-year-old for help," Marley laughed.

"You always talk to her about your problems?" Benny questioned, strolling up behind Marley with his hands in his pockets.

"What are you doing here?"

"I just thought it was time to visit." He hunched his

shoulders. “You did a beautiful job.” He motioned toward the tombstone.

“Harper picked it out, but yea, she did a great job.” Marley turned on her heels. “I’m going to leave and let you talk to her by yourself.”

“Wait, I’ve been calling you.” Benny grabbed her elbow but quickly released it when she shot him a hard glare.

“I know because I’ve been blocking them and I’m pretty sure it’s called harassment at this point. I mean after pointing a gun at me, I don’t know what you’d expect.”

“They told you?” He dropped his head, ashamed of how jealousy got the best of him.

“They didn’t have to. I saw the reflection from the car window as I was walking away. Were you really going to shoot me?”

“Nah, I was just mad. Embarrassed as fuck. Everything you said was the truth. I fucked up, and every time you’ve paid the price.”

“Why did you even come back?”

“Because I’m fucking selfish, Mars. What do you want me to say? Yea, I have a situation, but I want you too. After all we’ve been through, I thought our past was enough to keep us going, but I’m guessing our past wasn’t that good, huh?”

“Our past is just that. The past. And I’ve learned the hard way that you can’t rewrite it. You have a whole family now, and I think you should go back to them.”

“And what if they weren’t a thing, would we have stood a chance?” Benny asked, already knowing the answer, but he needed her to say it.

“No. I thought having you back would fix the hole in my heart, but that wasn’t the case. I used you dying as a crutch to wallow in my own sadness. I’ve been struggling for a long time, but that accident gave me a reason to hide in the darkness without feeling guilty. I missed you and Billie every day, but I also thought about my childhood, the love/hate relationship I have with my mama, and my daddy taking his life. It was a lot to deal with, and that accident was the last straw," Marley confessed for the first time in her life. "Then I met him."

"The rapping nigga?"

"His name is Julius, and yes. He's an asshole and gets on my nerves half of the time, but he only wants to make me happy. He wanted to love me, and I couldn't give him all of me because I felt like a piece of me still belonged to you. I'm realizing that even that was a mistake. I'll always have love for you, but I'm not in love with you anymore."

"Ouch!" Benny held his chest. "That hurts."

"It's true."

"Aight, I guess it's time for me to let you go."

"It is."

"Can I at least get a hug?"

"Nigga, no!" Marley frowned. "You got a bitch pregnant and tried to take me there on some sister-wife bullshit. Go meet your daughter. I'm going back to my car."

"You have a car now?" He grinned.

"Yea, Jaxon took me to get one. It's nothing fancy, but gets me from A to B."

"You know I can put you in something nice, right?"

"No. I'm fine with my lil Jeep. Save that money for your baby's college fund or something."

"It was good seeing you, Mars." Benny tucked his lip into his mouth, feeling kinda emotional that he was closing such a big chapter in his life.

"I wish I could say the same." She rubbed her hand across Billie's headstone once more before returning to her car. "Let me know when you leave so I can come back up."

"We can stay together," Benny suggested.

"No. I'll wait in my car."

Taking her time, Marley walked back down the hill with a smile on her face. For so long, she had been asking God to send her a sign, and because it wasn't the sign she wanted, she ignored the ones that were meant for her. The signs came in the form of family, because without Harper, she would have lost her mind. As hard as it was, Harper never gave up on her sister, and that was the true meaning of unconditional love. Loving a person through one of the most difficult times of their life took patience and selflessness. Then there was her business, a true blessing in disguise. When she wanted to hide in the shadows, *Sippin' Tea* made her shine. Everyone wanted to know the person behind the brilliant blends, making it impossible for her to hide. Then there was Czar. He was the distraction she needed and her sign to move on. Getting to know him made her feel human again and reminded her that she was capable of love. Finally, her sign came in the form of forgiveness. She forgave Benny, because holding a secret grudge against him didn't bring her the satisfaction she thought it would. For the first time in a long time, Marley was thanking God for never giving up on her.

The minute Marley slid into the front seat and removed her phone from her pocket, it started to vibrate. Seeing his name dance across the screen surprised her, since he made it clear that he wasn't fucking with her. Marley had even swept her loft, removing everything that his money paid for and left it at the front door. By the time she was finished, all she had was a bed in her room and her kindle. Harper called her stupid, but Marley was washing her hands with the situation… and now he was calling.

"Hey." She propped the phone up on the steering wheel.

"Where you at?" His deep voice filled her car.

"In my skin," Marley sassed. "Why do you sound like that?" She sat up, noticing that his background was pitch black. "Are you ok? Is your mom home?"

"The fuck you asking for? It's been two days and you haven't called to check."

"I called Biggie."

"Stop calling my people."

"They're my people too."

"No the fuck they not," Czar reiterated. "But she straight. The PR team is working with her to sort everything out."

"How are you, Julius?"

"Come see."

"I thought you didn't want to fuck with me anymore?"

"I didn't, but now I do. Come see me after you leave from visiting baby girl."

"How do you know where I'm at?"

"I always know where you're at," he smirked.

Marley opened her mouth to say something smart, but the tapping on her window caused her to jump, making her drop the phone. Czar's eyes zeroed in on Benny, who was standing on the other side of the window grinning.

"You still fucking with that nigga?" he barked.

"No, he-" Marley started to explain before he cut her off.

"I swear you moving like a fucking bird. I thought you was better than that." Czar ended the call without allowing her to explain.

Rolling the window down, Marley glared at Benny, who stood there looking stupid.

"What do you want, and why are you standing outside my car?"

"I was hoping we could go get something to eat."

"Are you slow?" She squinted. "I don't wanna do shit with you. Go take your baby mama and baby out."

Marley rolled up the window and put her Jeep into drive.

"Shit," she hissed. If it wasn't one thing, it was another.

∞∞∞

On the other side of the phone, Czar reached for the pain pills on the table next to him. Opening the bottle, he dropped three into his hand and closed the top. Lifting his hand to his mouth, Czar anticipated the pills falling on his tongue, but they were slapped across the room.

"You don't need that shit." Nova plopped down next to him.

"How the fuck you gone tell me what my pain level is?" Czar reached for the pill bottle, and again, Nova slapped it across the room. "I'll knock you the fuck out."

"You can barely move, so I highly doubt you knocking anything out, and didn't you just take something?"

"I was trying to take a nap."

"Then close your fucking eyes, nigga. You don't need that shit."

"Take your ass home," Czar grumbled.

"This my mama's house."

"Where she at?"

"Back there sleep," Nova replied, removing the blunt from behind his ear.

Czar rested his head on the couch and sighed.

"Aye. I tried to kill myself when I was sixteen."

"What?" The lit joint fell from Nova's mouth and onto his lap. "Fuck." He picked it up and patted his lap.

"I had got a letter from Cain. I didn't tell Mama. Shit, I don't even know why I checked the mail that day, but the shit was addressed to me," Czar continued. "I opened it and he was asking me to talk to the parole board on his behalf. Of course, I wrote back and told the nigga to suck my dick because if it was up to me, he'd never see the free world again." He paused. "I waited for him to write me back, but he never did."

"And that's why you tried to do it?"

"Nah." Czar shook his head. "He sent a letter to Mama a couple of weeks later. I got that one too and he said some real fucked up shit to her. Like the nigga was still behind bars and he was talking to her like he could touch her. Like he had people out here that could hurt her. Then he started talking about me. Saying shit like I wasn't his son, I was a nobody, and he knew I wasn't his. He told her he couldn't have kids and that she got pregnant by a random nigga. The nigga was calling me slow, saying I wasn't gone be shit because my mama was a young hoe and my daddy was a nigga who paid for pussy. The shit fucked with me for weeks. I started acting out, which was the first time I got locked up. Being alone with my thoughts and stuck in a cage fucked with my head. I started believing all the shit I read, and the darkness that loomed over me, trapped me. When I came home, I took all the pills in Mama's cabinet and laid in the bathroom on the floor."

"The fuck, why I don't remember this?" Nova swallowed,

sitting up.

"Because Slim took care of it. He knew a hood doctor that came to the house and pumped my stomach. After that he beat my ass and made me promise not to do the shit again. We never talked about it."

"So why you telling me now?"

"I'm tired of holding on to all this shit. It's weighing me down and I'm fucking tired."

"Tired of living?"

"Tired of everything."

Closing his eyes, Czar rested his head on the back of the couch. For two days, he had been sitting on his parents' couch waiting for his life to blow up.

"You know we took care of all that shit, right?" Nova whispered, scooting closer to his brother.

After ending Cain's life, Czar passed out. The blood leaking from his side and the pain was unbearable. He tried to fight the intense feeling, but he gave in to darkness as his brothers, Slim, Biggie, and Shortie stormed the back door. The sight of all the blood and bodies caused lumps to form in all their throats, but Ada's moaning snapped them from the trance quickly. Slim stepped over his brother's dead body and picked up his wife. Biggie and Romeo carried Czar to the car while Nova and Shortie worked to get rid of the other bodies.

Cutting on all the gas, they walked around the bar, setting multiple fires until everything started to burn. Picking up bottles of liquor, they tossed them onto the fire, causing it to spread faster. As they pulled out of the alley in unmarked cars, the old building went up in flames, and minutes later, it exploded.

"Yea, I know." Czar wiped his face. "Thank you."

"No thanks needed. You're my fucking brother and I'mma

look out for you always. You ain't gotta worry about shit. Shortie hacked into all the cameras in the surrounding area and removed any traces of your truck. As far as anyone knows, you were at home playing the game all night, and Mama was with Pops. If and when they come around asking questions, that's all you need to say."

"Oh yea?" Czar thumbed his nose.

"Yea nigga, now get up. You sitting here like you just had a fucking baby," Nova jested.

"I know you better get off my couch with that weed before I pop you in the back of the head," Ada threatened, walking into the room.

"Are you supposed to be up?" Nova quizzed. "Where Pops at?"

"He back there. Let me talk to your brother for a minute."

"Aight, I'm about to go out for a bit. Call me if yall need me."

"Aye," Czar called after him. "Good looking."

"I'mma always look out for you, bro," Nova promised, bopping out of the door.

Ada slid on the couch next to Czar, resting her head on his shoulder. The bullet that entered her shoulder went straight through, leaving her with a clean injury. If anything, the shock of being in a gun fight almost gave her a heart attack.

"How you feeling?" Czar questioned.

"Good. Slim hasn't left my side, and as crazy as it sounds, I feel better knowing that you're in the house."

"Cause I'm that nigga, Ma."

"Oh boy, please." Ada rolled her eyes. "How are you?"

"Better, Nova thinks he a therapist."

"Talking isn't always a bad thing. It's going to take some

getting used to." She rubbed his hand. "Um, thank you Julius, for everything." Her eyes welled up with tears. "You are truly my blessing in disguise and I love you."

"What's understood don't have to be explained, Ma. I'mma always step behind you." Czar kissed her forehead. "I set up a meeting with Terri. I have this album I've been working on for a while. It's really just a bunch of freestyles, but they tell a story. They tell my story. I'm going to clean it up and drop it."

"You ready for that?"

"I'm ready to be mentally free. Holding on to the past is hindering my growth as a person and artist."

"And what do you need from me?"

"I need you to write the book. The pictures are out there and it's only right they get the story. It's the story of a million girls around the world, and you might be able to help them. I can work on it with you, cry with you, and when it's done, we'll release the book and the album together. Turn your tears into dollars. Dead or alive, he doesn't get the last laugh. You do."

"Ok." Ada nodded. "I'll do it. Go get my laptop. We'll do it now."

"Like right now?"

"Yea, you got somewhere else to be?" She leaned up.

"Nah, but we both down bad. How we supposed to type?"

"I'll do it." Slim strolled in the room. "We good, C."

"My fault-" Czar started, but Slim stopped him.

"You were right. She's mine, and it is my responsibility to make sure she's straight, and it'll never happen again."

"You apologizing?"

"Nah, letting you know that I got my wife, nigga, and the

next time you say some smart shit, I'm going to blow your chest out."

"You'd hit a rich nigga?"

"I'd knock the Super Mario coins out yo ass," Slim promised.

∞∞∞

"So what do you ladies think?" the realtor asked Harper and Marley, who were walking around the empty space with their arms crossed.

"It's giving boss bitch." Harper spun around. "Like I can see myself twisting between tables with a platter of tea and gluten free crumpets for some bougie hoes."

"Harper, please," Marley snickered. "But I like it too. The kitchen is big and we can do a lot with this space. A couple of tables, extend the counter space, a couple of couches in the back."

"And this space offers a backyard." The realtor walked toward the back of the shop. "In the winter, you could do heated igloos, and in the summer, cute tents and tables." She held her hand out, motioning for them to step ahead of her. "The previous owner used the space for storage, but I think so much more can be done back here."

"I agree." Marley nodded, walking around.

"Oh my god, we can host tea parties back here!" Harper clapped her hands. "We want it."

"Wait, you don't wanna talk about it first?"

"Excuse us, can we have a minute?" Harper smiled tightly at the realtor, who was acting like she wasn't listening.

"Of course." She stepped inside, leaving the sisters alone.

"Ok, hoe, what's the problem?"

"I don't know." Marley glanced around the yard. "I mean it's not a problem, but you don't think we're jumping into this?"

"Girl, no!" Harper nearly shouted. "I've been dreaming about this for years. I just needed you to get on board. I need something else to do. Being a housewife is cool, but I like the idea of having a business. Jaxon is going to give us the money to put down and we don't have to worry about paying him back because he's still trying to make up for the situation with Mama."

"Bitch, are you blackmailing your husband?"

"No, I'm milking the situation for as long as I can."

"You are hell," Marley giggled.

"And I wasn't going to say anything yet, but some man named Fro reached out to me. He said he met you in Asia when Czar put on the concert for his son."

"How did he reach out to you?"

"Czar gave him our business card and a couple of tea bags," Harper explained. "He said his wife had been having digestive problems. She started drinking our tea before Christmas and she swears by it."

"Really?"

"Yep, and he's been asking if we could meet with him. He's flying here in a couple of weeks, and there's talk of finding a manufacturer so that we can produce large orders at once. You were going through the motions with Czar and Benny, so I didn't say anything, but I think we should do it. I think it's a good move. We can hire lawyers and all that good shit."

"You think we can handle this?" Marley chewed her lip.

"Look, bitch, you've been asking God for a blessing and this is it. You don't get to pick the size and timeframe, just strap up your boots and enjoy the ride. We got this, sis. I believe in you."

"You ladies ready?" The realtor poked her head through the door.

"Girl, calm down. You're going to get your commission," Harper sassed.

"Oh no, I –uh."

"Ignore her...we'll take it." Marley smiled.

"Ahhh!" Harper twerked. "Boss bitch alert," she danced. "Can you take our picture?"

"Um, that's usually after the bank approves the loan and-

"Girl, hush and take the picture," Harper snapped, handing her the phone. Marley snickered but hugged her sister as they posed for the picture.

#Newshopcomingsoon.

Chapter 32

Three months later

"Anybody wanna try my chicken?" Sammy asked, walking into the living room with a tray of half-done chicken. Not only was the middle a little pink, but she also made a mistake and used cinnamon instead of paprika.

"Hell nah." Czar, Nova, and Shortie turned their noses up. "And who the fuck told you to cook in my kitchen?" Czar added.

"My man," she sassed.

"Yo man don't live here. You done made my smoke detector go off three times and it smell like burnt feet. Go the fuck home."

"Baby, you gone let him talk to me like this?" Sammy pouted, holding her flat stomach.

"Chill, bro," Romeo warned. "You know she sensitive. Make me a plate, bae."

"And you about to eat that half-done shit?" Nova looked on disgusted.

"Yep."

"Just make sure yall don't feed my nephew that shit," Czar

voiced.

"How you know it's a boy?" Sammy asked, handing Romeo a plate of chicken that made his stomach turn, but he'd never tell her. His plan was to take some couples' cooking classes before she gave birth because his baby couldn't grow up eating shell-filled eggs and overcooked noodles.

"Because I do." He shrugged. "And go sit outside. I can't even smoke in my own shit."

Sammy gave Czar the finger and twisted back into the kitchen. He prayed to God that Sammy was having a boy because two of her in their family was way too much personality. She was only four months pregnant and giving his little brother a run for his money. Ada wasn't thrilled about the idea of them having a baby, but Romeo was stoked. He was already looking for a bigger house and even started a savings account. Slim reasoned that a baby was just what their family needed.

"You need to forgive my girl before somebody snatches her up. She went on a date with Yaro and they looked kinda cute," Sammy taunted, standing in the doorway.

"Who?" Nova quizzed. "LB?"

"Yep. They been dating for a month and she looks happy."

"Get the fuck outta here." Romeo waved her off. "My sis not dating that nigga."

"She is and I like it for her."

"Put yo shit on and get the fuck outta my house," Czar snarled.

"You gone put me and yo nephew out?" Sammy giggled.

"Yep."

"Why you jealous?"

"I'm not jealous of shit. I don't want her lying ass. She probably somewhere still fucking on that dead nigga."

"Well, actually, Casper went back to Ohio."

"How you know?" Biggie asked, coming from the back.

"Nigga, did you just shit in my bathroom?" Czar frowned.

"Yea. Them pancakes Sammy made fucked my stomach up." He rubbed his stomach.

"Yall can stop talking about my cooking," she pouted. "And if yall would get a girlfriend, I wouldn't be the only woman in this circle."

"News flash, you're not part of the circle," Nova responded.

"Nigga, I make the circle." She flicked him off, and she wasn't lying. Sammy was the sister they didn't ask for but loved like they loved each other. "Now like I was saying, the dead dude went back to Ohio, and his girlfriend even pregnant again."

"How you know all this shit?" Biggie quizzed.

"Instagram. People tell their lives on these apps."

"Nah, you just nosey as fuck," Czar growled, now in his feelings. Marley messing with Yaro rubbed him the wrong way, but being that he cut her off, there wasn't shit he could say. Even when he wanted to reach out to her, his pride wouldn't allow it. "And shut up, Mama's segment is about to start." He cut up the volume on the TV.

"Period, Mama Ada!" Sammy clapped her hands as Ada glided across the stage in a cute white and cream suit with matching YSL pumps.

Her self-titled book, *Ada's Reasons*, hit the bookshelves like a whirlwind. Terri shopped the book around and got Ada a six-figure book deal. Everything happened so fast that she was still processing but didn't slow down for a second.

Collaborating with Czar's album, *Diaries of a Real Nigga* turned out to be better than expected. Czar's album was the soundtrack to her book and the world loved it. The mother-son duo was just what the world needed. Czar became that much more appealing in women's eyes and everybody wanted a piece of him. With the help of Biggie and Shortie's expertise, they were able to remove 80% of the pictures. They were still underground websites that sold the images, but they were no longer floating around on social media.

Tati called herself getting on Live trying to go off on Czar about his mommy issues, but it backfired. Not only did someone post a video of her with nut leaking down her face, but somehow, a recording of the ordeal in the hotel room surfaced. Fans found out Tati lied about the miscarriage and she was canceled in the blink of an eye.

"Oh my God!" Sherri, the host, clutched her chest. "I'm so happy to have you on the show."

"Thank you for inviting me," Ada smiled.

"You are so beautiful."

"Thank you, so are you!"

"Girl, your book." Sherri held her chest. "It touched my heart. I loved it."

"Thank you. I'm happy you enjoyed it."

"I did more than enjoy it. I laughed, cried, learned from it and all. On behalf of all the victims of domestic violence, I wanna say thank you. I think you gave a lot of women the courage to stand in their truth. You are brave and we love you."

"I appreciate that. You know it wasn't easy, but I have a great support system. My family has been by my side, and I don't know what I'd do without them."

"And your son!" Sherri paused, because the audience started clapping their hands. "He is so talented, and that album was

everything. I felt like I was watching a movie. Like he talked about his feelings in a way that was poetic and that was amazing."

"Julius is amazing. You know, I named him Julius because of the leadership he possesses. A name like that comes with great responsibility, and my son wears it proudly. My story was a rough one, but life granted me three amazing, talented boys, and I wouldn't trade my journey for anything in the world."

"You know the album and book collaboration was brilliant. You are both number one on several charts around the world, and you've been on tour for a month now. How's that going?"

"It's going good. My husband travels with me, and my boys are grown, so I don't have any attachments at home. We actually like traveling from state to state. Seeing the world with a fresh set of eyes is a beautiful thing."

"It is! I tell people all the time to step out of their comfort zones and live a little," Sherri agreed. "Can I ask what made you want to write this story?"

"I didn't want to," Ada admitted. "Writing that book was really hard and I went through every textbook emotion, but it was worth it. I'm living in my truth. I was young and I made mistakes."

"Say that shit then, Mama Ada!" Sammy clapped her hands. "I'm about to clean up the kitchen, yall want anything else?"

"Girl, no, and stop offering that dry ass chicken like it's our last meal," Nova joked.

"It can be," she threatened, stepping toward him.

"Let him make it, baby." Romeo held his hand out, stopping her from advancing.

While they went back and forth, Czar logged into Instagram, and as the universe would have it, *Sippin' Tea* was the first thing he saw. Their grand opening was a few days away and Harper was walking around, recording the inside of the shop. Czar had to give it to them, it was beautiful. The decor was simple yet breathtaking. He liked the blends of beige and pastel green. Harper danced around the shop, pointing the camera at Marley, who was strategically adjusting the jars of tea on the counter.

"Girl, if you move them jars one more time, I'm going to scream."

"Get that camera out of my face," Marley hissed. "I need them to be perfect."

"Girl, shut up and tell people when we open!" Harper urged her.

"Hey yall." She plastered a fake smile on her face. "If you are in the Detroit Area, this Friday we'll be opening the doors. We have prizes, games, and free cups of tea. Come show up and show out but keep it cute because I have the pepper spray tucked."

Harper giggled and ended the video. Czar liked it and shared the video to his story.

"You going?" Biggie asked, leaning over his shoulder.

"Nah." Czar dropped the phone in his lap and focused on the TV. "Is she really dating that light skin nigga?"

"Not that I know of. She asked me to come by Friday and control the crowd for her grand opening, so if they together, he'll be there."

"The fuck? Tell her nappy headed ass to get her own security, and if she fucking with that non-rapping nigga, I'm going to burn that shop to the ground."

"I thought you wasn't worried?" Sammy yelled from the kitchen.

"I'm not worried about shit because LB know better and

hurry up so you can go home."

"It's been what, three months?" she continued. "I don't think you have the same effect on her as you once did. I love you, B-law, but I'm pretty sure you fumbled the bag with this one."

Czar didn't bother responding. He pushed up from the couch and went onto the balcony to smoke his blunt.

∞∞∞

Marley sat on the counter and blew smoke out of her mouth. The shop looked completely different from two months ago and she was proud. The hiring process was a nightmare, and almost everybody who applied wanted the job thinking that Czar was going to make frequent stops. Half of them couldn't even focus without asking Marley about their relationship status. The other half didn't have any customer service experience, and every other word out of their mouth was *period*. By the third day, Marley was over it and hired a retired teacher from JJ's school. She was slow but her customer service made up for her lack of speed.

"You ready for this?" Harper asked, hopping up on the counter and reaching for the joint.

"Yep. You know we're going to be here every day until we can get a reliable staff."

"I'm good with that. I'm just happy to have something we can call our own."

Marley gushed at the thought. Before she could agree, someone started beating on the glass door. Both Harper and Marley stopped moving, hoping the person would go away, but the person on the other side of the door cupped their hands to peek through the decal.

"I see yall!" Pam screamed, yanking on the handle.

"Oh hell no." Marley shook her head. "That's yo mama. When was the last time you talked to her?"

"Not since she showed up on my doorstep in December. I'm good on her." Harper glanced at the door. "Aht aht. We don't allow homeless people in here."

According to Jaxon, Pam was evicted from her place for non-payment of rent and living in the same homeless shelter she once worked at. She was having trouble finding a job and spent most of her time trying to seduce young dope boys into taking care of her. Harper nearly fell out when she found out that Pam had an Only Fans and was shaking her wide ass for a $7.99 subscription fee.

"Open the door," Marley insisted. "See what she wants."

"You sure?" Harper eyed her.

"Yea, and if she messes up anything, I'mma drag her ass right back out the door."

"I love you and all, but sis, Mama will beat you up."

"Then you better jump in." She shrugged, putting out the joint.

Harper slowly dragged her feet to the front door and undid the locks. She was on a high and didn't need her mother's negativity in their space, but Marley looked like she needed to get some stuff off her chest, so she sucked it up.

"What's going on, Ma?" Harper asked, pulling the door open.

"I should be asking yall that. We haven't spoken since Christmas," Pam snorted.

"Ok, and?"

"Harper, you need to get over that. We are family."

"Ma, what is it because I'm not about to keep revisiting

the same conversation?"

"I guess I miss you." Pam gazed down at her wet boots. "We didn't have the best relationship, but I'm still your mother. Maybe we can go to counseling or something so we can move pass all this mess."

"No, I think you miss what I can do for you."

"That's not true."

"What about my sister? You miss her too?" Harper questioned. Only then did Pam look up at her baby girl. She couldn't even muster up a smile to support the lie that began to form on her lips, so she cleared her throat and shifted her weight.

"You know me and your relationship is different from the one I share with her."

"Mm. Yea, well we no longer share a relationship. I don't trust you and can't have you around me. I need to protect my peace, and that means keeping my distance from people and situations that trigger me."

"I'm a trigger?" Pam frowned.

"Ma, every time I look at you, I want to punch you in the back, so yes, I'd say you're a trigger."

"You feel the same way?" Pam's eyes rolled over to Marley.

"You've been a trigger since before I even knew what the word meant, but I'm learning that I can't keep blaming you. I'm trying to live in my peaceful era, so I apologize."

"Huh, apologize for what?"

"I apologize for you not being loved correctly as a child and that you never learned how to reciprocate it," Marley started, hopping off the counter.

"Aw shit." Harper held her forehead.

"I apologize that every man in your life left you, and it

chipped away at your insecurities every time they walked out the door. I apologize that you weren't taught the necessities of life before you started a family of your own and passed down your toxic childhood traits to your children, causing you to see them as competitors versus a lineage to carry your name. And lastly, I apologize that you won't witness me in this season of winning. You sending Benny here almost broke me, but I forgot we serve a man with a plan and He'll never let me fall."

"Amen!" Harper clapped.

"Look, I didn't come here for all that. Y'all got a lil shop, cool. I need a few dollars because the shelter food taste like trash and the soap is drying out my skin." Pam sucked her teeth. "Yall obviously not hurting for money." She loosely flung her hand.

"I can't help you." Harper held her hands up.

"Oh, here." Marley patted her pockets, pulling out a set of keys.

"Wait, I can come live with you?" Pam's eyes doubled in size. She was expecting Harper to bend, not Marley.

"Heck no! These are the keys to the van. It was good enough for me and will help you get on your feet."

"I'd sleep under a bridge before I live in that piece of shit."

"Well, bundle up. It's going to be cold tonight and them beauty supply boots not gone cut it." Harper ushered Pam to the door.

"So that's it? Y'all can open up shops and live in fancy houses while leaving me to rot in a public shelter."

"I offered you my van." Marley bucked her eyes. "It's way more than you ever offered me."

"You know what," Pam chuckled, not believing they weren't going to help her. "This lil shop shit only gone last for a month or two."

"Yea, well luckily for us, we have money in the bank." Harper held the door open. "Gone on, you letting the heat out."

"God don't like ugly," Pam hissed, storming out the door.

"We know, that's why nothing is going in your favor. Bundle up and use the bridge on I94. They just repaved the roads and it looks a little warmer." Harper shut the door behind her.

"You ok?" Marley asked.

"I'm good. It just took me some time to realize that I don't owe her shit. I found myself doing stuff for her because she didn't have anyone else and she's my mama, but I don't have to be a fool for her."

"Period."

"Ugh, don't say that. These new lil hoes wear that word out."

"You want some tea?" Marley asked, stepping behind the counter.

"Yea, and relight the joint," Harper suggested, grabbing her phone off the counter.

Since posting the tour video of the shop, her notifications had been blowing up. A lot of people congratulated them, while others talked their hating shit that went in one ear and out the other.

"Oh!" Harper grinned, staring at the phone. She was wondering why Instagram was blowing up, and now she knew. "When's the last time you talked to Czar?"

"A couple of months ago, why?" Marley paused.

"He just shared our video."

"Oh."

"Oh, bitch bye. You know you miss him."

"I do, but I'm not about to kiss his ass. I said sorry, like what the fuck else does he want?"

"Girl, you broke up with him after he took you out of the country and plugged our business with a rich ass dude and his weak stomach wife, decked out your place, laced you with good dick, ate your ass, and sucked your toes!" Harper ranted. "Would you want a stanking ass *I'm sorry*?"

"No." Marley dropped her head.

"What would you want?"

"A grand gesture," she sighed.

"Then I'd advise you to think of a master plan before he links up with another Instagram hoe."

Chapter 33

Czar stepped on the stage and couldn't control the grin that spread across his face. Everybody couldn't sell out Ford Field, but he did. The exclusive concert was his first concert of the year, and the ticket sales did numbers, proving why he was the best at staying in his lane. Being that the concert was exclusive to Detroit, everybody wanted a piece. Romeo worked with Terri and the label's production team to make sure everyone got their money's worth. They came equipped with fireworks, bands, dancers, and much more.

"What up doe, Detroit," Czar bellowed into the microphone, feeling the energy in the stadium.

"What up doeeeeeee," the crowd replied.

"Before we get-" The microphone went out, causing Czar to frown. "The fuck?" he whispered, tapping the mic. "Aye, what's wrong with yall cheap ass equipment?" he hollered behind his back. "Come fix this shit before I take this party to the parking lot."

The crowd started chanting his name, thinking that the concert was over before it started. It wasn't a secret that the fire marshals were waiting to shut shit down due to all the smoke, but his fans weren't having it. There was no way they paid $300 plus to see their favorite rapper perform for twenty minutes. He was cool and all, but the nigga wasn't $300 for twenty minutes cool. A few of them were booing, hoping they didn't waste their money on the Lauryn Hill experience. When the lights were cut off, people started getting nervous, and Czar was pissed! He promised Terri he'd be on his best behavior, but Ford Field was on some straight bullshit.

"I know damn well the lights didn't get cut off in this big ass stadium." He dropped the mic on the ground and started walking backstage.

"*Here we are face to face.*" The voice blared over the speaker, stopping Czar in his tracks. He knew her starchy voice all too well. He dreamed about it, he missed it, hell, he beat his dick to it, but he wasn't ready to face it.

"*With the memories that can't be erased,*" she sung off key, causing the crowd to laugh at her. Czar wiped the corners of his mouth and slowly turned around.

A single spotlight shined on Marley as she made her way through the crowd. Czar's heart did what he'd describe as the corniest shit ever...it skipped a beat. Her bushy hair was pushed to the side, just the way he liked it. Her lips glossy and she even looked a tad bit thicker. Just a bit.

"*Although we need each other, things have changed. It's not the same,*" Marley continued to sing, making her way toward him. The closer she got, the harder Czar's fingers drummed against his thigh. He couldn't wait until this shit was over because he was firing everybody. At this point, if his mama said the wrong thing, her lanky ass was getting the axe too.

With the help of the security guards, Marley made it on the stage, and Romeo and Nova guided her up the stairs. She gave them both a quick hug before straightening her posture. As bad as she wanted to run and hide, she couldn't. It was her who fucked up and it was on her to make the grand gesture to get her man back.

Czar watched Marley walk toward him as Monica sang over the speaker about remembering the good times. The crowd had even begun singing, enjoying the scene that played out in front of them. Czar wished he could tell them to shut the fuck up, but his mic was off, and again, he wanted to know who did that shit because they were getting fired.

Dressed in a pair of ripped boyfriend jeans that hung off her hips and a tee shirt with his face on it, Marley advanced toward Czar until she was standing in his face. Thanks to the platform heels she wore, Marley stood at his nose. He glared at her bare neck, pissed that some sucker niggas had snatched her jewels. Czar made a mental note to replace them but had to remember she wasn't his girl anymore. He tried not to stare at her glossy lips, but she made it impossible. Marley knew what he liked, which is why the mint scent he loved so much consumed him.

"I made the choice, I was wrong, you were right," she bellowed off-key, further embarrassing herself and at the top of her lungs, Marley finished it off. *"Deep down inside, I apologizeeeeeeeeeeeeee."* She held the note like her life depended on it, and when she stopped the crowd picked it up, finishing the chorus. Somehow, his concert turned into a horrible karaoke session and Czar was pissed.

"I never meant to cause you no painnnnn."

"The fuck you doing here?" he asked, glaring down at her. He hadn't talked to her in over three months, and he hated the way her sad eyes still affected him. Deep down, he wanted to pick her up and whisk her off stage, but his pride wouldn't allow him to touch her. As far as he was concerned, Marley made her choice, and it was one she'd have to live with.

"I owe you an apology," Marley said into the microphone, and he pushed it away from her mouth. The world had heard enough, they didn't need to hear her beg.

“And you chose to do it in the middle of my concert? Who helped you? I’m about to fire they ass right now. I bet it was Biggie soft ass.”

“Julius, I miss you and I didn’t know how much I needed you in my life until I no longer had you. I’m sorry, I messed up.”

“So, what the fuck you want me to do? Forgive you for making me fall in love with your ass, only for you to shit on my heart? You want me to forgive you for making me a second choice?”

“Yesss!” the crowd answered. Czar took the microphone from her and looked at them.

“Shut yall ass up. She cutting into yall show and you friendly muthafuckas helping her sing,” he spoke into the microphone before turning his attention back to Marley. “I’m straight on you, shorty. I can’t play this game with you. You wanted that back from the dead ass nigga and you got him. I don’t have nothing for you.”

“Booooooooo,” the crowd hooted.

“Aye, throw something else up here and see what happens!” Czar pointed when a cup landed at his feet. “Now, can you leave so I can finish my show?” He turned toward Marley, who had tears streaming down her face.

Not only was she embarrassed as fuck, but she was also heartbroken. It wasn’t the same pain she felt when she lost Benny the *first* time. Marley didn’t want to take her life, but she wanted to crawl into a dark hole until her stomach stopped flipping. She wanted to lay on the beach until the sounds of the ocean drowned out her thumping heart. Marley wanted to breathe again without feeling sharp pains in her chest.

“Bye Felicia.” Czar waved her off as if she was an annoying

gnat. As if she wasn't the woman who showed him what happiness felt like, what real love felt like.

"Fine, bye asshole." Marley stormed away, causing the crowd to boo Czar.

"Aye," he hollered in the microphone. Marley stopped walking, thinking he was talking to her, but she was sadly mistaken. "Cut my shit back on," Czar demanded, and just like that, he resumed his concert.

∞∞∞

Marley moved around *Sippin' Tea* with a smile on her face. Their grand opening had come and gone, and the shop was popping. Every day, they had a line that was wrapped around the corner, and while they loved it, the sisters were overwhelmed. Jaxon had even stepped in to assist them with the load until they hired a few more waitresses. He tried to front as if they were taking up all his time, but he liked the idea of having a legal business and wanted them to expand.

"Welcome to *Sippin' Tea*. What can I get for you?" Marley asked, peering down at the computer screen.

"What can pregnant women drink?" Sammy asked, causing Marley to pop her head up.

"Aw heyyyyy!" she sang, moving around the corner. "You're pregnant?"

"Girl, yea. Ro think he slick, tryna sit a bitch down for the summer, but little does he know, I don't need liquor to turn up. A bitch get hype off the vibe."

"Oh my God, congratulations!" Marley hugged her.

"Thank you boo, and congratulations to you! I love this shop! It's so you." She spun around, checking out the space. "Plants, paintings, and shit. It's a vibe."

"Thank you."

"You're welcome, but as my baby's god mama, you need to go get her god daddy back."

"God mama?"

"Yea, but you and Pooh gotta share. She already started claiming my baby, not knowing I wanted you to be the god mama, but I didn't wanna hurt the hoe feelings, so I went with it."

"You are crazy," Marley laughed. "Do you want something to drink?"

"Yea, can I have the white raspberry tea with one of those vegan lavender bars? Biggie swears they the best thing he ever tasted, but then again, Biggie eats damn near anything."

"Stop it, don't do my friend."

"Anyway, so I saw what happened at the concert, and I'm on your side," Sammy assured her. "I would've clocked Romeo in the face with that damn microphone because nigga what. I love my B-law, but that man is stubborn."

Sammy left out the part about her cussing Czar out when he walked off stage. Ada had even called him a fool, and his brothers had no words for him. They were all aware that Marley had fucked up but reasoned that under the circumstances, he should forgive her.

"Yea, well there are no sides because he made it clear that he wasn't fucking with me, and I'm not about to keep putting myself out there."

"I get that, but I will say he just went through some shit, so his mind kinda everywhere. Plus, I told him you were dating Yaro, and he nearly choked."

"You what?" Marley bucked.

"Girl, calm down. He didn't believe me, but that's not the point. You a bad bitch, and he needs to know that you're not going to be single forever."

"Finding a man is the last thing on my mind. I need to keep working on me."

"So if B-law come around, you not gone pop that shit for a real nigga?" Sammy cocked her head to the side.

"I'm not saying all that, but I'm not about to chase him." Marley slid the tea and pastry across the counter.

"Period, but he's about to go on tour, and I think yall should make up."

"You can't make up with someone who doesn't wanna talk to you."

"You right." Sammy nodded. "Well, don't be a stranger. I feel like we can hang without them niggas. I like wine, yoga, and all that other Zen shit you into. Just don't invite me rock climbing or hiking. I'm not that kinda friend."

"I got you," Marley snickered, walking her to the door. After hugging one another, Sammy hopped in her Jeep, and Marley went back inside.

"You good?" Harper asked, passing by her with a tray of glasses.

"Yes, I'm about to go to the back and make a couple of batches. Let me know if you need me."

"Will do."

"What the hell?" Marley groaned, rolling off the couch. She didn't even remember falling asleep, but because she was tired as hell, it didn't take long before she was out like a light. The blaring sound of sirens and bells rang out, alerting her that something was wrong. Dressed in a pair of yoga shorts and a tank, Marley grabbed her cell phone and hoodie before stumbling into the hallway. Sleepy residents filed into the stairwells, carefully holding on to the wall while talking shit.

"This is some bullshit. Who up burning shit at 2 in the morning?" someone complained. "Got me walking down ten flights of stairs in a damn housecoat."

"Probably 9B. All they do is argue and smoke that shit," another resident chimed in.

"Fuck both of yall," 9B blurted. "I pay rent just like the rest of yall. I could have a meth lab in this bitch if I wanted to."

"Lord." Marley shook her head, pushing the exit door open. She made a mental note to look for another loft. This was the second time the alarm had been pulled, and she was over it. Buying a house didn't sound too bad.

"Oh god, and it's raining," she mumbled.

Firefighters bypassed the crowd as the building manager tried to assure everyone that everything was ok. His words meant nothing to the angry mob that was standing there in bed sheets, towels, and their nightclothes. Marley stood off to the side with her arms tucked at her side. She didn't feel the need to communicate with the other residents who argued about getting money knocked off their rent for the inconvenience. They swarmed around the manager as if he was going to start handing out credit memos on the spot.

"These muthafuckas rowdy," the voice said from behind her.

Marley could feel his breath tickle the back of her neck, and she could smell the weed and cologne mixture that lingered on his clothing. He was so close that she could feel his hard body pressing into her, leaving no space between them.

"Did you pull the alarm?" Marley probed, chewing the corner of her lip.

"Yep, and they big mad," Czar chuckled. "I'mma tell them you did that shit."

"You better not!" She elbowed him.

"Turn around," he demanded.

"No."

"Why?"

"Because." Marley ignored the feel of his arms wrapping around her waist. "You just embarrassed me in front of thousands of people, and now you wanna talk? I wanted to talk to you then, and you played in my face."

"I wasn't over it." Czar shrugged. "You hurt my feelings. What you want me to say?"

"What changed?"

"I had some time to think about what I wanted out of life, and I want you."

"Welp, I don't wanna talk no more." She shrugged.

"Turn around."

"Julius," Marley groaned, turning to face him. "Oh my god, you cut your hair!" She ran her hands over his fresh Caesar cut. "You look so fine," Marley gushed but quickly snatched her hands from his head.

"I needed a fresh start. Cutting my locs made me feel like I was headed in the right direction." He ran his hand over the waves that swarmed around his head.

"It looks nice, but I'm sure I would've seen the picture on Instagram. You didn't have to come over here disturbing people's peace for that, and what if I have someone upstairs?"

"Then I'd toss his ass off the balcony. The fuck."

"All that for someone you don't want?" Marley folded her arms across her chest.

"Aight, look. I was being an asshole," Czar admitted. "You're the first woman I've ever wanted, and I felt played as fuck when you went back to that nigga. I had other shit going on, and you leaving set off a motion of events. It was easier to say fuck you than to fight for you."

"And what changed? Why you wanna fight now?"

"Because I miss sucking your toes," he joked, causing Marley to giggle and punch him for getting a laugh out of her. "For real though, you cool as fuck and we vibe on a different level. I miss talking to you, smoking with you, drinking tea with you, and I miss this pussy. You're my homie, lover, and friend, and I love you, LB."

"I-I love you too," Marley stuttered, pulling at her fingers.

"Don't say the shit like I'm forcing you to say it. Say it like you sung that horrible ass song at my concert."

"Shut up." She hit him in the chest. "I love you, Juluis, and I only wanna be with you."

"That's what the fuck I'm talking about." He grabbed her by the back of the neck and placed soft kisses on her lips. "And this time I'm never letting you go."

"Good, because I only wanna be with you."

"That's what the fuck I know."

"Alright, everyone, it was a false alarm!" The firefighters announced as they exited the building.

"Aye, she pulled that shit," Czar said aloud, causing everyone to look back at them.

"Julius!"

Epilogue

Two years later

"Welcome, welcome, welcome!" Nesha Re excitedly clapped her hands together.

"What up doe," Czar spoke.

"Hey." Marley waved, leaning into Czar's side. He knew she hated it when they did interviews, but he had a way of making her do things she didn't want to.

"Girl, please, not that soft *hey*," Nesha Re smirked. "I've seen you go off, and baby, that tongue is slick."

"I'm chill until someone pops off. I don't play about a few things in life, and people take it overboard all the time," Marley explained.

"And what are the things you don't play about?"

"Well, for starters, my husband." She glanced at Czar. "I'll pepper spray the shit outta somebody about my man."

Czar chuckled, but it was true. Marley and her pepper spray were lethal. There had been a couple of people on the other end of the nozzle, and he didn't feel bad for them. His wife was nothing to play with, and people often underestimated her because of her size.

"Oh my god, how could I forget that you two eloped last year? How was that?" Nesha Re asked.

Marley and Czar jumping the broom in Cabo San Lucas broke the internet. Their wedding pictures flooded every social platform for weeks, and of course, it came with a great amount of hate. People swore she was pregnant or that he cheated and was trying to make it up to her. They acted as if it was hard to believe that Detroit's bad boy had met his match and couldn't allow her to slip from his grasp. In front of their family and a few friends, the couple vowed their lives to one another, and then Czar kicked everyone off their private beach. He wanted the pleasure of fucking his new bride in a cabana off the coast of the Pacific Ocean.

"It was perfect," Marley blushed, remembering all the nasty things Czar did to her body. The amount of sex and toys they used would've made Mr. Marcus blush.

"And are we expecting any babies in the future?"

"Of course," Czar answered. "But right now, I want to enjoy my wife as much as possible before we have a few crumb snatchers."

"Not crumb snatchers," Nesha Re giggled. "Of course, you'd say that."

"I'm just saying. When it comes to my wife, I'm selfish. I want all her time and attention, and I'm not afraid to admit it. I love getting up flying across the country at the drop of a hat. I love waking up getting my shit off without babies crying in the background."

"Julius." Marley jabbed him with her elbow.

"But when the time is right, we're going to purchase a big ass house, I'm going to fall back on the music shit, and we're going to raise our babies together."

"I love that," Nesha Re smiled. "So, Marley, I have a question. With Czar being in the limelight, how do you keep your own identity?"

"It's easy." She fell back into his arms. "I have a life outside of him."

"True, she be busier than me. Shit with her, I'm the help," Czar snorted.

Thanks to Fro, *Sippin' Tea* was now a household brand. Their teas were in every Whole Foods store across the country. Harper, being the CEO and founder of the company, was always on the go. It was nothing for her to attend a meeting and then fly back home to a PTA meeting. Marley still played the background and managed the shop while coming up with new products. They had hired more people, but Marley still visited the shop every week.

"Really?" Nesha Re laughed.

"Listen, the world knows the rapper Czar, but I married Julius, the man. So after he's done performing, he's at *Sippin' Tea*, packing orders and working the counter. When I'm not at the shop, I'm listening to beats and up late in the studio with him. It's balance. He's my help when I need it, and I'm his producer."

"I love that. Czar, I'm not going to lie. I've seen a big change in you within these last couple of years. Is she the reason for the growth?"

"She's a big part of it, but I did it for me. Changing for another person will only last for so long. I think you need to change for yourself in order for it to work."

"Facts, but even your music is different. How do your fans like the new Czar?"

"I mean, it is what it is. I can't rap about being in the trap and freaking on hoes forever. I'm hoping they matured and moved on with me, but I really don't care. I rap what I want, and if a certain song or album don't hit you, move on, and that's that."

"Yea, I'm not a creator like him, but I agree. Fans need to allow artists room to grow, to create." Marley rubbed Czar's arm.

"I like yall." Nesha Re nodded, moving the conversation in another direction. For the next hour, they chatted about everything from Czar partnering with homeless shelters to Marley's pop-up shops during the summer. Usually, wherever Czar had a concert you could find her mobile tea shop. If she wasn't on stage with him, she was slanging bottles of tea like crack.

Before either of them knew it, the interview was over, and Marley and Czar were in the back of their truck while Biggie drove them to their next destination. It was a little after five, and as bad as they wanted to go home, it wasn't an option.

"Biggie, you still coming with me to my yoga class tomorrow?" Marley asked, looking up from her iPad.

"Yea, but it's not that hot yoga shit again, is it?"

"No," she giggled. Taking Biggie to hot yoga was one of the worst decisions she'd ever made. Not only did he complain the entire session, but the instructor slipped in his sweat and ended the class early.

"Good," Biggie replied.

"You see this shit?" Czar asked, handing his phone to Marley. She glanced at the screen and rolled her eyes.

Tati writing a tell-all book wasn't a surprise. Life had humbled her in the worst way, leaving her exploring every avenue for a few coins. No more was she flying in and out of town on private jets or behind stages at concerts. She was no longer invited to red carpet events, and the only attention she received was from D-list celebrities. Tati couldn't even get a brand endorsement because after her fake miscarriage claims, nobody was fucking with her.

"Get ready because you know she's about to drag you in this book." Marley handed him back the phone.

"Fuck that girl and anybody that believes that shit," Czar snorted.

"You know people are nosey, so they gone buy it. Mmh, maybe I need to write a tell-all,"

"What would you put in it?" He scooted closer to her, slipping his hand under her skirt.

"Stop!" Marley hissed, glancing up to make sure Biggie wasn't watching them.

"Y'all nasty asses just don't give a fuck," he grunted, hitting the button to raise the partition he had installed.

"See what you did!"

"Fuck all that, what you gone put in your book?" Czar caressed her swollen bud.

"How you're always being so mannish," she moaned.

"What else?" He kissed her neck.

"And you bullied me into a relationship." Marley slowly rode his fingers.

"Don't sound like a bad book to me." Czar massaged her insides. "You gone cream on my fingers?"

"Uh huh."

"Good girl." He grinned, watching her face twist in pleasure as he dug her out.

Never in Czar's wildest dreams did he think he'd be content with just one woman, but he was. Marley was everything he needed and more. She was his best friend, his freak, his inner peace, his fitness guru, and more. With her around, he didn't feel the need to take medicine to stabilize his mood. Marley explored alternative ways to keep his mind clear, and it normally ended with her ass in the air. When she couldn't go with him on tour, Czar was flying home every other day to lay eyes on her. There was no more after partying in clubs, and if he did host, Marley was right there by his side.

Terri was fond of Marley and called her the *Czar Whisperer*. She was the only one who could talk him off the edge. When Czar didn't want to attend label events, Terri called Marley, begging her to put in a good word for him. All in all, she was a good look for him.

"We here, nasty asses." Biggie tapped on the window.

"You love me?" Marley puckered her lips.

"Fuck yea." Czar kissed her lips before pulling his wet fingers out of her.

"Good, because I promised Ro I'd be on his team."

"You got me fucked up." Czar sat up. "Why you lie to that man?"

"He called last night while you were in the shower, and I said yes. I felt bad."

"Yea, well you about to feel worse because you lied to that nigga. You belong to me." He hovered over her.

Before Marley could respond, the back door was pulled open, and Romeo was standing there with Sammy's twin in his arms.

"Come the fuck on, we been waiting on yall." He shifted his restless daughter in his arms.

"I'mma fuck you up! What I tell you niggas about calling my wife?" Czar scolded.

"Nigga, she was our friend before she was your wife," Romeo bucked.

"You know this nigga live in her skin," Biggie snorted.

"So the fuck what?" Czar shrugged, not ashamed that his world revolved around his wife.

"Gimme my big girl." Marley held her hands out, and Abby jumped into her arms. "Hi, my pretty girl."

"I pitty." Abby grinned, trying her hardest to repeat after Marley.

"You're the prettiest," Marley assured her, walking toward the backyard.

Abby was almost two and giving her parents a run for their money. Since she was the only kid, everyone spoiled her, especially Ada and Slim. She had her own room at their house and everything. Romeo swore they weren't having any more kids, and Sammy agreed. The pregnancy had dragged her through the mud, and her body paid the price.

"Bout damn time," Goose grumbled, watching the couple walk through the backyard. "Game night started an hour ago," he slurred.

"And you already drunk," Czar taunted.

"I wake up drunk, for your information," Goose corrected him.

"Alright, yall know the deal. Drop the phones, tablets, and all that other shit in the red bucket," Slim announced, walking through the backyard.

"We know, we know," Romeo commented. "I'm ready this time."

"You be so in a hurry to lose," Pooh taunted.

"You need to be in a hurry to stop wearing them tattooed edges. You start sweating and them shits start sliding down your face. Plus, I have a new partner this time."

"Who?" Sammy and Nova quizzed.

"LB," he revealed like she was his superpower.

"Tell him," Czar whispered in Marley's ear.

"Nooooo. He's so happy."

"Tell him or I'm not sucking your toes for a month."

"I can't be on your team," Marley blurted out, sending the backyard into an uproar. She sat down on the bench while everybody argued. Sammy no longer wanted to be on Romeo's team, and asking Nova was out of the question. "See what you done started?"

"I didn't start shit, you lied to the nigga." Czar sat beside her, pulling one of Abby's ponytails. "Get off my wife."

"Mine." Abby hugged Marley's neck.

"You ready for some babies?"

"No, you know I prefer to swallow them for the time being," Marley flirted. "It keeps me youthful."

"Keep talking like I won't take you home and put that mouth to work." Czar licked his lips.

"Don't threaten me with a good time. Tell them we're leaving and you'll get nothing but throat."

"Aye, come get yall baby!"

The end!!!!

Before you go...

I just have one question...What would you do?

If you thought the love of your life died and right when you moved on, he reappears. Would you leave your new lover for the old one?

I asked this question to a lot of people while writing this book and the answers amazed me. So, I'm asking you. Drop you answer in my reading group or in your review :)

As always, thank you!

Rate. Review. Recommend.

Follow Me

Instagram: Author_Nesha

Facebook: Nesha Williams

TikTok : Author_Ladii_Nesha

Website: www.authorladiinesha.com

Made in the USA
Columbia, SC
10 October 2024

43420532R00320